THE ST. CLAIR SUMMER

THE ST.CLAIR SUMMER

A NOVEL BY
MARVIN WERLIN &
MARK WERLIN

NAL BOOKS
NEW AMERICAN LIBRARY
TIMES MIRROR
NEW YORK AND SCARBOROUGH, ONTARIO

NAL BOOKS TRADEMARK REG. U.S. PAT. OFF. AND FOREIGN COUNTRIES
REGISTERED TRADEMARK—MARCA REGISTRADA
HECHO EN HARRISONBURG, VA. U.S.A.

SIGNET, SIGNET CLASSICS, MENTOR, PLUME, MERIDIAN AND NAL
BOOKS are published *in the United States* by The New American
Library Inc., 1633 Broadway, New York, New York 10019,
in Canada by The New American Library of Canada Limited,
81 Mack Avenue, Scarborough, Ontario M1L 1M8

Library of Congress Cataloging in Publication Data

Werlin, Marvin.
The St. Clair summer.

I. Werlin, Mark, joint author. II. Title.
PS3573.E67S24   813'.54   80-26214
ISBN 0-453-00395-8

Designed by Alan Steele

First Printing, April, 1981

1 2 3 4 5 6 7 8 9

PRINTED IN THE UNITED STATES OF AMERICA

ACKNOWLEDGMENTS

Our gratitude to Nathan Raisen and Charles W.
Yeiser of the Far Gallery, Rita Norton,
Kent Gerard, Bobby Abrams, and especially
to Jane Rotrosen.

Dedicated to the memory of my father,
Arthur Werlin, who taught me the value of
integrity, the meaning of love, and the joy
of living.   *Marvin Werlin*

To my grandparents, Paul and Flora Mundel,
whose humor, compassion, and understanding
of human nature are a constant inspiration.

Mark Werlin

Prologue:
November 1973

༄

New York

A COLD WIND gusted across the icy waters of the East River. The faint light of dawn slowly penetrated the darkness lying over the city and filtered down concrete canyons into the streets. Glass and steel monoliths crowded together like an army fighting to hold back the encroaching day, their long shadows turning the crosshatch of avenues and boulevards into a wasteland devoid of life and color. It was late in November, and a dry tingling snap in the air promised flurries of snow.

Olivia St. Clair stood at the bedroom window of her Beekman Place town house and stared down at the small park that lay behind the street of elegant residences. Shrubs stripped of foliage curved and whipped in the wind, and a nearby elm tree stood dark and solid, its naked limbs stretched in protest against the icy onslaught. Fallen leaves that had lost their autumn color and turned black were tossed across the barren stretch of ground. A veil of gray light hung over the FDR Drive, making ghosts of the sparse traffic, and in the distance the slate-colored silhouette of the Queensborough Bridge wavered against leaden skies.

Olivia turned from the windows, pulled the drapes tight, and got back into bed, moving restlessly under the warmth of a satin quilt. She had not slept well for the last few weeks and wondered if it was worth seeing a doctor. After all, she was almost sixty—something was bound to start giving way. Maybe she was doing too much, too many committees and board meetings. But there were so many problems: the newly organized World Arts Foundation was floundering in a mass of indecision and red tape; the National Endowment for the Arts was in the midst of allocating funds for a new series on Public Broadcasting about the lives of American artists, a

3

project she herself had organized. The St. Clair name carried a lot of prestige, not to mention the weight of money, in these endeavors. She knew she couldn't depend on Alexander and Vivian for anything other than their usual contributions, so it was left to her to do the work. The thought of her brother and his wife and their pretenses to culture made Olivia chuckle. She reached to the night table for a cigarette, lighted it, put an ashtray beside her and lay back against the pillows, carefully tapping the ash before it got too long; no point in dying like those silly women who fall asleep while smoking and send the bed and themselves up in flames.

She watched the early morning light grow stronger, dispelling shadows and bringing the room to life. Favorite pieces of furniture emerged from the darkness: an English breakfront housing a collection of porcelain figures, a Queen Anne armchair by the windows, the nineteenth-century satinwood table she used as her desk. On the walls were a few of her art treasures: paintings by Degas and Renoir, a Matisse, two first-state etchings by Rembrandt, the group of Americans—Hopper, Marsh and Eakins. And the large painting in the corner of the room, the first one she saw upon opening the door: a double portrait by Alan Conway of her niece and nephew, Dorian and David St. Clair.

Once when Olivia was being interviewed for an article in *Art in America* magazine, she was asked what, of all her pursuits in the arts, gave her the most pleasure. The writer was a humorless man with a reverence for her that was annoying, and she had impishly replied, "Going to bed and getting up in the morning with the great masters."

He had stared at her dumbly until she explained about the collection hanging on her bedroom walls.

"Owning great art is one of the pleasures of being rich," she had concluded frankly, relishing the disapproval on his face.

Olivia stubbed out her cigarette, put the ashtray back on the night table and closed her eyes, hoping for a few more hours of sleep. The wind moaned against the windows and somewhere in the house a floor squeaked. She wondered if Maggie, her housekeeper, were up making a cup of tea to soothe her own restlessness. We're like two old cats, Olivia thought, stirred by the slightest noise and moving around our rooms at all hours, seeking a quiet corner until we have to rouse ourselves and take up the chase of the day.

"But more slowly than we used to," she muttered, rubbing a stab of arthritic pain in her leg. "A lot more slowly . . ."

Suddenly the phone by her bed rang, its shrill sound a jarring shock in the silence. It was her private line, a number known only to a select group of personal friends and her family. Olivia sat up and glanced at the ormulu clock on the fireplace mantel. It was a few minutes to seven; who would be calling at this hour of the morning? The phone rang again, and with a worried frown she picked up the receiver.

"Hello . . . ?"

It was her brother's housekeeper, Mrs. Childress. A large, formidable woman with iron gray hair and a long face, she had long ago been nicknamed Chilly by David and Dorian, and the diminutive had stuck. Olivia asked, "Chilly, what is it? Why are you calling so early?"

The housekeeper's voice was choked by gasping sobs.

"For Christ's sake, Chilly, get control of yourself and tell me what's happened," Olivia commanded sternly. "Is Mr. Alexander ill?"

Mrs. Childress caught her breath and began to speak, slowly, her words punctuated by sharp intakes of breath and small cries. As Olivia listened her face drained of all color and one hand clutched at her breast to still the sudden pounding in her chest.

"Chilly, my God! Do you know what you're saying?" she half-whispered. "Are you sure?"

Olivia held the receiver in a tight, white-knuckled grip and pressed trembling fingers to her lips, struggling to control an overwhelming impulse to scream. When at last she could speak she said, "Call Dr. Steiner immediately. No—don't call the police! Don't do anything until I get there! Chilly, please, for God's sake stop crying! I'll be there as soon as I can."

Olivia hung up the phone and sat on the edge of the bed, trying to comprehend what she had just been told. Her body felt cold and her hands shook uncontrollably. She clasped them together tightly, hoping to quiet the tremors that were spreading into her arms and legs. Tears trickled down her face, but she didn't make a sound, afraid to open her mouth, to let go of the shriek inside her. The clock on the mantel

5

struck seven, and the unexpected sound startled her into movement. She stood up, slipped on a robe and walked stiffly to her desk, where she dialed Maggie on the house line.

"Maggie, I'm sorry to wake you so early, but I have to go out to my brother's house on the Island right away." Her voice began to break and she paused to gain control of herself. "What? Yes, I'll need some clothes for a few days. Wake Albert and tell him to get the car ready, I want to leave as soon as possible. And would you make some coffee . . . What? No—I'll tell you about it later—"

Olivia hung up before Maggie could ask any more questions. She wasn't ready to tell her what had happened, to make a reality of the nightmare Chilly had described. Everyone would know soon enough, but right now she needed time to think as decisively as possible. She began to pace the room and caught sight of herself in the vanity mirror. Her eyes were like a madwoman's and her face was white, the skin stretched tight over the fine bones of her cheeks. Her short gray hair was a disarray of tangled strands, like a thin wig placed slightly askew on a chalky skull.

"Oh God!" she cried aloud. "I'm too old, too old—"

She wept, covering her face with her hands. A bloody, grotesque image of what had happened flashed into her mind, and her stomach churned with nausea. She stumbled into the bathroom, turned on the cold water, and splashed it over her face.

A few minutes later, pale, still trembling, she came back into the bedroom and went to her desk. She picked up the phone and placed a call to her niece in London. "That's right, operator. Miss Dorian St. Clair. Yes . . . please keep trying and call me back. It's an emergency."

Olivia hung up and looked around the room, at a loss for what to do next. Her eyes fell on the portrait of her brother's children. She stared at it for a long time, then picked up the phone again, called the operator and sent a cable to Ireland. Her voice broke several times as she composed the message. When she was finished, she went to the windows and pulled back the drapes. The raw bleak day rushed in at her like a blow; she sank into the armchair, staring out at the clouds massing in the sky. Traffic was moving heavily now on the FDR Drive, and people began to appear on the esplanade along the bank of the river. They leaned into the wind, faces buried in scarves and turned-up collars, as if they sensed an imminent disaster in the air, a force of nature that was about to explode.

What would happen when the events of the morning were revealed to the world? It would become an international scandal, Olivia thought; the press would make a circus of the story with lies and half-truths. Everyone in the family would be touched by the horror—nothing would be the same ever again.

She turned to look again at the portrait of David and Dorian. Alan had painted it more than eight years before, at her request. In the corner of the canvas the scarlet letters of his signature seemed to burn with as much life as he had infused into the faces of the brother and sister. His presence was stamped on the painting with every brushstroke, just as he himself had become part of their lives.

Olivia shuddered and gripped her arms tightly, thinking of the agony that lay ahead of all of them. Then she took a deep breath and stiffened her back with determination; the next few weeks would have to be dealt with one day at a time. It was the only way any of them would be able to survive.

❦

London

A steady, driving rain beat against the houses around Regent's Park. It was a little after eleven in the morning, and despite the weather traffic moved in a clamor through the streets. A small army of glistening umbrellas was all that could be seen of people hurrying down the wet sidewalks of Marylebone Road.

The small garden behind Number 8 Ulster Terrace had the desolate look of a mire. Water flooded over the brick walk and up against the wooden gate off the back drive. The low stone wall enclosing the garden ran in rivulets like a mass of tiny waterfalls, and the house behind it, with its rain-streaked walls and shuttered windows, looked abandoned.

Dorian St. Clair lay half awake under a tangle of sheets

7

and blankets in the large bedroom on the second floor. Her dark hair was spread across the pillows; one arm pressed close to the man sleeping beside her. She stared at the ceiling, listening to the pounding of the rain and trying to ignore the growing pressure in her bladder. Finally she sat up and swung her legs to the floor. Her feet touched the slick surface of a bottle. She kicked it away and stood up, reaching for a robe. The room was icy cold; she shivered violently as she staggered to the bathroom.

A few minutes later she made her way back into the semi-darkness of the bedroom. A stale odor of damp walls and cigarettes assailed her nostrils; the room had not been aired in days. She searched through crumpled packages on the night table to find a cigarette and knocked over an ashtray filled with butts. It fell to the floor, spilling its contents and clinking lightly against several overturned glasses.

"Christ! The place is a pigsty," Dorian muttered, getting back into bed. She stacked some pillows behind her and sat up, clutching the blankets around her shoulders. The man beside her had not stirred. She looked down at him blankly, trying to remember who he was. Had they met at a party? No, that wasn't it. Where, then? Hell, it didn't really matter.

The man suddenly sighed deeply and turned over on his stomach, tossing the covers off his body. Dorian examined him idly. His back was broad and tapered to a slim waist that flared into muscular buttocks and strong thighs. His profile was sharp against the white pillows; young, dark-haired, with sulky, petulant features made almost childish in sleep. His full lips were parted slightly and his steady breathing made a small rasping sound.

She remembered where they had met—in a pub, near Piccadilly—when was it, a few nights before? He had approached her as soon as she'd walked in, and seeing him, she had thought for a moment of Alan. He wasn't really anything like Alan, she decided after a few drinks, but the illusion made it easier for her to bring him home, to close her eyes and remember Alan as they made love.

Now she observed him warily, trying to recall his name and wondering how long he had been here. He woke with a start and grabbed at the blankets to cover himself.

"God, I'm freezing!" he said in a thick, scratchy voice. "What time is it?"

Dorian picked up her watch. "After twelve," she replied.

"Day or night?"

Dorian laughed. "I'm not sure . . ."

He moved up on the pillows beside her and threw an arm across her body, his large hand resting on her breast. "I'm hungry," he mumbled.

An acrid, dank odor rose from his flesh, a two-day stubble of beard covered his chin and jaws. His arm was heavy and the hand on her breast felt possessive, threatening. Dorian suddenly wanted him to leave without knowing who he was or anything about him.

"There's nothing in the fridge," she said. "Why don't you go out and get something to eat?"

He yawned and slipped his hand down to her hips. "In a bit, love." His fingers moved lightly across her stomach and down between her legs. She tightened her thighs against them and said quietly, "No."

He looked up at her, blinking sleep out of his eyes. "Just a quick romp before breakfast—or dinner, whatever the hell time it is?" he smiled.

"No . . ." She drew her knees up to her chest.

"Want me to go, do you?"

"Yes."

He grabbed the covers and yanked them away so that she was naked, uncovering himself at the same time. He had an erection. He stroked it with one hand and with the other tried to pry her knees apart.

"Stop it," she said tonelessly. "It's too bloody cold." She pulled at the blankets and covered herself. "Why don't you just get the hell out?"

He sighed and gave her a mocking half-smile. "Finished with me, are you? All through having your fun?"

"I'm through," she said stonily, "—and so are you." She reached for her purse on the night table and opened it. "Here's some money . . ."

He looked at her in amazement as she held the notes out to him. Then he laughed, shook his head and got out of bed. "I have a feeling you've done this before," he said, slipping on his shirt, "—many times."

Dorian shrugged and put the money back in her purse. It always ended this way, she thought, with her feeling indifferent and then being alone—until the next time. It was a comfortable pattern; there was no need to think—just wait until the indifference passed and the ritual began once more.

He was almost dressed when the phone rang. Dorian ignored it and he looked at her curiously. The phone rang again and he asked, "Aren't you going to answer it? Do you want me to go into the other room?"

She shook her head no and reached for the receiver. "Yes?" she asked with a note of impatience. "What? Yes, this is Dorian St. Clair. Who? Who did you say was calling?"

She frowned and looked puzzled as the connection was made. "Olivia, is that you? This is a surprise . . . What? Speak louder, I can't hear you."

The young man was putting on his shoes when he heard Dorian draw in her breath sharply. He looked up and saw that she was deathly pale, her eyes wide with shock. Her mouth opened as if she were gagging. She nodded at the receiver, tried to answer, but could not. Finally she muttered a few words and hung up.

"What is it?" he asked. "What's the matter? You look ill— can I get you something—?"

Dorian stared at him wildly. Her hands clutched at the covers, her body began to crumple and a low moan rose from her throat, bursting into an anguished shriek.

ॐ

County Wicklow, Ireland

Alan stood at the easel staring at the large canvas he had been working on for months. He picked up a brush from the taboret, filled it with paint and touched it to the surface of the painting with light strokes. His dark eyes were intent on his work, his tall, lithe body swaying with the movement of his hand.

He picked up other brushes to mix paint on the palette and stopped to wipe a brush on his work pants, adding a daub of fresh color to the streaks of paint that had dried into the rough cloth. Once he paused to search through a stack of photographs lying scattered across a nearby table: pictures of Dorian and Olivia, David and the others, and himself.

After a few hours he stopped for a cigarette and a cup of coffee. It was almost noon and the sun had broken through the heavy morning clouds, filling the studio with light. He snapped off the lamps he had been working by and took his coffee to the large windows that overlooked the gardens. His cottage was set in the serene beauty of the Vale of Clare, and in the distance the morning mists drifted away from the Wicklow mountains, disappearing into the magical light he had sought many times to capture on canvas.

Sitting on the wide, cushioned window seat, Alan stared out at the pastoral scene, thinking of the distance of time and events between the past he was recreating on canvas and now. Seven years. He looked back at the canvas, examining the arrangement of figures and their relationship to each other. Much closer in paint than they ever were in life, he thought.

He could look at his work dispassionately now. The tension he had felt when first planning it had abated through long weeks of rough sketches and blocking out the composition. Evenings had been spent drawing from photographs and memory, but the memories were painful and many times he had given up the idea altogether. Lonely hours tramping through the countryside had not relieved his depression; he found himself drawn irresistibly back to the project. Now the painting was almost finished, the memories captured on canvas. Later, after being varnished and framed, they could be viewed from a safe distance.

The sputtering sound of a car drew his attention; the vintage station wagon of Liam O'Neal, the postmaster, was approaching the cottage. It was a rattling trap of loose bumpers, dents and scratches and an explosive exhaust, so noisy that Liam's arrival was heard long before he was seen. Alan opened the window and waved down to him as the car chugged up the lane to the house. Liam was leaning out the window, holding an envelope in his hand.

"It's a cable!" he called. "From New York!"

"I'll be right there," Alan called back.

When Alan first moved to County Wicklow he was regarded with suspicion by most of the townspeople. But Liam, a big, red-faced man with a hearty smile and a cheerful, good-natured manner, had made him feel welcome. To show his appreciation Alan had done a pastel portrait of him and presented it to his family as a gift. Since then Alan was no longer viewed as an outsider, and the two men had become friends.

Alan was at the front door as Liam got out of his car and came up the walk, waving the envelope. "A cable, it is!" he exclaimed again. "Something important, I'm sure."

Alan laughed. "Maybe . . ." He took the envelope and tore it open.

"A big commission?" Liam questioned. "Some famous person wanting you to paint him?"

Alan unfolded the cable and read it. A sudden weakness seized him, and he sat down on a bench by the door, shuddering.

Liam asked anxiously, "What is it, Alan? Could I be doing something for you?" He reached into his back pocket and pulled out a bottle of whiskey. "Take a swallow, there. It'll do you good . . ."

Alan tilted the bottle back and let the fiery liquid run down his throat. He gasped, coughed a little, and handed the bottle back to Liam. "Thanks, that helped," he said dully. Making an effort to pull himself together, he asked, "Liam, can you drive me into Dublin? I have to leave for New York immediately."

"Of course I can. Is it bad news?"

· "Yes—something terrible has happened."

"Will you be gone long?"

"I don't know."

The next few hours passed in a blur: driving to the city, making necessary arrangements, getting passage on a flight to New York, finally racing to the airport to catch the plane. Once in his seat Alan closed his eyes, overtaken by a desperate need to sleep, to escape the awful message that was taking him home.

Faces and voices fluttered behind his closed eyelids, echoing the past in random images: himself as a boy of twenty, glimpses of his parents and his home, and the sudden bright wash of a day in the summer of 1966 when he had gone to the St. Clair estate with his father, the day he had first met Dorian St. Clair . . .

Part One

1

San Francisco: June 1966

GRAY-SHADOWED CLOUDS lowered across the sky over Golden
Gate Park; it was a cool, crisp Sunday morning. Hundreds of
young people were scattered across the green stretches of
lawn. In their tie-dye shirts, embroidered vests, painted jackets, beads and headbands they looked like clumps of wildly
colored flowers. Some of them swayed to the soft strumming
of guitars, chanting the lyrics of a Dylan song, while others
lounged in the deep grass, smiling vacantly. Conservatively
dressed neighborhood residents avoided the open areas and
stayed on the gravel walks, scowling at the invasion of their
park by this strange teenage army.

David St. Clair hurried across the meadows, stepping
gingerly around kids asleep under blankets, cartons of take-
out food and bags filled with personal possessions that littered
the grounds. He looked conspicuously out of place in neatly
pressed slacks, sport shirt and cashmere sweater. Where other
boys his age had long hair, beards and moustaches, his own
thick blond hair was cut conventionally short and his face
was meticulously clean-shaven. It was altogether a striking
image, like an artist's conception of the ideal all-American
college boy. But it wasn't just his appearance that set him
apart. His disdainful expression and supercilious manner
clearly expressed contempt. To him the hippies were no more
than a gang of unruly children indulging in an absurd game.

The smell of unwashed bodies and urine cut through the
cool morning air. David grimaced in disgust. He headed for
Stanyon Street. A makeshift tent blocked his way and he
paused to look through the half-opened flap at a couple making love. The girl wriggled dirty toes and made strangled
sounds of pleasure, but David's attention was caught by the
sight of the naked boy crouched over her. Lean and muscu-

17

lar, his legs were tense and his pale buttocks clenched energetically. David watched them nervously for a few minutes, then tore himself away and hurried on.

A crowd was milling around a man sprawled across the sidewalk on Haight Street. A girl with a chalky face and drug-glazed eyes sat beside him, holding his limp hand, while a cop bent over the man and slapped him sharply. David shouldered his way past them, angrily ignoring a long-haired boy who was aggressively panhandling for spare change. He hated their neighborhood and the people in it. He could see that once it might have been an inoffensive middle-class business district; a few stores still retained their former identity. But the greater number of them had undergone a terrible metamorphosis, reemerging as head shops, rock clubs and stalls of cheap handicrafts. The whole area suffered from an eruption of psychedelic designs and Day-Glo colors, giving it the appearance of a broken-down carnival trying to breathe some life into its attractions. David's step became more urgent, his eyes fixed ahead of him to avoid the ugliness of the surroundings.

At the corner of Haight and Ashbury he glanced at his watch. Dorian had told him to pick her up at eleven; it was almost that now. She was staying with a young rock musician named John Silver. They had met one night at the Avalon Ballroom, and David had taken an immediate dislike to him. But Dorian had ignored his objections. As he started to climb the steep incline of Ashbury Street, he grew anxious; they were supposed to leave for home tomorrow. Now he wasn't sure she would go with him because of Silver. But she had to, he thought desperately; he couldn't go back alone.

At the top of the street he stopped to catch his breath, berating himself for being out of shape; he detested physical weakness, ridiculing it in others and fearing any sign of it in himself. He glanced down at the Victorian houses lining the street. They looked as if they had been assaulted by the same mad brush used on Haight. Gables, turrets, fretwork and railings were painted in a wild array of blatant colors, like ugly exclamations against the natural dignity of weathered walls and gray stone steps.

He ran up the front steps of a large house on the corner and opened the front door. The hallway was dark; the house seemed strangely quiet. When he had left Dorian here the night before rock 'n' roll had blared from open doorways and the hall and stairs had been packed with kids. Now the only evidence of them were pieces of dirty laundry strewn on the floor and the stale odor of grass lingering in the musty air. They must all be out in the park, David thought, starting up the narrow stairs to the second floor. He tried to imagine living this kind of life, and smiled, knowing that it was impossible. Even though many of the kids he and Dorian had met were children of affluence like themselves, he couldn't understand their enthusiasm for this dreary escape from parental authority, this shabby expression of their freedom.

The second-floor landing was an obstacle course of sleeping bags, threadbare blankets and duffel bags. David made his way down the hall to the last room and knocked on the door. There was no answer. He knocked again, more insistently, and a hoarse voice answered, "Get lost!"

David called out, "Dorian? It's eleven o'clock."

"Oh shit, it's my brother," he heard her say.

"So?—tell him to fuck off!" the voice of John Silver replied.

David pounded on the door. "Dammit, Dorian, open up!"

A few seconds later the door opened a crack. David shoved it all the way and pushed into the room. A small lamp with a red scarf flung over it dimly illuminated the interior with a deep pink light. Dorian stood glaring at him; she had thrown on a denim workshirt and was clutching it with one hand to keep it closed over her naked breasts.

"What the hell's the matter with you?" she cried angrily.

"You said you'd be ready to leave at eleven," David snapped.

"You always bust in like that when your sister's getting laid?" The question came from a dark corner of the room.

David turned, narrowing his eyes. He saw Silver lying naked on a mattress on the floor. His brown hair fell in a tangle to his shoulders, and a long moustache drooped down either side of his fleshy lips. He made no effort to cover himself; in the eerie light his skin had the sheen of pale satin.

David looked at him contemptuously, then glanced at the small, cramped room. Clothes were thrown haphazardly

19

across the back of a chair or on the floor. Nearby stood a wooden table covered with dirty dishes and a rusted hot plate; pinned up on the walls were posters of the rock group Silver performed with.

"Your room suits you," he said caustically. "The only thing that's missing is garbage cans." He turned back to Dorian. "You said you'd be ready by eleven," he repeated.

"So I'm late! You know how time flies when you're having fun!" She went into the bathroom and slammed the door.

David found an empty chair in the corner and sat down. Silver stared at him silently, a smile playing across his lips. David shifted uncomfortably; the room was dank and seedy. There was a disturbing presence in the air, a tangible sense of sex having just occurred. An image of the couple in the tent flashed across his mind and he drew himself up stiffly, folded his arms across his chest.

Silver picked up a guitar and began to strum it softly, never taking his eyes from David's face. David looked past him, concentrating on a sliver of daylight showing through a torn shade on the window.

"Man, you are such an uptight asshole," Silver murmured. "You sit there like you own the fuckin' street."

"Man, you are so right," David mimicked him coolly. "Once we owned the fuckin' street. Does that get you uptight?"

Silver laughed. "Man, you don't understand nothin'. If money meant anything to me, I wouldn't be living here. I'm happy, man. Are you?"

"Oh man, don't hand me that bullshit. Once your group gets going, maybe a record contract and a tour, you'll dump this place in a flash."

Silver shook his head with weary patience. "Hey—you don't understand. The music makes me happy, makes other people happy, and that's all that really matters. Money and power, they just fuck up your life, fuck up the country, fuck up the whole world. All I want to do is groove on some peace and happiness, man."

A hard smile spread across David's face. "Listen, *man*," he said softly. "I talked with your manager the other night at the Avalon. All he could think of was the gig your group is going to play in L.A. in a few weeks. He's already contacted a publicist and on opening night he's going to have every record company rep he can get his grubby hands on in the audience. He's talking about nothing but contracts, *man,* nothing but business!"

Silver stared at him in confusion. "I don't understand. Why did he tell you all that?"

"Because he thought maybe I'd invest some money in his little enterprise, buy into the package. He's selling you, man, in bits and pieces. So peddle your peace and happiness crap somewhere else!"

Before Silver could respond, Dorian came out of the bathroom. She was dressed in a skirt and blouse, and had tied her long black hair into a ponytail.

"I'll get my shoes and we'll go," she muttered to David. "What have you two been talking about?"

She went to the mattress and knelt to search through the sheets until she found a pair of sandals.

"We've been discussing the vicissitudes of life," David replied.

Silver looked angry and sullen. He turned to Dorian and put a hand on her hip, ran his fingers lightly over her thighs.

David stood up. "Let's go, Dorian. We have a lot to do."

Silver pulled her close and whispered something. She hesitated, then whispered back to him and stood up. Taking David's arm, she led him into the hallway.

"What's happening?" he asked suspiciously.

"I want to stay a little while longer—another hour or two . . ."

"Damn you, Dorian, you promised!"

Her voice rose shrilly. "All I want is a few more hours! I'll meet you at the hotel this afternoon. I'm doing what you want—we're going home tomorrow. Isn't that enough?"

He glanced over her shoulder through the open door behind her. Silver was leaning against the wall with his legs spread. He grinned at David and made an obscene gesture.

"Please, David," Dorian said. "I'll be on the plane with you tomorrow, you know that. I just want a little more time before we go back . . ."

David put his hand against Dorian's cheek; he knew how

she felt about going home, and understood why she needed to be with Silver.

"Okay. Be at the hotel in time for dinner. I'll take care of everything."

She gave him a quick hug and slipped back into the room. The door closed and he heard the click of the lock. David remained motionless for a few minutes, feeling a sudden weariness overtake him. He thought of Silver's obscene gesture to him, and laughed. That single gesture had defeated him. It was a crude reminder that intellect and status were feeble weapons compared to the base force of sex.

From behind the door he heard a throaty laugh from Silver, a soft murmuring that grew in intensity. With a wrenching effort he turned and ran down the hall, down the steps and out into the sudden blinding glare of the morning light.

The St. Clair Hotel was located in San Francisco's most elegant district, Nob Hill. The entrance was a pair of tall leaded-glass doors, arched at the top, set into a deep frame of burnished walnut. Gaslights on fluted metal columns stood at either side of the doors, and an awning the color of old wine stretched to the edge of the sidewalk. On it, painted in a fine gold script, were the words "The St. Clair Hotel—San Francisco." It was a reassuring sign to all guests that they were entering one of the more famous and expensive of the smaller hotels in the city.

The lobby was thickly carpeted and draped, as if to seal off the interior from the outside world and create the soft hush of another, more genteel time. Tiffany lamps illuminated rosewood tables and embroidered chairs, and an Austrian crystal chandelier hung from the vaulted ceiling, beaming a golden glow over the polished mahogany front desk. Paintings in gilt frames covered the paneled walls. Velvet drapes were swagged around the archway leading to the dining salon, where the sound of a quartet playing Mozart could be heard above the tinkle of glass and silver. Doormen, bellhops and waiters were all garbed in a uniform of gold-braided jackets and dark trousers, stiff white shirts with high wing collars and small, neat bow ties. The guests, in their currently fashionable clothes, were the only incongruity to challenge the nineteenth-century ambience.

At the back of the lobby a wide curving staircase with gold and marble bannisters led to the mezzanine. Here French satinwood writing tables and plush easy chairs were arranged around a large white marble fireplace. Over the mantel, in a handmade frame that was deeply scrolled and decorated with gold leaf, hung a portrait of the founder of the St. Clair hotel chain, Augustus St. Clair. An imposing figure of a man with a mane of white hair and penetrating blue eyes, he gazed out over the room with an expression of indomitable strength and pride.

During the last decade of the nineteenth century, when Augustus was a young man, he visited the cities of Europe on a Grand Tour. A middle-class New Yorker with aristocratic aspirations, he gravitated toward elegant hotels and spas that catered to the wealthy and wellborn. Possessing an acute instinct for human weakness, Augustus saw that the rich depended on the hostelers who served them, and, for that reason, the hostelers themselves attained a special, unique position in society. He became determined to bring the beauty and splendor of the great Continental hotels to the United States, where, he felt, life was rapidly moving toward modernization, and old values were being discarded.

On his return, Augustus, whose organizational abilities were exceeded only by his reckless ambition, used a substantial family trust to begin acquiring old and beautiful homes in major cities in the country, and to convert them into small, exclusive hotels for the very rich.

In time he married Melissa Gorden, the daughter of a wealthy New York merchant. Melissa soon realized that her husband's desires were fired more by her money than by being in her bed. With the addition of her dowry and money borrowed from her father, Augustus continued to expand the chain.

As the years went by three children were born: Alexander, Jonathan and Olivia. Augustus insisted that control of the chain remain within the family, and so the principal stockholders were himself, his wife and their children. It was a curious phenomenon in a business becoming dominated by corporate management, yet it was in keeping with Augustus's

23

pride in his accomplishments. He had a fierce determination to create, in each hotel bearing his name, an oasis of charm and graciousness, a reminder of the gentle pace and refinement that was quickly disappearing from the face of the world.

When Augustus died, Alexander, being the eldest, took over the control of the business. As ambitious and ruthless as his father, he added to the chain several famous homes that were sacrificed during the economic blight of the thirties. In Europe, after World War II, he purchased villas and chateaux that were being sold by impoverished nobles.

After Melissa's death the shares in the chain were divided among Alexander, his younger brother Jonathan, and their sister Olivia. By agreement Alexander continued to control the business while Jonathan headed up the European chain and Olivia remained a silent partner. It was assumed that they and their children would carry on the tradition of management.

But so far only Alexander had produced offspring: David and Dorian.

David got out of a cab and hurried into the hotel. He checked for messages at the front desk, then walked briskly to the ornate, wrought-iron grill of the open elevator. It was a relic of the 1890s that his grandfather had helped to install after adding two floors to the building. A suite on the top floor was kept reserved for members of the family, and it was here that he and Dorian were staying.

David, along with a few guests of the hotel, waited for the elevator to return to the lobby. As the door slid open and they stepped in, he stared in shock at the operator, a slim young man with light brown hair and a sallow complexion. The boy turned dark, pleading eyes to David, silently begging him not to say anything in front of the others. David stood at the back, trying to control his rage. When the guests had been let off at their floors, the boy whispered, "David, please—"

"Teddy, what the hell are you doing here?" he demanded in a low voice.

"I need this job, man, I really do!"

"I want you out of this hotel immediately, or I'll have you thrown out!"

The elevator came to a stop at the sixth floor, but Teddy didn't open the door. He turned to David, his face pale and tense. "I'm sorry about what happened," he said miserably. "It wasn't my fault . . ."

"The hell it wasn't, you little whore!" David hissed. "When I fucked you, I fucked a sewer! Now open the goddamned door!"

"I didn't know I had the clap!" Teddy protested weakly. "If I had, I would have stopped you."

"Bullshit!"

"David, you gotta let me keep this job—I owe money all over town."

David grabbed the boy's arm, spun him around and twisted it up behind his back, holding him in a painful hammerlock. "Open the fucking door or I'll break your goddamned arm!"

Ted gasped from the pain; he reached out with his free hand, touched a lever, and the door slid open. David released him and stepped into the hallway, stalking off without a backward glance.

Once inside his suite he closed and locked the door, went into the sitting room and sank into a chair. His hands were trembling and he could feel his heart pounding. He took a pack of cigarettes from his shirt pocket, lighted one and drew deeply, waiting for his fury to subside. Then he reached for the telephone and dialed the hotel manager.

"Gene? This is Mr. St. Clair. I've received some complaints from the guests about an elevator operator named Ted Summers. I want him dismissed at once. And Gene, make sure that none of the other hotels in town hire him . . . no, no severance pay. Oh, and one more thing—my sister and I want reservations on a flight to Kennedy Airport tomorrow morning. Will you take care of it for me? Yes—we're returning to Long Island for the summer . . . Thank you, Gene. What? Yes—we'll be delighted to have dinner with you tonight . . . The report to my father is almost finished—you can look it over. Right. See you tonight."

David put the phone down and stubbed out his cigarette. In the silence of the empty room he could hear his own breathing, still harsh and ragged. He sat quietly in his chair.

The blinds were drawn against the afternoon sun; the air was very still. From somewhere outside came the sound of a street musician playing Bach on a flute, the silver peal of notes rising above traffic noises. David sat back and stared at the ceiling, trying to find some relief from the feverish sense of unreality gathering within him.

How had this happened to him? Why had he allowed it to happen?

He had come to San Francisco three weeks earlier on his father's orders to meet with the manager of the hotel and make a report on its operation. It seemed as dreary a prospect as a school assignment until Dorian eagerly asked to go with him. She wanted to see for herself the things they had both been reading about—the flower children and love-ins, the rock concerts, drugs and sex.

She had met John Silver during their first week in the city, and began spending time away from the hotel. Alone, David wandered the streets at night. His walks took him past gay bars and parks where young men gathered to circle each other warily. But if someone approached him he grew apprehensive, and hurried back to the refuge of the hotel.

He could not accept being homosexual. When he was in prep school he had dismissed his adolescent encounters with other boys as mere experimentation. In college, while having a relationship with his roommate, he struggled to maintain an appearance of normality by excelling in athletics and dating attractive girls. He even laid a few of them, reluctant to admit that they held little attraction for him. When the pressure of gossip about his roommate threatened to expose him, he callously rejected the boy, moved out and took a room alone. The boy dropped out of school with no explanations. David joined in the derisive sneers and malicious jokes; he covered his secret life with protective layers of lies to others, and pretenses to himself.

David got up and went to the bar to fix a drink, hoping it would steady his nerves. The alcohol hit him hard, made him flushed and dizzy. He rested his head on the surface of the bar and closed his eyes, trying to sort out the events that had made such a shambles of the last few weeks.

He had noticed Ted Summers soon after they arrived at

the hotel. The slender young man had a boyish, androgynous appeal and had subtly flirted with David whenever they met; but David ignored him.

One night he returned to the hotel from a walk, feeling frustrated and angry—at Dorian for leaving him alone, at the men on the streets for approaching him, at himself for being nervous and frightened.

Ted was waiting at the elevator, and when David stepped in the boy stared at him boldly. "I get off work in a few minutes," he whispered as they began the ascent.

David quickly calculated the risks. He was safe in the hotel—the boy was an employee, he wouldn't say anything for fear of losing his job. And if he did, who would believe him?

David nodded his head. "I'll leave my door open for you."

A week later David realized he had contracted gonorrhea.

The discovery terrified him; he thought of his body as contaminated. Even more humiliating was the fact that if he had gotten the dose from a girl, there would have been no shame—only further proof that he was like other men. But he had sought out Ted.

There was no one to turn to but Dorian; he had confided in her since his first experience with a boy when he was fourteen. She took him to a clinic in the Haight where, using a false name and address, he endured the humiliating examination and was given his shots in the company of young men who joked about "the hazards of the trade." Later, he tried to find Ted, but the manager of the hotel told him the boy had called in sick with the flu.

He stayed in his room for days, insisting they leave for home as soon as he was free of the infection. Dorian tried to argue him out of his decision, but he pleaded that he couldn't stay in the city or face being at home without her.

David raised his head from the bar and picked up his drink with trembling hands. Seeing Ted again had rekindled his rage; a moment more, he thought, and he would have killed him. He smiled grimly at the idea, remembering the soft yield of Ted's body sagging against him in pain. The thought stirred a wave of voluptuous pleasure, a sense of sexual power and strength. His hand went to his genitals. Suddenly he realized what he was doing and stopped, horrified.

27

"Oh Christ!"

He stumbled into the bedroom, feeling sick. He had to pack, get away from here and what was happening to him. He'd be safe at home, sheltered and protected by everything he knew and understood.

He ran to the closets and began pulling out pieces of luggage, flinging them onto the bed, then went to the chest and tore his clothes from one drawer after another in a frenzy, like a man pursued.

2

Bay Shore, Long Island

ALAN LAY NAKED in the rumpled bedsheets, feeling the warmth of the sun across his back and legs. It was seven o'clock in the morning and already stifling. Rays of sunlight slanted between the venetian blinds, making a ladder of stripes on the floor. Motes of dust floated on the still air in a slow, drifting dance.

He lay quietly, letting the process of waking up take place; he could never simply jump out of bed in the mornings, convinced that the shock would disorient him for the rest of the day. He heard his parents stirring in the kitchen downstairs, then his father calling out to him; they were working together today and would be leaving early. He gave a muffled reply and burrowed his head into the pillows. A morning hard-on made him shift his hips to get comfortable, producing a tremor of excitement. Tensing his buttocks, he rubbed slowly against the mattress, thinking of the girl from New York he had met on the beach the day before. His thoughts became vividly erotic and he slipped into a sensual half-dream state.

A noisy argument in the kitchen disrupted his reverie and brought him fully awake. He turned over on his back, his excitement dissolving away. Shit, they're at it again, he thought, listening to the voices of his parents slice at each other.

A few minutes later his mother called up the stairs, "Alan, are you awake? Breakfast is almost ready . . ."

"Be there in a minute."

He yawned, stretched, sat up and surveyed his room with dissatisfaction. There was no space; everything was cramped. The bookcase bulged with art magazines, books on anatomy, drawing, perspective, painting in oil and watercolor, and volumes on the works of great masters. Nearby stood a drawing table with sketches pinned across the top, and on the easel by the windows was a half-finished canvas of the boats down at the marina. A shelf mounted on the wall above the bookcase contained plaster casts: a foot, a hand, a male torso, the figure of a woman. He examined the play of light and shadow over the chalky forms, then looked at an array of drawings tacked up on the wall. His attention focused on a sketch of the girl he had met on the beach.

What was her name? Terry something. She was a pattern cutter at one of the fashion houses in New York, out on the Island for the weekend to escape the swelter of the city. He'd spotted her in the late afternoon and started the sketch to attract her attention. She came on to him with sexy looks and double entendre jokes, and they'd finally made it that night, under a blanket in a secluded area of the beach. Alan smiled, remembering the tangle of their limbs, the salty taste of her skin, the thrilling fear that someone might come along and discover them fucking. She'd asked him to call her when he came to the city in the fall, and he had written her name and phone number on the back of the sketch.

"Alan!" His mother's voice was sharp.

"Coming, coming!"

God, he couldn't wait to get out of here, to have his own place, a real studio where he could sleep in, have girls stay over, work when he felt like it. Soon, soon—just a few more months. He got out of bed and went to the sketch, picked up a piece of charcoal from the drawing table and quickly darkened a shadow under the breasts, emphasizing their fullness. He stared critically at what he had done.

"Better," he muttered. "Not terrific, but better."

A few minutes later, his hair still damp, Alan left the bathroom and started back to his room to dress. A loud exchange between his parents made him pause; his mother's voice was raised in an angry protest.

"He shouldn't have to spend the summer working with you when he has so much to do on his presentation! We could give him the money he needs!"

Alan winced, hating the hopeless tone of his father's reply.

"Marie, please try to understand—Alan was ready to look for a job doing something else. He doesn't want to just take money from us, he wants to earn it. I'm proud of him for that, and you should be, too . . ."

"My pride lies in his talent, his creativity. He's an artist! That's something you don't understand!"

"That's not true, and you know it!" George shouted. "I have as much pride in his abilities as you, but I also know that he's independent, and wants to earn his own way, as a man should!"

"As a man should," she mimicked him, then added in disgust, "You and your ideas of what a man should or should not be!"

A rattle of pots and pans covered the silence that followed. Alan hurried to dress, knowing that he would have to mediate, as he had so many times before. He wondered what would happen to them if he weren't there to keep the peace. By some mysterious process that he didn't understand, they had become the children in the house, and he the adult, settling arguments and soothing injured feelings. The thought of living alone in New York in the fall grew more enticing with each passing day.

He came downstairs, walked into the kitchen with a prepared smile on his face and said cheerily, "Good morning!"

His mother turned from the stove with a dour expression and offered him her cheek to kiss. *"Bonjour. Assieds-toi, manges ton petit déjeuner."*

As always, when she was angry with his father, she spoke to Alan in her native tongue. It was her way of allying herself with him, creating an immediate division between them and George.

Alan replied in French, knowing that it was expected. *"Oui, je meurs de faim."*

He turned to his father and asked, "What time are we due at the house?"

"Ten o'clock," George replied with a wary glance at his wife. "It's out in East Hampton, near Amagansett. The drive will take about an hour and a half, depending on the traffic."

"Then you will be home late for dinner?" Marie asked sharply.

George sighed. "I don't think so. Mr. St. Clair and I are going over the costs and materials, the man-hours needed to do the restoration. I've made up a budget and schedule I think he'll approve. We should be finished by late afternoon."

Marie took a frying pan off the stove and scooped some eggs and bacon onto Alan's plate. Then she sat down and lifted her coffee cup, glaring at her husband over the white rim with dark, sullen eyes.

Alan made an effort not to laugh at the way the scene was being played out—a precise routine of exact actions: the dialogue with him in French, snappish questions and weary replies, the glowering exchange of looks. The expected outburst from his father came on cue.

"You should be pleased that we got this contract! I happen to know that St. Clair went to four other firms before coming to us. New York firms!" he added for emphasis.

Marie made a show of not listening to him. George raised his voice, determined to get a response from her.

"St. Clair told me that none of them had any feeling for the effect of charm and tradition he wanted. But he saw our work on the Kensington place and the Bellingham house, and knew we could do the job. And he made special mention of the interior design work that you did."

Marie remained silent, sipping her coffee with a doleful expression, refusing to acknowledge the compliment.

George finally exploded: "Alan agreed to work with me this summer! It was as much his idea as mine!"

"You're taking advantage of him!" Marie flared, her voice hard and accusing. "Preparing his portfolio is far more important than being an *ordinary workman!*"

George's pale blue eyes blazed. "There's no shame in working with your hands! That's how I started, and I've managed to give you a good home, with no debts and savings in the bank!"

Alan broke in angrily. "This is silly! You're arguing over nothing!"

Marie stared at him, furious. Alan lowered his voice and continued, "Working with Dad's crew was my idea. I'll have plenty of time to sketch and paint in the evenings and on weekends."

Marie turned away to conceal tears that were forming, signaling an end to the scene. "Talking to your father is—*c'est inutile,* there's no point to it. *Il ne comprend rien.*"

"No, I'm sure he understands," Alan replied, afraid that

the quarrel would flare up again. He stared at his mother imploringly.

She shrugged her shoulders and sighed, "All right, do what you want. I'll make something special for dinner tonight, just for you, eh? *Tu comprends bien ta mère, n'est-ce pas?"*

"*Bien sûr.*" Alan glanced at his father and saw the relief in his eyes.

They finished the meal in silence. Marie began to clear away the dishes and George went to get his jacket and briefcase. Alan poured himself another cup of coffee, opened the back door and stepped out on the small porch facing the backyard. It was a bright clear day, with wisps of white clouds in an intensely blue sky. Sunlight flowed over the green lawn and beds of hydrangeas, wild violets and geraniums. At the back of the garden, under the spreading limbs of an oak tree, sat a wicker table and chairs.

Marie joined Alan on the porch, her face set in an expression of resignation. He offered her a cigarette, and took one for himself. It was something else they shared; George didn't smoke. She settled herself on the railing and leaned against a post, letting the smoke curl from her lips in a deep sigh. When Alan was a child they had worked in the garden together, planting flowers and weeding the beds, watering the grass so that it never browned in the heat of summer. In the early evenings Marie would bring out a bottle of wine and some cake and they would all sit under the tree. George would give Alan a glass jar with a lid punched full of holes and, as it grew dark, they chased fireflies and put them into the jar. Then it was set in the center of the table where they glowed and sparkled like imprisoned jewels.

"You worry too much about me," Alan said to his mother.

"I don't like him taking you away from your drawing."

"I have plenty of time. I'm only twenty."

"There's never enough time." Marie's eyes were clouded with concern. "Never," she repeated softly, turning to stare at the garden.

Alan watched her out of the corner of his eye, observing her dispassionately, as he would a painting he was studying. The line of her profile and curve of her throat were like a young girl's. Masses of dark hair emphasized her clear, pale complexion, and there was a sensual pout to her lips, a hint

33

of mystery in her dark eyes. She had kept her figure; at forty she was petite, with small breasts, softly rounded hips and shapely legs.

But something about her eluded him, a haunting poignancy that he had never been able to capture in the many sketches he had done of her. There was something she kept concealed, a secret self, guarded and protected against—what? His father, him, the world?

George called from the driveway at the side of the house. "Alan, let's go. It's getting late."

Marie leaned forward and kissed him on both cheeks. "Have a good day, *chéri.*"

"Oui—I will."

She followed him down the steps to the driveway, waited as they climbed into the car and drove off, then returned to the house. When she was finished in the kitchen, she went upstairs to collect soiled clothes for the laundry.

In Alan's room she stripped the bed and gathered up dirty socks and shirts from the floor where they had been haphazardly thrown. As she was about to leave the room she noticed a new drawing tacked up on the wall, a sketch of a young woman sitting on the beach. The girl was leaning back on one arm, her long smooth legs bent at the knees, her breasts arched provocatively; her half smile and heavy-lidded eyes made Marie think of an Ingres odalisque.

Suddenly she wondered if Alan had made love to the girl—on the beach, perhaps, late at night, hidden by the darkness? She imagined her son hunched over the girl—his broad shoulders and straight back, his lean muscular thighs. He was *her* work of art, Marie thought proudly: his dark hair and intense blue eyes fringed with black lashes, the full red lips that were so expressive. Did the girl recognize his beauty, understand his passion and tenderness? When she received him, was she aware of that special quality that set him apart from other boys?

Marie was moved by an aching sense of loss; she had given so much of herself to him, and soon he would be leaving to study in New York, live a life she would know little or nothing about. The moments they had shared together were almost at an end. He would take what she had taught him, and all the new things he learned, and share them with someone else—like the girl in the sketch. Another woman would know her son as she never could.

And when he was gone, what would she do? What of her life then? She imagined herself standing in his room when it would be empty, and her face was suddenly wet with tears.

❦

George turned the car onto Sunrise Highway, squinting against the glare of the sun. They drove in silence for a while, grateful for the light midweek traffic. By Friday afternoon the highway would be clogged with people streaming out from New York to escape the burning city streets. The Island had changed a great deal since George and Marie had moved into Bay Shore twenty years before. Whole stretches of rural areas were taken up now with split-level developments, shopping centers and motel chains. Land values had gone up as much as ten times in the last fifteen years, leading to exploitation of the beach areas, which had suddenly become crowded with apartment houses, hotels, clubs and small private cottages, all squeezed side by side.

"So many people," George complained. "I've never seen it so bad. Ever since they built those cheap tract houses in Nassau—"

"—things just haven't been the same," Alan finished for him, smiling.

"It's no joke," George said morosely. "Everything has changed. We've lost the quiet and the peace, the contentment we used to have."

Alan looked over at his father. George's face betrayed none of the anger he had seen at breakfast, but his eyes were heavy, lending a sadness to his otherwise impassive expression. The weight of unspoken emotion hung in the air like the moment before a cloudburst in summer.

"Christ, it's hot," Alan said, slouching back in his seat.

"I think I'll get an air conditioner for the car next week." George gestured to a Sears catalog lying on the floor by Alan's feet.

"Swell. I'll help you install it."

35

They drove on, not speaking. Alan wondered if he should mention the argument or let it go. He always felt caught in the middle of their quarrels, trapped into having to take sides. It had started so long ago that he couldn't remember when, but simply accepted it as a fact of their lives. His parents were so different from each other. George was ten years older than Marie, and where she was still youthful in appearance and spirit, he had quietly slipped into middle age. His hair was thinning on top, and his body had thickened through the waist. There were lines across his brow and around his eyes, and the beginning of a double chin marred the lean strength that had once made him attractive. He was a man who resisted change, content to follow a pattern of living with which he was comfortable, despite the irritation it caused his wife.

Alan felt uneasy; he wasn't close to his father and often had feelings of guilt about it. He had comforted Marie before leaving the house, but had not yet said anything to George. He turned to him and began tentatively, "Dad, I want you to know that I'd rather work with you this summer. I mean, I needed a break from drawing anyway. The stuff I was doing was getting stale. I just don't understand why Mom got so upset."

George sighed, "Neither do I. She loves you very much, has great hopes for you becoming a fine artist. But I want that for you, too, you know that."

"Of course I do."

"Yes, but does she?" His voice grew thoughtful. "Sometimes she's like a stranger to me, a woman I hardly know. I love her. I've always loved her . . . but sometimes I think she sees me as no more than a clod, without a brain in my head, with no appreciation of anything fine or beautiful." He turned to Alan, resentment filling his eyes. "That's what she thinks, isn't it? She tells you everything!"

Alan was momentarily silenced by the intensity and anguish in George's voice. When he finally answered, he chose his words cautiously. "That's not true. We both think you're a fine craftsman, a true artist. I've seen you start with a ruined, useless building and transform it into a beautiful home that anyone would be proud to live in. You're like an architect and designer; you understand color and texture and form.

You're the very best at what you do—and whatever talent I have I've inherited from you."

They were stopped at a red light and George turned to look at his son. The boy had never spoken to him like that before; they were not pals, like the fathers and sons on television and in the movies. He had often been surprised by Alan's accomplishments, even felt a little inferior beside his quick intellect and artistic talent. He had always believed that Alan's sensitivity came from Marie, not himself.

"Thank you, Alan," George said gruffly. "That was a nice thing for you to say."

The light changed and they drove on. Alan watched the landscape become more rural; they passed small duck farms, weathered shingle windmills and long flat stretches of potato fields. They slowed down as they entered the village of East Hampton. A touch of pre-Revolutionary beauty had been maintained here: there were well-kept store fronts, a white colonial church, and neatly trimmed lawns bordering quiet streets.

Alan glanced back at his father, wondering what he was thinking, wondering if his praise, which was genuine and deeply felt, had helped to soothe George's anger over his mother's outburst at the breakfast table.

Almost as if in reply to his son's thoughts, George said, "I hate it when the two of you speak French."

※

George turned the car off Montauk Highway and onto a private road that meandered lazily through a green meadow dotted with fir and elm trees. A sweeping curve suddenly brought them to the gates at the edge of the St. Clair estate. Alan's eyes widened at the sight of grounds that seemed to sweep in from the Atlantic and sprawl over acres of velvet green lawns and thickly wooded groves. Terraced gardens fell away to moss-covered slopes leading to a private beach. As they went around the circle drive to the house, he saw an Olympic-sized swimming pool surrounded by colorful lawn furniture. A few hundred feet away lay the neat rectangle of a tennis court.

The house made Alan catch his breath; it was dazzlingly white, a palatial jewel of neoclassic architecture, with broad steps and stately columns suggesting an Italian villa, all set in a bower of tall, leafy trees. George parked the car and Alan felt momentarily embarrassed; the Ford sedan was several years old, and its appearance marred the perfect symmetry of the setting. Like a boil on the ass of Michelangelo's David, he thought sourly, getting out of the car.

They walked up the steps to a door that was arched at the top and set with deep moldings. George lifted the heavy bronze knocker and let it drop. The clang it made against the metal plate sounded like a gong pealing out over the grounds. Alan wished his father had just rapped instead. A maid opened the door and looked at them with sharp, inquisitive eyes. His father said with an authority that surprised him, "Mr. Conway and his son to see Mr. St. Clair."

She shrugged a bony shoulder and stepped aside to let them in. The foyer was a huge circular affair with a black and white marble floor and a long, curving staircase that divided at the top and flowed into hallways leading to separate wings. There were tall ferns in white ceramic urns, marble and bronze sculptures. Ionic columns formed the perimeter of the hall; a crystal chandelier floated above it like a sparkling icy cloud.

The maid led them across the foyer and down a short hall to Mr. St. Clair's study. In a nasal voice that complemented her narrow, pinched face she told them that Mr. St. Clair would be with them in a few minutes. Then she left, her scrawny body swaying on perilously thin ankles.

Alan looked around the study and gave a long, low whistle. High ceilinged and paneled in rosewood, the room was filled with antique furniture and gold-framed drawings on the walls.

"Jesus, this place is wall-to-wall money!" Alan exclaimed. "What does St, Clair do?"

George replied: "He owns the St. Clair hotel chain. There's one in New York, and in other big cities here and in Europe. This house was built by his father, Augustus St. Clair, back at the turn of the century." He walked to the center of the spacious, richly appointed room. "Just look at that scrolled ceiling, Alan, and the carved wood molding around the doors and the fireplace."

"Fantastic," Alan muttered. But he was only half aware of the room itself; a Géricault drawing of a charging chasseur, his horse rearing up against a cloud-filled sky, had captured his attention. He was fascinated by the moment of violence and energy the artist had achieved with such economy and precision, and was so engrossed in the sketch that he hardly noticed Alexander St. Clair enter the room.

"Good morning, Mr. Conway," a ringing baritone called out.

His father hurried up to a tall, broad-shouldered man dressed in a soft sport shirt and linen weave slacks.

"Good morning, Mr. St. Clair," George answered, shaking his hand. "This is my son, Alan. He'll be working with me for the summer."

St. Clair turned to Alan and held out his hand. He had an imposing appearance. A thick shock of gray hair was neatly cut around his long, deeply tanned face, giving him a military look. His eyes were a cold, emotionless blue, and his long straight nose dominated the high rugged planes of his cheeks and jaws. A thin white scar ran from his hairline across his forehead to his left eyebrow, drawing it down and giving the effect of a permanent scowl.

Alan took the large, strong hand that was offered. St. Clair's grip was tight, almost deliberately painful, and Alan set his teeth to keep from wincing.

"I like the idea of a son working with his father," St. Clair said. "It's the best way to learn a trade—from a man with experience."

Alan withdrew his hand from the forceful grip and said quietly, "I'm just working for the summer, not learning a trade. I have a profession of my own."

"Oh?" St. Clair's smile was patronizing. "And what might that be?"

"I'm studying to be an artist."

"Really?" The word was clipped with disapproval. St. Clair turned to George. "Shall we get down to business?" He gestured to a chair by his desk, ignoring Alan completely.

"I want the restoration of the guest house finished by the middle of August, Conway," St. Clair said.

George began to go over the list of repairs needed, quietly protesting the lack of time to do all of them. But St. Clair was insistent. Alan moved away from them, humiliated at the way he and his father were being treated. He wanted to grab George by the arm, tell St. Clair to fuck off, and leave. Then he heard George say firmly, "Mr. St. Clair, if you want the job done, and done well, you'll have to give me more time— or find someone else to do it."

Alan looked at his father in surprise. The old man had balls! He suddenly felt better, and almost laughed aloud at the stunned look on St. Clair's face.

"I take great pride in the work I do," George went on. "And I'm sure you'd prefer to have the best of my craftsmanship than a job that was done quickly and sloppily."

St. Clair made an effort to control his temper. "Yes, yes, of course, Conway. Well—what do you suggest in the way of a schedule?"

Alan smiled and turned away to examine the drawings on the walls. He studied the pictures until he heard the two men rise and Mr. St. Clair say, "Let's take a look at the cottage again, Conway. I have a few ideas of my own about how I want it done."

He glanced over at Alan. "Since you're so interested in art, young man, would you like to see the collection in the library while your father and I go over these plans?" The offer was made brusquely, as if to indicate that Alan wasn't needed for the more important business at the guest house.

Alan looked to his father for agreement, and George nodded. "Thank you, Mr. St. Clair. I'd like that very much," he replied, making an effort to sound polite.

"Come along, then. I'll show you where it is," St. Clair said, striding out of the room.

They followed him down the hall to the foyer, where he gestured to a pair of closed doors. "That's the library," he said curtly, then led George out of the house.

Alan opened the doors, stepped into the room and stopped, astonished by what he saw. Deep chairs and low tables were arranged around a magnificent marble fireplace and one wall was filled with floor-to-ceiling shelves of books. An Oriental rug covered the center of the polished teak floor and sunlight flooded in through the French doors, washing a deep amber light over pieces of sculpture and fine china vases. But even more heart-stopping was the collection of paintings and drawings hanging on the paneled walls: examples of the Venetian school, a selection of French Impressionist masterworks, a group of Rembrandt etchings, early works by Picasso and Matisse. A Mary Cassatt pastel hung over a side table, and nearby were a group of Ingres drawings.

Admiration, envy, and resentment swept over him in a wave of conflicting emotions. It was inconceivable to him that any one man could possess such an extraordinary treasure of art for his own private pleasure. He found it difficult to reconcile what he saw with St. Clair's imperious manner and obvious disinterest in his desire to become an artist.

He moved into the room softly, as though entering a shrine, and began to devour the paintings with his eyes. A large portrait by John Singer Sargent hung over the mantel of the fireplace; he stepped closer, studying the canvas intently, examining the facile brushstrokes and quick, perfectly placed shots of color. The painting was of a middle-aged man, commanding in appearance, with fierce blue eyes and a stern face. He was wearing a brocade dressing gown and a white scarf, and stood in dignified solemnity, his hand resting lightly on the back of a chair.

"Formidable looking old bull, isn't he?" a voice behind him asked.

Alan turned, startled. At the far end of the room a woman was standing by the doors leading to the gardens. A wide-brimmed straw hat shadowed her face and he couldn't distinguish her features. She was dressed in a light cotton blouse knotted under her breasts and a colorful wraparound skirt. Her feet were bare, and she carried a basket filled with flowers over one arm. He thought that perhaps she was one of the maids.

"He looks a little like Mr. St. Clair. They both have that arrogant, rich-bastard expression," he said, glancing back at the portrait.

The woman laughed and came into the room. "He was a rich bastard. That's Mr. St. Clair's father, Augustus St. Clair, and you're right—they both have the same arrogant expression. But before you go any further, I think it's only fair to tell you that I am Olivia St. Clair, the rich bastard's daughter and Alexander's sister."

Alan's face fell. "Oh Christ, I'm sorry!" he said miserably.

Olivia smiled and put the basket of flowers down on a table. She took off her hat and he saw that she was older than he had thought, about fifty, although it was hard to tell. Short dark hair was casually styled around the cameo beauty of her small, oval face. As she came closer he saw a single streak of gray sweeping back from her brow, which only seemed to heighten her youthful appearance.

"Don't be sorry," she said, her brown eyes sparkling mischievously. "Many people have referred to them as rich bastards, even worse, and with proper justification. Now tell me who you are."

Alan was surprised and delighted by her frankness. "I'm Alan Conway."

"One of David and Dorian's friends? But they're still in San Francisco, didn't you know?"

He looked at her, bewildered. "No, I mean—I'm not a friend. My father was contracted to restore the guest house. I'll be working with the crew." Alan swallowed nervously, feeling awkward at the admission.

Olivia asked gently, "Then what are you doing here?"

"Mr. St. Clair said I could look at the collection."

"Oh? Then you must be interested in art."

"Yes—I paint." Alan felt a need to offer some credentials, some proof of his ability and intentions. He said quickly, "I'm going to New York in the fall to study with Jordan Shaw."

"Are you really?" Olivia looked surprised. "Jordan doesn't take many pupils. You must be very good."

Oh shit, she knows Shaw! Alan thought, feeling trapped. He shifted uneasily before her steady gaze, then burst out defensively, "I am very good—but what I said wasn't altogether true . . . Mr. Shaw has agreed to see my portfolio and decide if he'll take me as a pupil—but I know he will."

"I'm sure he will." She went to the basket of flowers she had brought in and began to arrange them in a large delft vase. "You have a great deal of self-confidence, and that's very important for a young artist. Perhaps you'll show me your work one day?"

"Yes, I'd like to." His eyes strayed back to the paintings on the walls.

"It's a hell of a collection, isn't it?" Olivia chuckled.

"I've never seen anything like it, outside of a museum. I didn't think Mr. St. Clair was that interested in art . . . oh, I'm sorry, I shouldn't have said that."

"Stop apologizing for what you think of my brother." Her voice was suddenly sharp. "You're right—he's not much interested in art, except as an investment. This collection is mine, and when I leave here I'm taking it with me. Alexander will have to find something else to fill the empty spaces on the walls. I've no doubt that some smart dealer will take advantage of his bourgeois taste and fill the place up with nineteenth-century kitsch."

She finished the flower arrangement and set the bowl on a table, then said, "Will you join me in a glass of iced tea and tell me more about yourself and your work?"

Alan nodded and she went to a bell cord hanging on the wall and pulled it. "I always feel like I'm appearing in an old English play when I do this. A bad play, I might add," she said with a grin.

A maid appeared at the door and Olivia ordered the tea. "Are you hungry?" she asked Alan. "Would you like a sandwich?"

Alan glanced at his watch and Olivia said, "Don't worry about the time. My brother is wretchedly methodical—I'm sure he'll go over every inch of the guest house with your father before he's satisfied."

Alan sat down in a chair and Olivia settled herself comfortably on a couch opposite him, tucked her feet up on the seat and regarded him curiously.

"Now, tell me about your work. What kind of painter do you want to be?"

"A successful one," Alan answered quickly.

"Successful? You mean financially or artistically?"

"Both."

"My God, what nerve!" Olivia laughed. "So—you're going to be rich and famous, and a fine artist."

"That's what I want. I'm very ambitious." His statement was a firm declaration of intent; he wanted to impress her with his sincerity, to make her understand how serious he was. "I'm going to be a portrait artist," he went on, "the best since Van Dyck."

"What an extravagant, boastful statement! I admire you for that—and for choosing Van Dyck as a model; his portraits are extraordinary. But watch your egotism—most artists put more of themselves in their portraits than the person they're painting. A good portrait artist is like a cruel thief—he steals something from his subject, some secret aspect of his soul, and puts it on canvas. Then he shows it to the world while the client, poor bastard, stands by hoping that whoever looks at the painting will be dazzled by the frame, or the room it's hanging in—anything but what's there in front of him in the portrait. That's why so many people that Thomas Eakins painted hid their portraits in attics and cellars!"

"I don't intend to compromise myself," he said. "I think an artist has a duty to paint whatever truth he sees, flattering or not. If the painting is good, it becomes more than a portrait—it stands alone, as a work of art."

Olivia listened to him, intrigued by his enthusiasm and attracted by his dark handsomeness and lithe figure. Had Alan been a homely boy she would have paid him less attention; Olivia cheerfully admitted to preferring things and people that were beautiful.

"And you think with that philosophy you're going to be a financial success?" she asked humorously.

"I'll do my best," Alan stated firmly.

"Well, perhaps . . . I was married to an artist very much like you. Yes, you remind me of him a great deal; he, too, was all fired up with ambition . . ."

"You make it sound like a curse."

"Do I? Well, maybe it is—maybe ambition is a curse, though God knows, without it artists are like snowflakes—each of them perfect and unique until they hit the ground. Then they melt and become so much slush."

Alan laughed. "You have a pretty tough view of artists."

"I've been around them a long time," she said. "You're right to be ambitious; you're young and have years of struggle ahead of you. But be judicious with your ambition, Alan. Use it—don't let it use you. Otherwise you're screwed!"

Outside the library there was a sudden sound of an argument, and then the doors flew open.

"Olivia, there you are! I've been looking all over for you!"

A woman stormed angrily into the room. Alan stood up and Olivia introduced them.

"Alan, this is my sister-in-law, Mrs. St. Clair. Vivian, this is Alan Conway. His father is restoring the guest house."

Vivian St. Clair glanced at him disinterestedly and sank into a chair with the willowy grace of a model.

"What's the trouble?" Olivia asked, irritated by Vivian's sudden intrusion.

"It's Dorian and David!"

"What about them?"

"They're coming home!"

"What happened to their plans to stay in San Francisco?"

"I don't know," she answered peevishly. "They never tell me anything. They sent a telegram, which that stupid maid forgot to give me—she just told me about it a moment ago—and now they're arriving at Kennedy in about two hours. Alex will be furious!"

"Well, there's no reason for an anxiety attack; Charles can pick them up."

"No, he can't," Vivian snapped. "No one can. Charles is out doing errands that should have been completed hours ago, Alex is busy with some carpenter, and I have too much to do to simply take off on a moment's notice to accommodate the idiosyncratic travel plans of my children!"

Alan listened to her tirade, observing the two women with interest. Where Olivia's beauty was natural and devoid of artifice, Vivian St. Clair had the manicured appearance of a woman who labored before her mirror with infinite care and diligence. Her blond hair was shoulder length and brushed smooth to frame her face. Artful makeup heightened the color of her large green eyes, but lines of tension drew down the corners of her mouth, giving her a petulant expression. He couldn't help noticing her figure; the pale blue knit dress she wore was designed to emphasize the curve of her breasts and hips. She was obviously younger than St. Clair, and Alan wondered if she fucked around when the old man wasn't looking. The idea pleased him.

Finished with complaining, Vivian leaned back in her chair and absently stroked her throat, as if to make the lines that had begun to show magically disappear.

"Why don't they simply take a cab home?" Olivia asked.

"That's ridiculous! I'd never hear the end of it!"

"Excuse me," Alan interrupted. "If you like, I could pick them up."

Vivian sat up and, for the first time since entering the room, looked at him directly. "That's very kind of you—" She searched for his name.

"Alan Conway," Olivia repeated it for her. "His father is the man with Alex at the guest house."

Vivian's face grew distant. "Oh, yes . . . Mr. Conway is repairing it—"

"Restoring it," Olivia corrected her.

"Yes, of course," she said indifferently.

"I think Alan's offer is your only solution. If it makes you feel better, he could borrow one of Charles's caps, even a jacket, take the Rolls and pretend he's a chauffeur, so as not to embarrass the children." Her voice betrayed no hint of sarcasm. "Of course, if that isn't enough, Dorian and David could always hide in the back seat," she concluded with a straight face.

"I don't think all that will be necessary, Olivia." Vivian glared at her. She said to Alan with a forced smile, "Thank you, Alan, I'm very grateful for your help. David and Dorian are coming in on TWA, flight 207, at three o'clock."

She stood up and left the room, closing the door behind her sharply.

Olivia sighed and offered Alan a cube of sugar from the tray of sandwiches and tea. "To sweeten the aftertaste of that little encounter?" She smiled wickedly.

Alan released the laughter he'd been holding in. "How do they put up with you?"

"Not very well, I'm afraid. But I'm moving to New York in the fall, and I'm sure they'll all breathe a sigh of relief when I'm gone."

"Then I'll be able to see you there!" he said impetuously. Olivia responded with a broad smile, "That was pretty much what I was thinking. Now let's get you off to the airport. I'll tell your father where you've gone. I'd like to talk with him anyway; I hear he's a marvel at what he does."

"Who told you that?"

"The rich bastard, my brother," she grinned. "He only

hirès the best, you know. Now let's go—you don't want to keep the heirs apparent waiting."

As they walked out of the house, Alan asked, "What are they like, David and Dorian?"

"David is twenty-one and Dorian is nineteen. They're beautiful and spoiled, autocratic. You've met their parents—take the best and the worst of both, stir well, then judge for yourself."

"That bad, is it?" he laughed.

"Wait and see."

3

THE ENGINES DRONED a deep, unpleasant sound that grated on David's nerves. His throat was dry, his head buzzed and his eyes burned slightly. In a few minutes they would be landing at Kennedy—they'd be home. There would be confusion, and endless, irritating questions. Later, perhaps, he and Dorian would be left alone. If they were lucky. He gripped the armrests and involuntarily bit his lip. There was a panicked expression on his face.

Dorian glanced up from her magazine. "You look awful. What are you so fucking nervous about? Everything's all right, now."

"I know that."

"Then relax, for God's sake!"

"Keep your voice down!" he hissed.

"David, sometimes you give me a pain!" Then she added more gently, "There's nothing to worry about. Nobody will ever know what happened. You'll feel better after we've been home for a couple of weeks."

David looked at her gratefully. "I've really spoiled your summer, haven't I? But I just couldn't stay in San Francisco—you know that."

"I know, I know," she replied with a sigh. "It doesn't matter. I probably would have 'freaked out,' as the flower children say, within a couple of weeks." Suddenly she laughed. "Oh God, David, weren't they awful? Those clothes! Why do they have to rebel against the establishment dressed like something out of *The Grapes of Wrath?*"

David chuckled. "I thought they looked like a cheap high school musical—all that embroidery and bad design. But I like *Grapes of Wrath* better; it's more to the point—and literate!"

"What a pair of snobs we are. We have the same gripes they do—"

"—but a lot more style!"

They giggled together and David relaxed into his seat, feeling more comfortable. Once they were home, everything would be all right. He'd think of a reason to give his father why they had left San Francisco so suddenly, and his mother wouldn't be much of a problem, she'd be so delighted to have him close by for the summer. He knew Dorian would help smooth over the rough spots; between them they could keep their parents at bay.

"It's just as well that we left when we did," David said. "The city was getting bizarre, even unsavory." His voice took on a smug sound. "Kids panhandling in the streets, sleeping in doorways and parks—and they were so filthy!"

Dorian gave him a noncommittal nod, and he went on, warming to his subject, "I didn't think much of the music, did you? That band we heard at the Avalon, what were they called—?"

"The Thirteenth Floor Elevators."

"Yes, that's right. Ridiculous name! And that girl who was screaming 'I'm God' during their encores? Remember—she had fluorescent paint all over her body? Christ!"

"They weren't that bad," Dorian responded mildly. Then, with a slightly malicious edge to her voice, she added, "They just bruised your refined sensibilities. The trouble with you is that even when you say hello you sound like you're issuing an edict. I really think a lot of the kids we met thought *you* were freaky!"

He turned on her angrily. "Not now, Dorian! I'm in no mood for your perverse little game of agree and disagree. There's time enough for that later—all summer, in fact."

"Yes, *all* summer," she said with emphasis.

"You're just pissed because you had to leave your sexy rock musician—what was his name? Silver Dust?" he asked tauntingly.

Dorian laughed harshly. "Very funny. And you're right, I am pissed! He was great in the sack—the best I've ever had!"

"He had the brains of a swan!"

"It wasn't his brains I was interested in! You must have noticed while you were in his room!"

"Stop it!" he warned her under his breath.

"Okay, okay," she shrugged, and turned to look out the window, growing quiet, pensive.

The trip hadn't worked out as she had hoped. Not that she was surprised; anticipated pleasures had often turned into fiascos. She couldn't blame David; she'd been as scornful as he of what they had encountered in the city—she had just tried harder to enjoy it, to lose herself in what was happening. But, in the end, she had felt like a guest in the midst of a wild party who suddenly perceives despair underlying the frenzy; all excitement evaporates and only a dismal self-consciousness remains. And worse, she had not been able to escape the conflicts that raged within her.

Dorian's anger had always taken the form of small rebellions, outbursts of frustration and resentment that never accomplished anything. She'd hated the schools she was sent to, and frequently got herself expelled for insulting teachers and administrators. She felt no affinity for girls who were carbon copies of each other, and she ridiculed boys destined to reincarnate their successful fathers. After losing her virginity to a football player in a deserted locker room, she used her nascent sexuality to manipulate a series of boys with whom she had brief, passionless affairs. Shrewd enough to keep her escapades secret from her parents, she managed to enjoy the benefits of wealth and privilege while pushing to the limit the social boundaries that constrained her.

Now she was nineteen, and beginning to fear that money and beauty were her only strengths. She distrusted men, tolerated her parents, and loved only her brother. She had little self-respect.

The No Smoking and Fasten Seatbelts signs flashed on as the plane banked and curved over the city. White shreds of clouds floated past, and below the skyscrapers and towers of Manhattan looked like an outdated model for a futuristic metropolis. The plane swooped lower, and tiny moving forms of traffic became visible, appearing sluggish and aimless.

Dorian rested her face against the window. "It's going to

be so goddamned boring on the Island," she said in a voice filled with disgust.

❦

The car was a 1950 Rolls-Royce Silver Cloud. For the first time in his life, Alan felt the power of an expensive car under his hands. He had never been so close to great wealth; it was as if he'd opened a door to a fantastic country where the color and texture of life were heightened to a brilliance that transcended everything he had known. And he'd made a friend of Olivia St. Clair, a beautiful, cultured woman whose perception and understanding was as startling to him as the discovery of a new emotion.

A sleek convertible with the top down drew alongside him. An attractive young woman sat behind the wheel. Alan glanced over at her; she was wearing a summer dress in a floral print, her full breasts cupped by large red flower petals. He stared at her, imagining what she looked like naked. She saw him looking at her and, with an angry frown, raced away.

He laughed out loud, wondering what would happen if he pursued her. After all, he was driving a Rolls—he could do anything!

A blare of horns jolted him out of his reverie. He spotted the Kennedy offramp and began to worry about getting the car safely through airport traffic. One scratch, one dent and, he had the feeling, Mrs. St. Clair would cheerfully skin him alive.

Once the car was parked he hurried into the TWA terminal and checked to see if the plane were on time. He was told it had just landed and was disembarking. On his way to the arrival area, he stopped abruptly; he had no idea what David and Dorian looked like! Berating his stupidity for not asking Mrs. St. Clair or Olivia how to recognize them, he rushed back to the information desk and had them paged. A few seconds later their names were being called over the PA system, adding to the noise and confusion of arriving and departing travelers.

Alan stood near the desk, peering anxiously into the crowds. A group of young people dressed in sandals, jeans and t-shirts came into view. They were conspicuously colorful in their headbands, beads and long hair. One of the girls carried a baby wrapped in a Day-Glo-painted blanket. Alan smiled, knowing that David and Dorian weren't among them, but wondering what Mrs. St. Clair's reaction would be if he returned with two flower children in the back seat.

A few more people hurried by, and then he saw them. He would have recognized them anywhere. They came across the lobby at a brisk stride, with the assurance and slightly irritated manner of film stars who travel incognito but hope that someone will recognize them. At the desk where the girl was still paging them, Dorian snapped, "We're the St. Clairs— now turn that damned thing off!"

David had the lithe grace of an athlete or dancer. His blond hair was neatly cut to collar length, and he was casually dressed in a lightweight summer suit that looked crisp and expensive. Dark wraparound glasses hid his eyes, but Alan could see that he was extraordinarily handsome. He had a tawny complexion, with a splash of high color across his cheeks. His nose was long, with small, tight nostrils, and his lips were full, sensitively shaped. He stood quietly beside his sister in an attitude of complete calm, while Dorian seemed to crackle with energy as she angrily looked around to see who had paged them.

Alan decided without any reservations that she was the most beautiful girl he had ever seen. Slim and of medium height, she was the opposite of David in coloring: her long dark hair gleamed as if it had just been washed, and her complexion was a rose-tinted ivory, pale, cool, and flawless. Dark glasses similar to her brother's masked her eyes. The delicate curve of her cheeks and supple line of her throat reminded Alan of the haughty beauties painted by Sargent. She was dressed in a simply cut pants suit that clung to her body, accentuating the long line of her thighs and small firm breasts. Her mouth was the flaw that made her exciting; it was large and sensual, with a curiously vulnerable expression, even when her lips were tightened in anger, as they were now.

Alan walked up to them and said, "Hello, I'm Alan Conway."

Their dark glasses stared at him, blunt and opaque.

"Your mother sent me to pick you up," he added hesitantly.

"Why?" David asked. His voice was quiet, almost a whisper.

"Your telegram arrived late, and there was no one else available."

Dorian was furious. "Was it your idea to blast our names all over the terminal? Exactly who the hell are you?"

"I told you," Alan said, bristling, "I'm Alan Conway, and yes, it was my idea! Since I've never seen you before, can you think of a better way for me to get your attention?"

David handed him their baggage stubs and without another word they turned and walked toward the exit. Alan followed them until they were outside. They stopped at the wide circle of traffic moving to the various terminals. David finally turned to him and asked, "Where's the car?"

"In the parking lot," Alan replied stiffly, "—it's the Silver Cloud . . ."

"I know our car!" David cut him off. He took Dorian's arm and they started across the cross-walk, ignoring the signal light, looking neither left or right. A cab squealed to a stop, narrowly missing them. The driver's curses reflected Alan's thoughts.

He watched until they disappeared into the parking lot, and smiled; the car was locked. Then he went to the baggage department and waited until everyone else had collected their luggage. To his dismay he saw ten pieces of matched top grain cowhide left, and they all belonged to David and Dorian. Fitting as many bags as he could under his arms, he slogged toward the parking lot.

David was leaning against the front of the car, smoking a cigarette; Dorian was pacing back and forth. When she saw Alan, she faced him with her arms crossed in front of her like an angry schoolteacher.

"The car is locked!" she exclaimed.

Alan dropped the bags at her feet and grinned. "Yes, I know. Keep your eyes on these. I don't trust the kid with the cigarette—" He nodded at David, then trotted off, leaving her openmouthed. When he returned with the rest of their luggage, he saw that David hadn't moved; Dorian was perched on one of the bags. He unlocked the trunk and filled it with as many pieces as he could. The last to fit in was the one she was sitting on. Alan looked over at her and asked, "Would you please bring that here?"

She got up and went to David, leaving the bag where it was. Alan walked over, picked it up and put it into the trunk. He unlocked the car doors, finished stacking the remaining pieces in the rear seat, then sat down behind the steering wheel and waited. David slid into the back, next to the bags, but Dorian came around to the driver's side.

"Move over," she said flatly. "I'll drive."

Alan looked up at her. Dorian's mouth was set in a firm, resolute line. He shifted into the passenger seat without a word and she took his place behind the wheel.

As they edged out into traffic Alan remained silent. He was more amused than upset by their childish behavior, and wildly curious about them both. Dorian seemed charged with a restless, jolting energy, but David, quietly self-assured and impassive, appeared more mysterious.

Once they were out of the airport and on the parkway Dorian began to drive with calculated recklessness, rushing through afternoon traffic, completely disregarding other motorists. It had taken Alan a little over two hours to make the trip in from East Hampton; she seemed determined to return in half that time.

David said nothing, unmoved by his sister's erratic performance. He knew that she was a very able driver, and simply putting Alan to the test because he was handsome and intrigued her. She was reacting typically; trying to get the upper hand, to gain control over him.

Alan wasn't sure what Dorian was doing, or why. He sat quietly, but with his feet braced against the floor, determined to remain unshakable as she weaved in and out of traffic at high speed.

By the time they were on the Sunrise Highway she was driving dangerously. Roadside businesses flew past them in a blur, red lights were raced or ignored. When another driver began to cross an intersection Dorian bore down on him, then threw the Rolls into a dizzying turn, barely avoiding a collision. Tires screeched as the Rolls lurched heavily back onto the road and straightened out.

Christ, we'll all be killed! Alan thought, going pale. He saw her flicker a glance in his direction, but stared straight ahead, wondering if the highway patrol had all gone to lunch at the same time.

They were just past Southampton when a motorcycle cop came tearing out of a side road after them.

David said quietly, "Dorian, the law . . ."

"Fuck 'em," she answered.

Gripping the steering wheel tightly, she hit the accelerator and the car jumped forward. The road ahead led into the village of East Hampton. At the outskirts she suddenly swerved, taking a sharp left onto a residential street that ended in a dirt road. Clouds of dust billowed out behind them as she turned the car again, this time into an open field, and plowed across it toward a grove of trees.

Alan saw her plan: to come around the back of the estate and lose the cop. He couldn't hear the sound of the motorcycle anymore, and resisted the impulse to look back for it. He saw her press her foot down on the accelerator.

Dorian guided the car around the trees with incredible agility, raced across an open space and finally landed on an asphalt drive that led to the gates of the estate. She brought the car to an abrupt halt, leaned back against the seat and smiled.

"Bravo," David said in a bored tone. "Next year the Grand Prix."

Alan said quietly, "We've got company."

Dorian looked up and saw the cop bringing his motorcycle to rest a few hundred feet away. "Shit!" she muttered, then turned to Alan and commanded: "Change places with me— fast!"

"What?"

"You heard me! Move! I don't have a driver's license!"

She tugged at his shoulder, and Alan shifted to let her squeeze under him.

The officer walked toward them, wiping his dust-streaked face with a large white handkerchief that fluttered in his hands like a flag of truce.

Dorian opened the door and swung out of the car with cool assurance. David silently went to stand by her side.

The cop looked from one to the other for a moment, then at Alan sitting behind the wheel.

He returned his attention to Dorian. "Weren't you driving, young lady?" he asked.

"No, he was," she contradicted him.

The cop shook his head, confused, and looked at David, who nodded in agreement with Dorian.

"I was driving, officer," Alan said loudly, to get his attention. "I was just showing off for my—" he hesitated before saying the word "—friends. I'm sorry—I got carried away."

"You sure did, mister. Let's see your license."

Alan took the citation and the lecture that went with it stoically. When the officer left, Dorian and David got back into the car. No one said anything as they drove through the opened gates and up the circle drive to the house. Alan cursed her silently for the way she had used him, dumbfounded by her casual attitude about the incident.

He brought the car to a stop a few feet from his father's car. Mrs. St. Clair was at the front door, and Dorian flew into her mother's arms with a big smile. David followed and received a fervent embrace. They all spoke together for a few minutes, then Vivian and Dorian disappeared into the house. David turned back to Alan.

"I'll give you a hand with the bags," he offered.

Alan nodded and they began to unload the luggage. "Are you working on the estate?" David asked.

"Yes. My father's firm was contracted to restore the guest house and I'm on the crew." He kept his voice aloof, thinking that David wasn't much better than his sister; he hadn't said anything to the cop either.

"Are you learning the trade by working with your father?"

"That's funny," Alan said coldly. "Your father assumed that, too. No, I'm not learning the trade."

David seemed puzzled, but Alan offered no further explanation. When they were finished David took off his sunglasses and patted his brow with a handkerchief. Alan glanced at him. It was the first time he had seen his eyes; they were darkly lashed and amber in color. Alan had hoped he might be cross-eyed.

56

"You were very patient with Dorian," David said. He smiled, revealing even, white teeth that added an irritating perfection to his handsomeness. "She tends to be a bit headstrong," he added.

Alan stared at him in astonishment. "Headstrong! Are you kidding? What a fucking understatement! She's not headstrong—she's nuts!

David's eyes narrowed angrily. A tense silence ensued. He reached into his jacket and pulled out his wallet.

"Here, this should take care of the fine," he said quietly, handing Alan some bills.

"Fuck off—I can take care of it myself."

David stood unmoving, his hand still extended. Then he put the money away, turned on his heel and walked toward the house.

Alan looked after him, seething with indignation. The son of a bitch. They had all treated him like a servant: St. Clair, his bitchy wife, and these two fucking kids who thought they could get away with anything because they had money! He wasn't even sure about his feelings toward Olivia; maybe she had just been putting him on. Shit!

He slammed the trunk of the car closed and started toward the guest house to find George. Hurrying across the wide green lawns, he felt a stab of longing that surprised him. Everything here; the house, the Rolls, the pompous behavior of the St. Clairs, all represented power, the power of money. Despite his anger, he could taste his envy. Even the idea of being so close to that power was exhilarating. He felt like a thief whose fingertips were only inches away from a fortune.

Suddenly Alan sensed that he was being watched. He looked back at the house, but there was no one near the entrance. A fluttering drape at a second floor window caught his eye, and he stared intently, positive that he saw a figure through the curtains. Was it Dorian? Vengefully, he gave whoever was watching the finger, then hurried on.

It was almost twilight by the time he and his father reached Bay Shore. To Alan's eyes the quiet, tree-lined streets appeared drab, and when they pulled up to the house it seemed shabby, drained of all color and vitality. A deep melancholy took hold of him, and he couldn't help wondering what Dorian and David were doing at this very moment. Were they talking about him? Or laughing at him.

David finished unpacking and carefully put his clothes away. Drawing a deep breath, he waited for the safety of being home to soften the bands of tension that still held him in a tight grip.

He looked around, letting his room enfold him like a soft blanket. The decor and furnishings were neat, almost severe: shelves of books and hammered brass lamps, a large walnut desk and several deep leather chairs. Dark brown rugs covered the floor, and a lighter brown spread lay tight over his bed. He had chosen the monochromatic color scheme himself, despite his mother's objections, finding it restful and less ostentatious than her florid taste. Olivia had given him a few eighteenth-century prints and a sketch by Thomas Eakins of two young men wrestling. These were simply framed and hung near a shelf of athletic trophies he had won in college; otherwise the walls were bare. A large dressing room and bath connected to the bedroom, and he had converted an adjoining room into a gym with mirrored walls, weights, a slant board, and an exercise bench.

He went to the French doors at the far end of the room, opened them and stepped out onto a balcony that overlooked the beach. A slight breeze wafted in from the ocean. The sun, brilliantly orange against a cloudless sky, was low on the horizon; he could hear the soft murmur of the tide rolling in against the shore.

The bedroom door opened and Dorian walked in. He turned to her with a frown and said, "Don't you think it's time you learned to knock first?"

"Why? Afraid I'll walk in and catch you jerking off?" she asked flippantly.

"When you were little, your vulgarity was amusing. It isn't anymore. Neither was your display of brainlessness driving home from the airport."

"Think I scared him away?"

"He knew what you were doing. He's not that stupid."

"Then maybe you scared him off."

"What do you mean? What the hell are you talking about?" He tried to keep his voice casual.

Dorian flung herself into a chair and looked up at him with a disarming smile. "I saw what happened—I was watching from my window. You tried to give him money for the ticket and he refused it."

"As father would say, it was a gesture of pride from the middle class," David replied loftily.

"Oh shit, come off it! He's no more class-conscious than I am. You're the one who's class-conscious—at least, sometimes," she added sweetly.

"As always, you're dodging the issue," David said with a knowing smile. "The fact is, you're very aware of your status, and that's why you go after football players, parking-lot attendants—and, I might add, rock musicians!"

"Go to hell!"

"You like to feel superior, don't you," he persisted. "That's why you roll in the mud, then come home to get cleaned up."

"You should talk," Dorian answered with a derisive laugh.

David's voice was triumphant. "Whenever I'm right about something, you get bitchy!"

She gave him a look that was full of charm. "If I'm not mistaken, I believe your credo is 'We are all in the gutter, but some of us are looking at the stars.' Oscar Wilde, isn't it?"

David looked away from her, his face suddenly filled with pain. Dorian got up and threw her arms around him. "Oh, David, don't look like that—I was just kidding."

He shrugged out of her embrace and walked back to the balcony. The sun seemed to be falling into the ocean, taking the last rays of daylight with it. For a few moments the whole landscape was bathed in the fiery sunset. Dorian came to his side and they stood watching the water turn into liquid gold.

"He is beautiful, isn't he," she murmured, more to herself than to her brother.

David felt uneasy at the hint of excitement in her voice. He glanced at her and saw that she was staring into space, her eyes remote and thoughtful. The deep amber light from the dying sun added a luminous cast to her beauty and a halo of bright gold around her dark hair. She reminded him of a Madonna in one of Olivia's paintings, and he wanted to say something about the deep love he felt for her. But instead, he said in a strained voice, "The summer isn't going to be as boring as we thought, is it?"

❦

"What is it, Alan? You've hardly touched your dinner," Marie said.

"He's had quite a day," George smiled. "Being at the St. Clair estate with me won't be so bad, will it, Alan?"

"No, of course not," he answered, then added, "Even if they didn't have that collection of paintings."

"Or their daughter?" George kidded him, his eyes twinkling. "I caught a glimpse of her before we left—"

"Oh?" Marie raised an eyebrow. "So there's a girl too, besides all the great art. You didn't mention her, Alan. Is she pretty?"

Alan grew quiet. "Yes, she is."

"And the aunt, Miss St. Clair—are you going to show her your work?"

"Yes—I think so . . ."

Marie looked at him expectantly, waiting for him to go on, but Alan remained silent, picking at his food moodily. She wondered what had happened to make him so quiet. Something with the girl, possibly? Would he tell her about it, later? Probably not. She felt a stab of jealousy. George was describing the house and its furnishings, and she tried to listen with interest, laughing when he described their meeting with Alexander St. Clair.

"The man sounds *un peu fou*," Marie said, turning to Alan for his opinion.

"Yeah, he's crazy all right," he replied absently. Suddenly he stood up and said, "I'm a little restless. I think I'll go for a walk."

Marie looked at him worriedly. "Are you feeling all right?"

"Sure, I'm fine." He smiled and bent to kiss her cheek. "I'll be back later."

"Not too late," his father said. "We have to be up early."

Alan left the house and walked to Montauk Highway. The warm, still air enveloped him like a stack of sodden blankets. There was a bustle of people on the Highway; summer visitors in shorts and gaudy shirts were shopping at the Grand

60

Union supermarket, and a few blocks away a crowd was lined up at the local movie house to see *The Sound of Music*. A small carnival filled the vacant lot next to the Howard Johnson's and a noisy crowd of teenagers had gathered, shouting and laughing.

It was the same as every summer he could remember; the people, the noise, the yellow glow of street lamps reflecting in store windows. All the shops were old, squeezed together side by side on the narrow street, as if they were holding each other up. Their displays of clothes and furniture had a tired, musty air, like an exhibition of faded relics in a seldom-visited museum. Nothing had changed since he was a child.

But he had changed. Something had happened to him, and he felt displaced here, as though he were a stranger wandering once-familiar streets.

Alan turned down Clinton Avenue, a quiet street lined with oak trees. Pale light filtered from the open windows of old houses, along with the sounds of TV sets and low murmurs of conversation. Someone was playing a Beatles record on a stereo, and he paused, nodding his head in time to "Eleanor Rigby."

The street ended at Benjamin Beach. Heat shimmered over the sand like ripples of water. In the nearby marina boats rocked in the stalls, their dark shapes resembling cut-out silhouettes pasted against the sky. Near the water's edge sat a group of long-haired kids, passing joints and singing softly to a guitar accompaniment. White swirls of foam rushed in over their feet, then sluggishly retreated into the murky depths of the water.

For a moment Alan thought he might join them, take a few hits and relax—he never kept any grass in the house, afraid that his parents would find it, and depended on friends for an occasional high. But he decided he wanted to be alone, and walked further up the beach to a secluded area. He took off his shirt and slipped out of his shoes. The night air played across his skin. He lay back on the sand and sighed deeply.

The solitude of the beach usually helped to clear his mind of problems, but tonight was different; moonlight cast amorphous shadows across the dunes and broke into a thousand gleaming flashes over the water, lending an eerie, Dali-esque mood to the scene.

Alan began to draw the outline of a woman's face in the sand. He thought about Dorian, and realized that he had not seen her without her sunglasses. He wondered if her eyes were the same as David's—amber and long lashed, faun shaped. She appeared in his mind like a strange drawing of a beautiful young woman who is masked. He remembered the pale ivory skin, the line of her throat, the smooth sweep of her back as it moved down to small buttocks. He could see her naked except for the sunglasses, and the image was mysterious and exciting.

"Alan—is that you? Alan Conway?" a voice called out from the darkness.

For one transcendent moment he thought it might be Dorian. "Yes—who is it?" he called back, his heart pounding.

"It's me—Terry. What are you doing out here all by yourself?"

Alan stood up as she came closer. It was the girl from New York he had met the day before. Her sudden appearance was momentarily disconcerting. "I thought you had to go back to the city last night," he said.

"I decided to play hooky for one more day. I'm going back in the morning." She looked around to see if there was anyone nearby, then stepped closer to him. "Want some company for a while?"

For a few seconds Alan couldn't answer, not knowing what he felt or wanted. The still, dark beach and faint moonlight made everything seem illusory. Terry took his hesitation for shyness, and said, "I had a terrific time last night. I was hoping I'd see you again—that's why I stayed over."

"I'm glad you did," he replied, not meaning it. In the moonlight her face was shadowed, her eyes hidden, and he thought of Dorian. He knew Terry was waiting for him to do something. He reached out and touched her shoulder. She moved into his arms. Her flesh was warm, yielding, and he grew aroused; yet he had the sensation of being outside himself, removed from what was happening. Terry's mouth opened as they kissed. He tore at her dress and clamped his hands roughly over her naked breasts.

Terry pulled away from him. "Hey, not so hard, baby! I bruise!"

"I'm sorry," Alan said hoarsely. "I didn't mean to . . ."

She smiled. "I didn't say I didn't like it. Now relax, and let me—"

She fell to her knees and fumbled with his belt, unzipped his fly and pushed his levis down to his ankles. His body tensed as she ran her hands up the back of his thighs and inside his shorts. She shoved them down over his ass, freeing his cock, and leaned forward to take it in her mouth. At the touch of her lips he wanted to grab her head and push himself into her throat all at once. Her mouth was hot and wet; he felt her tongue flick lightly over his balls.

"Take it easy," he groaned.

She let him slip out of her mouth, wiggled out of her dress and lay back in the sand, holding her arms out to him. Alan fell awkwardly to his knees, kicked off his pants and shorts, moving slowly, as if he were in a dream. She pulled him against her and ran her tongue over his throat, darted it playfully into his ear. Her hand snaked down between their bodies and grabbed his cock. She held it for a moment, teasing it along the inside of her thighs.

Alan shut his eyes tightly, his mind separated from the sensations tingling through his body. He felt the warm sand under him, heard the dull thudding of the surf, and the distant voices of the group further down the beach.

Terry grew impatient and pulled him over on top of her. "C'mon, honey, do it," she moaned.

Her legs wrapped around him like a fleshy vise, her body rubbing against his urgently. He felt trapped by her suffocating embrace, her insistent demands. An inexplicable anger welled up in him and he began to kiss her harshly. She ran her hands over his body, down his back to his buttocks, pulling him closer. Suddenly she jabbed a finger into his ass. His anger exploded and he shoved himself into her with one quick hard stroke, ignoring her cries, not caring if they were of pain or pleasure. He pulled her up until she was lying on her shoulders; her legs flailed wildly as he crouched on the balls of his feet and hammered away at her.

"Oh baby, I'm almost there!" Terry screamed. "Alan! Oh God, I'm going to come!"

Through clenched teeth he answered in guttural cries, heedless of everything except the hot rush of coming, draining away his fury. A final thrust held him motionless, and he abandoned himself to a small, exquisite death.

Alan fell to the sand, his head reeling. Terry was making small whimpering sounds. She reached out and touched his arm, but he shook her off and rose to his feet. Staggering slightly, he began to run toward the water and threw himself forward. The icy current hit him with a shock.

Hours later Alan lay in his room, staring into the darkness. He thought about what had happened on the beach with the detachment of a witness. He hadn't hurt Terry—if anything, she had loved it, made him promise to call her as soon as he got settled in New York. But that was little comfort. He still couldn't fathom the reason for his fury, or the acute sense of desolation he felt now; even the air he breathed seemed filled with it. There were so many things about himself that he didn't understand. He had hoped that the confusions and small terrors of boyhood were over. Yet he was still being caught unawares, faced with puzzling thoughts and unexpected reactions. Like tonight, with Terry.

Like meeting Dorian and David.

The whole day rushed back into his mind, and he went over it, incident by incident, trying to make some sense of what had taken place. Had all of it simply been an act? Dorian's recklessness and David's galling air of superiority? Or had they merely engaged in a teasing game, like children in a schoolyard?

He saw Dorian's face, vivacious and mocking, and David's, quiet and mysteriously intense. He remembered the moment when he thought Dorian was staring at him from the house. Now he was sure. She had been watching him.

Dorian . . . David and Dorian—Dorian and David; their names began to sound a persistent rhythm in his mind, lulling him into uneasy sleep.

4

DURING THE FOLLOWING week Alan worked with the crew on the guest house, and saw little of David and Dorian. Once he passed them as they were on their way to the tennis court; they nodded to him and continued on, as if he were a stranger. Another time he saw them coming across the grounds from the beach. When they caught sight of him, they began whispering to each other. The silvery peal of Dorian's laughter rang through the air, and Alan turned away self-consciously. He felt angry at himself for being infuriated by them. He was jealous of their private, seemingly inaccessible world, and more fascinated by Dorian each time he saw her.

One afternoon, while taking a cigarette break, he sat on a stone bench near the cottage and sketched. An unexpected breeze had drifted over the grounds, leaving in its wake a gentle sultriness. The lawns shimmered in the heat and long shadows of trees made secret places among the shrubs. Seagulls hovered in the sky, their raucous cries an abrasive dissonnance in the tranquil setting.

Alan examined the drawing he had been working on. It was of the main house, done in quick pen strokes, and designed to make the mansion look remote from its surroundings. He had drawn it at the top of the page, leaving the rest of the space blank except for a faint indication of shrubbery and trees. But without thinking he had filled in the space with sketches of Dorian and David, overlapping the house, making them part of the quality of isolation he had been trying to achieve.

He heard his name being called and looked up to see Olivia coming toward him. She was wearing a white blouse and a long, pastel-yellow skirt that created the illusion that she was gliding over the grass.

"You look like an Impressionist painting," he said as she drew near.

"Exactly the impression I was hoping for," she laughed, making a face at her pun. She floated into the seat beside him and said, "I haven't seen you for days." She glanced toward the cottage. "The work going well with your father?"

"I guess so—I'm just an apprentice where restoring is concerned; my father and the crew are the experts."

She looked down at the pad he was holding. "Are those some of your sketches? May I see them?"

He gave it to her and she studied the drawing. "Did you plan it this way—making the children part of the design?"

"No, that was just an accident," he admitted.

"One of those lucky accidents artists always talk about," she smiled. She flipped the pages and stopped at some quick sketches of his father working. "These are excellent—you're very good."

Alan wondered if she were being sincere. "Do you really think so?"

"I do indeed," she replied, closing the pad and handing it back to him. "I want to see more. In fact, I'd like to see what you are going to show Jordan. He's an old friend, and a few words from me could be very helpful . . ."

Any doubts about the sincerity of Olivia's interest in his work vanished with her offer. "Do you mean it?" he exclaimed. "Would you do that? . . . I'll bring out my portfolio tomorrow! Is that all right? I mean—will you have time . . . ?"

Olivia patted his hand. "Tomorrow is fine—but don't get too excited. I'm very critical."

Alan could hardly contain his excitement. He felt suddenly more energized than he had ever been. "I don't know how to thank you . . ."

"Time enough for that later, when there is something to thank me for," Olivia said.

Just then there was a shout of laughter; Dorian and David were running across the grounds toward the pool. Alan stood up, following them with his eyes. Olivia saw the longing on his face and started to say something, then thought better of it and remained silent.

The next day, in the late afternoon, Alan hurried off to the main house carrying his portfolio and a case of paintings. At the front door his knock was answered by a tall woman wearing an old-fashioned gray dress with a small white collar. She had a long, stern face, topped by a tightly wound coronet of hair the same color as her dress, as if they had been matched. There was a permanent crease above the bridge of her strong nose, and she stared at Alan with cold gray eyes.

"I'm Alan Conway . . ."

"Yes, I know," she said gruffly. "Miss Olivia is expecting you in the library." Then she added, "I'm Mrs. Childress, the housekeeper." The tone of her voice suggested that she wanted no misunderstanding about the possibility of her being a maid.

"I'm glad to meet you," Alan said respectfully. He followed her into the foyer.

"There's the library . . ." She gestured to the door and went off down the hall, the starched gray dress rustling like old newspapers.

Alan opened the door and Olivia looked up from the couch. "Ah, there you are! Come in, come in."

"I just met Mrs. Childress," he said, closing the door behind him. "She reminds me of a tough Whistler's Mother!"

Olivia laughed. "I think of her as 'The Relic,' but the children named her more accurately; they call her 'Chilly.' " She stood up and took the portfolio from his hands. Now, let's see what you've brought me."

While she put the portfolio on a table and opened it, Alan took his canvases out of the case and set them up. His throat was dry and his hands felt sweaty. Olivia looked at him and smiled. She reached for a decanter of sherry.

"Here, drink some of this," she said, pouring a glassful. "It's very old and perfect for nervous young artists."

He took the glass gratefully, and she began to examine his work. He had included everything he was going to show Jordan Shaw: quick sketches, finished drawings, watercolors, pastels and oils. He tried to appear casual but there were trickles of sweat under his arms, and the sherry was making him light-headed. He stepped to the French doors opening onto the garden for some air. Out of the corner of his eye he could see Olivia standing quite still in front of his paintings.

"Alan," she said finally, "I'm a little overwhelmed."

The sudden sound of her voice startled him, and he turned jerkily, spilling some of the wine.

"What? I mean—are they all right—?"

"They're a lot more than just 'all right,' " she said. "You are a superb draftsman for someone so young, and your brushwork and color sense are marvelous. You have a way to go, but your talent is obvious in every line. I shall certainly tell Jordan how I feel about your work."

Alan tried to smile and a nervous laugh escaped his lips. "Now may I say thank you?"

Olivia went to him and took his hand. "I think you'd better sit down before you fall down."

She led him to a chair and he sank into it. "You don't know what this means to me . . .," he stammered.

"I think I do, and it's just as exciting for me. I had a feeling about you the first time we met . . ."

Just then the library doors opened and Dorian walked in, followed by David. "Oh, I'm sorry," she said to Olivia. "I didn't know you were busy." She glanced at Alan and started to leave, motioning David to come with her.

"Don't go," Olivia called out. "Come look at the remarkable drawings and paintings Alan has done."

Dorian hesitated, but David turned back. He went up to the table and looked at the drawings, then at the canvases. "You did these?" he asked.

Alan stood up, nodding, but his attention was fixed on Dorian. She was standing uncertainly by the library doors, trying to avoid his eyes. Her dark hair was brushed into full, soft waves, and she wore a pale blue summer dress that left her arms and shoulders bare. For the first time since they had met he was seeing her without her sunglasses. Her eyes were dark, almost black, and fringed with long lashes. They had a tense, electric luster that added an unexpected radiance to her beauty.

David turned to him from the canvases and said, "These are all very good, but I don't understand why you work so academically. Compared to the new movements in art, this kind of realist painting seems very old-fashioned."

Olivia regarded her nephew with raised eyebrows. "Why

David, I had no idea you were aware of new movements in art," she chided him.

David frowned, and went on. "It's impossible to ignore the influence of Abstract Expressionism, Pop Art and the more radical developments in Minimal and Kinetic art. Surely, Alan, you've seen the work of Frank Stella, Jackson Pollock, Robert Motherwell . . .?"

Alan shifted his attention from Dorian to David's question. "Yes, I've seen their work," he answered.

"Well?" David asked.

"Well what?" Alan countered.

"Don't you think you're a bit—out of step, to put it as tactfully as possible?"

"That's a little more tactful than 'old-fashioned,' but not much," Alan replied irritably.

David acknowledged the barb with a condescending smile. "Now, now, Alan, don't be thin-skinned. After all, the kind of painting you're doing has been done—" he gestured to the masterpieces hanging on the walls. "The art of today should be new, a mirror of the present, not a reflection of the past. It should be involved with what's happening now." He paused, glancing at Alan's canvases. "Or are these merely a warm-up, until you find your own voice, as it were?"

Alan's irritation turned to anger. "Do you always talk like that, or are you just putting it on for my benefit? Or for yours?" he asked Olivia.

"I'm not sure," she replied with a puckish grin. "Though I must admit I was about to start taking notes . . ."

"I think David is right!" Dorian said defensively, coming to her brother's side.

"Ah, another expert heard from," Olivia rejoined.

"David has a right to his opinions!"

"Of course he does," Alan broke in angrily. "Just as I have a right to paint in any style I fucking please! It doesn't matter if it's 'out of step' or 'old-fashioned.' What does matter is if it's any good!"

"Exactly!" Olivia exclaimed. "That's what painting is all about—whether or not it's any good. And Alan's work is good, that much I can tell you out of my own experience and knowledge, which I think both of you will agree is considerable."

She stared at her niece and nephew challengingly and there was a long moment of silence. David picked up a sketch of Alan's mother and studied it. "This is really beautiful," he admitted, "but I still don't understand why you draw this way—"

"It's very simple," Alan said quietly, a little ashamed of his outburst in front of Olivia. "I try to put down what I see and what I feel so effectively that you have a kindred response. I'm not comfortable with nonobjective and conceptual art. That doesn't mean I don't admire it, just that I get no emotional reaction to that kind of expression. A realist style is my particular vehicle, as abstract expressionism is Motherwell's."

Dorian interrupted, "Do you always talk like that or are you just putting it on for us?"

"I don't have to put anything on for you."

"Touché!" David smiled. "I think you put your feelings very well, in words and on paper."

He turned back to the portfolio to examine the other drawings, but Dorian moved away from him, sullenly refusing to accept his sudden change of attitude. Alan, emboldened by his victory, stepped up to her and asked, "Would you let me do a sketch of you?"

She stared at him, her dark eyes hard and unyielding, her mouth turned down in a sulky pout. Then, as if she were lifting a veil, her expression changed. Her eyes softened, searched his face slyly. A smile hovered at the corners of her lips.

In that single glance, Alan knew that she had made some subtle alteration in her feelings toward him. He felt a sensual current flow between them, an understanding that isolated the space they stood in, separating them from David and Olivia.

"Why do you want to draw me?" she asked teasingly.

"You know why," Alan murmured.

"I'm not a good model—I'm too restless."

"I'm not demanding. I'll give you rest breaks," Alan answered softly.

Her face grew warm with color, and for an instant her eyes glittered a promise that made him catch his breath. Then she turned abruptly to David and Olivia and announced, "Alan wants to do a drawing of me."

David looked up at them, frowning, and Olivia said,

"That's a wonderful idea, Alan. And David, too. I'd love to have some portrait sketches of both of them. Will you do it, for me?"

"Well—yes, of course," Alan said hesitantly, seeing his hopes of being alone with Dorian diminish.

"Splendid!" Olivia cried. "As a matter of fact, I have an even better idea. I'd like a painting, a double portrait of Dorian and David. That's a commission, Alan, and I'm making it here and now, in front of witnesses."

Alan stared at her in disbelief. "Are you joking?"

"Not at all—and I shall pay you a very good price for it. I'm sure you'd prefer to paint the portrait than work with your father's crew, wouldn't you?"

"But—I'll need time," Alan stuttered, "I mean—there's preparatory sketches to do, and—"

"You have time. The children will be here all summer . . ."

Alan turned to the brother and sister, his face glowing with excitement. Dorian was watching him with an amused smile, but David appeared upset by Olivia's suggestion.

"I'm not sure I want to have my portrait painted," he said.

"Oh, David, don't be silly." Dorian looked at him accusingly. "We're stuck here for the summer, so we might as well do something constructive."

David's hands clenched into fists. "Posing for a portrait is not my idea of doing anything, constructive or otherwise!"

Olivia was puzzled by his sharp rejection of her idea. "Come on, David," she pleaded charmingly. "Do it for your old auntie. Please?"

Alan stood by quietly, hoping David would refuse; it was Dorian he wanted to paint, to be alone with. But David reluctantly shrugged his shoulders in assent and asked Alan, "Do you think you're up to it?"

Alan heard the skepticism in his voice. "Time will tell."

"The two of you make this painting sound like it's going to be a test of strength," Olivia said. "Before the gauntlet is thrown down, let's have a glass of wine to celebrate the occasion."

The glasses were poured and lifted. Olivia made the toast: "To Alan, and to a long successful career painting out of your own vision."

Alan looked around at all of them, fixing the moment in his mind. This was his first portrait commission, a thought that was at once thrilling and somehow frightening. He felt like a diver poised on the edge of a chasm, confident of his strength and ability, but unaware of what hidden dangers might lie beneath him.

5

"OLIVIA, YOU NEVER fail to amaze me. I can understand
your pride in being a patroness of the arts, but commissioning a twenty-year-old boy to do a portrait of David and
Dorian seems a bit extreme, even for you!" Vivian's flutey
voice had a tone usually reserved for servants: commanding,
and with a slight edge of contempt.

"One of my great pleasures in life is doing things that
amaze you," Olivia replied with a smile.

Alexander sipped some wine from a long-stemmed crystal
glass, looked up at the maid hovering anxiously by his side
and nodded. While she hurriedly went around the table filling
glasses, he turned his attention to his sister.

"I'm afraid I have to agree with Vivian," he said in a
mildly disapproving tone.

"Don't be afraid," Olivia replied. "It won't be the first time
we've disagreed."

The family was gathered in the small dining room for dinner. Dorian and David sat next to each other, concentrating
on their food. A few minutes earlier, over cocktails, Olivia
had told her brother and his wife about commissioning the
painting, and now the subject was beginning to create an air
of tension around the table.

"I don't particularly want that boy hanging around the
house for the entire summer," Alexander said firmly.

Olivia sighed and put down her fork. "Alex, *that boy* is extraordinarily gifted. I know your interest in art is rarely excited beyond the value of your investments, but someday you
may find yourself bragging to your friends that Alan Conway's first commission was of your children, and painted
right here, in your cozy little palace!"

"Olivia, be sensible," Alexander said. "The boy is brash and common . . ."

"—and we certainly don't want to risk another incident like the one we had with that little thief a few years ago!" Vivian interjected.

Dorian glanced quickly at David. Except for a flush of color that spread across his cheeks, he appeared unmoved by what his mother had said, and continued to eat methodically, as if he were dining alone.

"Alan is not a thief," Olivia said patiently. "If you want to talk about thieves, I'll remind you of some of Father's more intricate business deals!"

Alexander shot a hard look at her and squared his shoulders like a general about to go into battle. "Olivia, I find all of this very disagreeable—"

"Of course you do! You preside over this house as if it were one of the hotels and we were members of the staff! Honestly, Alex, you grow more like Father every day, with your silly pretensions and grand manner. You insist on maintaining an attitude that is as stuffy as it is outdated!"

Vivian broke in angrily, "Really, Olivia, sometimes I think your association with artists has damaged your sense of values!"

"Don't you dare refer to my marriage to Scott as an 'association!' " Olivia said harshly.

"I don't think we should go on with this discussion in front of the children," Alexander barked.

"It's not a discussion, it's an argument!"

"And don't call us children," Dorian broke in. "It's demeaning."

"Careful," David whispered under his breath.

"After all," Dorian went on heedlessly, "it's hardly a secret that Olivia's husband deserted her, or that Grandfather swindled any number of people to start the hotel chain!"

"That's enough!" Alexander bellowed. "Dorian, leave the table at once!"

"Not until I've had my dessert," she replied calmly. "It's chocolate mousse, and I wouldn't miss it for anything."

David suddenly broke into a gale of laughter. Vivian turned to him, a shocked expression in her eyes. "I don't see that anything humorous has been said here, David."

"Of course there has," Olivia said, beginning to smile herself. "We've played these scenes so many times we sound like the road company of a Victorian play. But I shall shortly relieve you of one of the cast; I've taken a flat on Beekman Place in New York that will be available in September."

"No one has asked you to leave, Olivia," Alexander said.

"I almost wish you had. I've been here much too long as it is. I should have taken my own place a long time ago . . ."

"We were happy to have you," Vivian said with a forced smile.

Olivia chuckled at her effort. "And you'll be just as happy to see me leave."

Vivian's smile faded. "Well, of course, I'm sure you prefer to live alone—"

Olivia's eyes widened innocently. "Oh, I never said I was going to live alone. There's a perfectly beautiful doorman down the street from the house—"

Everyone except Vivian began to laugh, Alexander the hardest of all. "Olivia, you're incorrigible! You always have been, even when we were children," he gasped, wiping his eyes.

Dorian seized advantage of the moment and asked, "Then it's all right for Alan to do our portrait?"

Alexander looked at his daughter shrewdly. "You'd make a wonderful salesman, Dorian—you know exactly when to be persistent and how to get your own way." He smiled grudgingly. "Well, since the young man has such an unqualified endorsement from your aunt, then—yes, he can do the portrait."

Vivian threw up her hands in exasperation. "Alex, you're impossible!" Seeing the stubborn set of his jaw, she added quickly, "Sometimes you're simply too considerate. Where is he going to set up all of his paraphernalia? We certainly don't want the house smelling of paint and turpentine!"

"He could use the guest room on the second floor," David suggested. "The light is good and the furniture could be moved . . ."

"That's impossible, dear," Vivian replied, refusing to lose ground. "Jonathan is coming in from Paris in a few weeks, and he'll be using that room."

"Uncle Jonathan is coming here? That's wonderful!" Dorian exclaimed.

Vivian turned to her daughter. "Yes, isn't it? I was so hoping he could use the guest house, but I understand that the man repairing it won't have it finished in time." She looked at Dorian meaningfully.

Dorian refused to acknowledge the sarcastic reference to Alan's father. "We can find a place for Alan to set up," she said. "The house is big enough."

Vivian sat back and sighed. "Well, I shall leave that to you and David. But do be careful—with all the valuables lying around, I wouldn't want anything broken." She smiled cheerily at Alexander.

God, how does she do it? Dorian wondered admiringly. She glanced at David and realized that he wasn't sharing her amusement at Vivian's maneuverings. His face was pale and there was a strained expression in his eyes.

"Why is Jonathan coming here?" he asked his father.

"Because I told him to," Alexander replied. "There are some things we have to discuss about his management of the Paris hotel and the European operation in general. We'll have meetings here, and in New York, and I expect you to attend them."

"Why? I've told you I don't want to get involved in the business . . ."

"I don't wish to discuss it now," Alexander cut him off.

"Don't I have anything to say about it?" David demanded.

"Nothing."

"When *do* I get a chance to say something about my own life?" David went on hotly. "You've directed every move I've made since I was a child."

"A direction you needed then and need now."

"In your opinion only!"

"An opinion you should pay more attention to!"

"I don't agree," David said grimly. "I'm twenty-one—old enough to make my own decisions."

"And have you made any? What, exactly, are you planning to do with your life?"

Vivian interrupted her husband. "Alex, perhaps you could go into this another time . . .?"

"Why? He'll be as indecisive later as he is now. Tell us,

David. What are you going to do? Speak up—I'm giving you the opportunity you asked for. Take advantage of it!"

David seethed with rage at the unexpected confrontation. It was the kind of insidious manipulation his father used in all of their quarrels to catch him off balance, leaving him as insecure as a chastised schoolboy.

"Well?" his father pressed him. "We're all waiting to hear what you have to say."

David put his napkin on the table, rose to his feet and started from the room.

"Come back here!" Alexander commanded. "I'm not finished with you yet!" His face was flushed with anger and the scar across his brow showed a deadly white.

"You were finished with me a long time ago," David muttered. He crossed the entry hall and went out the front door, slamming it behind him.

An uncomfortable silence fell over the table. Olivia pushed away from the table and stood up. Alexander glared at her.

"Are you leaving us too?"

She looked at him reproachfully. "Alex, you're a very silly man," she said quietly. Then she left the room.

Dorian was furious with her father. It was an old, familiar anger, like a recurring headache, made more intense by repetition. But she remained silent, afraid that anything she said might ruin Alan's chance of doing the painting. For the moment, that was all she cared about.

"David can be so stubborn sometimes," Vivian said, breaking the silence. "I'm sure he'll grow out of it." She gave Alexander a bright smile. "By the way, I was thinking we should give Jonathan a party, to welcome him home. What do you think, dear?"

Alexander nodded his head in agreement. His face was still flaming with color, and he tapped his fingers against the table in a staccato rhythm. The maid came in to clear the table, and Vivian told her to bring a bottle of his favorite brandy.

Dorian watched her mother behave as though nothing had happened. She understood; it was Vivian's way of dealing with her husband's rages. She would placate him with inane chatter, the brandy would dissipate his anger, and for a while the fight with David would be forgotten. But it wouldn't change anything; it never did.

Dorian tried to think charitably about her mother; she was an uncomplicated woman who hated scenes and avoided making decisions. But the order of her life was flawed by a volatile, demanding husband and two children about whom she knew absolutely nothing. For as long as Dorian could remember, Vivian had hovered on the periphery of their lives, more a gracious hostess than a loving mother. That was the consequence of playing by Alexander's rules; she was not so much disinterested in her children's lives as afraid of upsetting her tyrannical husband. And by now, Dorian sadly realized, she probably couldn't think of any advice to offer, even if she wanted to.

The maid returned with the brandy. Vivian dismissed her with a nod and set a glass before Alexander. On an impulse Dorian picked up the bottle and gave her mother a conspiratorial wink. Then she turned to her father.

"Shall I pour?" she asked sweetly.

❦

David lay stretched out on a flat rock in a cove a few hundred yards up the beach from the house. It was isolated from the rest of the grounds by tall sand dunes covered with sparse shrubbery and wild grass, and had always been his place of refuge. Here, like the rocks, he felt fixed in place, resisting the onslaught of the waves without yielding. But it was only imagined strength; he always yielded to his father. Was there ever a time when he didn't give in to Alexander's demands? No, not really. Opposing him was like shoveling shit against the tide.

David laughed at the expression and tried to remember where he had heard it. Oh yes, from Chilly; she claimed it was an old New England saying: "Trying to defy the inevitable is like shoveling shit against the tide."

He turned over on his stomach and stared out at the horizon. The long evening twilight had begun and the sky was touched with traces of pink and gold from the setting sun. Seagulls hovered over the water, their widespread wings catching glints of color, and in the distance he saw the pale silhouette of a sailboat making its way back to shore.

Jonathan was coming; the thought struck him like a chill.

It was going to happen and there was nothing he could do to stop it. The summer trips to the hotels in Europe, language classes, studies in business management, European history, everything he had learned—all geared to prepare him for working with Jonathan. Alexander would finally get what he wanted. David bowed his head under the weight of defeat. Would his father like him then? Had he ever liked him—as an infant, as a child? He couldn't remember. It seemed that there had always been Alexander's dictates, decisions, aspirations to live up to, and he had never been equal to the task.

Did he suspect that his son was queer? David said the word silently, testing it in his mind's ear. He tried to add it to the words: "I am—."

Did they know, his father and mother? Is that why Vivian was afraid to have Alan around, why she had mentioned "that little thief a few years ago" at dinner?

That little thief . . .

David would never forget him.

The incident had occurred during the summer of 1959.

David was fourteen years old, a shy, slender boy, introspective and inclined to secrecy. Even though he attended one of the best private schools in the country and was a better-than-average student he remained aloof from other boys, preferring the world of his imagination, where he was a bold, decisive figure, free of his father's demands and disapproval. His classmates shared a life that he had no part of: rowdy games and whispered secrets, exchanged confidences about the mysteries of sex. Except for his friendship with his sister, he was alone.

That summer Dorian was banished to an exclusive girl's camp as punishment for smuggling whiskey into her room at school and getting some of the other girls drunk. David was supposed to accompany Alexander on a hunting trip to South America, a prospect that filled him with dread; his father would be there to criticize and belittle any effort he made. But at the last minute a business crisis had forced Alexander to cancel the trip.

With his father in New York most of the time and his mother busy with her social schedule, David had the run of the estate. He read and swam, took long walks along the beach, piloted a small sailboat around Montauk Point. The summer was languid and peaceful, even though he was lonely for Dorian.

Then Vivian had an argument with the cook and fired her. A few days later she hired a Mrs. McGuire to take her place. That night the woman and her seventeen-year-old son Don moved in. He was put to work helping with the gardening.

The first time David saw him, Don was weeding a flower bed at the back of the house. Out of curiosity he approached him.

"Hi, how is it going?"

"Lousy! I'm bustin' my balls and getting sunstroke. Who are you?"

"I'm David St. Clair."

"Yeah?" Don looked up at him and grinned. "Hiya."

Don stood up and they shook hands. He was husky and had black curly hair and black eyes that sparkled when he laughed. David liked him.

"Can I help you?" he asked.

"I don't think your folks want you working with me."

"But I want to. They don't care. They don't even know."

"You do a lot of things your folks don't know?"

"Sure."

"Bullshit!" Don laughed, and handed him a rake.

In the days that followed the two boys became better acquainted. Don was different from anyone David had ever known. His coarse speech and crude manners were somehow attractive, and his disrespect for authority made him even more appealing. He seemed independent and free, qualities that David longed to possess. He began looking forward to seeing Don every day.

Don talked openly about his life; he had grown up in a poor neighborhood in New York, had run with a gang that stole cars for joyrides and got into fights with other gangs. He'd been on the streets since he was twelve. David was fascinated.

They were working together on the grounds one afternoon when a maid came out to tell David his parents would be staying overnight in New York. As she walked back to the house, Don stared after her with a sour expression.

"Too bad all your maids are such old ladies," he said absently, and went on with his digging.

"Why?" David asked innocently.

Don looked up at him and winked. "Cause I'm horny, kid—and there's nothin' doin out here. Christ, if I only had a car . . ."

"Do you have a girl back in the city?"

"Yeah, I used to—" he stopped, then laughed. "What the fuck do you know about girls? You're too young."

"I'm not! I've read some books—I know all about it!"

"You don't know shit! Reading isn't the same as doing," Don said with a leering smile.

"Tell me."

Don was reluctant at first, but David coaxed and wheedled until he relented and began telling him about his sexual exploits. His crude words and graphic descriptions were more exciting than anything David had ever imagined. He kept pestering him for more stories, more details. Compared to the dry explanation of the reproductive process his father had given him, and the few things he had overheard at school, Don's tales were magical evocations arousing sensations that were new and a little frightening. He became greedy to learn everything Don knew. And Don, relishing the hero worship and adulation he was receiving, became endlessly inventive.

At night, alone in his room, David's thoughts were filled with the images Don had described. He began to have sexual fantasies about himself being like Don and doing all the things Don had described. He masturbated, conjuring up visions of a man and woman locked in a passionate embrace, their shadowy bodies a single form of tangled limbs. But it was Don he saw having the woman, not himself.

One day Don made an unexpected offer. "I got some magazines hidden in my room, the kind with pictures you'd like. Wanna see them?"

"Yes! When can I see them? Now?"

"Later, while Ma is preparing dinner. We can be alone then."

David waited impatiently until late in the afternoon, then stealthily made his way to Don's room in the servant's quarters. All around him the sounds of the house seemed magnified and unreal: pots clattering in the kitchen, a maid vacuuming the carpets, the voice of his mother on the phone. Moving quickly through the rooms, he felt as thin and light as air, as if he were separated from that reality and part of another, more thrilling, dangerous world.

The room was small and dimly lit. It smelled of cigarettes and the odor of Don's body. He saw Don waiting for him, lying on a narrow bed with the magazines spread out around him, like a pagan ready to perform a strange ritual.

David sat down beside him and grabbed up a magazine. He raced through the pages, his heart pounding with excitement. Don offered him another one, laughing softly at his wide-eyed astonishment over the photographs of naked women.

"Christ, lookit the tits on this one!" Don exclaimed. "I'd like to stick my cock between that pair and rub off!" He looked up at David and grinned. "You got a hard-on."

David flushed with embarrassment. "So do you!"

"Yeah, and it aches like hell." Don rubbed the bulge in his pants and stared steadily at David. "I'm going to beat off." He opened his belt and pulled down his zipper.

David watched him nervously. He had seen other boys playing with themselves in school, in the bathroom or late at night in the dorm. But this was different; Don was older—a man, and they were together in his small room. He began to perspire; Don had shoved his pants down and was stroking himself. Magazines lay open, surrounding him in garish pictures of women holding their breasts, opening their thighs. The scene blurred before David's eyes into an image of writhing flesh, of Don fondling their legs and hips while slowly caressing his cock.

"Wanna touch it?" Don asked in a low voice.

"No—I'm afraid," David whispered.

"Of touching it? You baby! C'mon, take yours out—we'll do each other . . . See, there's nothing to be afraid of . . . Feels good, doesn't it?"

". . . Yes."

They climaxed together in shuddering gasps, holding each other tightly, spurting over the magazines and themselves. David lay in a daze, feeling Don's hand still firmly grasping his cock, his body still twitching beside him. He put his head against Don's shoulder and closed his eyes, trying not to cry from the overwhelming happiness he felt. For the first time in his life he was close to someone, connected to another human being. The world outside this moment had disappeared; nothing else existed.

After that there were other times, in the dunes along the beach and in hidden places on the grounds. David was deliriously happy; thoughts of Don and the secret pleasures they enjoyed filled his every waking moment. Don had told him that what they were doing was something shared only between close buddies, and David trusted him completely.

Late one afternoon, in the boat house near the small dock where the family kept their cabin cruiser, Don showed him a magazine more shocking than the others. It was filled with glossy color pictures of men and women in a variety of sexual acts. They were doing all the things Don had described, and more.

Sprawled on the floor with the magazine between them, the two boys became furiously aroused.

"Suck it, Davey," Don pleaded. "Like in the pictures! C'mon, you're my friend, do it."

Don's hands reached out to him, touched and caressed his body, closed over the tangle of his hair. "Do it now, Davey."

Don's touch fired his excitement, made him breathless. Yes, they were friends, but even more than that, he loved Don! A torrent of emotion swept through him, leaving him weak. He felt Don's hands tighten on his head and submitted, unresisting, to his demand.

For days afterward David avoided Don, sickened by what had happened. Don's climax had been terrifying. Caught in the steel grip of his hands, like a trapped animal, David had choked on fear and semen.

The bitter taste lingered in the back of his throat, haunting him late at night in his bed and making him relive the scene over and over, until finally he realized with a shock that he wanted to do it again.

Anguished and confused, he found his days once again long and lonely, made more painful by the knowledge of Don's presence close by. He took to watching him from behind the blinds of his windows, hoping he would look up from his work in the garden, make some sign that he missed him. Once they came face to face near the tennis court. Don started toward him, smiling, but David turned and ran.

He began to eat less and sleep fitfully, plagued by doubts and guilt, but driven by his desire to be with Don.

Early one evening he sauntered out onto the grounds as Don was finishing up his work. David stood with his hands in his pockets in an attitude of nonchalance where Don could see him. The two boys stared at each other through the darkening twilight. Don smiled, then turned and began walking toward the boat house.

David followed him slowly.

A week later, Don asked a favor. "I need some money, Davey. Can you lend me ten?"

It was easy to comply with his request—David was given a generous allowance in cash every month.

And then, a few days later, "Listen, kid, something's come up—I need another twenty."

And then, "David, I can get a car! The guy only wants fifty for a down payment!" David put the money in his hands and Don hugged him happily. "I'll be able to take you for rides in the country—"

But after a while the requests became demands and David began to object. At first Don was angry. Then he found a more effective means to get what he wanted; he became indifferent to David. Days passed and David grew distraught. He relented and continued to give Don money until all that he had for the month was gone; it would be a few weeks before he received more.

But Don insisted. "You can get it—there's gotta be some cash in the house! Get me some more money and I'll make you feel good, I promise . . ."

David stole the money from his mother's purse; she never knew how much she was carrying. He felt ashamed and guilty.

Don continued to pressure him until he finally cried out, "I can't steal any more money! I can't!"

Don's eyes turned hard, like black stones, and his voice was threatening. "I need more money. If you don't get it, I'll tell my mother you been chasin' me, that you're a little cocksucker! She'll tell your dad, I know she will!"

David stared at him, devastated by a far more powerful emotion than fear of exposure. He'd been betrayed by someone he had trusted, had worshiped. He ran to his room, convulsed with outrage and grief. Everything had been a lie! Don had used him, exploited him!

Hours passed. David lay on his bed, wide-eyed, his face streaked with dried tears. Hatred seeped through him, destroying all vestiges of the love he had felt. The strength of it surprised him. And with the hatred came cunning. Don had threatened him, now he had to protect himself. Worse than Don's betrayal would be his father's wrath. He had to do something—and quickly.

The theft of his mother's ruby choker was discovered early that evening. Everyone was questioned. David's face was a mask of innocence when he told his father that he had seen Don in the house that afternoon. Alexander went to the servant's quarters and Don's room was searched. The choker was found in the box he kept hidden under the bed, beneath the pornographic magazines. Don's mother cried, and no charges were pressed. They left the house that night.

David watched from the window as they drove away. He felt no trace of remorse, but a sense of triumph, of vindication. Don had forced him to discover a strength he had never known, and he had used that strength to protect himself, used the security of his position as a St. Clair to keep from being intimidated. How ironic, he thought, that his father would never know *how* he had learned a doctrine that Alexander had been trying to instill in him for years.

A breeze stirred the long swaying stalks of wild grass. David shivered. It was almost dark. The light had turned to deep silver over the water, and the beach looked like a ragged strip of gray gauze made damp at its edges by the gentle touch of the surf. A few yards up fom the cove he could see the boat house, a small cottage-like structure of white frame and a peaked, shingled roof. He smiled sadly, remembering what the place had once meant to him.

Suddenly he heard Dorian calling his name. He sat up and saw her running along the sand, her black hair lifted out behind her, white dress fluttering like a ghostly sail in the dying light.

"I thought you'd be out here," she said breathlessly, and threw herself down beside him. "Everything is quiet now. Mother plied Dad with brandy, and they're in the library, where he's putting her to sleep with reminiscences of the good old days and how the world is going to hell."

David smiled. "Did he change his mind about the portrait?"

"Nope. You made him forget all about it."

They laughed together for a moment, then she asked, "Are you worried about Jonathan—I mean, what will happen while he's here?"

David nodded slowly. "I know what will happen, and there's nothing I can do to avoid it, that's what's so frustrating." He sighed deeply. "It's my own fault—I never could stand up to Dad. And the truth of it is, I really wouldn't know what else to do except get into the business."

He leaned back and cushioned his head with his hands. "I'm very weak. Charming, but weak."

"Oh David, that's silly! You're not weak." She looked at him with a mock-serious expression. "Are you?"

They laughed again, then were quiet for a while.

"David, you don't really mind Alan doing the painting, do you?"

He understood what she was asking, and replied, "No, of course not. He's very talented." He saw that she still regarded him questioningly, and added, "Don't worry—he only has eyes for you."

She gave him a quick smile and lay down beside him. He put his arm around her and she rested her head on his chest.

"David, I love you."

"I know."

❦

Marie was thrilled with Alan's news of the commission. During dinner she and her son speculated about his future while George listened, relieved that he wouldn't have to endure his wife's reproaches about Alan working on the crew for the rest of the summer.

"Do you think it may lead to doing portraits of the rest of

the family?" he asked at one point, trying to enter into their discussion.

"It might, if it's good enough—" Alan replied.

"Of course it will be good enough," Marie interrupted. "You must believe in yourself, Alan, and be prepared to advance in your career with every opportunity that comes your way. And you will, I know you will."

George heard the censure of his own lack of ambition in her words, and continued to eat his dinner silently.

Later in the evening, Alan lay on the living room floor, scribbling thumbnail sketches in a large drawing pad, while Marie sat quietly in a nearby chair, writing in a leather-bound book. George was in the den adjoining the living room, watching television. A blaring musical theme announced the nightly newscast, followed by the anchorman's sober recitation of the week's death toll in Viet Nam.

"Marie," George called, "do you want to watch the news?"

"No, no—and close the door or turn it down; I don't want to hear it!"

"All right, all right! Sorry I asked . . ."

A moment later the sound was lowered. Alan went on working, undisturbed by the sharp exchange, but Marie shook her head wearily; how could George be so thoughtless? Had he forgotten that her entire family had been murdered by the Nazis during the occupation? Or was it simply that he didn't care any more? Yes, that was probably the answer, the reason there was so little left of their marriage; he had stopped caring for her—or was it that she had never really cared for him at all?

As a child, Marie had lived in Paris, the daughter of a successful playwright and an accomplished actress. Their home had been an elegant town house near the Place de la Concorde. She had attended private school, played with her friends in the Tuileries, and watched her mother perform at the Comédie-Française. But that world was shattered when the Germans invaded France and occupied Paris. She saw her parents and older brothers shot in the streets for their work in the Resistance.

After that, she survived from one day to the next by whatever means were necessary. By the time she arrived in New

York in 1945, Marie was toughened by years of war and suffering to the point of indifference to life.

She lived with distant relatives for whom she had no regard, and who, in turn, had little interest in her. During the day she studied English, and at night she drifted through the noise and turbulence of city streets like a spectre.

In a subway station one night a group of drunken servicemen just returned from Europe started to harass her. A man stepped up to them, they exchanged some heated words and he pulled her away to safety. He invited her to dinner, and when they were finished, offered to take her home. But it was late, and if she woke the family, there would be an unpleasant scene. When he suggested that they go back to his place, she agreed; they spent the night together. And that was George.

He asked to see her again, and she said yes, not because she liked him but because he insisted. For Marie the idea of romantic love belonged to the lost world of her childhood. The war had left her emotionally inert; her only response was to his kindness. A few months later she discovered she was pregnant. George was elated, and insisted they marry at once; he would take care of her and she wouldn't have to worry about the future. She accepted, preferring to let someone else direct the course of her life. She was only nineteen years old.

With the birth of Alan, Marie became aware, as if for the first time, that life contained beauty. She realized that the horrors she had witnessed as a child had not destroyed her capacity to love; she adored her son. When he began to evince his talent for art, memories of the grace and culture that had once been part of her life were reawakened.

After Alan started school she joined George in his business as an interior design consultant, bringing to his work her own flair and taste. His small firm grew and they became moderately prosperous. George was content to keep things as they were; he had no desire to expand or compete with larger companies. Never an ambitious man, he enjoyed working directly on the job, and shunned the idea of becoming a desk-bound executive.

His attitude infuriated Marie, who watched with mounting frustration the opportunities to make more money and gain social advancement pass them by. In time she became increasingly resentful of their unchanging upper-middle-class existence. She thought of leaving George, but didn't want to hurt Alan, and years of concessions and submission had left her with an overwhelming sense of her own weakness. She grew short-tempered, taciturn and withdrawn, and finally unresponsive to George sexually. Only Alan provided an escape from her discontentment.

Marie looked up as Alan ripped a sketch in half, rolled over on his back and stared soberly at the ceiling.

"You're trying too hard," she suggested. "You've told me yourself that nothing happens if you try too hard; it has to come by itself."

"You're right," he sighed. "I guess I'm just so excited about the painting I can't think."

"Are they coming here to pose, these *enfants terribles?*"

Alan smiled. "That's a perfect description of them—*les enfants terribles . . .*" He sat up and rubbed the back of his neck. "No, I don't think they'll come here. There's barely enough space in my room for me and the easel. Besides, I don't think they'd be very comfortable here." He saw a look of dismay on his mother's face, and hastened to add, "Not that I wouldn't be proud to invite them; you've made this house into a beautiful home . . ."

He paused, looking around the room. Marie had taken great pains to decorate it: soft, muted colors, with accents of texture in the rugs and drapes, comfortable furniture, including a few fine antique pieces that George had carefully restored, and some of Alan's best paintings hanging on the walls.

Alan went on, "It's just that I have to find the right background for the painting, something that reflects them—that is, if I had any idea of what the hell they're all about."

He chewed thoughtfully on the end of a pencil. "They're not like any kids I've ever known."

"I'm sure you'll find a way," Marie reassured him. "Perhaps if we talk about them, it will help?"

"I don't think so, but thanks anyway. Maybe after you've had a chance to meet them—when do you start working on the house with Dad?"

"Not for a couple of weeks yet. As soon as he and the men finish the interior repairs, I'll go out to the estate."

Alan stood up and stretched, then gathered his drawings and pad from the floor. "I think I'll go look through some of my art books; maybe that will help give me some ideas for the portrait."

He went to her and leaned over to kiss her cheek. She closed the book on her lap as he approached so that he couldn't see what she had written.

"Ah, the mysterious journal," Alan said, smiling. "Will you ever show me what you write in it?"

"No, never," Marie answered gaily. "These are the secrets of my soul." She made a theatrical gesture of clutching the book to her breast.

Alan placed his hand on his heart and solemnly declaimed, "Your secrets are safe with me, dear lady. And now I shall say goodnight—" He made a sweeping bow and started to back out of the room. ". . . Goodnight, and yet again, goodnight . . ." His voice trailed off as he disappeared from the room.

Marie laughed and called after him, *"Bon nuit, chér enfant."*

Then she was alone. She sat in the quiet room, not moving. George had fallen asleep; his rhythmic snoring drifted through from the den, a wheezing accompaniment to the television monotone. She felt a surge of anger, but almost immediately it dissipated into despair. This was the measure of her life, she thought, the passing of days and nights in a vacuum of routine. She opened the book and stared at the page, written in French in her small, fine hand.

A quiet day, like so many others. A quiet not of peacefulness, but of emptiness. With Alan away during the days, the house dries up, like a dead flower. The noonday heat was almost suffocating. By the time the worst heat was over it was late, and I had to race like a madwoman to fix dinner in time. And of course I broke something, an old plate that my grandmother gave me, a beautiful china plate with a peasant girl painted on it. It made me very sad, but it was, after all, a small loss.

She stopped reading, and for a moment her grandmother's house was illuminated in her mind: the clean white plaster walls and dark wood beams, the large fireplace in the kitchen and the scrubbed, gleaming floors, the delicate scents that wafted through casement windows from the garden. With a deep sigh, she lifted her pen and finished the day's entry.

My son's first commission is cause for happiness and rejoicing. Yet this news comes also as a shock, like swimming in the ocean when it is calm and tranquil, and then suddenly being raised up high by an enormous wave; either it will carry you to the shore or crush you beneath its terrible weight.

6

For the next few days Alan continued to work with the crew until George hired a replacement. During that time Dorian and David ignored him as if their commitment to sit for the portrait had never been made.

Alan's exhilaration turned to disappointment and anger. There was too much at stake; not only the fee that Olivia had offered—money that would help help establish him in New York—but his chances of impressing Jordan Shaw.

Late Friday afternoon, while finishing up his work, he saw the brother and sister returning from the beach.

Alan wiped his hands, slipped on a shirt and started after them, determined to crack their shell of indifference.

"Dorian, David—wait a minute!"

They turned at the sound of his voice. "Yes, what is it?" David asked as he caught up to them.

"I'm finished working with my father today, and I'd like to start on sketches for the painting tomorrow," he said bluntly.

David hesitated. "Well—I suppose we could arrange some time for you—" He turned to Dorian. "Do we have anything on for tomorrow?"

She knitted her brows in a look of studied concentration. "I'm not sure. I'll have to check. Can we let you know later?" she asked Alan.

His impatience boiled over. "Look, let's cut the crap! If you don't want me to do the painting, say so now. You two have been putting me on since I met you, and I've just about had it!"

David raised an eyebrow at his outburst. "He has a temper," he said to Dorian.

"I think it's called artistic temperament."

"Okay, that does it!" Alan exploded. "Fuck the painting!" He turned his back on them and stormed off.

"We'll meet you at the pool tomorrow morning," David called after him.

Alan stopped and turned around, regarding them suspiciously.

Dorian gave him a dazzling smile. "We always take a swim before breakfast, so don't be late."

"Is that a promise?" Alan asked.

"That's a promise," David answered quietly.

Alan looked to Dorian, but she was already walking toward the house.

"And no more games?" he yelled to her.

She glanced over her shoulder and replied, "Don't be greedy."

Early the next morning Alan drove through the gates of the estate in his Volkswagen. His parents had given him the car as a graduation present two years before. With four previous owners, and of indeterminate age, it bore the scars of countless sideswipes and street-rammings, and the color had faded to what Alan thought of as closely resembling a skin disease. While he was guiding it up the circle drive the engine sputtered and started to die.

"This is no time for a heart attack," he muttered to it, and eased around to the garages. As he got out he saw David's red Corvette Sting Ray, carelessly left out all night, glistening with early morning dew. Alan gazed at it longingly for a moment, then pulled an oversized clipboard holding a pad and a box of pastels from the back seat of his car and trotted off in the direction of the pool.

It was almost nine o'clock, and the sun was high and bright. As he neared the pool he shaded his eyes with his hand; there was no sign of Dorian and David. White wrought-iron tables and chairs and colorful lounges sat on the flagstone patio like guests waiting for a party to begin. Silence hung over the grounds, broken only by the soft murmur of the surf rolling in against the nearby shore.

Alan put his materials down and sprawled on one of the lounges. He looked at his watch; it was a few minutes after nine—he'd wait until nine-thirty, then leave; he was finished catering to them.

He opened his pad and looked at a sketch of Dorian he had done from memory. It was wrong, like all the others—too idealized, false.

How could he capture all the things he saw in her face? Her changes of expression were so mercurial: mature and womanly one minute, petulant and childish the next. She reminded him of dozens of paintings and sketches; the wistful beauties of Rossetti, the imperious women of Sargent and, in a way, of his mother; there was something in the cast of her face that was remote and mysterious, like Marie.

Suddenly he saw them coming across the grounds. They were dressed in white terry cloth robes, and appeared like a pair of white swans drifting across a lake of green grass.

"Good morning," Alan called, getting to his feet.

They didn't answer his greeting, but went to the edge of the pool.

"Would you like to join us in a swim?" David asked.

"Thanks, but I didn't bring a suit."

"Well, then, you can watch," Dorian said, barely glancing at him.

They stepped out of their sandals and slipped off their robes, tossing them on a chair. David wore a narrow black bikini that set off the graceful lines of his muscular body.

Dorian was naked.

"What the hell are you doing?" David exclaimed, more in exasperation than surprise.

"I couldn't find a suit I liked," she replied innocently. "Anyway, don't artists want their models to pose nude?"

Alan was speechless; she was even more beautiful than he had imagined. She stood waiting for his answer. "Well, don't they?" she asked again, with a demure smile.

"Not always," he answered, stammering slightly. "And under the circumstances, I think your family would find it less than amusing if I were to paint you nude and David clothed."

"Oh? Well, couldn't you do something like Monet's '*The Picnic*'? You know, the naked lady and the two fully dressed men?"

"Yes, I know the painting—and it's by Manet."

Dorian gave him a devilish grin. "I always get those two confused."

"Now you never will again."

"I'm going swimming," David announced impatiently. "Dorian—?"

Alan watched her stroll to the edge of the diving board. Her body was a tantalizing complex of small movemets: a light swaying of hips and buttocks, tiny breasts too firm to do more than just spring a little as she walked.

He waited until she was ready to dive, then suddenly said, "You know, I think a swim might be a good idea."

Dorian looked over at him, startled, and David said, "I thought you didn't bring a suit."

"I didn't," Alan replied grimly. He began to strip out of his clothes.

Dorian watched with frank interest, and David, sitting on the edge of the pool, leaned back on his hands and stared at him openly. For a moment Alan felt like a prize horse up for sale; he wondered if they would examine his teeth and feel his legs.

"Do I have everyone's attention?" he asked, then took off his jockey shorts. He held Dorian's gaze, defying her to look anywhere but at his face. Moving leisurely, he struck a pose, then began to parade around the pool, flexing like a contestant in a muscle man contest.

"Well, do I pass inspection?" he asked. "Can I swim now?"

David whooped a burst of laughter, ran up onto the diving board with arms outstretched, and before Dorian could get out of the way, the two of them sailed into the water. Alan dove in after them and they thrashed around each other, shrieking.

David called for a race, and Dorian played timekeeper. Alan had a longer reach, but David drove himself madly to win, his body whipping through the water with frantic energy. They ended up floating on their backs, and Dorian joined in, the three of them circling each other lazily. Alan saw her hair floating gently on the water, her breasts just breaking the surface. She caught his glance and lifted her hips for a moment; black silky curls glistened at the juncture of her thighs.

Alan turned away and David rolled beside him, their bodies touching lightly with the movement of the water.

"Are you good at tennis?" he asked.

"Terrific."

"You'll have to prove it."

Alan laughed. "Of course."

Dorian's head appeared between them. Tiny drops of water were beaded like jewels on the dark fringe of her lashes. She leaned one arm across David and put her hand on Alan's chest to steady herself. The tip of her breast grazed his side and he felt a sudden tightening in his scrotum.

"I'm starved," she said. "Let's get some breakfast. Can you cook?" she asked Alan.

"Well enough to make breakfast, if that's what you're hinting." He slid away from the touch of her body. "What about your cook?"

"She went off to do some shopping in the village, and the family's gone to New York for the day. We're on our own."

"Okay," Alan agreed. "I'll make us breakfast. But I don't cook fancy."

"I'll make the coffee—that's my specialty," Dorian said. She swam to the edge of the pool and lifted herself out, then used her robe to dry herself before slipping it on. "Don't linger, you two—I'm famished!" she called before turning toward the house.

The boys got out of the pool and David offered Alan his terry robe to use as a towel. While slipping on his clothes, Alan said, "I've never met a brother and sister like you two. You're very close."

"Yes. In many ways, Dorian is the only friend I have."

"Why?"

"She understands me better than anyone else I've ever known."

"Are you that complicated?"

David lifted his head and stared at the sky. His hair clung in wet ringlets to his head like a golden cap, and his faun-shaped amber eyes glinted with flecks of light.

"Yes, I am," he replied thoughtfully.

By the time they arrived at the kitchen, it was redolent of fresh coffee. Dorian poured a cup and handed it to Alan, saying, "Here, this will keep you going while you make breakfast. I put out butter, eggs and bacon on the stove."

She had changed into a blouse and shorts; wet hair curled around her face like silken strands, and the tight points of her breasts were dark accents under the soft folds of her blouse. A sweet, fresh scent rose from her body.

Alan went to the stove and started breaking some eggs into a dish. "Where did you two go to school?" he asked.

"That's not a subject we care to discuss," David answered. "There were too many, and we were thrown out of most of them."

Alan smiled. "I bet you drove them crazy."

"They got what they deserved," Dorian chimed in. "Do you have lots of girls?" she asked, changing the subject.

"Lots."

"One in particular?"

Alan glanced up at her; she was waiting for his response with a bemused smile. "Five, as a matter of fact," he said airily, and went back to his cooking.

"All at once?" David asked in mock seriousness.

"Sometimes. Orgies can be fun. Somebody put on the toast—this is almost ready."

Dorian came to his side. "What is that?" she asked looking down at the frying pan.

"It's an omelette, country French style. My mother taught me how to make it."

"I thought you said you didn't cook fancy."

"I lied."

They filled the plates and carried them to the table, sat down and began to eat.

"This is delicious," David said. *"Mes compliments au chef."*

Alan made a quick bow.

Dorian nibbled on a piece of toast. "Do you really want to become a famous artist?"

"Of course. And your portrait will start me on the road to fame and fortune. It may even make you famous."

David chuckled, but Dorian frowned. Then she said archly, "I think that if you stick with us, we'll make *you* famous."

Alan leaned forward and looked at her seriously. "Dorian, did anyone ever tell you that your high school dramatics get a bit trying?"

David began to laugh, and Alan sat back, feeling smug at the expression of surprise on her face. But Dorian had the last word.

"I bet we beat the shit out of you at tennis!"

❦

For the next few days Alan tagged after them, sketch pad and pencils in hand, while they played tennis, went swimming, or took long hikes along the beach. Occasionally David piloted them around Montauk Point or into Block Island Sound in the family cabin cruiser.

But most of the time they preferred to stay close to home, rarely driving into the village, and flatly refusing Alan's suggestions of going to a movie or any of the local clubs.

"The summer people are noisy and boring," Dorian stated, closing the subject. Then she added with a challenging glare, "We enjoy our own company. Don't you?"

"Oh, I've always enjoyed my own company. It's yours I'm not sure about."

"Smartass!"

As the days went by, Alan found being with them alternately exhilarating and exasperating. When the mood took them they could be bright and articulate, commenting scathingly on the current political and social disasters taking place in the country, or gossiping furiously about famous people they knew. They took a lofty attitude toward the spreading use of drugs, yet thought nothing of polishing off several bottles of wine on their expeditions, claiming that it had a lot more style than smoking grass.

"It smells like decaying socks," Dorian said.

"And I don't like the idea of losing any part of my self-control," David added. "I can handle wine."

Other times they withdrew into long, moody silences that left Alan feeling completely alienated from them. During these periods he filled his sketch pad with drawings, trying to capture that "secret part of the soul" that Olivia had talked about. Dorian was little help, even when she was silent. If she caught Alan sketching her she grew restless and energetic and began moving about, leaving him frustrated and angry. But he kept up with her, catching varied moods and expressions,

98

covering page after page with sketches, some no more than quick indications of her running across the sand, others more detailed studies of her face and figure.

David was easier; apparently unconcerned about being sketched, he sat reading or staring out at the ocean. His face always had a calm expression that Alan began to think was purposeful, fixed in place to disguise whatever he was thinking. Only in his deep-set amber eyes did Alan see a hint of something more, a troubled, almost fearful aspect that puzzled him.

Alan learned that Dorian had a passion for photography. When he least expected it he heard the click of the Nikon she had taken to carrying with her all the time. She had her own darkroom in the lower level of the house, but when he asked to see it and her pictures she refused, appearing flustered by his interest, even a little shy. It made him more curious than ever about her.

He began to use ink washes and watercolors for his studies and the number of drawings increased. David suggested using the gym adjoining his bedroom as a studio, explaining that it was the only room in the house where he wouldn't have to worry about making a mess and could work undisturbed. Only he and Dorian occupied that part of the house; Olivia and his parents had suites in the other wing.

Alan brought out his easel and taboret, and he and David set about turning the gym into a studio. It was a large, high-ceilinged room with mirror-lined walls and strong light from a bank of windows that overlooked the grounds. David moved his workout equipment to a far corner and Alan put the easel by the windows.

Dorian was a constant distraction; her sleek, tanned body was always so close, yet out of his reach. Alan was beginning to think that she had dedicated herself to the single purpose of keeping him in a constant state of excitement. She was succeeding admirably; he thought about her all the time, and could even draw her from memory. Sketches of her covered the walls of his bedroom, and at night he lay staring at them, making them come alive in his mind.

One morning she marched into the studio while Alan was working and declared, "Today we picnic."

"What, again? I wanted you two to sit for me."

"We have sat, we will sit, but today we picnic. David's in the kitchen getting a hamper of goodies made up. Put on your swimsuit and meet us on the beach."

"Why don't we skip the suits today?"

"I'm only naked when the mood takes me," she answered flippantly.

"What happens when the mood takes me?"

Dorian's mouth tightened defensively. "How the hell should I know? I've never been around to watch, except that morning by the pool, and that wasn't particularly amusing." Then she smiled. "Tell me the next time the mood takes you, and I'll bring my camera. I've always wanted to shoot dirty pictures."

She started for the door, waving cheerily over her shoulder.

"Does your camera have a self-timer?"

She stopped and looked back at him thoughtfully. "I never thought of that. Silly of me, I've missed a lot of terrific opportunities."

Alan laughed and threw his hands up in a gesture of surrender. "Okay, I give up. Where on the beach will I find you?"

"Just listen for the sound of girlish laughter—that'll be David . . ." She stopped, realized what she had said, and added quickly, "—giggling at having his picture taken."

Alan managed to do a drawing of both of them before Dorian insisted that they have lunch.

"Why do you always take candids?" he asked, seeing her snatch up her camera and click away as he bit into a sandwich.

"It's more fun catching people unawares."

"Why not take a proper picture of us?" He threw his arm around David's shoulders and smiled broadly.

"That's junk for family albums." Dorian looked through the viewfinder: David had a tense, uncomfortable expression on his face from being embraced by Alan.

"David, open the wine," she asked. "I'm parched."

He gave her a grateful nod and slid away from Alan's arm to search through the picnic hamper.

"Go back to eating or drawing," Dorian called out to Alan. "Forget that I'm here."

"Christ, I wish I could," he muttered.

David laughed and offered him a glass of wine. "Here, this will help you relax."

"I doubt it." He accepted the glass and leaned back on one arm, watching Dorian through half-closed eyes.

"Why are you squinting?" David asked. "It's not that bright today."

"It cuts the details and leaves only the forms—it's a way of seeing the large masses and colors. Try it . . ."

David narrowed his eyes and looked at Dorian, then at the expanse of beach and pale blue water. "Yes, I see what you mean—" He turned to look at Alan, who turned and looked at him, the two of them with their eyes screwed up into slits.

"Oh my God, it's Charlie Chan and Number One Son!" Dorian shrieked, clicking the shutter again and again.

A few days later Alan told them he wanted to do some oil studies for the painting. "I'd like you to decide what you want to wear. Most people prefer to pose in something they feel comfortable in—"

"How does that affect the portrait?" David asked.

"Your attitude is different, depending on what you wear. In jeans you feel casual and slouch around, whereas in more formal clothes you might hold your body differently, assume a manner that goes with the costume. The only difference it makes to me is that I want you to be relaxed. I can paint you in whatever you chose to wear."

Dorian started to say something, but Alan anticipated her. "No—not nude. Another painting, perhaps . . ."

She gave him a smile that sent a tremor along the backs of his legs.

Dorian said, "I think that's a good idea. About the clothes, I mean," she added slyly. "I'll go through my wardrobe and see what I can find."

Alan watched the pert movement of her buttocks as she walked out of the studio.

"You're getting sweaty," David observed wryly.

"I know," Alan groaned. Then he apologized: "David, I'm sorry—I mean, I know she's your sister and all, but every move she makes, every word she says—I never know if I'm being put on or put down. Has she always been like that?"

"Always."

"I think I'm in big trouble."

"I could have told you that the first day we met."

"What the hell does that mean?"

David didn't reply; he was looking at himself in the mirrors lining the walls. "You're right about the clothes," he said finally. "I'll go look for something else to put on." He went into his bedroom and closed the door behind him.

Alan paced before the easel. David was right—he was sweaty. And not just because of Dorian. He stopped and wiped his brow with a clean paint rag, looking at the empty canvas on the easel. The white surface stared back at him challengingly. This wasn't the same as doing a portrait of his mother or father, or his friends; those had been done with some feeling for them, some knowledge of their lives. What the hell did he know about Dorian and David, besides the hots he had for her? And David was confusing, with his alternating moods of warmth and reserve, his oblique humor that only Dorian seemed to understand.

Nervously he began setting out his paints and brushes. He glanced at his watch. They had been gone for almost fifteen minutes. He studied the shape of the canvas, trying to determine a composition that would be pleasing to the eye and interesting in its design. God, there was so much he didn't know!

Outside of what he had learned in high school, Alan was self-taught, a choice he had made not out of disregard for art schools and qualified teachers, but from a desire to follow his own course and not be influenced by current trends. A biography of Jordan Shaw published in *Art News* had validated his decision; Shaw was self-taught, had learned by trial and error. Now he was one of the most successful artists in the country, with paintings in major museums and private collections.

Alan looked at his watch again and realized that Dorian and David had been gone over a half-hour. What were they doing? They'd had enough time to change into ten outfits!

Just then he heard a small noise at the door leading to the hall. He looked down and saw a slip of paper being shoved under the door. By the time he crossed the room, picked it up and opened the door, the hall was empty. He looked down at the paper. It was a note from Dorian and David.

Dear Alan—
We have discovered that we don't have any clothes we like for the painting. So we've gone to New York to do some shopping. Please start without us.

Alan stared at the message, dumbfounded. "They couldn't have!" he said in astonishment. "It's a trick!"

Suddenly the door to David's room burst open. Alan looked up and saw the two of them; David was laughing and Dorian was holding her camera. Before he could move, there was a rapid series of clicks.

"Wait until you see the look on your face!" she cried gleefully.

Late one afternoon, after a week had passed, David came into the studio and stood quietly behind Alan, watching him work out the details of a large charcoal drawing.

"That's beautiful," he said softly. His eyes moved from the sketch to the nape of Alan's neck, lingering on the firm muscles of his back.

"Thanks. I feel good about the composition, and I think when the portrait is finished it will say something."

"About what?"

"You and Dorian, what you mean to each other. I've begun to understand that, a little. It's what prompted this composition."

"You understand more than you give yourself credit for," David said, examining the drawing more closely. "God, I envy your ability to do this."

"David, please, too many compliments and I get dizzy."

"I think some compliments are in order, considering what we've put you through."

"You mean it's all over? We can be serious grown-up folk now?"

David laughed. "You know better than that! In the words of my sainted sister, 'Don't be greedy!' When are you going to transfer the sketch to canvas and start painting?"

"Tomorrow. I have a canvas at home that is primed and ready to go!"

"I think this calls for a celebration. There's a bottle of very good Scotch just a few feet away in my room."

"What about Dorian? Shouldn't she be in on this party?"

"She's out shopping with Mother—there's just us."

"Okay—lead on to the Scotch!"

They talked deep into the evening, exchanging ideas on a variety of subjects, discovering mutual tastes and dislikes. Dorian came in while they were involved in a heated discussion of U.S. foreign policy, and they waved her away. She accused them of having a stag party and insisted on seeing the dirty pictures, until finally they chased her out.

Under the euphoric influence of the Scotch they made foolish, extravagant late-night conversation. Alan confided that a football accident had wrecked his knee and kept him out of the draft, and David told him that a childhood fever had left him with an inner ear problem and saved him from going to war. They both solemnly agreed that otherwise they would have seriously considered skipping the country.

David listened to Alan talk at length about art, captivated by his energy and passion and trying to ignore his own keen awareness of the grace of Alan's body, so casually sprawled in an easy chair. Alan's t-shirt and faded denims seemed to cling to him like a second skin, and his vitality threatened to burst the confines of the room. David had to make a concerted effort to keep his eyes on Alan's face.

It was late by the time Alan left. Alone, David felt as if a blazing light had suddenly gone out, leaving afterimages of himself and Alan in a series of vidid scenes: boating, playing tennis, swimming. He imagined them together in the silence of a dying twilight, walking across the grounds to the beach, sitting on the rocks in the cove, two men deeply conscious of each other's feelings.

But he had forgotten about Dorian: she would be with them all summer. A burst of anger, mingled with the pain of frustration, went through him. He couldn't ignore the fact that it was Dorian whom Alan wanted.

He and Alan might be friends, but they would be lovers.

7

EXCEPT FOR THE sound of breathing, the studio was silent. Alan stood at the easel, moving his brush lightly from canvas to pallet, his eyes darting over Dorian and David, then back to the painting.

David sat completely still, his gaze fixed straight ahead, calm and detached as though he were in a trance. Dorian, too, was motionless, but her eyes were beginning to bulge from the effort and her muscles were twitching with tension. She moved her arm.

"Dorian, please, try to keep still for longer than three seconds at a time," Alan said.

"God; you're a pain in the ass!"

"No, I'm a talented, verging on brilliant, young artist. You're the pain in the ass. Now shut up."

"If I don't move in one minute—I repeat, one minute—you will hear a shriek that will turn your black hair white!"

"Please—I'm working on your lips," Alan muttered. "I've never been able to understand why people always start talking when you're painting their lips . . ."

"That does it!" She screamed at the top of her lungs and scrambled to her feet, banging her knee in the process, and hobbled toward the door to David's room.

Without breaking his pose, David asked, "Are you all right?"

"Fuck you both!" She left, slamming the door.

David said to Alan, "She'll be fine in a few minutes."

"I wasn't aware that anything was wrong," Alan said, and continued to paint.

"Dorian has a short attention span. Frankly, I'm amazed she's been able to pose like this for almost two weeks."

"Umm—yeah, it's amazing . . . Good discipline for her."

Dorian opened the door with an angry flourish. "Discipline, hell!" she shouted. "All artists are sadists!"

"But not all sadists are artists," he answered.

A shoe came flying through the room, narrowly missing Alan and almost striking David.

"That's some arm she's got," Alan laughed. He stopped painting for a moment and searched for another brush.

David squirmed in his chair. "May I leave the room?" he requested in a small voice.

"No!"

"Then I shall pee all over the floor."

"Oh God!" He put the brush down and sighed, "Okay, that's it—I'm through for the day."

"In that case . . ." David fled from the room.

Dorian stormed back into the studio, looking for her shoe. "You're going to wreck both of us! Our bladders are being ruined! I thought you said you'd give us breaks!"

Alan picked up a large drop cloth and began to cover the painting. "I'm giving you a break," he said. "I'm immortalizing you on canvas."

"Very funny. Let's see what the master is accomplishing—" She started for the easel.

"No— not yet. Not until it's finished." He straightened the cloth and then turned to her. "How's your knee?"

"I'll never dance again."

"Sit down and let me take a look at it."

"Why—you thinking of adding medicine to all your talents?"

"Oh for Christ's sake, sit down and stop being cute!"

He shoved her gently into a chair and knelt at her feet. "Where is it?"

She pulled the skirt of her dress up. "There. See?—it's still bleeding. Your lousy painting is drawing blood!"

He touched the small bruise with tender fingers. "It's not bleeding," he murmured. "Just a little red—" He pressed his lips to her knee, and moved his hands up a little under her skirt, holding her thighs.

"Stop it!" Dorian whispered. "Alan, please—"

She put her hands on his head, tangling her fingers through his dark hair, then leaned forward and kissed him lingeringly.

Just behind the door to his room, David stood watching them, overcome by an incredible longing, a yearning to be in his sister's place, to be in Alan's arms. Suddenly he heard someone in the hall, and made a noisy entrance into the room.

"Cheezit, the cops!" he whispered. "Somebody's coming!"

Alan and Dorian broke apart as Vivian entered the studio.

"Sorry to interrupt, but I need you to help me, Dorian." She looked around the studio critically. "What in the world have you done to this room?"

Watercolors and pencil sketches lay everywhere, and small oil studies were piled against the wall. In the center of the room was a platform covered by a Persian rug that Olivia had rescued from the basement. In the middle of the platform sat a French love seat from Dorian's room and next to it a Queen Anne side table holding an Italian vase filled with flowers.

"It's the setting for the painting," David explained. "Rather nice, isn't it, considering the mixture of styles and periods?"

Vivian didn't look impressed. "That side table is very valuable," she said to Alan.

"We're being very careful with everything, Mrs. St. Clair," he answered quickly. "As a matter of fact, my father is standing by to refinish even the slightest scratch."

She gave him a frosty smile that broke fine lines in the perfection of her makeup, and turned to Dorian. "You've been so busy with these portrait sittings that I haven't seen you for days. There are still a great many details to be taken care of for Jonathan's party. I could use some of your time."

"You have a secretary. You don't need me to lick the stamps for the invitations."

Vivian bristled. "You're absolutely right—you wouldn't be much help. Speaking of invitations, do either of you wish to invite any of your friends to the party? It wouldn't do you any harm, socially, to begin mixing a little more with a few of the better—"

"No!" they both answered her in unison.

"It's your party," David added. "I really don't think any of our school friends would be comfortable."

"That's nonsense!" she declared. "It will be one of the social events of the season!"

"No, Mother," David said firmly.

Vivian looked at her children with an expression of despair. "I don't understand you," she said quietly.

Alan felt uncomfortable listening to the exchange. Since their first meeting he hadn't given Vivian much thought. The few times he saw her she reminded him of the society women in old films on the Late Show—always impeccably dressed and completely self-possessed. Now, however, he was moved by her inability to cope with her children; facing Dorian and David, she looked vulnerable and defeated.

Sensing that the strained moment called for some diplomacy, Alan said, "Mrs. St. Clair, I feel I should apologize for monopolizing so much of Dorian and David's time."

She seemed surprised by his statement. "Thank you, Alan, that's very thoughtful of you, but not necessary. They usually do exactly what they want." She glanced at the easel. "Is it going well?"

"Yes, it is." Alan smiled. "I hope you like it. In fact, if you ever have the time to sit for me, I'd like to do a sketch of you."

Out of the corner of his eye he could see a slow flush of anger suffusing Dorian's face.

Vivian recognized the effort Alan was making on her behalf and smiled at him warmly. "If your painting is as good as Olivia thinks it will be, we just might arrange something."

Her large green eyes lingered on him for a moment, and she fingered a strand of pearls around her throat in a girlish gesture. Then she glanced briefly at Dorian and left the room.

David began to laugh and applaud. "Very good, Alan! You've won over the mistress of the house!"

"Well—I just . . ." He faltered under Dorian's stormy glare. "I just thought it would help to—"

"To what?" Dorian demanded. "Get yourself another commission? You lousy little opportunist! I could see the wheels turning during that exchange of hot-eyed looks! Christ! I hate sycophants!"

"Are you crazy?" Alan shouted. "All I wanted to do was make her feel better! You treated her like shit, for which you should be soundly spanked!"

"You don't know anything about my relationship with my mother, so keep your fucking criticism to yourself! As for spanking me, you're either very old-fashioned or into kinky sex—and knowing you, it's probably the former!" Tears suddenly began to fill her eyes and she rushed from the room.

"Wow!" David said with admiration. "I haven't seen her that upset in years!"

"She's a spoiled, self-indulgent little bitch!"

"You're right!"

"And she *should* be spanked!"

"Right again! Struck regularly, like a gong, to quote—"

"Noel Coward!"

"Very good!"

They both started to laugh. Alan picked up a pillow from the love seat and flung it at David's head. He caught it, wound up like a pitcher and sailed it back across the room. Alan ducked and tumbled to the floor, still laughing. David raced toward him, nimbly leaped over the edge of the platform, landed on the floor beside him and pummeled him with a flurry of light blows.

"Stop, stop!" Alan cried through tears of laughter. "I'm a weak, sensitive artist!"

They finally lay still, gasping for breath and breaking into giggles. David looked at Alan fondly. "I understand why you said what you did to Mother. It was very decent of you. We do treat her like shit."

"I shouldn't have criticized Dorian," Alan admitted. "It wasn't any of my business. But Jesus, she really pisses me off sometimes."

David sat up abruptly. "I just thought of something!"

"What?"

"A friend I want to invite to the party."

"Who?"

"You, that's who!"

Alan struggled to sit up and stared at him, incredulous. "Are you nuts? Me, at your mother's fancy party?"

"Alan, if you're going to be any kind of success in this world of toadies and parasites, you've got to stop thinking of yourself as the poor boy from the streets! It's demeaning to your talent, and positively Dickensian in attitude. You are not Oliver Twist!"

"My God, you're right!"

"You're coming to the party."

"Dorian will never allow it."

"Allow it? She'll love it!"

"David, did you hear the way she talked to me? Bullets couldn't have done more to rip out my guts!"

"That's a bit florid, but accurate. However, I repeat—she'll love it. She's not really angry at you. You just aroused one of woman's most basic instincts."

"I did? What?"

"Jealousy."

ॐ

One morning a few weeks later, as Alan drove through the gates of the estate, a bewildering sight greeted him. A line of trucks, delivery vans, and automobiles crowded the driveway to the house. Dozens of workmen were everywhere, unloading the vans, stringing lights up on the trees and spreading out a large multicolored canvas in the middle of the lawn. He maneuvered his car past them and parked near the garages, then hurried into the house through the back entrance.

Inside, all was chaos. Movers were transferring furniture from one room to another, tables covered with silver and gold services were lined up in the hallway, manned by a corps of maids busily polishing, while men streamed through the front doors carrying boxes and cartons. Alan made his way to the stairs in the center hall and managed to get to the second floor landing, where he paused to watch the frantic activity below. Workmen cursed and collided with one another, their voices rising in anger over the shrill cries of maids scurrying about carrying dust mops and brooms. The house sounded like a battleground.

Vivian suddenly appeared in the middle of the throng with Mrs. Childress at her side. The housekeeper looked agitated, but Vivian stood calm, unruffled by the confusion. She clapped her hands sharply, calling for everyone's attention. The clamor died down to a low grumble, but she waited until there was complete silence. Then, hands behind her back, she surveyed the situation and quietly began issuing commands. Within minutes a smooth flow of activity moved around her as she stood in the center of the hall, directing traffic with the agility of a Times Square cop. At one point she glanced up the staircase and saw Alan watching her. He smiled broadly and shook clasped hands above his head in a salute. She smiled back at him, and took a quick bow. Just then Olivia came out of her room and joined him on the landing.

"Alan, how is the painting going? I'm very anxious to see it."

"It's shaping up, but I don't want you to see it until it's finished. Do you mind?"

"Of course not—I'd prefer it that way. We'll have a proper unveiling when it's ready, a little party."

"Not like this, I hope." Alan nodded at the noisy activity in the foyer below.

Olivia chuckled. "Isn't it ghastly? Vivian is determined to make it the social event of the year. Did the children tell you it's a costume ball? An Arabian Nights fantasy. I can't imagine what possessed her! But we'll have fun—David told me he invited you—I would have myself, but he beat me to it. And I invited a few of my friends, who should liven things up considerably."

"Is Jordan Shaw coming?"

"No—he's ensconced in his summer home in Maine. Nothing could root him out, not even my pleas." She paused, hearing Vivian call to her. "I must run—I'm helping to supervise the decor. By the time we've finished I'm afraid the whole place will look like a Moroccan whore house!"

Alan started down the hall to the studio when he saw Dorian tearing out of her room. She was dressed in sneakers, old jeans and a sweatshirt and her hair was tucked up under a scarf. Alan thought she looked like a little girl rushing out to play.

"David and I have been drafted to help Mother," she told him breathlessly. "We can't pose today, so can you work on something else? The background or the bowl of flowers?"

"Sure. There's a lot I can do without you."

"It's not our fault," she said. "We just couldn't get out of it."

"I told you, it's okay," Alan reassured her.

"Well, if you're sure—and listen, you can't get near the kitchen, so I'll have a maid bring you some lunch on a tray

111

later—okay?" She had an anxious, motherly concern in her voice.

A slow smile spread across Alan's face. "Things are looking up—you're worrying about me." He stepped closer to her. The hallway was deserted and they were hidden from the landing by an archway. He touched her face with his fingertips.

"Stop it," she said, her voice faltering. "Someone will see us."

"I don't care," he replied softly. "Dorian, kiss me . . ."

"No."

"Please. Kiss me—"

She threw her arms around his neck and they clung together. Her mouth was soft and open, her tongue moving inside his lips. Alan held her tighter, forced her mouth to open wide as his hands ran over her body.

"Stop it, let me go—" she whispered, trying to pull away.

"No." He held her close and kissed her again, more fiercely.

She wrenched herself out of his arms. "Dammit, that's enough!" Her eyes were blazing.

"Not for me, it isn't!"

"Fuck you!"

"That's exactly what I want!"

Her face suddenly crumpled and tears sprang to her eyes. She turned, ran through the hall to the landing and disappeared down the stairs.

༅

For the next couple of days Alan saw Dorian only when she came to the studio to pose for the painting. She was civil, if somewhat remote, and didn't mention the incident in the hallway.

"I've never seen her like this before," David said to Alan when they were alone. "What's it all about?"

"I guess I came on too strong and frightened her."

"You frightened Dorian?" David asked, incredulous.

"Didn't she tell you about it? I thought she told you everything?"

David looked at him thoughtfully. "I guess she doesn't—at least, not about you. That's a first." He patted Alan's shoulder. "Well, whatever it is, she'll get over it—she always does."

"What do you mean, 'always'?"

"You don't think you're the first man in her life, do you?"

"No, of course not," Alan said quickly.

"Then why do you look so angry?"

The next morning, when Alan arrived at the house, Mrs. Childress told him that David and Dorian had gone to New York with their parents to pick up Mr. St. Clair's brother Jonathan, who was arriving from Paris. Alan spent the day trying to concentrate on the painting, but all he could think about was Dorian. She confused him as no other girl had, stirring emotions that were new and puzzling.

The following day Dorian came to the studio and told him that David had remained in New York. "He had some work to do with father, so Mother and I brought Uncle Jonathan home last night."

"Then I'll just work with you today."

"I can't. It's Uncle Jonathan's first day here, and I want to spend some time with him."

"That's just an excuse," Alan retorted. "You're still mad about what happened in the hallway the other day."

"Don't be silly," Dorian replied coolly, lighting a cigarette. "That sort of thing happens to me all the time. You're no different from any of the other boys I've known. Just a little more talented, that's all."

Before Alan could respond, she gave him a cheerful smile and walked out of the room. He threw his brushes down furiously.

"Goddamned bitch!" he muttered, then picked the brushes up and returned them to the taboret. He stood in front of the easel and stared at the canvas. Christ, it all looked so flat! He began to mix some color on the pallet and made a few tentative strokes, then wiped them out in disgust. To hell with it, he thought, throwing a cover over the painting.

There was a knock at the door and Alan called out, "Dorian?"

Olivia stepped in. "No, it's me. I was on my way to the

guest house and thought I'd stop by." She glanced at the easel. "Not working today?"

"No. Dorian's busy, and David's in New York, so—"

"Is there anything wrong?"

"Not really—I just can't make it work this morning, thought I'd give it a rest . . ."

"Good idea. No artist is inspired every minute he's painting. Why don't you come over to the guest house with me? Your father and his crew are doing wonderful things with it, and I've been having a ball working with your mother. She's a lovely woman, and very creative."

"Yes, I agree," Alan replied. "I'll clean up here and join you in a few minutes—I'd like to see what Dad's been doing."

Olivia began to leave, then glanced back at the easel. "I can't wait to see what you've been doing. Dorian and David told me they haven't seen it yet, either; not even sneaked a peek at it when you weren't around," she laughed. "You've obviously had a great effect on them."

"I doubt that," Alan said glumly. "But they've certainly had an effect on me."

"Have they? Now I'm more anxious to see the painting than ever. An artist needs shaking up every so often—it improves his vision."

"It may improve his vision, but it plays hell with his life."

"Only if he allows it to," Olivia said, smiling shrewdly. "I understand how you feel, though. Everything that's happening to you is new and exciting, very romantic. But I suggest you take as much time with your life as you do with your painting."

Alan recognized the warning, and knew that she understood how he felt about Dorian. He smiled at her gratefully. "Thanks for the advice."

"I hand it out with all my commissions. Just remember: for your own sake, don't rush. There's nothing in the world more enchanting than romance—or more destructive."

❦

Marie pointed to a fabric in the sample book she was holding.

Olivia said, "I see what you mean—the mauve velvet would be lost on that chair in the corner."

"Precisely," Marie smiled. "Mrs. Ellis used that color against my advice and the room suffered for it. But then, she can be—how does one put it politely—?"

"One doesn't," Olivia chuckled. "The woman's an idiot. I've had to deal with her more than once at my Art Council meetings—"

"And more than once is two times too many, yes?"

"My dear, you're a very good judge of character."

There was a sound at the front door and they looked up to see Alan standing in the entryway.

"Ah, there you are!" Olivia called out. "Well, how do you like it?"

He crossed the foyer and stepped down into the living room. "It's terrific! Beautiful!" Polished floors and fine wood paneling gleamed in the morning sunlight. An Aubusson rug defined a seating area of chairs and tables grouped around a scrolled Italian marble fireplace. White china vases filled with flowers added spots of bright color, and paintings and prints were artfully hung on the walls. "Is it all finished?" he asked.

"Not hardly," Olivia replied. "As your father and his men finish with each room, Marie and I come in and work. We make a hell of a team, don't you agree?"

"It's incredible. The place looks ready to live in."

"Alan, is that you?" George's voice called out from the dining room. He came in, smiling at the expression on his son's face.

"Dad, it's fantastic! Just fantastic!"

George beamed with pride. "I think it's some of the best work I've ever done," he said, walking into the room.

"George, be careful," Marie said curtly. "Your coveralls are full of plaster dust—you're making a mess."

He stopped, his face reddening. "Oh, I didn't realize—"

Marie kept a fixed smile on her face, furious at her husband. Couldn't he have at least brushed himself clean before joining them? Even his face was streaked with white smudges, and his hair—*mon Dieu,* the man was so *gauche!*

"We can clean it up," Olivia said cheerfully. "Alan, take a look at the decorative scrollwork in the study—you'd never know it had been chipped and cracked from the way George has restored it."

"Yes, it's really wonderful," Marie said quickly, wanting to make amends for her tactlessness.

There was a sound of voices in the foyer, and Vivian came into the house, followed by a tall man dressed in a beige linen sports coat and matching slacks.

"May we join you?" she asked gaily. "I want Jonathan to see how nicely the house is coming along."

"Come in, come in," Olivia said. "Mrs. Conway and I were just choosing some fabrics for the drapes and chairs."

Jonathan was introduced to Alan, Marie and George, and for the next few minutes everyone talked about the progress of the restoration. George was explaining his work to Jonathan and Alan, while Olivia and Marie showed their selection of fabrics to Vivian. But Marie's attention was drawn to Jonathan. Out of the corner of her eye she watched him chatting with her husband and thought how different they were. Jonathan was a handsome man in his early forties, trimly built, with short dark hair lightly touched with traces of gray. Arched black brows shadowed deep-set brown eyes, and his smile was dazzingly impudent and infectious. He had a self-assurance and poise that demanded attention.

Alan broke away from the two men and came over to Vivian. "Where's Dorian?" he asked.

"She's helping my secretary with the preparations for the party. She'll be through in a little while. Is the portrait going well?"

"Yes, it should be finished in a couple of weeks . . ." He paused and looked at his watch. "I really have to get back to it—there's still a lot of work to do."

He kissed Marie on the cheek, said his goodbyes and hurried out of the house. One of the men on George's crew came in and said something to him; George made his excuses and they went into the dining room.

Jonathan joined the women, professing interest in the choice of colors they were discussing, but paying more attention to Marie. "Olivia tells me your son is a very talented artist," he said to her. "I understand he's painting a portrait of my niece and nephew."

"Yes, we're all very anxious to see it. Your sister has been most kind to Alan, and we're very grateful to her."

"He deserves all the help he can get," Olivia said. "He has a prodigious talent."

Vivian took Jonathan's arm. "We must be going—Alex and David will be home soon, and I have so much to do. We're giving a party for Jonathan to welcome him home," she explained to Marie.

"I hope you'll be there," Jonathan said, taking Marie's hand. "You and your husband, of course."

"That's a wonderful idea," Olivia chimed in. "Marie, you and George must come. It's a week from Saturday."

Marie grew flustered. "Thank you, that's very kind, but—"

"Mr. and Mrs. Conway may already have an engagement for that evening," Vivian said pointedly, throwing Olivia an angry glance.

"If you do—won't you please break it and come?" Jonathan asked, smiling persuasively.

He was still holding her hand, and she felt the pressure of his fingers. "Well, we'll see—" she answered softly, withdrawing her hand.

As Jonathan and Vivian left the house, George came into the room. "Have they gone?" he asked. "I wanted them to see the repairs I made on the wainscoting in the dining room."

"I shall come and look at it, dear," Marie said, "as soon as Miss St. Clair and I are finished."

"Why don't you go ahead," Olivia offered. "I have some calls to make. Besides, I agree completely with your choices—your taste is exquisite. With parents like you, I can understand where Alan gets his talent."

"Thank you, Miss St. Clair—for everything."

"Please, call me Olivia—and do try to make the party. I'll put an invitation in the mail this very afternoon."

Marie smiled and went to her husband. As they left the room, Olivia watched them, musing on the striking contrasts between the husband and wife. George was a plain, simple man, with little social grace, whereas Marie carried herself with almost aggressive poise and chic. She reminded Olivia of many women she knew—the ambitious wives of complacent husbands, struggling to achieve some social distinction. Perhaps she shouldn't have invited them to the party; the idea certainly didn't please Vivian. But Jonathan seemed anxious that they attend, at least as far as Marie was concerned. Olivia frowned, thinking about her brother; he had more charm than a room full of diplomats, and quite often used it carelessly, especially with other men's wives. But Marie had looked so pleased at the invitation, so grateful to be included.

Yes, she decided, she would send them an invitation; it would mean a great deal to Marie just to receive it, whether they attended the party or not.

8

ALAN FINISHED BRUSHING his hair, trying to ignore the argument that had been raging between his parents all day. It was the evening of the party, and George was adamantly refusing to go, insisting that Olivia had sent them the invitation merely to be polite. Marie had used every tactic at her command, saying that the invitation was sincere, insisting that it was necessary to his business to be with people who might offer him more work, and finally pleading with him to go as a favor to her. But he had remained unmoved, stubbornly reminding her how out of place they would be, how uncomfortable he was at such affairs. Alan had wisely elected to stay out of it, knowing that nothing he could say would help; George had always resisted social involvements with his clients.

Before he left the house Alan went to say goodbye to his mother. He found Marie sitting in her bedroom, holding her journal on her lap. Her eyes were red from crying.

"I have to leave now," he said softly. "David and Dorian asked me to come out early."

She looked up at him and nodded. "You look very handsome," she whispered. In the late afternoon light she looked wan and fragile, like a child who had been through a long illness. Her hands, resting on the journal, were pale and limp with defeat.

"I'm sorry about Dad," Alan said.

Marie gave him a sad smile and pulled him down to kiss his cheek. "Go, and have a wonderful time. When you get home, you can tell me all about it."

"It may be very late."

"No matter—I'm sure I'll be awake," she said ruefully.

It was almost seven o'clock when Alan drove through the gates of the estate. He stopped the car and stared at the scene before him. All the trees and shrubs were lit with tiny diamond-like lights, and a huge tent, festooned with banners and surrounded by potted palms, rose up from the lawn. The tent flaps were pulled back to reveal a circular bar and deep cushions on a Persian rug. Turbaned servants were setting out silver goblets and lighting small flames in gold-painted braziers. Around the tent sat rattan peacock chairs and low tables, and nearby a portable dance floor had been set down on the grass. Young men looking ill at ease in Arabian Nights costumes stood waiting by the entrance of the house to park the cars of arriving guests. They stared down the driveway at Alan's Volkswagen.

"They probably think I should be using the servants' entrance, and they're right," he said to himself, backing up the car.

He drove around to the rear and parked near the guest cottage, walked across the grounds to the back entrance, made his way through the confusion in the kitchen and went up the back stairs. He saw David coming down the hallway.

"Ah, you're here," he called out. "Good! Come into my room—we have a surprise for you."

"Where's Dorian?"

"She's getting dressed. We'll go get her in a few minutes."

They went into David's room and he closed the door. "What's the surprise?" Alan asked.

David went to his closet and brought out a large box. "I hope all this stuff fits. We had to guess at your measurements."

"What the hell are you talking about?"

"This is a costume ball—remember? So we picked one out for you."

"But I told you I was going to wear a suit!"

"Yes, I know. For an artist, you certainly can be stodgy. Now don't argue, just get dressed."

"What are you wearing?"

"Never mind! I'm going to change in the dressing room—I don't want you to see me until I'm ready."

Alan opened the box and looked at the costume they had gotten for him. "You're crazy!" he yelled to David. "I can't wear this!"

"If you don't, you'll finish the portrait without us!" David called from behind the door.

Alan muttered obscenities under his breath and began to take off his clothes. A few minutes later, wearing the costume, he stared at himself in the mirror. White silk trousers clung to his hips and thighs, then flared out to huge bells that gathered at the ankles. A red vest embroidered in gold and silver thread fitted snugly over his bare chest, and a red turban covered his hair. On his feet were black slippers with curved, pointed toes, and a gold sash was tied around his waist.

"Christ, I look silly!" Alan groaned. "I can't go downstairs dressed like this!"

David opened the dressing room door and came into the room. "You look sensational—just like Sinbad the Sailor!" he exclaimed. "How do I look?"

David was dressed in the white silk raiment of a rajah. His coat was studded with red stones, a black scarab was affixed to the center of his turban, and around his neck lay a heavy silver chain supporting an intricately jeweled medallion. A light makeup deepened his tan, making the strong bone structure of his face gleam like chiseled marble.

"You've got to let me paint you in that get up! You look like an Edmund Dulac illustration come to life!"

"Now that's what I call a compliment."

"I can't wait to see Dorian."

"She should be ready by now."

At Dorian's room, David tapped lightly on the door. "Can we come in?"

"Wait, I'm not ready!" she cried. "Okay—now!"

They stepped into her room. Dorian stood in front of an alcove of mirrors, facing them. For a moment Alan stopped breathing. She was Scheherazade. Yards of transparent blue veil swirled to the floor from her hips. A silver chain was clasped around her loins, jeweled cups with thin silver straps covered her breasts, silver bracelets were wound around her arms and wrists. A delicate headdress of peacock feathers sat atop her head, falling gracefully to her shoulders and framing her face. A tiny diamond clung to one nostril, and a larger one gleamed and sparkled from her navel. Her feet were bare except for rings on her toes, and slave bracelets flashed at her ankles.

Alan stood transfixed. Suddenly she began to move in the delicate steps and gestures of a temple dancer. Flashes of light from her jewelry were reflected in the mirrors, swift gleamings that flowed and eddied like a veil around her slender body. She was dazzling, enchanted, a princess encircled by shimmering iridescence.

David clapped his hands sharply and she sank to the floor, her head bowed. He walked up to her and gave her his hand in a royal gesture. Lifted to her feet, she twirled gracefully and came to rest at his side. She held out her hand to Alan, who moved toward her slowly, caught up in the rapture of their mystical game. He took her hand and knelt before her, pressing his lips to her fingertips. David raised his hands, as in a benediction.

"We are beautiful, we are perfect," he whispered.

"And we are going to be late for the party," Dorian added.

ႜ

"It's dying," Dorian said.

"Mother's parties always die," David commented.

"It looks wonderful to me," Alan said.

"Everything looks wonderful to you," Dorian replied.

The three of them were standing at the banister on the landing overlooking the foyer. The ceiling was covered with a canopy of softly draped chiffon that gathered around the crystal chandelier to create a tentlike effect. On the marble floor stood tall palms in white urns. Velvet drapes were swagged to the columns circling the hall. Music came from a small dance orchestra in the ballroom, and servants in colorful Oriental costumes were passing among the guests carrying silver trays of drinks and canapés. Small groups wandered from the main dining room into the ballroom and out onto the terrace. The measured pace of their movement lent a dignified air of restraint to the proceedings.

"It's positively funereal," Dorian groaned. "We'll have to do something to liven it up, or the whole group will turn in their turbans and go home."

"Nothing rash," David warned her.

"You know I never do anything rash." She saw a maid standing by one of the opened bedroom doors and went to her.

A few minutes later Alan and David saw the woman go down the stairs and hurry toward the ballroom. Dorian returned to them, a mischievous smile on her face.

"What's happening?" David asked.

"You'll see. In a few minutes, we'll stand this party on its head!"

꒲

Vivian and Olivia were chatting with one of the directors on the board of the Metropolitan Museum. Vivian smiled and nodded, impatient to speak with Olivia alone. When he had moved away, she asked her anxiously, "What do you think? The evening seems very low-key so far."

"It's a nice party—quiet, but nice."

Vivian sighed. "That's what I was afraid of. And Alex is no help! He's in the library with that awful man from the Hilton chain."

"You know Alex—business first. Oh, look who just came in—it's Mrs. Conway . . ."

"Why, so it is." Vivian's dismay was thinly disguised.

"Don't be such a snob!" Olivia snapped. "Look at her, she's absolutely beautiful."

Olivia left Vivian and crossed the foyer to Marie. "My dear, I'm so pleased you could come. But where's George?"

"He sends his regrets. He's had a summer cold these last few days, and tonight I insisted he stay home and rest—he was so anxious to be here, but I didn't think it wise."

"Oh, I am sorry. But at least you came, and you look wonderful. Where did you get that gown?"

Marie was wearing a rose-colored Empire gown with touches of fine lacework at the throat and sleeves. A thin pink velvet cord was knotted under her breasts, and the dress fell in soft folds that clung to her slender figure.

"It belonged to my mother," she began to explain, when Jonathan suddenly appeared. His dark eyes swept over her approvingly.

"My dear Mrs. Conway," he said, taking her hand and kissing it lightly. "So you came after all. And you look exquisite."

Marie blushed a little. "I was just telling Olivia that the gown belonged to my mother. She was an actress with the Comédie-Française, and wore this in Molière's *L'École des Femmes*. It is one of the few treasures I saved during the German occupation."

"Then we must show off the treasure and the beautiful woman in it," he said, taking her arm and sweeping her away.

"You must forgive me if I am clumsy," Marie said to Jonathan. "I haven't danced in a very long time."

"You're anything but clumsy, and should be taken dancing more often. Tell me, when were you last in Paris?'

"Oh, it's been years. Do tell me about the city—I miss it so."

"It still produces the most beautiful women in the world. Even if she hasn't been there in years, when you see her, you know she's from Paris."

"I see that Paris still teaches *savoir faire* to expatriate Americans."

༡

"Why are we just standing here?" Alan asked. "When are we going down to the party?"

"In a few minutes," Dorian answered. "Look, Truman Capote just came in. And there's Lennie Bernstein with Angela Lansbury!"

"Where?" David asked.

"There, near the door, talking with Olivia, of course. What could they have to say to Mother?"

David peered down at a group of new arrivals. "The ballet people just came in—Olivia must have invited them; maybe the party will pick up . . ."

Dorian leaned over the banister. "There's Uncle Jonathan coming out of the ballroom. I wonder who that woman is with him—she's beautiful."

Alan followed her gaze and exclaimed, "That's my mother!"

❦

"Are you enjoying yourself, my dear?" Vivian asked Marie.

"Oh yes, very much. But where are the children? I was hoping to meet Dorian and David—Alan's told me so much about them."

"They haven't come down yet. I can't imagine what's keeping them. Oh, there are more guests—I must greet them; please excuse me—"

Vivian hurried away and Marie said to Jonathan, "She's very charming."

"Not at all," he said, laughing. "I'm the only charming member of the entire family."

"And certainly the most modest," she teased.

"Hardly. No one ever achieved anything by being modest. Now, let me get you something to drink."

"No, please—I'm keeping you from your friends—and I really should go soon. My husband's not well, and I promised I'd return early."

"Believe me, I have no friends here, and—" He was suddenly serious. "You don't really want to leave, do you?"

Jonathan's lips were touched with a faint smile that was at once assured and hopeful. Marie returned his smile, and in a quick, covert gesture he lifted her hand and kissed her fingers.

At that moment a violinist from the orchestra appeared in the foyer and the lights dimmed. From the ballroom came a steady roll of drum that increased in volume.

❦

"Dorian, what are you up to?" Alan asked.

"This is it," she laughed. "Just follow me. We're joining the party!"

A low murmur of anticipation ran through the crowd; had the St. Clairs planned an entertainment? The violinist began to play the solo passage from the *Scheherazade Suite* in a clear, sweet tone, and the guests grew quiet. The chandelier glowed with a faint, mysterious light, and the palm trees circling the foyer cast long shadows on the walls and across the canopy. Suddenly there was a movement on the stairs. Everyone looked up and saw Dorian slowly descending, moving in a swaying dance step, followed in regal solemnity by Alan and David. The illusion that Vivian had failed to achieve was finally accomplished; the artifice of her decor, muted by the dim light, provided the perfect setting for the three costumed figures moving slowly down the stairs. They appeared like a vision, almost mythic in their beauty. There was absolute silence until they reached the foot of the stairs, where they waited, poised like a triptych, until the violin solo was finished.

Then the lights came up and the orchestra broke into a medley of themes from Broadway musicals. Dorian glided across the floor past her astonished parents and whirled Jonathan off into a dance. David took his mother in his arms and followed them, while Alan led Marie onto the dance floor. The guests broke into a round of applause and joined in, filling the ballroom.

❦

Marie said to Alan, "Everything is so magical, and the *enfants terribles* are beautiful!"

"They're not so *terribles* anymore," Alan laughed. "We've become friends. I'm so glad you decided to come; I wanted you to see all this and meet them."

"It is an evening I shall never forget."

Marie caught a glimpse of Jonathan dancing with Dorian. But he was watching her.

❦

Jonathan said to Dorian, "My dear, you are bewitching!

You've made this dismal affair come to life."

Dorian glanced over his shoulder at Alan dancing with Marie. "Doesn't he look wonderful?" she asked.

"Yes, he's very handsome. It's easy to see where he gets his looks; he and his mother look almost like brother and sister. She's a charming woman."

"I saw you dancing with her. Just remember, uncle, she's married."

"How can I forget? She's been reminding me of it every minute since we met!"

🐛

The party was in full swing now. Dignified restraint gave way to noisy drinking and dancing. A cabaret entertainer sang an impromptu medley, and a couple of musical comedy stars did a dance number. The terrace was crowded, the buffet tables in the dining room looked ravaged, and couples were dancing across the lawns.

Vivian was ecstatic. "It's exactly what I hoped," she said to Alexander and David as they stood by the doors to the terrace. "David, I've never seen you look so handsome! And your sister! She's absolutely taken over the party!"

David smiled at his mother wryly; there were few times he could remember when Vivian was so pleased with her children that she gushed.

Alexander glanced around the room, nodding to guests. He saw two men dancing together and stiffened. "Will you look at that?" He sounded outraged.

"At what?" David asked.

"Those two men dancing over there. Some of Olivia's pansy friends, no doubt," he snorted contemptuously.

"They must be," Vivian said, frowning. "The men we know wouldn't be dancing together."

🐛

Alan cut in on a young man dancing with Dorian and swept her across the floor to a less crowded corner of the room.

"You're the belle of the ball," he said. "All the women in the place are wildly jealous and every man wants you."

"I know, and I love it!"

She was radiant with success. Her face was flushed and her eyes glittered in triumph, as if she had proven something of great importance. Everything about her was charged with an electrifying vitality.

Alan held her close. "This is a dream," he whispered. "Nothing is real, except you, and I'm not so sure about you."

Dorian drew away from him. "I'm real, Alan. I promise you, I'm real."

She took his hand and led him toward the doors to the terrace.

※

David had a fixed smile on his face as he gallantly led one of his mother's friends around the dance floor while she kept up an incessant chattering. As soon as the music stopped he excused himself and went to the bar. Drink in hand, he leaned against the bar and watched Dorian and Alan.

"Are you having a good time?" someone at his side asked.

David saw Alan and Dorian leave the dance floor and go out onto the terrace.

"I said, are you having a good time?"

David turned. "What?"

It was a young man dressed in costume. He was in his early twenties, swarthy, with large dark eyes and a sharp, slightly hooked nose. His full lips were very red and had a soft, bruised look. His short open vest studded with colored beads revealed a tanned chest and muscular arms. Black satin pants clung to his strong legs, and on his feet were soft embroidered slippers.

"I asked if you were having a good time."

"No, not very," David replied. "But I'm getting a little drunk, and that should help."

The young man smiled, showing very white teeth against his dark skin. "Aren't you Olivia's nephew—David St. Clair?"

"I am, and you look like a dancer. Ballet Theatre?"

"Yes. I'm Jennings Talbot. We met once, backstage, after a performance of *Swan Lake*."

"Were you the prince?" The drinks were beginning to make David light-headed, and he slurred his words.

"No, just one of the courtiers. I've only been with the company for a season."

"Oh? That's too bad. I only speak to princes . . ."

David started to move away from the bar. He staggered slightly and Jennings grabbed his arm, steadied him.

"Thank you, Jennings." David giggled. "Jennings? That's a hell of a name. Do your friends call you Jenny?"

"No, they call me Butch," the dancer replied sarcastically. "I think you'd better get some air before you fall down."

"Some air? Yes—I can't hold my liquor very well . . . must go into training for that, I think drinking will be important to me . . ."

Jennings followed him as he walked unsteadily toward the doors to the terrace. "Can you make it alone? I'd better help you—" He took David's arm.

"Very good of you," David mumbled. "You are not a courtier, you are a prince. But I shall not call you Butch—or Jenny . . ."

The dancer held his arm tighter and looked at him with a swift, brazen intimacy. "What will you call me?"

David felt his hand warm and firm on his arm, and leaned against him.

"Sinbad."

༃

"I'll walk you to your car," Jonathan said.

"No, please. I've taken enough of your time." Marie glanced at him nervously.

"I insist." He sounded angry.

They waited while an attendant brought her car around. Jonathan stood close to her, scowling. Marie made an effort not to look at him. The boy brought her car up and she got in. Jonathan leaned down to the window, forcing her to face him.

"I want to see you again."

She answered quickly, as though prepared for his request. "That's impossible."

"No, it's not impossible, is it?" His voice was low and insistent.

Marie's hands moved uneasily on the steering wheel. He was so close she could feel his breath on her face, smell the light scent of his cologne. She struggled with herself for a moment before answering, "No, it's not impossible."

ళ

Out on the grounds, away from the house, Alan held Dorian in his arms. They danced slowly. The faint music of the orchestra drifted from the ballroom in distant, incomplete sounds, as if heard in passing or in a dream. They turned and moved in time to the music, melting into the sultry darkness of the night, feeling close and hidden.

"What are you thinking, Alan?"

"I'm feeling more than thinking. Sensing would be a better word . . ."

"Sensing?"

"Yes, feeling everything with my senses—the whole evening, the colors of the house and the costumes, the people's faces, the music. The night feels like a soft glove. And you—I'm sensing you—" He held her closer.

She laughed softly. "What are you sensing about me?"

"Everything. The incredible way you look, so exotic, yet so real. The way you move in my arms, the way you feel . . ." He stopped and kissed her, "—and the way you taste."

A burst of laughter came from the terrace. They looked up to the pale glow of light encircling the house."

"Can we go someplace—be alone?" Alan asked huskily.

"Yes. Come with me."

ళ

David led Jennings toward the cove on the beach.

"Where are we going?"

"To my castle, Sinbad. To a place that's secret and safe. That's what you want, isn't it? To be alone with the rajah?"

David's hand moved down the dancer's back to his hips. His fingertips traced over a satin-clad buttock, and gave it a painful squeeze.

Jennings slipped his arm around David's waist. "Not too hard," he murmured.

"Why not? You've got a tough ass, baby. Like a rock." David giggled. "All you dancers are hard assed. Hard assed!" he shouted.

"Shh," Jennings cautioned. "There's some other people over there."

David looked around dully. "Where?"

"There, coming down the beach . . ."

Through the darkness, David made out two figures walking toward the boat house. They looked like pale phantoms floating across the sand. The light tinkle of Dorian's bracelets carried in the air like the sound of wind chimes.

"Another couple slipping away to be alone," Jennings whispered.

David remained silent until Dorian and Alan disappeared inside the boat house.

"Is that what we are?" he asked Jennings, "a couple slipping away to be alone?"

The dancer put his hand on David's crotch and pressed lightly. "If that's the way you want it." There was an excited catch in his voice.

David stared at the boat house. "Nothing is the way I want it," he said grimly, pulling him close.

※

From the moment Alan entered the boat house with Dorian, a curious change overtook him: the sense of unreality he had experienced earlier in the evening suddenly passed, leaving him in a state of heightened awareness. Dorian lighted a candle and placed it on a low table near an old divan. The lambent flame illuminated the room, revealing each object in chiaroscuro like a painting by de La Tour: a pair of oars leaning against the wall, netting hanging from a hook, a coil of rope half hidden in a shadowy corner. A breeze floated through an open window, carrying with it glimmers of moonlight and the sound of waves surging against the dock. He could hear his own breathing, and it seemed as if the room were breathing with him.

Dorian came toward him with hesitant steps, her expression oddly timorous, unsure. She touched his face, then let her fingers drift from his eyes to his throat and rest on his chest. Her body rippled slightly, like the surface of a pond disturbed by a cast pebble. Closing her eyes, she swayed against him and felt him lift her into his arms so gently she might have been suspended in space.

Alan lowered her to the divan and kissed her mouth, her eyes. He touched her, savoring the contrast in texture of the silk veils and her skin beneath them. She clasped her arms around his neck and drew him down hard against her. Her kisses were feverish and uncontrolled, she sucked his tongue deep into her mouth, bit his lower lip. He felt her heat rise through the folds of silk. They stood up, helping each other to undress with trembling hands. In the yellow light from the candle, Dorian's body gleamed soft tints of color. She appeared fragile and yielding, so different from the first time Alan had seen her nude, that morning at the pool. There was no trace of the hardness and calculation that underlay all her gestures that day. He turned her around to explore her back and hips, pressed himself into the warmth between her buttocks and cupped her breasts. Her head fell back against his shoulder and he kissed her throat, feeling the beat of her pulse under his lips.

They fell to the divan, limbs entwined like the fleshy vines of a tropical flower, their mouths seeking the most tender parts.

Dorian felt as if she were experiencing sex for the first time. With other men she had held back from giving, divorced her emotions from the act. Now she was open, pliant, seeking frantically to satisfy Alan's pleasure as well as her own. She threw her legs around his waist and cried out for him.

He penetrated her so quickly that she moaned in surprise. For a moment her hands quivered helplessly in the air, then moved to grip his thighs, urging him on. She drew her legs up to his shoulders, a final gesture of surrender that drove him deep inside her. Then she answered his thrusts with a frenzied succession of movements that left her shattered.

Alan saw her eyelids flutter wildly, her face go pale. He felt his orgasm upon him and held himself absolutely still. At the instant of his ejaculation Dorian whimpered and opened her eyes. She looked up at him with an expression of child-like wonder, tears flooding down her cheeks; he remained poised above her, unmoving, until he was spent. With a deep shudder, he collapsed, cradled in her arms. She brushed away strands of hair that had fallen across his face, and he kissed her tears. She began to sob, small choked cries that grew into unashamed weeping. The candle had gone out, and they clung to each other in the darkness.

"Dorian, I love you," he whispered.

"Yes," she wept.

9

DAVID STOOD BY the French doors in the library and gazed out over the grounds. He patted his face and neck with a handkerchief. It was the last week in July, and waves of heat flowed and wavered in the air like slowly moving sheets of white silk. Insects droned lazily over flower beds, and low fountains of water jetted from sprinklers, creating a fine mist over the grass.

Behind him, David could hear the voices of his father and Jonathan; they had been talking business for the last hour. Now they were discussing his future, but he paid them scant attention; from his vantage point he could see Alan and Dorian walking toward the beach. They were both dressed in swimsuits—probably taking a break from the portrait. Alan was working with them separately, now that the painting had been completely blocked in.

David wondered if they were going to the boat house. He knew that in the weeks following the party they had gone there many times; it had become their love nest. He smiled at the old-fashioned term, yet it seemed appropriate; their affair had turned them into romantic children. They exchanged swift, secret glances, laughed over silly jokes, touched hands whenever they were close. Alan was tender and considerate and his effect on Dorian was obvious; she was softer, less brassy, warmer. Blooming like a goddamned flower!

He ached with envy when they were together and fantasized about what they did to each other—imagined how Alan looked, what his body was like while making love. The images turned in his mind like a knife. In some perverse way, it was as if he were sharing him with Dorian. Sometimes, when the three of them were together, he daydreamed of Alan making love to both of them, turning from Dorian to him with lips still moist from her kisses. David imagined holding Alan in his arms, kissing him more passionately than Dorian had, exciting him to a frenzy. Dorian would vanish and they would be alone . . .

David heard Jonathan loudly saying: "No, I disagree! He isn't ready to come to Paris. He doesn't have the necessary experience to work with me."

David turned to see his father looking at Jonathan with an angry scowl that wrinkled the scar across his forehead. "I think it's vitally important to David's future that he go back with you," Alexander retorted.

David listened with amusement to the two men; he suspected that his father wasn't happy with how Jonathan was directing the European chain, and that Alexander's desire to send him to Paris was a subtle maneuver to keep his brother under observation.

He wants me to be his spy, David thought. There've been too many rumors about Jonathan's gambling and his affairs with the wives of visiting diplomats. With me hanging around, he would have to be more discreet.

David smiled, thinking of how he had outfoxed his father. A few nights before he had played on his uncle's fear of having him in Paris by eagerly declaring his willingness to go. When Jonathan protested that David lacked experience in hotel protocol, David had managed to look unhappy, and had finally agreed that he needed more authority for the job. Now the decision was being argued out between the two brothers.

"Alex, be sensible," Jonathan said. "When I return to Paris in September I'll have too much to do—there won't be time to give David any training. There are new hotels going up all over the Continent, issuing massive advertising campaigns and promising unheard-of luxuries. It's true, of course, that we don't try to compete with them, that we deal in a service geared to older, wealthy clients who return each year rather than the transient tourist. But we must maintain, if not increase, our service and our publicity, if only to pick up more of the rich Americans who are traveling abroad. They must become part of our clientele, to replace the older ones who are, quite frankly, dying off."

David listened to his uncle's impassioned plea with a look of intense interest, trying desperately not to laugh aloud.

What a shrewd bastard you are, he thought, spinning out your rhetoric like a politician. David knew that Jonathan did little more in Europe than see to it that the management of the hotels was in capable hands.

He saw his father weakening and stepped in to reinforce his uncle's stand.

"Why don't I spend the next couple of weeks working with Uncle Jonathan at the hotel in New York? We could stay a few days at a time, and he could teach me some of the finer points of management."

"You'd be willing to do that?" Alexander asked suspiciously.

An expression of sincerity masked David's feelings. "Dad, I want to do that," he replied in a voice filled with contrition. "I know my behavior in the past has been a great source of worry to you, and how difficult I've been, making up my mind about what to do with my life. But these last few weeks, being with Uncle Jonathan, and hearing all your stories about the hotels, well—"

He hesitated, as if making a momentous decision, then went on earnestly, "I want to be part of it, as you want me to be."

He stopped, afraid he'd gone too far in his performance. Alexander stared at him hard, then his eyes softened.

"That pleases me very much, David," he said quietly.

David smiled at him. You old fart! he thought viciously. Aloud, he pressed home his advantage.

"When Uncle Jonathan leaves in the fall, I'd like to move into the hotel, stay there and actually take part in managing it. Then, if you think I'm ready, I'll go to Paris and begin to work there."

"That's a splendid idea," Jonathan said vigorously, with as much relief as enthusiasm. "A year at the most should do it, David."

A year, David thought. A year in New York.

And Alan would be there.

🜨

"Alan, stop it! Someone may come along and see," Dorian giggled.

He had slipped off the top of her suit and was covering her breasts with a soft flurry of kisses.

"Let's go to the boat house."

"I can't, not today—"

"That time of the month?"

Dorian nodded. "I'm sorry."

He rolled away from her with a groan. "It's okay. I'll survive—somehow."

Dorian moved close to him and put her hand between his legs. "Is it bad?" she asked, smiling.

"It's always bad when I'm around you. And if you keep that up, it will get worse."

She sat up and slipped on her top. "Alan, is sex all we have between us?"

He turned over on his stomach and wrapped his arms around her thighs. "You bet. Soon as I've had my fill of you, I'll throw you away like an old shoe."

"I'm serious!"

"So am I! I should be finished with you in about fifty or sixty years, and that's it!"

She laughed and ran her fingers through his thick hair, pulling it slightly. "What's going to happen when the summer is over?"

"I'll go to New York to study with Jordan Shaw, you'll come with me and we'll live together in a little den of iniquity."

"And then what?"

"I'll become a famous artist, we'll travel the world and you'll be the woman behind the man. You'll take photographs detailing my sittings with stars of theater, royalty, men of letters, et cetera, and when we're old we'll publish a book and retire gracefully to a villa in the south of France."

"Jesus!"

Alan looked at her wide-eyed. "You don't like my plan?"

"I think I hate it."

"Oh. Well, okay—then I'll just paint and let you support me."

"Now there's a romantic idea," Dorian said sourly.

"That's me," Alan sighed. "The last of the old-fashioned romantics."

He closed his eyes against the sun's glare and lay with his head nestled in her lap. Dorian stroked his hair softly, knowing that despite his joking Alan meant what he said about their future together. The idea made her uneasy; he was presuming a commitment from her that she wasn't sure she could give him. Every time they were together she felt that she was losing a part of herself, sacrificing some irreplaceable fragment of strength to him. Sometimes she thought of herself as standing on the edge of a crevice with Alan waiting impatiently on the other side, urging her to jump.

๛

Marie finished brushing her hair, took one last critical look in the mirror at her dress, and sighed; it was too young. She contemplated changing it, then shook her head; there wasn't enough time. She didn't want to keep Jonathan waiting. She had been late the last time, and knew that it irritated him. She had to leave now—the inn was almost a half-hour's drive.

As she started down the hall, she passed Alan's room. The door was open and she glanced in. The walls were covered with sketches of Dorian, tacked one on top of another. Wherever she looked she saw the girl's face. The effect was startling; Dorian's presence seemed to overwhelm the room.

He's in love with her, Marie thought. In love . . . The words sounded strange, like a phrase heard in one's youth, then forgotten until a moment in later years, when it is remembered wih bitter nostalgia. A curious feeling of sadness settled over her, and she closed the door of Alan's room as if to shut out the lavish, youthful display of romance.

The Cherbourg Inn was located a mile or so off South Country Road near Westhampton Beach. In an effort to be true to the inn's name, the main building hinted at French Normandy with white plaster walls, dark wood beams and leaded glass windows. It was surrounded by a cluster of cottages in the same style, all well removed from each other to afford privacy. Beds of wild flowers and sunlit shadows cast by old trees almost completed the picture of French country charm that the owners were striving for.

Marie avoided the half-circle drive in front of the inn, and pulled off the road into the lane beside the cottage Jonathan had kept booked for their assignations. They had been meeting here several times a week for over a month. The first few times she had seen him alone they had met in New York, while Marie was shopping for fabrics for the guest house. They had lunch at small, quiet restaurants, occasionally stopped in at one of the galleries on Fifty-seventh Street, or took a stroll in Central Park. Jonathan was ardent and persuasive, and finally she agreed to go to bed with him.

Marie turned off the motor and sat in the car for a few minutes. He had not yet arrived; his car was nowhere in sight. She took a cigarette from her purse and lit it, trying to quell a sudden impulse to leave. It happened every time she came here. The very act of driving to the inn filled her with a sense of dangerous excitement, sharpened by the thought of Jonathan's hard body pressed against hers. When she was with him, she felt drugged with sensual pleasure.

But when she left him, the terror began. Driving home was like reentering a prison after having been mistakenly set free; the walls were close and stifling, the routine of her days as oppressive as dying.

And always there was the pretense, stretched thin and taut, that she had to maintain in the presence of her unknowing husband and son. Deception had suddenly become an important part of her life.

She saw Jonathan's car round the turn in the lane and pull up behind her. At the first sight of him all doubt and confusion fled. She got out of her car as he came up to her, and at the touch of his hand she knew that she was powerless to alter the course she had taken.

ະ

Jonathan reached out to the night table for cigarettes and handed one to Marie. He put an ashtray between them and turned on his side to face her.

"You look sad, Marie. Has something happened?"

She smiled up at him. "Yes, something has happened. You."

"But I'm supposed to make you happy, not sad."

"And you have, *mon amour,* you have." She touched his cheek with her hand. "With you I am a *jeune fille,* experiencing her first love. There is nothing else when I am with you, no other life, no other world."

"Good. That's the way it should be." He kissed the palm of her hand and lay back against the pillows with a smile of satisfaction.

Marie sat up, put out her cigarette and moved the ashtray so she could be closer to him. He enjoyed watching the delicate gestures of her hands and slender arms, the small movement of her breasts. He thought of the many other times he had played this scene: in bed with a beautiful woman, lingering over a cigarette together in the warm afterglow of sex. It seemed to him that of his few accomplishments, this was one he had perfected; the art of the tryst.

Marie had more than fulfilled his expectations. She had acquiesced to every subtle suggestion, responded even to the inflections in his voice, the change of expression in his eyes. Getting her to agree to these clandestine meetings had been a careful maneuvering, alternating pleas and demands, a show of attention and then indifference, a hint of pain and then a promise of pleasure and fulfillment. She had followed his every move with the grace of a dancing partner. Yes, she was perfect: hungry for passion and safely trapped in the respectability of home and family. When the summer was over, they would part wise, mature lovers, with gratitude and promises to remember their idyll. That she was French only added to his convenience—American women could be so difficult when the time came for farewells.

Excited by the realization of his own finesse, he took Marie in his arms. In moments the swift, sure touch of his hands had her ready once more. He crouched above her, slipped his hands under her hips, and entered her smoothly, bringing a guttural cry from her throat. Then he sat back on his haunches, pulling her up into his lap. She flung her arms around his neck, raising and lowering herself on him while his hands played over her body. At the moment of their climax, her face was wet with tears.

A classic touch, he thought.

ॐ

That night, after George and Alan were asleep, Marie took out her journal and made another entry.

My happiness is beyond measure. Jonathan and I were together again this afternoon. He is tender and exciting, sympathetic. We understand each other. I know that he wants me, and will help me escape. I will return to Paris with him in the fall, leave George, to whom I am nothing more now than a burden. And an ungrateful one, at that.

I feel in my heart that Alan will forgive me whatever pain I may cause him and his father. And I feel, too, that he will understand, eventually, why I have made this choice. He is in love himself, and is beginning to realize what it means to care for someone deeply, as I care for Jonathan. And one day, perhaps, he may join us. Paris! The name alone is like a dream to me. But soon it will become the reality I have hungered for.

☘

One morning Alan arrived at the studio. Dorian had told him that David would be in New York all day, working with Jonathan, and that they would be alone. After Alan had worked on the painting for a few hours, they had planned to drive up to Montauk Point for lunch. But Dorian wasn't there.

He waited for a few minutes, then went to her room and knocked on the door.

There was no answer. He was about to knock again when he saw her coming down the hall from the back stairs. She was carrying a large, flat box and a stack of manila envelopes.

"Hey, thought I'd lost you," Alan said. "We have work to do. And lunch to eat. And love to make . . ."

"Sounds like a dull inventory," Dorian said grumpily. "I was in my darkroom, that's why I'm late. Open the door, my hands are full."

He followed her into her room, puzzled by her mood. "What's in the envelopes? Photographs?"

141

"Yes." She dropped the box and envelopes on the bed and sat down.

"May I see them?"

"No."

"Dorian, what's the matter?"

He kneeled down in front of her and took her hands in his. "Is it the pictures? Don't you like them?" He pressed her palms to his face and kissed them.

Dorian threw her arms around his neck and held him tightly. He kissed her hard until she pulled away, breathless.

"You have a hot mouth," she said, smiling a little.

"I have a hot everything. Feel better now?"

She nodded slowly, the smile growing.

"Want to talk about what's wrong?"

"Sure, doctor. But move away a little—you're very distracting."

Alan sat down on the floor at her feet. "Okay, let's hear it. I'm all ears."

Dorian reached for the flat box and handed it to him. He opened it and saw a large close-up of himself on top of a number of other photographs. The picture had been taken on the beach while he was sketching, snapped during a few seconds when he had looked up from his drawing pad and was staring into space. A breeze had whipped his hair across his forehead, and his eyes were deeply shadowed; sunlight emphasized the planes of his face. Careful cropping had turned the photograph into a thoughtful, serious study.

Alan took the other pictures out of the box and spread them out on the floor. There were dozens, of himself, David, Olivia, and her parents. But most were of him. He suddenly felt as if he had stepped into a house of mirrors at a carnival, seeing his face and figure reflected in myriad angles: long shots of him walking on the beach, close-ups of his face, his hands, cropped pictures that focused on his body.

"What do you think?" Dorian asked anxiously. "Are they terrible? Say something, goddammit!"

"I'm not sure what to say . . . ," Alan began slowly. "I think they're—wonderful, exciting. Now shut up and let me look."

He sifted through the pictures, overwhelmed by the sheer

number of them, feeling strangely vulnerable and exposed. She had captured some quality, a gesture, a look in his eyes, a turn of his head, something particular about himself that revealed his moods, his personality. It came as something of a surprise to realize that she was as much an observer as he.

"You're being too quiet," Dorian said. "Tell me some more how good I am."

Alan looked up at her seriously. "These are amazing," he began quietly. "You have a terrific sense of composition, a perfect instinct for when to snap the shutter, they're lyrical and moving, surprising. Not only are you beautiful, but you are an artist."

"That's exactly what I wanted to hear. Now tell me the truth."

"You know, I'm as surprised by your work as I am by this sudden glimpse of your insecurity. What the hell do you mean, tell you the truth? I'm telling you the truth! The worst thing you can do to any creative person is to lie about what they've done."

He had begun to shout and Dorian held up her hands in a gesture of surrender. "Okay, okay—I believe you."

"Good—now, what are you going to do with all this talent?"

She stared at him blankly. "Do? Well—I'm not sure . . ."

"I am. It's very obvious to me that you have the makings of a photographer—in photojournalism, perhaps, or fashion work; look how sensational Avedon's work is."

"You think I'm that good? Oh, Alan—I'm not sure . . ."

"Stop saying that! You won't be sure until you get into it!"

"All right! Stop crowding me!" she cried. Then she said tentatively, "As a matter of fact, I've been thinking about enrolling in the New York Academy of Photographic Design for the fall semester . . ."

Alan jumped up and pulled her into his arms. "That's wonderful! Then we can be together in New York! We'll find a place in the village, work together, live together—"

Dorian clung to him, laughing. "You're crazy, but yes! I want that too! Oh Christ, do you think we can really do it?"

"We can do anything, *anything,* as long as we have each

other," Alan whispered, drawing her down to the bed. "God, I love you."

"I love you, too, But I'm worried."

"About what?"

"My family is going to shit bricks when they hear about this!"

10

THE ST. CLAIR Hotel in New York was near Park Avenue in the middle sixties. Once the home of a Swiss industrialist who had come to the city after World War I, the Romanesque-styled mansion was acquired by Augustus St. Clair in 1930, after the industrialist had been wiped out by the Crash.

Augustus had added ten floors to the structure in the same massive architectural style, and decorated every room in opulent *fin de siècle* furnishings. In contrast to the modernist and art deco hotels that were becoming popular at the time, the St. Clair provided a Continental ambience that appealed to the wealthy, more conservative international visitors who had frequented the chain's hotels in Europe.

This was David's favorite of the American St. Clair hotels. He saw it as his grandfather's most successful effort to preserve the charm of prewar Europe. The dining room walls were hung with Dutch landscapes, there was an English suite with Chippendale furniture and Victorian engravings, bound sets of Hugo and Voltaire in French could be found on the shelves in the writing room, and a Tiepolo graced the foyer.

David was spending several days a week working with Jonathan and Alexander, determined to learn everything he could as quickly as possible. He knew that when the summer was over his parents would be off to visit some of the other family hotels across the country. David's plan was to gain his father's trust so that he could remain in New York, perhaps indefinitely.

There was still some question about what Dorian would do. She had spoken to him privately about enrolling in the New York Academy of Photographic Design. He knew that being with Alan had inspired the idea; up to now she had expressed little interest in a career. It was always assumed that she would become a part of their parents' society until she found "someone suitable," as Vivian was fond of saying, to marry.

David thought about the changes Alan had made in their lives. *He* was getting involved in the family business and taking the shit his father handed out without a word, and now Dorian was talking about doing something serious with her interest in photography. Neither of them was acting out of any burning ambition of their own, but only because they both wanted to be near Alan. More than that, David was aware of a division growing between him and Dorian. For the first time in their lives, they were not confiding in each other—at least, not where Alan was concerned.

Late one afternoon in the middle of August, David was going over some of the hotel books with Jonathan in the manager's office. The secretary interrupted to say that there was a call for his uncle, and Jonathan picked up the phone. When he heard who it was, he frowned.

"I'm sorry," he said. "Yes, I know you've been waiting. No, something unexpected came up. What? No . . . I'm afraid not. No, I can't." His voice was edged with irritation. "You really shouldn't have called me here . . ."

There was a click on the other end and he hung up. He tapped his pen on the desk impatiently, then turned to see David smiling at him.

"A liaison gone awry, Uncle?" David asked. "Who is she this time? A dancer? An actress?"

"Nothing quite so romantic, I'm afraid. Just an appointment I forgot."

He closed the ledgers before him with a snap. "I think that's about all for now. The Baroness Geschwitz won't be arriving until midnight, and I think you should be here to meet her; she has an eye for handsome young men. She usually travels with a large entourage, so checking her in may get a bit complicated. Why don't you take the next couple of hours off?"

"All right—if you're sure you don't need me."

"No, I don't. It's quiet now. I may take a nap before dinner."

After David had left, Jonathan rose from the desk and

stood by the windows overlooking Park Avenue. His dark eyes narrowed as he thought about the phone call from Marie. Their affair was beginning to grow tedious; she was becoming difficult to deal with. The last few times they'd been together she had talked more and more of wanting to go with him to Paris. One word of encouragement, and he knew she would leave her husband. He couldn't blame her; he had met George.

Jonathan glanced at himself in a mirror hanging on the wall near the desk. He was looking more fit than ever, tanned from hours on the beach, his eyes clear and sparkling. He'd let his hair grow a little, and it waved softly over his fore- head. Almost boyish, he thought. When he returned to Paris he would go directly to Gino and let him disguise some of the gray that was getting too apparent. But he'd keep the streaks at his temples; they gave him a dashing look.

There was a knock at the office door, and he turned as a slender young girl in her early twenties came in and closed the door behind her. Jonathan heard the click of the lock and smiled, starting toward her with outstretched arms.

※

David walked toward the Plaza Hotel. The August heat seemed to rise from the pavements, enveloping the early eve- ning traffic. Tourists slogged alongside New Yorkers, their ir- ritable complaints mingling with the impatient blare of horns and motorists' frantic cries. The tourists swore they'd never come to the city in summer again, and the natives wondered aloud how to escape to cooler climes.

At the Plaza David went directly to the Oak Room. He stood in the entrance for a few minutes and looked around. There was the usual collection of middle-aged and elderly men in business suits sitting at tables. Some of them looked up and stared at him for a moment, then returned to their conversations, glancing surreptitiously in his direction as they talked. Compared to the heat-streaked people on the street, the men here were cool and neat, well-barbered, nails glisten- ing from recent manicures, cheeks flushed from too much drinking.

The aged faces were interspersed with younger ones, companions or lovers who appeared more handsome by contrast. They exuded healthy young executive or college-boy charm in their carefully pressed summer suits and casually tousled hair styles. They were quick to smile, and flourished lighters whenever a cigar or cigarette appeared. Their laughter was low and discreet, and interest in their companions seemed to pour out of their faces. Even so, they swiftly noted the presence of a new man in the room, especially someone who was young and good-looking.

David ignored the appraising glances he received and searched for someone who was alone, rather than play the game of eye-contact with a young man already entrenched at a table with a friend. He noticed a boy standing at the bar, and for a second he thought it was Alan. Tall and dark-haired, the youth had the same straight profile and strong jawline. But when he turned in David's direction David saw that he was older, about twenty-four, and that his face was rougher, not as fine-boned as Alan's. But there was a resemblance that intrigued him. The young man caught David's glance and held it, smiling a little, as though he had recognized him. There was something insolent in the way he stared that made David shift his eyes to another part of the room. When he looked back, the boy was coming toward him.

David felt that everyone was watching them. All the faces in the room seemed intent on their impending meeting, bright to the possibility of these two desired beings getting together; hope and envy stared out from every table. With a last quick glance at the boy coming nearer, David left the room, looking back once to make sure he was being followed. He went out the Grand Army entrance of the hotel and walked across the street to the small plaza.

Dusk was settling over the city, diffusing the light into warm gray tones, like a theater dimming before the beginning of a play. Hansom cabs were gathered at the curb, glum-faced drivers and patient horses waiting for the evening's business to begin.

David sat down on a stone bench near the Pulitzer fountain and lighted a cigarette. He avoided looking toward the hotel and stared up at the sky, trying to appear nonchalant.

A few minutes later he sensed someone approaching the bench and sitting down beside him.

"It was cooler in the Oak Room," the young man said.

The register of his voice reminded David of the bellhop in San Francisco: soft and undemanding, a little passive. He turned and looked at him. Up close, the rough features were even less like Alan's. But the insolent smile and intense eyes held an exciting promise.

"I don't like putting on a show for those old queens," David replied. He glanced at his watch and saw that it was a little after six. "Do you have any plans for dinner?" he asked. "I only have a few hours."

"In that case, let's skip dinner. Your place or mine?"

"Yours."

They climbed a dimly lit staircase in one of the many crumbling old buildings on Fourteenth Street, just off Seventh Avenue. The boy preceded David up the stairs. He had taken off his jacket in the cab on the way over, and David saw sweat stains on the back of his shirt and under his arms. The air in the building was stale, and a sound of harsh voices came from other apartments—people arguing and complaining about the heat. A man yelled something unintelligible and a woman cried out; a baby made fretful noises. The walls were scrawled with graffiti, the floors littered with scraps of paper and garbage.

Christ, this place is a dump, David thought nervously. Why the hell did I come? He could beat me, steal my wallet, even kill me. Nobody would know, or care. It was stupid to come here with him, dangerous.

On the third floor David hesitated as the boy went down a narrow hallway. I could leave now, he thought. I don't have to stay. Then the boy stopped at a door, opened it and turned to David. In the pale light his face looked more like Alan's. David remembered what Alan had told him and squinted to further the illusion. He hurried forward, forgetting his fears.

"It's not much of a place, but rents are getting higher all the time," the boy said, closing the door and locking it.

A neatly made bed disguised with many pillows to make it look like a couch dominated the small room. An effort had been made to decorate with prints and posters, and a galley kitchen was revealed by half-opened folding doors that were mirrored to make the room appear larger.

"It's very nice," David said.

"So are you." The young man's voice was eager. "You're really a terrific-looking guy. I have a weakness for blonds."

"You and everybody else," David laughed, pulling him into his arms. "What's your name?"

"Don."

David stiffened slightly, then smiled. "That's perfect. The guy who brought me out was named Don."

"Yeah? Was he nice?"

"No. But that doesn't matter now."

David pressed him closer and they kissed, tentatively at first, then more intensely. Their hands moved over each other, feeling the resilience of muscle and flesh. Behind David's closed eyes, an image of Alan appeared, and he grew more forceful.

Don pulled away, breathing hard. "Hey, you're wild! Let's get out of our clothes. I really want to enjoy this."

"You will," David said, slipping out of his jacket.

❦

For the next few days, on one pretext or another, David avoided sitting for Alan. The knowledge that he was gradually becoming a third wheel when they were all together made him uncomfortable, and he began to think that his plan to live in New York just to be close to Alan was a foolish one. Doubts plagued him, and he grew withdrawn.

Finally, at Alan's insistence, he joined him in the studio one afternoon and assumed his pose. Dorian was printing in her darkroom for a few hours, and for once he wished that she were there with them; he was in no mood to be alone with Alan.

As soon as David was settled, Alan picked up his brushes and started to work, patiently repainting David's eyes for the third time.

"Don't move," he muttered. "I think I've finally got them right."

"What's wrong with my eyes?" David asked, keeping his head still and barely moving his lips.

"Nothing. They're beautiful," Alan replied absently, mixing a color on the palette. "Eyes just give me trouble, that's all. If they aren't perfect, then nothing else in the face really works."

While Alan worked David fell into a recollection of his few hours with Don. The boy had proved to be nothing like Alan; even his resemblance had done little to make the encounter more exciting. When they had finished David had barely been able to conceal his eagerness to leave.

"Let's take a break," he heard Alan say, and roused himself from his thoughts. He stood up and stretched, slipped off his shirt and did some deep-knee bends.

"I'm getting out of shape, posing for you," he said.

Alan glanced at him from the easel and smiled. "You don't have to worry; you have a terrific build, and you're very graceful. I really should do a few figure sketches of you— that is, if you'd be willing to pose for them."

David stopped moving. "You mean nude?"

"Sure. Why? Are you shy, or modest? I know a lot of guys are."

David sat down on the floor. Alan reached for some cigarettes and handed him one. "Once I asked the coach of the basketball team to pose for me. He was a big, rangy man, long muscles, heavy veins in his arms and legs, a terrific subject for a charcoal study. He agreed and showed up wearing boxer trunks. When I asked him to strip, he went nuts, got cadmium red in the face and said posing in the buff—that was his expression—was for fruits."

David tensed. "What happened?"

"I had two fights in the locker room that week because he hinted that I was queer for wanting to draw him 'in the buff.' I finally convinced the other members of the team that the reason he got so angry was because he didn't want anybody to know he had a two-inch dick. Poor son of a bitch could never go into the showers after that without everybody trying to sneak a look at his cock!"

David joined Alan's laughter half-heartedly. "I didn't know you were so tough—two fights in one week to defend your honor?"

"Well, I hate boneheads who automatically think that any man who is sensitive or creative is queer."

David looked up him guardedly. "But a lot of people do, you know."

"Yeah, but it's stupid. If a guy gets his kicks sucking cock, that's his problem. A *chacun son goût.*"

David frowned, irritated by Alan's vulgarity.

"Anyway," Alan went on, "do I get to immortalize your body as well as your face? When you're old and paunchy, you can show the drawings to your grandchildren."

"I have no intention of getting old. or paunchy," David muttered. "And I'm not shy or modest—and I can't be threatened about the size of my equipment. Maybe in the fall I'll come to your studio and give you a thrill," he concluded flippantly.

"That's a deal," Alan said. "I still can't believe that we're all going to be in New York together. When Dorian told me she wanted to study photography, I almost fell over!"

David suddenly wanted to say something that would undermine Alan's enthusiasm, to make a dent in the perfection of his hopes.

"If I were you, I wouldn't get too eager yet. She hasn't told the family about her plans."

Even as he spoke, he knew how cruel he was being. Yet he felt a certain satisfaction at seeing the light go out of Alan's eyes.

"You think they'll try to stop her?"

"Well, it's hard to say . . ." Then, ashamed of his bitchiness, he added, "Dorian usually gets her way. She has a very strong will, and just as strong a won't."

Alan grinned in relief. "That's what I wanted to hear."

David stretched out on the floor, cushioning his head on one arm. He was disgusted with himself for hurting Alan. After all, if nothing else, they were still friends, and he was certainly strong enough to keep that friendship from degenerating into something ugly. The truth was that he could never manipulate Alan into going to bed with him; that was one of the reasons he felt so strongly about him—knowing that he was unobtainable.

"You ready to go back to work?" Alan asked.

"In a minute—I ache in muscles I never suspected I had."

"Sitting still for so long is a strain," Alan agreed. "Turn over and I'll rub your back."

"No, that's okay—lying on the floor helps."

Alan knelt down beside him. "Turn over. I do this for my father a lot. I'm very good at it."

"No!" David protested, not wanting Alan to touch him.

"Don't be silly," Alan laughed. "I'm not going to hurt you."

David began to struggle as Alan tried to turn him over onto his stomach. For a few minutes they fought each other, more seriously than Alan realized; he was merely intent on making David feel better. Equally matched in strength, Alan found it difficult to hold David's flailing arms. David battled to keep Alan away from him, but he found it harder and harder to keep from giving in. All of a sudden, his last defense gave way, as if something inside him had broken. He quit struggling and let Alan tug him over onto his stomach and straddle his legs. He lay quietly, afraid to move or breathe, and felt the pressure of Alan's thighs against his own, the heat of Alan's hands on his flesh. The intimacy of the contact made his heart pound, and at the same time left him feeling weak and vulnerable. Turning his head slightly, he saw them reflected in the mirrors on the wall. Alan was bending over him, the muscles working in his arms, his faded denims pulled tight over his thighs and hips.

David closed his eyes, replaying the image in his mind. Only now they were naked, and Alan was making love to him. A nervous excitement took hold of him.

"Alan, stop," He pleaded softly. "I feel much better."

"Of course you do. I started giving my father rubdowns when I was fifteen. Another minute or two and you'll feel like a new man."

David grunted in reply, not trusting himself to speak. He felt reduced to helplessness, betrayed by his emotions and his body like a man felled by a terminal disease. Nothing would change, he thought; he would always want Alan. Up until this moment he had refused to admit that to himself. But it wasn't just wanting him, David realized with a shock. He loved him. Whatever happened, however they were together or separated, that would never change.

Toward the end of August Alan finished the painting. When Olivia heard the news she was delighted; George and his crew had completed most of the work on the guest cottage, and now she could plan a small party to unveil the portrait and the house at the same time.

"I promise you," she told Alan, "that I won't try to sneak a look at it until the party. Have you shown it to David and Dorian?"

"No—and I think they're ready to kill me!"

"Then I'd better work fast," she laughed. "I'll talk to your mother and see if we can plan to do it in the next couple of days."

That evening, after dinner, he and Marie talked about the party. "Olivia is so excited about seeing the portrait," she said. "Are you happy with it, *mon cher?*"

"It's the best thing I've ever done," Alan replied. "It's funny—Dad feels that way too, about the restoration of the house."

"I know. He's very proud of what he has accomplished, and I am proud of you both."

Later, when she was alone, she wondered what he would think if he knew about her affair with Jonathan. The summer was almost over, and she and Jonathan had still not discussed if she would return to Paris with him or follow later. She would have to face both Alan and George with her decision soon. She was positive that Alan would understand—they had always been so close, and besides, with this portrait, he was beginning to build a career, a life for himself. Sooner or later she would lose him anyway.

The day of the unveiling they all drove out to the estate early. Alan had some finishing touches to do before the painting was moved to the cottage, and George was anxious to go over some details with his men. Marie had offered to help Olivia set up the buffet.

Once at the estate, Alan hurried to the studio. Dorian and David were waiting for him, and as he walked through the door they began to applaud.

"Will you two knock it off?" he laughed. "I'm nervous enough as it is."

"We decided to have a little ceremony by ourselves," Dorian said. "After all, we ruined our bladders and our behinds sitting for the bloody thing—"

"—so we feel it is only fitting that we be the first to see it," David finished.

"Three great minds that think exactly alike," Alan said. "I was planning to do just that."

Dorian and David stepped up on the platform and sat down next to each other on the loveseat, folding their hands in their laps like children at a party waiting for the presents to be opened. Alan swung the easel around to face them, hesitating for a moment before he took the covering off the painting.

"Okay, you two, here goes. And for Christ's sake, no jokes—"

He lifted the cover and stood to one side, watching them. For a long moment there was silence.

The portrait had the strange quality of a moment seen in passing, as if the relationship of the figures had been determined afterwards, in the imagination of the artist.

Dorian, in a blue sleeveless dress with a full, filmy skirt, was curled up in a corner of the loveseat with one arm resting in her lap, her fingers trailing down to touch David's shoulder. He was seated on the floor, leaning back against the chair with one knee up and the other leg bent under him. One arm crossed his chest so that his hand touched Dorian's. He was dressed in a soft white shirt and slacks, a pale blue sweater tied loosely by the sleeves around his throat, so that it fell over his shoulders. Dorian's eyes were gazing at him fondly, while David seemed to be staring at some distant point beyond the canvas. Next to the loveseat was the side table bearing the bowl of flowers, and in the background the lawns of the estate stretched to the house, mistily delineated near the top of the painting. Despite the detail of the embroidered loveseat, the vase of flowers and their clothes, the focus of the painting came down to their touching fingers, uniting them like an endearment whispered in confidence.

Dorian stared, in awe of Alan's prodigious talent. At the same time she felt unexpected resentment arising from a sense of her own inadequacy. But she swept it aside and rushed to enfold him in her arms, her eyes wet with tears.

David sat, not moving, stunned. The portrait captured his grace and dignity, but Alan had also managed to suggest the weakness, the flaw in his nature that David was so afraid to admit. It's written into my face, he thought with sudden anguish. Yet he was positive that Alan didn't suspect his homosexuality. No, it's only my own fear, he told himself; no one else could possibly see it.

"David—why don't you say something?" Alan asked anxiously.

"It's wonderful, Alan. But very sad . . ."

"Sad?"

"Yes. We shall grow old, but this picture will remain forever young. If only it were the other way—if it were we who were to be always young, and the picture that were to grow old—"

Alan and Dorian threw themselves on him with a burst of laughter.

🦋

Vivian looked around the guest house in astonishment. "Mr. Conway, you've wrought a miracle!"

"Yes, it's very good, Conway, very good," Alexander agreed gruffly.

"Very good, hell—it's sensational!" Olivia said. "Even old bulldog Augustus, our revered father, would have had more to say than 'very good'!"

Alexander threw her an irritated look and stalked off, summoning George to follow him.

Olivia looked after her brother, exasperated. "For a man who professes an admiration for gracious living, Alex has the manners of a longshoreman!"

"Oh, Olivia, what's the point of getting angry? You know Alex will never change," Vivian said.

"I know—he thinks of himself as the lord of the manor— it's his idea of ensuring class distinction. Sometimes I think without it he'd collapse like a cripple whose crutches have been kicked out from under him!"

Marie stood by Alan, trying to listen to him describe the house as it was when he and George had first seen it, but her attention wandered; Jonathan had not yet arrived, and she was nervous about being near him while surrounded by their families.

"It's just incredible what Dad has done with this place—" Alan was saying.

She glanced over at George, who was talking enthusiastically with Alexander. He was wearing a new suit for the occasion and looked trim, younger, almost handsome. Marie suddenly thought of the first time they had met, how kind and patient he had been that night—and through all these years. The memory was painful, and she tried to dismiss it from her mind.

Just then, Olivia called for everyone's attention. It was time to see Alan's painting.

"I shall let the artist do the honors," she said.

Alan stepped up to the easel and smiled hesitantly. "I wasn't expecting all this formality," he said. "I feel I should have prepared a speech or something—" He paused, swallowing nervously. "I guess the best thing to do is let the painting speak for itself."

He pulled off the velvet cover draping the canvas and stepped back.

"Oh, my dear boy!" Olivia exclaimed in a hushed tone.

Vivian clapped her hands. "Alan, it's simply beautiful!"

The others joined in, applauding eagerly. Marie's eyes filled with tears, and George hugged Alan, then stepped aside to let Dorian and David near him.

"I told you we'd make you famous," Dorian whispered in his ear.

"I think Alan has outwitted both of us," David laughed.

Alexander stared at the painting and muttered, "Astonishing. I never realized that my children were so beautiful . . ."

David and Dorian had to make an effort to keep from laughing aloud, but Vivian gave her husband an angry glance.

Suddenly a voice rang out from the doorway. "Am I in time for the party?"

Olivia looked up. "Jonathan! You're just in time!"

He strode through the room to where they were gathered. "Ah, the unveiling of the painting," he said. "And it's magnificent! You are to be congratulated, Alan." He turned to George and took his hand. "Mr. Conway, you must be very proud. And Mrs. Conway," he said to Marie. "I haven't seen you since the night of our costume ball. How nice to meet again, especially under such exciting circumstances."

Vivian took his arm and led him away. "You must see the remarkable transformation of the house. Mr. Conway, come along and explain what you accomplished with this old wreck of a place!"

As George hurried out with them, Marie stepped away and sat down. Her hands were trembling, and she knew that her face was pale; when Jonathan had walked into the room she had almost panicked.

Olivia came over to her. "Marie, are you all right?"

"Oh, yes—" She laughed self-consciously. "It's just all the excitement."

"Can I get you something?"

"No, please don't bother—I'll be fine in a moment."

Marie glanced nervously through the archway to the dining room where George was talking with Jonathan and Vivian. Olivia followed her gaze, then looked back at Marie, noting with surprise the expression on her face as she watched Jonathan. And then she realized that they knew each other, had done more than just meet at the party.

Vivian joined them. "Mrs. Conway, I'm so pleased with everything you've done here. Your choice of colors, the drapes and fabrics for the chairs, the placement of the furniture—all absolutely perfect," she said breathlessly. "I will certainly recommend you to all my friends, and your talented husband, too!"

"Thank you—" Marie began, but Vivian had already hurried over to talk with Dorian and David. "She's very kind," Marie said to Olivia.

"A little condescending, and still a snob," Olivia remarked, smiling. "But she's getting better. Sometimes I almost like her."

Marie laughed. "You are the rebel in the family, yes? Very forthright and independent. I envy you for that."

"It doesn't always work to my advantage," Olivia rejoined ruefully. "Many times I've thought that there was no point to being a rebel unless you had a gift that would make the world pay attention to you. Unfortunately, I don't have one of my own—I'm only able to recognize it in others."

"But that in itself is a gift," Marie said warmly. "And one for which we are all grateful. Alan told me that you will be living in New York while he is there. It makes me very happy to know that you will be close by to keep an eye on him and his work."

"You make it sound as if you won't be seeing him," Olivia said. "Don't worry, though—I'll do everything I can to help him."

Vivian called to her, and Olivia left Marie alone. A few minutes later Jonathan approached, saying: "Mrs. Conway, you've done beautiful work in the house . . ."

"Thank you, Mr. St. Clair." Under her breath, Marie said anxiously, "I haven't seen you for almost a week."

"I know," he whispered. "I've been very busy."

"Can we meet tomorrow at the inn?"

Jonathan frowned, and a touch of impatience tightened his lips. Then he said, "Yes, I suppose so—"

Marie's eyes were pleading. "Please, I've missed you so—and we have so much to talk about."

"Yes, yes," he agreed hurriedly, seeing Alexander approaching. "I'll be there at two."

For Marie, the rest of the afternoon passed in a blur of fixed smiles and inane chatter. Even more difficult was the drive home; George and Alan were in high spirits, but all she could think about was being with Jonathan the following afternoon.

11

"I MUST GO," Jonathan murmured. "It's getting late."

Marie slipped her arms around him and reached to kiss his lips. "No, please, not yet—"

"Marie, please." He pulled away from her and stood up. "Would you like another glass of champagne?"

"Oh, yes . . ." She sat up against the pillows and smoothed her hair with her fingers. The room was warm, scented by fresh-cut roses that Jonathan had brought along with the champagne. She laughed softly, feeling content.

He handed her the glass of wine and she drank quickly, spilling a little down her chin. Jonathan dabbed at the trickle of wine with a handkerchief. "You're like an impatient child, my dear," he said.

"Happiness makes me careless," she replied gaily, then kissed him.

He disengaged himself from her and began to dress, watching her in the vanity mirror. She was gazing at him adoringly over the glass. The light filtering through the partially opened drapes was harsh, and she looked tired, a little worn. Well, after all, he thought, she isn't a young girl.

"I dreamt of Paris last night," she said. "Oh, I cannot wait to be there again, especially with you. It would be better, don't you think, if I wait until Alan is settled in New York, before I leave George . . . ?"

He hesitated for a moment before answering, then said quietly, "Marie, you cannot come to Paris with me."

"What?" Her eyes were wide, disbelieving. "Why not?"

He went to the bed, sat down and cradled her in his arms, saying, "My dear, there is nothing in the world I want more than to be with you. But my life in Paris is so complicated, so burdened with obligations that we would have little time together. What kind of life would that be for you?"

Marie nestled closer to him. "Ah, *mon amour,* no inconvenience would be too great for me to bear."

He put his finger to her lips to silence her. He had rehearsed the scene in his mind, selected the phrases and gestures he was certain would make things go smoothly; why couldn't she keep her mouth shut?

Marie held his hand to her cheek. "Forgive me—I know you are thinking of me, of my comfort, but you have nothing to fear. Being with you whenever I can will make me happy."

He pulled his hand away gently, hating her for clinging to him. As if he had nothing better to do than rescue a frustrated housewife from the prison of her marriage! Now he would have to be blunt, and there would be a scene. He sighed, wishing he could have done it over the phone.

"Marie, my sweet," he began, in a practiced facsimile of regret, "I cannot disrupt your life any further—and you cannot join me in Paris."

She saw that he was serious, and grew pale. "I don't understand."

"I thought you did; perhaps that was my mistake. When I first saw you, I was sure that you felt as I did—that we could have a lovely interlude together . . ."

"An interlude?" She stared at him blankly. "You mean—just an affair? You lied to me?"

"Not at all," Jonathan replied coolly. "I never deliberately deceived you."

Marie struggled wildly to collect her thoughts. "But you said you loved me." Her eyes filled with tears. "You said you loved me!"

"You must understand that a man in my position has to be free. That's why I never married. I could not offer you a home—"

"I've had a home! I want you!"

"Marie, it simply cannot be," he declared flatly, standing up. He went to the mirror and began combing his hair. "If I've hurt you in any way, I'm truly sorry."

She rose unsteadily to her feet and pulled on a robe. "Coward!" she cried hoarsely. "You never had any intention of marrying me!"

"My dear, I have no intention of marrying anyone."

Marie went across the room and grabbed him by the shoulder, forcing him to face her. "Are you telling me that we shall never see each other again?"

Jonathan gave her a look of absolute intransigence. The pain of recognition struck her like a blow from an unseen assailant, and, covering her face with her hands, she began to moan.

"Please, let's try to part with some dignity," Jonathan said coldly. "I find melodramatic scenes very distasteful . . ."

Her moans rose to a shriek and she hurled herself at him with clawed fingers, striking madly at his face. *"Bâtard!"* she screamed, ripping his cheek and drawing blood.

Jonathan caught her wrists with one hand and with the other struck her hard across the face, and threw her onto the bed.

"Menteur!" Marie wept helplessly, her cheek reddening from the force of his hand. *"Vous m'avez trompé—je vous déteste!"*

Jonathan put a handkerchief to his face to stanch the flow of blood. Then he slipped on his jacket and walked out of the room.

Marie heard the squeal of tires as he drove off. She lay sobbing uncontrollably, her breath coming in harsh shudders.

An hour went by before she could rouse herself to dress. When she was finished she sat down before the vanity mirror. Her face was blotched and her eyes looked back at her like the eyes of a dying woman, hollow and lifeless. A momentary panic gripped her; the present disappeared into a glimpse of the past and the future, and she was alone in both. With deliberate calm, she took out her makeup and began to apply it as if she were creating a mask.

Before leaving the cottage she looked around. The room was shadowy and dim. The only evidence that anyone had been there were the empty bottle of champagne, two glasses and bouquet of roses sitting on the dresser. As she left, her last impression was of the subtle odor of Jonathan's cologne still lingering in the air. Gripping her purse, she forced herself out the door.

In the following days, Marie went through the motions of

her daily routine like a sleepwalker. She complained of a summer cold to excuse her listlessness, and went up to bed when thoughts of Jonathan's betrayal became too overwhelming to bear.

George and Alan were solicitous and helpful, but her nerves were frayed, and she grew increasingly unstable, flaring up in anger, then dissolving in tears. Her sleep was broken by dreams that brought her awake, made her cry out in the dark. George held her in his arms, and she wept, despising herself for wanting him to be Jonathan.

She grew apathetic, withdrawn, reliving memories of her childhood and the horror and desolation of being alone after her parents were killed. Once, in the middle of the night, she awoke with a start, certain that she had heard the sound of gunfire. George lay beside her, asleep, and she looked at him, wondering if the pain she was going through were a punishment for all the loveless years they had spent together. She began to cry, and buried her face in the pillow, fearful of waking him.

A few nights later Alan returned from having dinner with Dorian and David to find his father sitting alone before the television set.

"You're home early," George said. "I thought you were going to a movie."

"Mr. St. Clair's brother is returning to Paris in a few days, and they had some people over to see him. Dorian and David couldn't get away, so—"

He went into the kitchen and got himself a glass of milk. "Where's Mom?" he asked, returning to the den and taking a chair beside his father.

"She went out to do some shopping at the market—said it was easier in the evening when it's cooler. She ought to be back soon, she's been gone almost an hour."

"What's the movie?" Alan asked, gesturing to the TV set.

"Something with Claude Rains—I missed the title—but it's pretty good—"

A half-hour went by and the movie ended. George looked at his watch. "Marie should be home; it's eleven o'clock," he said worriedly.

"She'll probably come walking in any minute."

Another half-hour passed and George insisted on driving up to the market. "Maybe she got sick—or had trouble with the car . . ."

The market was closed, and there was no sign of Marie; the street was deserted. George grew frantic. They went back to the house and he began to call their friends, asking if they had heard from her, if she had dropped by to visit. Alan made some coffee and tried to appear calm, but he was more frightened than he wanted to admit.

George finally called the police; then the waiting began. He paced the floor, cursing himself for every argument, every harsh word he had ever said to her. Alan tried to reassure him, but to no avail. The hours ticked by and a cold, apprehensive silence settled over the room. Alan stood by the windows, vainly searching the street while George sat on the edge of a chair, his hands clasped tightly.

Suddenly Alan saw a police car turn the corner and pull up to the house. He and George rushed to the front porch. Two officers with somber faces came up to them. An abandoned car matching the description of Marie's had been found near an inlet in East Islip.

Alan sat next to his father and held his hand tightly as the police car sped through the night. In the flash of street lamps, George's face was chalky, his eyes blinked rapidly, and a faintly sour odor of fear came from his breath. The ribbon of highway before them seemed oddly distorted, like a drawing that was out of perspective, and the buildings on the side of the road leaned at a crazy angle.

They rolled to a stop on a small beach at East Islip. Alan and George got out of the car, guided through the darkness by the officers. Other police cars were parked nearby with their searchlights on. A group of policemen were gathered around something lying on the sand. Their figures were shadowy and still, their faces half visible in the slashes of light.

They stepped aside as George and Alan approached, revealing a body covered with a blanket. One of the men knelt down and lifted the cover. For a moment Alan had a queer image of himself lifting the cover from his painting only a week before.

A flashlight was beamed down and they saw Marie. Wet

hair lay coiled in dark strands over her face like spilled ink. Her mouth was opened, the lips pinched and blue, and her eyes stared glassily, as if focused on a vision.

Alan felt his father crumple into his arms. He closed his eyes tightly, and screamed hoarsely to the police, "Turn off your lights! For Christ's sake, turn off your lights!"

❦

Throughout the long night George wept in Alan's arms, convinced that he was responsible for Marie's death. Alan, his nerves deadened by shock, could only repeat meaningless words of comfort, all the while tortured by his own self-recriminations. What despair had driven her to suicide? He had seen her unhappiness and anger, but never once questioned the source. Now he would never know.

Dorian and David were by his side in the days that followed, and Olivia helped him through the agony of the funeral arrangements. George was inconsolable; he sat alone in his room, clutching a picture of Marie and agonizing over his feelings of guilt and shame.

A week after the funeral George left Bay Shore to visit in Connecticut with his sister; she had insisted he needed some time away from the house and its memories. Alan told him to go, as much for his own sake as his father's; he wanted to be alone, to mourn for his mother privately.

Left to himself, Alan spent hours sitting in the garden, remembering how he and Marie had cared for it. He wandered through the house, touching pieces of crystal and china she had collected, looking at photographs and books about Paris and France that she had kept. In her room, he found a box of mementos of his childhood: sketches he'd done in school, an award he'd received in a competition, a newspaper article praising a painting he had entered in a local art show.

In the bottom drawer of her desk, he came across her journal. He held it in his hands, wondering if he should read it; she had always been so mysterious about the notes she made.

He would be worse than a thief even to open it—and yet written on those pages might be an indication, a clue to why she had taken her own life. He stared at it, hesitant, even a little afraid. But he had to know; he couldn't let her just slip away from him forever without some explanation.

ॐ

Dorian stood by the living room windows and watched the twilight wash long shadows over the ground. Clouds were massing on the horizon and the sky was shot with streaks of fading color. It was the second week in September, and there had been an autumn chill in the air all day.

Behind her she could hear Olivia arguing with her father. Vivian would break in with a comment, then David. Once, Jonathan added a few words, but it was Alexander's tirade that dominated the conversation. She lit a cigarette and drew on it nervously, wincing at the harsh sound of his voice.

"She will not go to any school in New York just to be with that boy!" Alex shouted. "I won't have my daughter running off to live with some adolescent! Dorian, you are going to Paris with Jonathan—if you're so anxious to study photography, you can do it there," he added sarcastically. "Do you hear me? Look at me when I talk to you!"

Dorian remained where she was, refusing to face him. Vivian came over to her and touched her arm. "Darling, you're only nineteen—give it a little time."

Dorian's eyes were stony. "Does it get better when I'm twenty?" she asked sullenly.

"I know how you feel about Alan," Vivian went on. "But have you given any thought to the future—your future, if you—" She hesitated, then finished, "—leave us, now?"

"You mean go live with him, don't you?" Dorian asked coldly.

"Yes, that's exactly what I mean!"

Dorian turned on her furiously. "You just want me to be like you! Do what he says, go where he tells me, cater to his demands the way you do!"

"I want you to think about living with no help from your father," she retorted. "Think about what you'd be giving up to live with a boy who has years of struggle ahead of him. He'll demand your support while he gives all his energy to his work."

"That's not true!" Dorian cried. "Alan loves me!"

"I'm sure he does, but he's very ambitious. If his work doesn't come first, if he has to worry about you, what do you think will happen to that love?"

"He's not like that—he'll take care of me!"

"All I want you to do is think about it," Vivian implored. "Don't rush into anything—"

Mrs. Childress suddenly appeared at the door. Unnoticed by the others, she beckoned to Vivian and Dorian.

"Yes, what is it?" Vivian asked.

"It's Alan—he's in the foyer, and he's in a terrible state!"

Dorian ran to the front hall and saw Alan coming toward her. He was pale, wild-eyed, and clutching a book in his hands.

"Alan, what's wrong?"

"Is your uncle here?" he demanded.

"Yes, he is, but why . . . ?"

He pushed her aside and ran into the living room, hurled himself at Jonathan and knocked him to the floor, punching him savagely.

"Alan, what the hell are you doing?" David cried, trying to stop him.

Alexander grabbed at Alan's flailing arms, pulled him roughly to his feet and slapped him hard across the face. "What's the meaning of this?" he said harshly.

"He killed my mother! The bastard killed my mother!"

"Alan, for God's sake, what are you talking about?" Dorian cried.

In a voice shaking with rage, he told the stunned group what he had read in Marie's journal.

"That's ridiculous!" Jonathan snapped. "I admit I took her to lunch once, but that was the only time I saw her! The rest is just some fantasy—the delusions of a woman trying to escape the boredom of a dull marriage!"

"You fucker!" Alan shrieked. He tore himself free of Alexander and lashed out at Jonathan.

"Mrs. Childress, call the police!" Vivian screamed.

"Alan, stop it!" David shouted, throwing himself into the fight.

Alan shoved him aside and David crashed into the coffee table, shattering a tray of sherry glasses.

"Stop it, stop it!" Olivia pleaded.

Dorian, her face ashen, ran to help David to his feet. Alexander sprang at Alan from behind and twisted his arm into a hammerlock. Alan tried to break his grip, throwing them against a table that fell over with a crash. Jonathan struggled to recover himself; his mouth was torn and bleeding and blood poured from his nose, spattering over his shirt. Enraged, he took advantage of Alex's hold on Alan and began to beat him until the boy sagged unconscious in his brother's arms.

Alan struggled to open his eyes; one was swollen almost shut. His face and body ached, and he could taste blood in his mouth. He saw two police officers standing with Alexander and Jonathan, talking in low voices. There was no one else in the room. He tried to sit up and discovered that he was handcuffed, his arms behind his back.

Suddenly one of the officers came over to him, pulled him to his feet and pushed him across the room. He stumbled, then straightened up. Alexander was watching him.

"Where's Dorian?" Alan asked hoarsely.

Alexander's eyes were cold, his voice harsh. "I'm going to make sure that she never sees you again."

The officer shoved him forward. Alan saw Jonathan standing near the door, holding a handkerchief spotted with blood to his mouth. The officer gripped his shoulder to hurry him along, but Alan wrenched free for a moment and thrust his face close to Jonathan's.

"I won't forget what you did," he muttered through clenched teeth. "I'll never forget, and I'll get you—I swear to God I will—"

Jonathan recoiled slightly before the fierce intensity, the murderous expression on Alan's face. The two policemen grabbed the boy's arms and marched him out of the house, threw him into the back of a police car and slammed the door. Alan fell across the seat and slipped into a dark, cold void.

A few hours later he awoke to find himself in the holding cell of the East Hampton jail, booked on an assault charge.

On an overcast morning two days later he was released. At

168

the front desk, an officer handed him a packet containing his valuables.

"The charges against you have been dropped," he said matter-of-factly. "You're free to go. You'll find your car in the lot—Mr. St. Clair had it brought over."

Alan went outside and started for the parking area. Olivia was waiting for him; she was standing by the Rolls, and for a moment he thought Dorian was in the back seat. But as he drew closer he saw only the chauffeur.

"Are you all right?" she asked anxiously. "You look terrible—"

"Your brother has fists like King Kong. I assume you got him to drop the charges?"

"Yes—Alan, we were all shocked by what happened. I don't mean the fight, but everything . . . dear God, I don't even know what to say to you, how to apologize—"

"You have nothing to apologize for. Where's Dorian? Why isn't she with you?"

Olivia looked away from him nervously, reluctant to answer.

"Is she all right? Did he hurt her?"

"Oh no, no—Alex never abuses his children physically; he's more cruel than that. I say it, even though he is my brother."

"Then where is she?" Alan asked urgently.

Olivia took a deep breath. "She left for Paris yesterday with Jonathan. She had no choice, Alan. Alexander made her go."

He stared at her uncomprehendingly. "I don't believe it!" he said harshly. "Why didn't she run away, take off for New York and wait for me there?"

"Dorian couldn't do that. She's not as strong as you, or as independent as she appears. She's still a child . . ."

"But she said she loved me, that she'd go with me!"

"I'm sure she cares for you very much, but she just wasn't ready to renounce the only way she knows how to live. She enjoys being privileged, and—"

"Don't say any more!"

Olivia remained silent. A chill breeze stirred around them and Alan shivered, drew his windbreaker closed and zipped it up. He took a cigarette from the pocket and lit it. "Where's David?" he asked. "In New York?"

"Alex decided to take him on his trip across the country to visit the hotels. They left this morning. David read the last entries in your mother's journal, and had a terrible fight with Alex, trying to defend you—"

Alan sighed wearily and gave her a strained smile. "Poor David—funny, isn't it, the way everything got so fucked up? It was all so perfect—the whole summer. Nothing that good ever lasts, does it."

"Some things do. You have one thing that's lasting, that belongs to you as no human being ever could—your work. Whatever else happens in your life, that's something you'll never lose."

Alan nodded, silent for a few minutes. Then he asked, "Do you have my mother's journal? Did David give it to you?"

Olivia shook her head sadly. "I'm afraid not. I think Alex kept it."

"He probably burned it. Well, it doesn't matter—at least my father will never know what happened. But I'll always remember what she wrote in it."

"I think we all will."

The chauffeur leaned out of the car window and said, "Miss St. Clair, it's getting late . . ."

"I have to go, Alan. I'll be moving to New York in a few days, and there's so much to do—"

"I understand. Thanks for coming down."

She reached into her purse and handed him an envelope. "It's the check for your painting; I'm having it moved to my place in town. And there's a letter of introduction to Jordan Shaw. As soon as I'm settled I'll call him. Oh, and you'll find an address of a studio or an apartment, I'm not sure which. It's in the Village—a friend of mine owns the building. Go and see if it suits you."

Alan took the envelope and held her hands tightly. His voice shook with emotion. "You've been very good to me, Olivia."

"No, I haven't been good to you at all. If anything, I've brought a great deal of pain into your life, and I never meant to do that."

Her dark eyes were wet with tears. She kissed him on the cheek and got into the car.

Alan stood looking after her as the car drove off, feeling

suddenly alone, deserted. He opened the envelope; Olivia's check was for more than she had agreed to pay him. A scrawled note was paperclipped to it: "You deserve this, and a great deal more."

A smaller envelope bearing Jordan Shaw's name was under the check, and in the corner of the envelope was a card with the address of the apartment in Greenwich Village.

Alan took it out and stared at it, seeing only a number and a street name. But gradually the address began to assume a meaning for him. This might be his new home, where he would live and work. It could be a place for Dorian, too; he was positive she would come back to him—Paris wasn't so far away. She had defied her father before, she would do it again, despite everything that had happened.

He began to walk toward his car, dreading the return to an empty house. He could leave now, he thought, there was nothing to keep him. A slight stir of excitement went through him; he could pack his clothes, books, canvases, paints, everything—and leave now! He started to run. Olivia was right— the one absolute constant in his life was his work. He ran faster, clutching the envelope tightly.

He felt as if he were holding the future in his hand.

Part Two

12

New York: January 1967

ALAN PUT DOWN his brushes. His eyes ached; and the colors
on the canvas in front of him blurred into a wavering flow of
brush strokes that had no form or meaning. He stood up and
stepped back from the easel. Blinking rapidly to clear his
vision, he studied the painting.

"Alan, can you hold that for a minute?" Jordan Shaw
called out from across the room.

Nodding his head, he stood motionless and continued to
examine the painting. It was lousy, he decided; flat, lifeless.
He shifted his gaze to the slender nude young woman sitting
in a Chippendale armchair a few feet away. The pearl gray
light filtering through the windows gave her white skin a soft
patina of ivory; only her dark hair and the rose pink of her
nipples provided a touch of color on her pale body.

Alan looked back at his painting and groaned aloud.

"Be finished in a minute, then you can move," Jordan said.

"I'm not groaning because I'm tired. That was an expression of disgust at the piece of shit sitting on my easel."

Jordan laughed quietly, worked for a few more minutes,
then put the sketch down. "Okay, that's it," he said to Alan.
Glancing at his watch, he gestured to the model. "Let's quit,
Myra—it's almost five-thirty."

She broke her pose with a sigh of relief and went behind a
Chinese screen to dress.

Alan was still before his easel, his shoulders slumped in defeat. Jordan went to his side and offered him a cigarette, then
took one for himself.

"I don't have a match," he said, searching his pockets.

"You never do." Alan pulled a lighter from his jeans and
flicked it first for Shaw, then for himself. It had become a

175

standing joke between them; Alan was always out of cigarettes.

Jordan shifted his tall figure into a relaxed stance and drew deeply, letting the smoke curl out the nostrils of his long, bony nose. He had the husky build of a middle-aged athlete, thinning gray hair, and a sensitive, mobile face. But despite his air of certainty, there was a hint of restlessness in his blue eyes, a searching expression that at times turned fearful, or veiled, as if to hide his thoughts and feelings.

"It's not so bad," he said, examining the painting. "I wish I had done as well when I was your age."

"It doesn't breathe, move or even wiggle a little," Alan said morosely. "And the light is all wrong. Everything is soft, like it's going to float right off the canvas and drift away."

Jordan chuckled and patted Alan's shoulder reassuringly. "With all your talent, you're very short on the one thing every artist needs—patience. You know what's wrong, so correct it. If it eludes you, put it away and start something else. Come back to it in a couple of weeks with fresh eyes."

"You're right, I am impatient," Alan said grimly. He took the painting off the easel and leaned it against the wall, facing in.

Jordan went back to his worktable and began to clean his brushes. He was tired, and his hands were trembling. A familiar pressure had begun to push insistently against his chest, and his breathing grew slightly labored. Thank God we're not going out tonight, he thought; if Grace just leaves me alone, I can deal with it. He glanced up at Alan, wondering if he could take the boy into his confidence, if there were any way he could help him. No, he decided, best to leave Alan out of it.

When Myra left the studio and they were alone, Alan asked Jordan, "May I see the sketch you did of me?"

Shaw nodded. Alan went over to his worktable and picked up the drawing pad. In a quick, flowing pencil line, Jordan had drawn Alan standing before his easel, capturing his mood of discontent. Roughly indicated was Myra sitting in the chair, the screen behind her, and even a suggestion of the painting Alan was working on.

"Christ, how do you do it?"

"I'm very talented," Jordan replied facetiously. "I am also

fifty-two years old, and I've been drawing since I was seven."

"That answers my question very nicely, thank you."

"I thought it would." He wiped his brushes, shaped them and returned them to a large white jar. "Why don't you get out tonight and have some fun? You seem a bit edgy."

"I don't have the time—I'm working on a couple of sketches for a new painting."

"All work and no play? What happened to the tradition of artists balling their models? Myra's been coming on to you ever since she started posing for us."

"She's not my type," Alan said curtly.

"Okay, okay, sorry I mentioned it. Grace and I are just concerned about your being alone so much."

"Thanks, but I prefer it that way."

"Well, then, how about having coffee with us before you leave?"

Alan followed him out of the studio and down a broad, well-lit hallway that was lined with paintings. He glanced at them, feeling the same thrill as when he had first seen them, five months earlier.

Those months were the bleakest in Alan's life; the anguish of loss was a dark nebulous background obscuring the light of his new beginnings. The lingering chill of Marie's death corrupted his vitality. He felt as if encompassed by a vacuum that absorbed every new impression, until his vision turned on itself and reflected only the morbid relief of his personal landscape.

Eventually he had settled into a routine of working with Jordan a few hours each day, and roaming the streets in the late afternoons and evenings. He was incapable of seeing New York as it was; instead, he unconsciously superimposed on it all the paintings, drawings and prints of the city he had ever admired: a woman leaning out of a tenement window became an Edward Hopper etching; the jostling Eighth Avenue crowds resembled scenes by Bellows, Marsh and Luks; his first sight of the Hudson from the Cloisters evoked paintings of the Hudson River school. Long hours were spent alone in galleries and museums, where he obsessively studied great works of art.

All the while he constructed in his mind a fantasy of

success, success that he would use as a weapon of violent retribution against Jonathan and Alexander St. Clair. Alan could not insulate himself from the shock of tragedy; he relived the terrible discovery of Marie's corpse and Dorian's betrayal over and over again.

This harsh regimen of bitterness and vengefulness isolated him from contact with people. Although he went to see his father every few weeks, if he hadn't been studying with Shaw, and hadn't occasionally visited with Olivia, he would have been utterly alone.

Jordan and his wife, Grace, lived in a many-roomed flat on the fifteenth floor of an old apartment building on Park Avenue in the middle eighties. They had occupied it for over twenty years, and had decorated it with rare pieces of art: paintings by famous friends, valuable works by old masters, sculpture, *objets d'art* they had collected on their travels, and fine antique furniture. Jordan had used almost everything they owned as props in his paintings of models and friends, of Grace and himself, prompting one critic to call him "a painter of his own environment, an environment of such charm and graciousness that we have all yearned to be part of it at one time or another."

Yet there was something strange about the carefully designed rooms, with every piece in its correct place, every bit of space perfectly balanced for weight and form. It was as if the Shaws, having completely filled their home with beautiful objects, had left no room for themselves. Grace, an accomplished cellist who taught a select number of students, generally kept to her studio during the day. The sonorous tones of a Bach unaccompanied suite or the melancholy sound of a Brahms sonata would drift like a ghostly tide through the narrow halls that separated her studio from Jordan's. As for Shaw, he didn't so much live in his home as paint it. Moving restlessly from room to room, sketch pad in hand, he would rearrange a vase here, a chair there to capture yet another grouping, a different perspective of the walls and furnishings he had endlessly examined.

Only when they entertained did the Shaws seem at ease. On these nights their home became a salon of New York artists, writers, and musicians. The drawing room resounded with music and conversation, white-jacketed servants attended the famous guests with fine food and wine, and for a few hours life and decor blended in a totally perfect creation.

Many times Alan was invited to attend these evenings. Jordan introduced him to the elite of contemporary artists: Pollock, the Soyer brothers, John Koch, Motherwell, Frank Stella, and many others. Although Alan remained politely quiet at first, it was not long before he acquired enough confidence to articulate his own views. As Jordan's protégé, he knew he was in a position to gain the attention of his teacher's friends, and rarely missed a chance to do so. Jordan was aware of Alan's self-promoting behavior, but found it more charming than opportunistic. Since Alan was his staunchest advocate in arguments about the merits of his academic style, he could scarcely fault him for being a little too openly ambitious.

What Jordan didn't realize was that something more dangerous underlay Alan's calculations; his determination to achieve success was becoming the driving force in his life.

Jordan hurried ahead of Alan and flung open the library doors. Grace had turned on the lamps and started a fire in the small, Italian-tiled fireplace. The room glowed with warm light, dispelling the early evening overcast.

She was standing by an English tea cart that was laden with pastries and a silver coffee service, and as they entered, she said, "Yes, yes, the coffee is ready," answering her husband's question before he could ask it.

Grace was slender and delicately boned, almost fragile. She had a kind, gentle face, with a small nose, sweetly curved lips, and calm, dark eyes that had a curious quality of innocence. Chestnut hair lightly streaked with gray lay in short, soft waves over her head. She was wearing a long black skirt and a white ruffled blouse. When she came across the room to kiss Jordan's cheek she moved with the grace of a young girl.

Jordan threw himself into an armchair by the fire while she fixed the coffee. Alan settled into the couch and lit a cigarette.

"How did it go today?" Grace asked him.

"Better than I thought, or so the master tells me."

"You're much too hard on yourself, my dear," she said

softly. "You have such an abundance of talent, but you're very short on patience."

Alan laughed. "Did anyone ever tell you two that you say the same things in almost the same tone of voice? Jordan told me that not more than five minutes ago."

"Oh dear," Grace sighed. "Soon we shall begin to look like each other, as they say people do who have lived together for many years."

"Impossible!" a woman's voice exclaimed from the doorway. "Jordan's too tall, you, my lovely Grace, are too short, and besides, he's losing his hair!"

Jordan leapt to his feet, upsetting his coffee. "Layla! Where the hell did you come from?"

"The bathroom, where else? It's so goddamned cold out, it took my pee twenty minutes to thaw!"

Jordan rushed to enfold her in a bear hug. "I simply can't believe you're here! When did you arrive?"

"About a half-hour ago. I told Grace not to disturb you." She kissed him on the mouth. "God, you taste good and look even better!"

The woman swept into the room, charging it with her presence. Swathed in a fringed red stole over a black shirt, wearing jeans tucked into high-heeled boots, she was at once colorful and exotic. Midnight black hair fell in full waves around her face, accentuating wide, sharply defined cheekbones. Her skin was the color of dark honey, and her full lips were a vivid red. But most startling were her eyes; they were large, darkly lashed, and supernaturally green; against her dark skin they had the lustrous gleam of jewels.

Alan stood up as Jordan led her to him. "Alan, this is Layla, a very dear friend, and the best model I've ever had or will have."

"What he says is true." Her voice was a husky purr that complemented the feline eyes. She held out her hand, giving him a swift but careful appraisal.

Alan guessed that she was in her late twenties. From the sinuous way she moved he thought she might be a dancer.

"Are you modeling for Jordan?" she asked. Before he could answer, she turned to Shaw. "He's gorgeous—very Delacroix, with that black hair and those blue eyes. He looks like he smolders—" She turned back to Alan. "Do you smolder? Speak up, who are you and what do you do?"

Alan let go of her hand, confounded by her barrage of flippant questions, and suddenly annoyed by her overbearing manner.

"Are you finished with the interrogation?" His voice was testy.

"I am," she replied, a mischievous smile playing at the corners of her lips.

"I'm Alan Conway," he said stiffly. "And I don't model or smolder. I paint."

"I'll remember that," she said solemnly. Then, leaning close to him, she whispered, "But I have news for you—you *do* smolder."

She swung around to Jordan and Grace. "I'm a guest!" she admonished them. "Lavish me with food and drink quickly!" She had suddenly slipped into a Jewish accent that bewildered Alan but made Grace and Jordan laugh.

"You haven't changed a bit," Jordan said, laughing. "Here, have some coffee."

"Do you want some brandy in your coffee?" Grace asked.

"Of course—I may look warm, but inside my body is frozen. Christ, I would pick the middle of winter to come home! But I just couldn't stay away another day."

"Tell us where you've been and what you've done," Jordan said. "It's been over a year since you left—"

"—and we haven't heard a word, not a single letter or a postcard," Grace chimed in.

"God, you sound like my mother! Okay, okay—from the top . . ." Layla took a chair close to the fire and began to describe her travels.

Alan sat back on the couch, not so much listening to what she said as observing her vibrant, theatrical manner. She had thrown the red stole over the back of the chair, creating a perfect background for her black hair and luminous skin. The shirt she wore clung to the firm curves of her breasts, and her jeans fit smoothly over long, shapely thighs. Everything about her seemed excessive and glossy; she gave the impression of constantly making a statement about herself.

"—so there I was in Rome on May Day, with every Communist in the city screaming 'Get out of Viet Nam!' and waving their signs and placards in my face! So I grabbed a sign and joined the march, yelling at the top of my lungs, 'Yeah, baby, let's get us out of Viet Nam!' "

"What happened?" Jordan asked between gasps of laughter.

"I got my tush pinched by every guy in the square! I couldn't sit down for a week! Oh God, those Italians are something else!" She looked over at Alan with a wicked smile. "You Italian, baby?"

"No—my mother was French and my father's family are English."

"Ah, so I was right about the Delacroix look," she said slyly.

Then she looked at her watch and groaned. "God, I've been here for hours!" She stood up, reached for the stole and threw it around her shoulders. "I've got to go catch up on what's happening in town."

"When are you coming to work with me?" Jordan asked.

"Give me a week to get settled, then I'm all yours."

Grace went to get her coat and Layla turned to Alan. "Are you busy this evening?"

"Yes, I have some work to do back at my place."

"Where do you live?"

"In the Village."

"That's just where I'm heading. Why don't we share a cab?"

Before he could reply, Layla whipped her arm through Alan's and hurried him toward the door. "I'll call you in a few days," she said over her shoulder to Jordan and Grace.

"Don't lose my star pupil," Jordan called back.

"Don't worry—he may be returned in pieces, but he won't get lost!"

As soon as they were gone, the genial smile on Jordan's face faded. Grace began to clear away the coffee cups. Jordan slumped into a chair, letting his head and arms drop with abrupt awkwardness. He stared at the patterns of grain in the hardwood floor until the lines blurred slightly and began to vibrate. When he looked up, his eyes were watery with emotion. "Did you talk to her? Did you tell her?"

"No, I didn't," Grace said coldly. "I won't have anything to do with it."

"I told you I just needed something mild—a stimulant—nothing hallucinogenic—you know I'm through with that." A pathetic note came into his voice. "I'll call her tomorrow. I just need something to calm my nerves, so I can work better."

"That's not what you need, and you know it!" She crossed the room, her heels making staccato clicks against the floor, and took him by the shoulders, forcing him to look at her.

"You *must* see a doctor, Jordan, and soon! This has gone beyond experimentation. You've lost confidence in yourself, and in your art. You'll never get it back with drugs!"

He shook his head. "You don't understand."

An expression of rigid opposition caused her face to look suddenly much older. "I do understand, and I'm not putting up with it much longer." She started to walk away toward their bedroom. "By the way, Walter Koehn called this afternoon."

"Ah, my redoubtable agent." He got up shakily, and ran his hands through his hair. "Well? Did I get the Venable commission?"

"No," her voice came back faintly. "They decided to buy a Rauschenberg."

Layla and Alan stood near the curb, searching for a taxi. Street lights shone on pavements that were still wet from an early evening shower, and a cold wind blew down the avenue. She shivered and pulled the cape more tightly around her.

"There's a cab, but he doesn't see us," Alan said, spotting one at the top of the block.

Layla put two fingers to her lips and produced a strident, piercing whistle. The cab stopped and backed up to them.

"That was pretty quick action," Alan commented.

"Just survival technique. I grew up in this wilderness."

They got into the cab and she told the driver, "Bleecker Street—the Cafe au Go Go."

"I live near there," he said.

"Oh, then you've been to the club."

"Yes, but not often. By the way, what's your last name?"

"I don't use one—just Layla." She settled back, stretched her legs and sighed, "I could be in Bali right now, drinking coconut milk, lying on warm sands, and here I am, freezing my tail off in this ruin."

"Why did you come back?"

"Because this is my home, and it's where everything is happening. I like to be in the center of *now*—in Europe I felt like I was in the middle of *then.*"

She sat up and peered out the window as the cab careened down Fifth Avenue. Despite the intense cold the street was crowded with people. Brightly lit store windows splashed blurred colors across the wet sidewalks.

"It's beautiful, isn't it?" Layla said in a half whisper. "All that energy, the life and colors flowing together like streaks of paint." She turned and shifted closer to Alan, holding out her hands. "Rub these poor things, honey. They are frozen!" Her accent had abruptly gone pure ghetto black.

He took her hands and asked, "What's with all the dialects? When you described your trip you slipped into a Jewish accent, and now—"

"Confusing, huh? No last name, green eyes and not quite black skin, and, you will admit, an abundance of style."

"An overabundance. But I suppose there's an explanation."

"Of course there is! My mother is Jewish, and used to be an actress in the Yiddish theater. In the thirties she turned to costume designing and the Communist Party, in that order. Either out of love, or political defiance—I'm still not sure which—she married my father, a black man struggling to make his way as an opera singer. So, I'm black and Jewish, or, if you wish, a black Jew."

"You must have had a hell of a time growing up."

"Sure did—to the niggers I was a kike, and to the Jews I was a *shwartze.* My life has been one long identity crisis. Momma got the brunt of it, what with her politics and me as living proof of her convictions. But we survived, baby. We survived." She sat back, face hooded by shadows, her green eyes catching sparks of light from the street.

The cab turned onto Bleecker and pulled up in front of the club.

Layla asked, "Are you sure you don't want to join me, just for a little while?"

"All right. For a little while, maybe."

The first band was setting up equipment and doing a sound

check. Layla rushed to greet the manager of the club and Alan looked around. The room was narrow and deep, and there were cables everywhere. Lighting equipment was mounted on exposed pipes on the ceiling, and PA speakers and instruments jammed the small stage. The club was shabby and crowded and smelled of stale cigarette smoke and the mixed scents of many bodies. People were dressed in Carnaby Street mod, the girls in miniskirts, the boys in Edwardian jackets, paisley shirts and long hair. Even the language sounded different—underground drug words and hip expressions were shouted back and forth across the room.

Alan found a table and sat down, observing the frenetic action until Layla finally broke away from her friends and came over to him.

"God, this is great!" she exclaimed, sitting down. "Now I really feel like I'm at home!"

She slipped off the cape, adjusted the red stole around her shoulders and looked over at him. "By the way, don't you have a girlfriend?" she asked unexpectedly.

"Sure. I keep her locked up in a closet with two day's supply of food and water."

She threw up her hands. "Okay, okay! Sorry I asked . . ."

Alan was ashamed of his unnecessary sarcasm. "Sorry—I didn't mean to be rude."

A guitar chord suddenly sounded through the speakers, shaking the club into momentary silence. Then the lights dimmed and everyone began to clap and whistle. A voice blared out, "Ladies and gentlemen, and all the rest of you freaks, please welcome the Blues Project!"

The music was loud, raw and intense. During the numbers the light changed dramatically from hazy red to hot white to mesmerizing strobe effects. Layla responded to each shift in sound and light; during a slow, elegiac blues she wrapped her arms around herself and bowed her head, as if the pain expressed in the lyrics were her own. But an up-tempo instrumental had her rocking in her seat, pounding the rhythm on the table.

Alan was less interested in the music than in watching Layla; absorbed by the way the soft light emphasized her dark skin and heightened the shape and color of her amazingly green eyes, he began to see her in sketches and paintings, and looked forward to her modeling at Jordan's studio. She had a feral, almost predatory quality that excited him.

The houselights came up; the set was over.

"Do you want to stay for the next band?" he asked her.

"Nope, I've had enough. I want to see your paintings. Let's go back to your place."

"Do you always have to be so aggressive?"

"Sorry," she said quickly. Then, assuming a demure, shy attitude, she whispered, "Alan, is there something else you'd like to do, someplace else you'd like to go?"

"Yes, I thought we might go back to my place."

Alan's apartment was on the top floor of a four-story house on Sullivan Street; it was one large room with a kitchen and a bath. The former tenant, also an artist, had installed a skylight, polished the bare floors and painted the plaster walls white.

Alan had picked up some furniture in junk stores on Second Avenue, built bookcases along one wall and set up his easel under the skylight. With everything in place, he finally had the studio he had longed for.

Layla followed him up the stairs and into the apartment. He turned on the lamps and put away her cape while she looked around.

"This is nice," she said softly. "Clean and neat. You don't make a mess, do you?"

"Only when I paint."

She stopped at a wall covered with drawings and watercolors of Dorian. There were a few of David, and some of the preparatory sketches for their portrait. Layla stood, silently examining his work.

"May I see your paintings?" she asked.

He went to a storage bin he had built, took out several canvases and set them up around the room. Layla went from one to another, her eyes roving back and forth over the surfaces.

"Do you have any other sketches?"

He lifted a large portfolio and set it down on the table he used for his meals. While she opened it and looked through the stack of drawings, he sat down on the bed and watched her.

When she was finished examining the sketches, she looked up at him and said, "I can understand why you wanted to work with Jordan, and why he respects your talent. These are all quite beautiful."

"Thank you."

"Don't be so quick to thank me—you might regret it."

"What do you mean?"

She walked toward him and he made room for her on the bed. But instead she sat down on a nearby chair, opened her purse and took out a joint. Alan reached for his lighter, leaned over and held it for her. She drew deeply, then let the smoke out with a deep sigh.

"Tell me about the girl," she said, gesturing to the drawings of Dorian. "Unless you'd rather not . . . ?" She handed the joint to Alan and he took a hit, then handed it back.

"No, I don't mind—she's a girl I met last summer. Her name is Dorian St. Clair—"

"Olivia St. Clair's niece?"

"Yes—why, do you know her?"

"No. I know Olivia, though." She hesitated, then added, "I met her at Jordan's one night, several years ago. But go on, tell me about Dorian."

It was nearly two o'clock in the morning before he finished. He hadn't intended to talk for so long, but under Layla's careful questioning, the whole story of the summer came out. It was the first time Alan had talked about the events since they had occurred.

"I'm sorry about your mother, Alan. It must have been horrible for you," she said softly. "Have you heard from Dorian or David?"

"Dorian wrote to me, trying to explain how her family had pressured her to go away, but I didn't buy it. She's independent and has more than enough money to get a plane ticket and come back to me, if she wanted to. But she doesn't. She never wanted to live with me; I was just the entertainment for that summer. I tore up the letter. As for David, well, we had lunch once but it was difficult seeing him again—"

Layla stood up and went to his portfolio. She began to separate the drawings into two piles. When she was finished, one pile was much thicker than the other. Alan got up and went to her side.

"What are you doing?" he asked.

She pointed to the larger group of drawings. "These sketches are all of young women around town—here's a girl sitting on the steps of the Met, one in the park, this one outside a store—"

"Yes, I know my own sketches," Alan smiled. "What are you getting at?"

"Alan, every girl's face in these sketches is the same."

"That's ridiculous—" He thumbed through the drawings.

"Look closely." She reached out to the wall and pulled off a portrait of Dorian, then placed it beside the sketches on the table. All of the faces had the same cast to the features, the same expression.

"I don't believe it," Alan murmured.

"It's a strange contradiction that artists can see the world and not their own work, but it's often true. You're still in love with her."

"Christ!" Alan swept the drawings off the table and threw himself across the bed, staring at the ceiling. Layla picked up the sketches and returned them to the portfolio. Then she began to unbutton her blouse. "Why don't you take off your clothes and get into bed," she said softly.

He sat up and saw that she was naked to the waist. Her breasts were firm and beautifully shaped, with small, dark red nipples. He held out his arms and she went to him, and pressed his face against her warm flesh. She stroked his hair, then tightened her fingers and tilted his head up to look at him. In the soft glow of the lamps her features were darkly shadowed, accenting the strong planes of her face. He saw her eyes and thought of them as pieces of jade against a velvet setting.

"It's time you had a new woman to think about, baby," she whispered.

"You know something? You're absolutely right."

The morning light forced Alan to open his eyes. He was lying on his side, facing the windows, and for a few minutes he stared at the bare branches of a tree visible through the frosted panes. A pattern of light and shadows was thrown against the wall where the sketches of Dorian hung, and he saw her face criss-crossed by the shadows as if slashed by dark scars. He closed his eyes against the disturbing vision.

Layla shifted behind him and flung a bare leg over his. The heat of her body was comforting, and stirred thoughts of the hours they had spent making love. He became aroused, and turned to face her. His hands moved over the satiny texture of her breasts and hips. She moaned softly, coming a little awake at his touch, and nestled her head sleepily into the hollow of his neck. Moving one leg under him so that he lay between her thighs, she opened herself to him. He entered her cautiously, slowly, until they were completely united, then began to move, clasping the firm flesh of her buttocks, directing the pace with the pressure of his fingers. Opening his eyes wide, he stared at her face, seeing sharply focused details, as in a painting: the light blue tint on her fluttering eyelids, the deep, reddish honey color of her cheeks against the white pillows, the blue black hair fanned out around her head. He snapped his hips more energetically and she arched her brows in surprise, and caught the pink tip of her tongue between her teeth as he pressed more deeply into her. She reached out and grabbed the back of his thighs, raked them with her fingernails and moved up to meet his thrusts with a fury that sent him into a final, ecstatic lunge. In that instant, behind the blazing red screen of his eyelids, he saw a glimpse of Dorian's face, heard her voice merge with Layla's as they cried his name in discordant unison.

For a long time they lay quietly, folded together like interlocking parts of a puzzle. Finally Alan rolled over on his back and stared into space. Layla lifted her face to him and he kissed her, but in his mind the vision of Dorian lingered—blurred, indistinct, yet present.

13

OVER THE SILENCE in the studio Alan heard Grace playing
Vivaldi. The deep sound of the cello floated in the air, as
pure in tone, he thought, as a line drawing by Beardsley. He
went on working for a few minutes, then stopped and called
Jordan to look at the painting.

"What do you think?" he asked.

Jordan stubbed out the cigarette he was holding, reached
into his shirt pocket for another one and put it between his
lips. Alan picked up his lighter from the taboret and lit it.
"Well?" he asked again.

"It's shocking, absolutely shocking," Jordan replied gruffly.

"What is?"

"What's happened to your painting in the last few weeks,"
Jordan answered, scowling. Then he broke into a wide smile.
"Look at that,"—he gestured to an area of the canvas—
"those tonal values, and the balance between those two
sources of light—you wouldn't have dared try that two weeks
ago. And the color you've used, here, in the hips . . ."

"It drove me crazy, trying to figure out the right combina-
tion for dark skin tones."

Jordan laughed. "You should have asked Layla—she
knows."

Without moving from her pose, Layla broke in, "I
wouldn't tell him. Goddamn if he didn't try to weasel it out
of me, but I said, 'Figure it out yourself—you've got eyes in
your head, use 'em!' "

Alan colored with embarrassment. "Pushy bitch!"

"Oh dear, the honeymoon is over," she wailed. "Last night
he called me his 'hip muse.' "

Alan picked up his brushes and continued to paint. "She

has no concept of privacy," he muttered to Jordan. "My life has become an open book!"

"And what a book!" Layla said. "Jordan, if that boy could let go in paint the way he does in—"

"Enough!" Alan bellowed, cutting her off. "One more word and I'll start painting you white!"

Jordan held up his hands in a gesture of peace. "No more, no more—these revelations are titillating and embarrassing. Let's quit for today—it's almost five-thirty and I've had it."

Layla swung out of her pose and began doing stretching exercises. Jordan moved to the windows and leaned against the frame, staring out at the gently falling snow. In the reflection of the cold light his face looked drained, bloodless.

Alan pulled on a sweater and went over to him. "Are you all right?"

"I wish this damned winter were over. I need the spring badly." His mouth tightened to a thin line and his eyes stared ahead vacantly.

Layla joined them. "Is something wrong?"

"No—no," Jordan replied nervously. He gave her a weak smile. "I was just thinking I could use a week in the Bahamas."

Her eyes narrowed slightly, then she glanced at her watch. "We should be going," she said to Alan.

"What's on for tonight?"

"It's a surprise."

Jordan walked with them to the foyer. As they passed Grace's studio she came out and joined them, glancing anxiously at her husband.

"Leaving so soon?" she asked.

"We've got a big night ahead of us," Layla replied. She turned to Alan. "Get a cab, will you, baby? I'll be right down."

"Sure—get some rest, Jordan. I'll see you Monday."

As soon as he was gone Shaw pitched forward into Layla's arms. His eyes were closed, his fists tightly clenched. Grace cried out softly, and helped Layla walk him to the library.

"Don't get sick now," Layla said to him. "You can make it, you can get through it."

The two women settled him on the couch. "Can you come

back with something for me later?" he asked in a strained voice.

"Yes—as soon as I can leave Alan."

She stood up and Grace went with her to the door. "Keep him warm until I get back," she told her.

"I will. Please hurry—he's been ill all day."

"I'll be back as soon as I can."

"Is Jordan all right?" Alan asked as she got into the cab.

"He's fine, just a little overtired, that's all."

"Grace looked upset."

"She's a worrier, especially where Jordan is concerned."

Layla gave the driver an address and sat back, staring out the window.

A few minutes later the cab turned into a street near Washington Square and drew up before a Greek-revival-style three-story house. As they went up the front steps, Alan heard strange wailing sounds and people shouting at each other through the second floor windows.

"What is this place?" he asked.

"You'll see . . ."

Before they could knock, the door swung open and a small, stout, dark-haired woman appeared. She was dressed in slacks and a blue workshirt that was covered with bits of thread and lint. A dressmaker's tape measure dangled around her neck.

Layla embraced the woman, then said to Alan: "This is my mother, Della Peake."

Della took him by the hand and led him into the house. "We were expecting you. Sylvester's upstairs trying to keep a riot from breaking out . . ." She sounded at once irritated and amused.

As if to point up her statement, there was a loud crash from the floor above, then screams of laughter and more weird wailing sounds. Layla started up the stairs, telling Alan to follow her. Della called up to them: "Tell Sylvester I need those sketches of the Pharisee's costumes—"

"I will," Layla answered.

"Pharisee? Like in the Bible?" Alan asked.

"Yes. It's a project Sylvester is working on . . ."

They reached the second floor landing and walked down a

broad hallway to a pair of doors. Layla flung them open and they stepped into an enormous room that had been converted into a workshop. There were young people everywhere, all involved in some activity: painting flats that hung from the ceiling, building a series of plywood platforms, and reading aloud from scripts. Over the noise of hammers pounding rose the strange wailing sounds Alan had heard earlier.

"What's that weird noise?" Alan asked, raising his voice over the din.

"That's Simon, playing a synthesizer," Layla replied, gesturing to a man at the back of the room.

A tall thin man in his early thirties approached them. "So, you finally brought him to meet me," he said, looking at Alan. He had a delicate face, wavy blond hair, and blue eyes.

"Alan, this is my brother, Sylvester," Layla said.

"Don't look so surprised," Sylvester laughed. "I'm her half-brother, from Momma's first marriage to an actor no one remembers, not even Momma, I suspect."

"Layla never told me she had a brother, especially a famous one."

"She's ashamed of me because I'm white."

Alan had read about Sylvester Peake in newspapers and art magazines. He was a critically acclaimed set designer, and a notorious underground artist whose Pop Art happenings and outrageous ideas had been compared to the work of Andy Warhol. Sylvester had caused a public incident with a performance art piece called "Saran" the year before. He and fifty friends had covered themselves in plastic wrap and invaded Grand Central Station at five o'clock in the evening to demand railroad timetable information from astonished commuters.

Layla glanced at her watch and made a face. "Omigawd! It's late and I gotta do a quick errand for Jordan. I'll be back in an hour, Alan. Sylvester will take care of you—"

Her brother looked after her as she left, shaking his head sadly. "That girl is a social disaster—but I'm glad we have a chance to talk. I'd like you to work with me."

"Doing what? I don't even know what this is all about."

"Yes, it would help if it were explained; Layla and I forget to do that sometimes. We're doing our version of the Corpus Christi plays—those fifteenth-century English play cycles that retold the history of the universe as it was written in the Bible. We're preparing a modern version for a happening that will take place Easter Sunday. I'm supervising the whole thing, and Della's doing the costumes. But we could use someone with your ability for an idea I have for the climax of the event."

"But I don't do Pop Art, or anything that's abstract—I paint in a realistic style . . ."

"I know. Layla's told me how good you are, that's why I want you to work with me. I have an idea for a painting that demands your expertise as a draftsman—you see, it must be absolutely classical."

"I'm not sure," Alan demurred. "I've been working toward a one-man show, maybe at a gallery—"

"What I have in mind won't hurt your ambitions—if anything, it might help. I plan to invite the cream of the New York art world. There could be a lot of publicity in it for you, even bring you to the attention of some gallery owners."

Alan listened carefully as Sylvester outlined his idea, growing excited at what the designer had in mind. This would be the first opportunity he'd had since coming to New York to do something that would be seen publicly. His thoughts raced with the possibilitities of being involved in an event created by Sylvester Peake, and the coverage it would receive in the press.

Sylvester went on describing the event to Alan and introduced him to members of his troupe. When Layla returned, she asked Sylvester: "Well, did he go for the idea?"

"Like a moth to the flame," he replied.

"What the hell was this—a plot?" Alan asked.

"Absolutely!" Layla laughed, hugging him. "When do you start to work?"

"I thought I might do some sketches tonight . . ."

"Oh Christ!" she groaned. "You are ambitious, aren't you? No, not tonight. Tomorrow," she declared.

"But—"

She slipped her arm around his waist and whispered in his ear: "Tomorrow—I have other plans for tonight."

14

Paris: February 1967

DORIAN BRUSHED HER hair so that it lay close to her head and fell in a straight line below her shoulders. She reached into her jewelry case for a slim diamond choker, fastened it about her neck, and stepped back from the alcove of full-length mirrors to view the effect. The shimmering metal Paco Rabanne gown clung to her body like a silvery encasement. Her arms and shoulders were bare, and the diamonds were a needle-thin flash of brillance at her throat. She smoothed her hands over the woven strips of aluminum hugging her hips and muttered, "If it rains, this thing will rust."

There was a knock at the door of her suite and she called, *"Entrez."*

"Where are you?" a woman's voice asked from the foyer.

"Madeline? I'm in the bedroom."

A moment later Dorian saw Madeline Gautier reflected behind her. "Well, what do you think?" she asked.

"My dear, *tu es formidable!*" Madeline exclaimed. "You will be the center of attention at the theater and I shall be furious!"

"I doubt that," Dorian laughed. "You look incredible, as always."

Madeline stared at herself critically in the mirrors. At thirty, she had the slim figure of a Parisian model, and carried herself with the assurance of a woman who took her acclaimed beauty for granted. Her shoulder-length golden blond hair, sensuous voice and figure and smoldering blue eyes had caused a sensation in many films, and rumors about her private life regularly filled the gossip columns.

Tonight she wore an iridescent red gown that gathered under her small firm breasts and stretched provocatively over narrow hips. A full-length sable coat was carelessly flung around her shoulders, adding a theatrical touch to her glamorous appearance.

"Yes," she said, "we complement each other perfectly. We must stay together all evening like sisters. That way we have the attention of the entire theater and the performers on stage will go mad!"

"Where's Jonathan?" Dorian asked.

"He'll be along in a few minutes—he's in his office, on the phone," Madeline replied. "Shall we have a drink while we're waiting?"

They went into the living room of Dorian's suite. Madeline stepped behind the bar and began to mix cocktails; Dorian perched on the edge of a stool.

"So, tell me what you've been doing—it's been a week since I've seen you," Madeline said.

"Oh, the usual things—nothing very exciting. There was a dinner for the Baron de Viliers a couple of nights ago, and a screening of the new Godard film. Claude and I went to Longchamps for the races, and I did some shopping . . ."

"What happened to the classes at the Beaux Arts?"

"I dropped them. I didn't think much of the instructors, or the students, for that matter. I prefer to work on my own. Claude and I spent an afternoon in Luxembourg Gardens, and I took some pictures there that are pretty good . . ."

"I heard Claude's name twice." Madeline smiled and handed Dorian a drink. "You are seeing a great deal of him?"

Dorian hesitated before answering. "He's fun, good company—that's all . . ."

". . . and he's very attractive, yes?"

"Well, he's not Alain Delon, but he'll do."

"My dear, no one is Alain Delon—not even Alain! He is a fiction, like all beautiful men. But what of your American Alain—or Alan," she pronounced the name carefully. "Have you heard from him?"

"No, he never answered my letter."

"You never explained to me why you left him. Was it something serious?"

Dorian didn't reply, and Madeline asked, "Am I intruding into your privacy?"

"It's not easy to explain," Dorian said, stirring her drink

moodily. "It's been over six months since I've seen him, and I still . . ." She lit a cigarette, her fingers trembling a little.

"And you still miss him," Madeline said softly. "Or aren't you sure?"

"I'm not sure of anything," Dorian answered with a shrug. She gave Madeline a hard smile. "I've never been sure of anything about myself."

Madeline's voice was sympathetic. "I know how difficult it can be, *ma petite*. I too had a young man, when I first began working in films. He was a playwright and we were very much in love. Then I was offered a film in Spain, and he went to London for the opening of one of his plays. By the time we saw each other again, he was married and I had a lover." She sighed wistfully. "I've had many lovers since, but he was a moment in my life that cannot be equaled or replaced."

Dorian listened to her, a smile spreading across her face. "Madeline, you said that almost as tenderly as you did in *Le Grand Amour,* with Charles Denner—I saw the film in New York."

The Frenchwoman stared at her blankly for a moment, then laughed. *"Merde!* In your blunt American way you unmask me! I am completely transparent with you. Ah, well— nevertheless, my intentions were true. But since you are so clever, I'll tell you what I really think; if this boy is causing you pain, then forget him. Life is too short for romantic nonsense. Take what you can get now, and enjoy it!"

"That sounds more like you," Dorian said humorously. "Save the bullshit for my uncle—he deserves it."

She reached out and touched Madeline's sable coat. "This is new, isn't it? A little gift from Monsieur St. Clair?"

The actress smiled demurely. "He's very generous. This is a little token of his esteem . . ."

"His what?"

"Ah, you are incorrigible!" Madeline cried. "No wonder we are friends—we understand each other."

"Well, let's say that I understand you," Dorian commented dryly.

"Bitch," Madeline said affectionately.

The phone rang and she picked it up. *"Oui?* Ah, yes—we will . . ." She put the receiver down and said to Dorian,

"Jonathan is waiting for us in the lobby, and Claude is with him. Shall we go?"

Dorian finished her drink and stood up. "I'll get my coat."

As they left the suite and walked toward the elevators, Madeline said, "Now, tell me—what did you think of my performance in *Le Grand Amour . . . ?*"

❦

It began to rain as they left the Comédie-Française. Jonathan's car drew up before the theater entrance and they ran quickly across the wet pavement. Jonathan and Claude took the jump seats facing Madeline and Dorian.

"I've booked a table at Tour d'Argent for dinner," Jonathan said as the car sped through the glistening streets.

"Well, I hope the meal is better than the play," Madeline sighed. "Giraudoux can be very trying—and those costumes! Positively shabby!"

"The speeches went much too fast for me," Dorian said. "My French isn't that good, or else their diction wasn't that clear."

"I think the cast was probably upset at the attention you were receiving from the audience—you are both so beautiful tonight." Claude looked at Dorian adoringly.

Madeline bowed her head graciously. Dorian smiled and said, "Spoken like a true public relations man."

The young man frowned and fell silent. Madeline gave Dorian a sharp nudge with her elbow, then said pleasantly to Claude, "What film are you working on now?"

"I leave for London in a few days to start work on a new picture starring Dirk Bogarde."

"You didn't tell me," Dorian said. "When did that happen?"

"I received a call this morning—I was going to tell you about it later. I thought that when I was settled, you might come over for a few weeks . . ."

"London in the winter?" Jonathan said. "My God, it's worse there than in Paris. Besides, Dorian—I was on the phone early this evening with Alex. He and Vivian will be here next week . . ."

"Is David coming with them?" she asked eagerly.

"No, he's going to stay on at the hotel in New York. Alex tells me he's doing very well there. They'll be coming here alone."

"Well, that's reason enough for me to go to London," Dorian said sullenly.

"I don't think they would appreciate your not being here," Jonathan said in a sharp tone of voice.

Dorian sat back and stared out the windows of the car. She'd talked with David several times while he and their parents were traveling, but not since they had returned to New York in January. She wondered if he had gotten in touch with Alan. A sudden yearning to be with her brother came over her; Madeline and Jonathan were little more than strangers, and she had come to regard Claude simply as an entertaining escort. They had met a few months before at a screening of a Lelouche film for which he was doing the publicity. Dark haired and attractive, Claude was easy to be with, undemanding and attentive. Now he was going to London and she would be left alone to cope with her parents. As the chauffeur drew the car up before the restaurant, Dorian suddenly said, "Do you mind if Claude and I get a cab and go out to one of the clubs? I'm not very hungry, and it's still early . . ."

"Whatever you wish," Jonathan agreed, preferring to be alone with Madeline.

They said their goodnights at the door of the restaurant and Claude hailed a passing cab. Once they were seated, he asked Dorian: "Do you want to go to the 'Blue Note?' "

"Not really—let's go to your place," she replied, satisfied with the look of surprise on his face.

The doorman ushered Jonathan and Madeline into the elevator going to the restaurant. When they were alone, Jonathan said, "After dinner, we're going to the club; I have some business there to take care of."

"What? But we are supposed to have drinks with Jean-Paul and the American distributors, to discuss my film!"

"Not tonight, my dear. I had to cancel the meeting—we'll make it for another time."

"But you know how important this is to me!"

"My business takes precedence," Jonathan said bluntly.

The elevator doors opened and the maître d' led them to Jonathan's table. Madeline fumed silently while he ordered. After the wine had been served, she said, "So, we spend another tiresome evening while you gamble away a few thousands and I entertain your gangster friends."

"Don't speak of them that way again," he said calmly. "They're businessmen, that's all . . ."

Madeline gave a brittle laugh. "You astonish me with your naiveté. But it your problem, not mine. To me those people are simply vulgar and crude. But to you—" She paused, hesitating to go on.

"What?" Jonathan asked coldly.

"I suggest you be more careful. They could be very dangerous."

Dorian lay on her side, waiting for Claude to finish. She felt his body pressed to her back, his face buried in her neck. His breath came in short, quiet gasps, and his hips began to move more urgently. Everything about him was so tender, she thought disdainfully: the hand clasping her breast was gentle, the lips against her shoulder were soft. He fucks like a child, she decided. She shifted her head on the pillow and let her eyes wander around the dimly lit room. Over the back of a chair she saw the gleam of her silver dress, and on the floor nearby, her coat and shoes. His clothes were nowhere in evidence—he'd hung them neatly in the closet before getting into bed. The thought made her giggle, and at that moment Claude gave a faint cry and came. His body tightened momentarily, and then, with a deep sigh, he withdrew himself from her and rolled over on his back. So much for the legend of French lovers, Dorian thought.

She got out of bed and went to the bathroom while he lay back, contented. A few minutes later she returned and slid under the covers beside him.

"Did I please you?" he asked in a husky whisper.

"Of course," she lied, kissing his cheek. "You make love beautifully."

They were silent for a few minutes, then she asked, "When are you leaving for London?"

"At the end of the week. Why?"

"Would you like me to come with you?"

Claude sat up and took her in his arms. "Of course I would! But don't you want to wait and see your parents?"

"No, I'd rather be with you. If I wait, they might not let me go, so it would be better if I left with you."

"I'll make the arrangements first thing in the morning!" Claude said happily. Then he asked, "Do you want to stay at your family's hotel in London?"

"I don't think so."

He leaned over her, hopeful. "Then—you will stay with me?"

Dorian shifted so that she lay under him. She put her arms around his back and pressed him close. "Isn't that what you want?"

"You know it is," he whispered, and kissed her breasts.

Dorian stifled a yawn as he began to make love to her again.

ॐ

New York

David nervously paced the richly carpeted floor of his father's office in the hotel. Gray winter light cast a cold color over the mahogany-paneled walls and period furnishings. Alexander was sitting behind the desk, impervious to his son's agitation.

"I still don't see why I can't go with you to Paris," David burst out. "Everything is going smoothly here. I won't be missed for a week or two—and I'm anxious to see Dorian."

"David, you can be very tiresome," his father muttered. He closed the account books he had been examining, put them away and straightened the top of the desk. Looking up, he saw that David was waiting to continue their discussion. "There's nothing more to be said," he declared with finality.

"There never is," David replied. "If you say it, then it must be so, regardless of what anyone else thinks or wishes."

"I'm very tired of your righteous indignation where my decisions are concerned," Alexander bristled. "I want you to remain here. I don't want to discuss it, I just want you to do as you're told."

He stood up, smoothed his jacket and touched the small knot of his tie to make sure it was straight. Then he looked at his watch and said, "It's late—you'd better go dress: Olivia has invited us to dinner. There will be important people there you should meet—it's time you became better known in New York society—"

"I'm not going," David said quietly.

Alexander glowered at him. "I insist."

"Insist all you wish, I'm not going. I find Olivia's dinner parties boring, and I don't give a damn about being better known in society."

David stared at his father obstinately. After years of battles with Alexander, he knew that he could only win the skirmishes. It was little comfort, but he relished every one of them. He was beginning to understand the complexity of his father's ego, his need to be right in all things concerning his family and his business, whether or not, in truth, he was. And, although David hated to admit it, he was still afraid of his father. It was a fear born of a childhood need for approval, and a nagging guilt at never having won it.

Before Alexander could say anything, David went to the door and opened it. "Give my regrets to Olivia—I'm sure she'll understand." He walked out, slamming the door behind him.

Hurrying through the lobby, he thought, If the sound of all the doors I've slammed on my father were put together, they'd create a noise that could topple buildings. But he'll never fall; when everything is crashing down around him, he'll probably just stand there and demand that it all rise up—"at once!"

In his bedroom, David stripped off his suit and changed into a turtleneck pullover and jeans. He took a heavy windbreaker from the closet and put it on, examining himself in the mirror. Perfect winter cruising clothes, he thought. The phone rang; it was Alexander or Vivian, calling to demand that he go with them to Olivia's.

"Not tonight, dear parents, not tonight," he muttered, leaving his suite and striding down the hall to the service elevator. "I've got to get out and get laid—God, it's been months!"

He stood in the shadows at the end of the hall, waiting for

the elevator to come. When it did, he slipped into it like a hotel thief making his getaway.

Snow drifts lay piled against the steps of houses and along the curbs, the sidewalk was coated with ice. David walked carefully, hands jammed into his pockets, his collar raised against the cold. The streets of Greenwich Village were deserted but for a few men and women hurrying along, their faces buried in caps and scarves. A gusty wind sent a chilling blast of air through the snow, raising white clouds that hurtled around his feet.

Christ, what a night to go looking for a piece of ass!

He remembered that Alan lived a few blocks away, and wondered for a moment about going to visit him. But the thought of them being together alone, the way he was feeling tonight, changed his mind. No, he decided, I need some action, not more frustration. He turned down Waverly Place and headed for a bar called Julius's.

The place was warm and noisy with music and conversation, filled with young men dressed in crewneck sweaters and slacks. The college crowd, or would-be college crowd, he thought, seeing a sprinkling of older men who were as youthfully dressed. He found a table at the back of the bar and ordered a drink from the waiter. Heads had turned when he walked in, and now a few men were glancing at him surreptitiously or staring openly. He sipped his drink and sat back, trying to relax; he was still nervous about coming to a bar, always afraid that he might be recognized by someone, afraid that what he was doing would somehow get back to his father. He imagined Alexander's shock and outrage at discovering the truth about his son, and hurriedly finished his drink, then ordered another.

By eleven o'clock he was a little light-headed. The crowd had thinned out and David concentrated his attention on a young blond boy he had been cruising for the last half-hour. Suddenly a voice at his side said, "David? Aren't you David St. Clair?"

He looked up, his heart quickening at hearing someone speak his name in this place. The man standing over him was smiling.

"Don't you remember me?" he asked. "I'm Jennings Talbot."

David tried to place the darkly handsome face, while at the same time keeping an eye out for the movements of the blond boy.

"Jennings Talbot?" he asked.

"We met at your place on Long Island last summer—you kept calling me 'Sinbad' all evening—"

"Oh, yes—at the costume party, now I remember." David recalled the moment they had shared on the beach that night. "Yes, I remember you very well. Sit down—what are you drinking?"

"Nothing for me, thanks, I've had enough tonight."

"You still with American Ballet?"

"You do remember," Jennings said, pleased. "Yes, I am. And you—?"

David hesitated before answering. "I'm—living in New York."

There was an awkward moment of silence between them. David cast a swift glance toward the blond boy, but he had disappeared.

"Were you waiting for someone?" Jennings asked.

David turned back and gave him a warm smile. "Yes, I was—and now he's here."

"That's the most encouraging thing I've heard all week." Jennings's dark eyes grew soft, caressing. He put his hand over David's and asked, almost shyly, "Are you into repeat engagements, or is it only one-night stands for you?"

David chuckled. "Are you asking me to go home with you?"

"Yes—if you want to."

"I want to."

Jennings lived in a large apartment on Fifty-Seventh Street. When they walked in and he turned on the lights, David looked around appreciatively. There were comfortable, expensive furnishings in muted tones of brown and rust, hammered brass lamps and a few fine antique pieces that blended with the modern decor.

"I always thought dancers lived in tiny, cramped rooms

that were flamboyantly decorated with scarves and fans," David said.

"That's exactly what I lived in until a few years ago—then I moved here with my lover. This was his place."

"Oh, did you break up? Did you get custody of the apartment?"

"In a way—but we didn't break up. He died."

"Jennings, I'm sorry—"

"Oh, that's all right, I'm over it now." He took David's windbreaker and hung it in the hall closet. "Can I get you something to drink?"

"No, I don't think so—" He waited for Jennings to come back, then reached out to take him in his arms. "Let's skip the formalities."

The dancer smiled and kissed him, flicking his tongue inside David's mouth. He pulled away and said, "I like a man who knows what he wants. The bedroom is down the hall."

"Oh God!" David moaned, feeling Talbot's mouth plunging down on him.

The two men held each other close on the large bed in the darkened room. Months of being without someone made David ravenous, he filled his hands and mouth with Jennings's flesh, groaning aloud at the sensations tearing through him. Furiously, he turned him over on his stomach and fell across his back, shoving his legs wide.

"Easy, David, easy," Jennings whispered softly. "There's plenty of time. Relax, enjoy it—don't rush. You don't have to rush . . ."

The soothing words calmed him and David buried his lips against the warm hollow in the dancer's neck. Jennings reached between them and grasped David's cock firmly. "Let me help you," he said gently, guiding him.

David was slowly enveloped by the heat of the man's body. They began a series of subtle movements, producing intense pleasure and an awareness of each other's responses. David sighed deeply, resting on the broad back, and felt a quiet peace come over him. Jennings raised his head so that they could kiss, then lifted himself slowly, taking David with him, until he was crouched on his hands and knees.

"Now," he muttered, pushing back against David's groin. "Now . . . do it now—now!"

Later, they lay side by side. There was some wine on the night table; Jennings poured two glasses and gave one to David.

"That's nice," David said, sipping it. "Very smooth."

"Gordon knew about wines—he taught me."

"How long were you together?"

"Almost four years. He was a costume designer—that's how we met. I went to his studio to have some fittings for *Billy the Kid*—I was one of the cowboys. He was very kind and considerate, different from the people I'd known."

"Who seduced whom?" David asked cynically.

Jennings laughed softly. "It was mutual, like in the movies. We fell in love."

"I find that hard to believe."

"Why?

"Because there's so much ass out on the streets. Two men can't be in love and be loyal or faithful to each other. Isn't that one of the fascinations of gay life? Its promiscuity?"

Jennings sat up and looked at him. "But David, ass is just ass—just sex. The only thing shared is lust. Gordon and I understood that. But we also understood that there was more to be shared, like trust, mutual respect—and love." Jennings saw the amused look on David's face. "You don't think that's possible, do you."

David looked up; the boy's liquid brown eyes stared at him with a puzzled, troubled expression. Talbot's dark hair was tousled around his face, and his full red lips were slightly parted, moist. David put down his wine glass and took him in his arms.

"I think this is possible," he said, kissing him. "And this." He slid his hands down to cup the firm, shapely buttocks.

"Okay, okay," Talbot said, smiling. "We'll skip the lectures—I can see that you're ready for Act Two."

"—and Three and Four; I have a lot of time to make up for."

The two men were quickly aroused, but now Jennings was the aggressor. He took David's body over with masterful, demanding force. David began to struggle, wanting to dominate as he had before, but Talbot refused to give in. They were like wrestlers trying to get a hold, to topple the other. Talbot was strong and quick, and David began to succumb, feeling a strange new pleasure in the passive role. Then Jennings was on top of him, kissing him wildly. "I want to fuck you," he said, trying to enter him.

"No!" David cried out. "I've never done that—"

"I'll be careful," Jennings said. "I won't hurt you . . ."

David tried to resist, but a flash of pain momentarily paralyzed him. Then Jennings was cradling him in his arms, crooning to him tenderly and rocking him, penetrating him more deeply until they were locked tightly together. For a few moments they were absolutely still.

Slowly, David's resistance gave way to an overwhelming feeling of languor. A new and powerful excitement began. Fear was transformed into a deep sense of pleasure, of being protected and revered. He threw his arms around the dancer's neck and gave himself up to the fantasy that had begun when he was fourteen years old.

David awoke to see the dawn light through the drapes at the windows. He moved his arm from under Talbot's body and reached to the night table for a cigarette. Jennings opened his eyes.

"Me too," he said sleepily, motioning for a cigarette.

David lit one for him and put it between his lips. "I thought dancers didn't smoke," he said.

"We smoke," Jennings mumbled.

David lay quietly, drawing on his cigarette and staring into space.

"Are you all right?" Jennings asked.

"Yes."

"What are you thinking about?"

"It's not important—"

Jennings slipped inside David's arm and rested his head on his chest. "Will you come back to see me?" he questioned softly.

"I don't know . . ."

Jennings raised his head and looked into David's eyes. "Tell me what you're thinking about."

David put his head back into the pillows and let out a sigh. "I'm thinking about my father."

15

New York: April

ON THE NIGHT of Easter Sunday, Sylvester Peake's version of the Corpus Christi plays was presented in a loft in Soho. Alan had worked almost up to the last minute on the painting Sylvester had asked him to do. Now he stood anxiously with Layla and Della as the guests began to arrive, wondering what the reaction would be to his work.

The swelling audience of art critics, journalists, newsmen, and members of New York society were greeted and led to their seats by sepulchral figures in black hooded robes that featured a whimsical touch in design—the skirt of each robe was made of separate strips of cloth that parted with any movement to reveal naked bodies underneath. The unexpected glimpses of genitalia and buttocks produced a great deal of nervous laughter, and news photographers popped a steady stream of flash bulbs taking pictures.

Finally all the lights in the loft went out and a single note on the synthesizer signaled the beginning of the event. Lights came up on the playing area to reveal a lovely young girl named Charlene, who was wrapped in a thin silvery material and lying on a mound of animal furs. Behind her loomed a bright red cycloramic screen. As she began a subtle, sexual movement of her body, a slow lamenting wail of electronic music based on Gregorian chants filled the loft. The tempo of the music increased, and Charlene's gyrations grew more frantic, until finally she cried out, "Oh God, you're terrific!"

An electronically altered man's voice, groaning and swearing, came through the music.

"Oh God!" Charlene yelled. "Deeper, deeper!"

The electronic voice instantly dropped an octave, bringing laughter from the audience. Charlene continued to take a pounding from her invisible lover and the music reached an ear-splitting crescendo, then stopped. Charlene rose from the bed of furs and slowly turned her profile to the audience. Before their stunned eyes, her stomach swelled to gigantic proportions.

Just then a naked shepherd appeared, carrying a shepherd's crook. He ran up to the girl, raised the crook above her menacingly, and cried, "What's happening?"

Supporting her ballooning stomach with both hands, she faced the audience and shouted, "It's a miracale!"

At that instant her gown split, the balloon burst loudly, and a doll with long hair and wearing a diaper ejected out over the heads of the guests. Blinding strobe lights flashed on and off, the cycloramic screen became a montage of people cheering, and Handel's *Messiah* was heard at top volume. The show was on.

One outrageous scene followed another and members of the audience grew furious. A few people began to leave, angrily denouncing Sylvester.

Others roared with laughter and cheered the players on, and the photographers had to be restrained from getting too close to the action.

Sylvester's depiction of the Last Supper, with himself as the central figure surrounded by leather-clad bikers lolling over the table drinking beer, brought a storm of protest and scattered applause. The bedlam died down as dimming lights brought the scene to a close. The stage was cleared, and as if from a great distance, came the sound of voices singing the "Hallelujah Chorus." A beam of amber light focused on something at the extreme back of the loft that was moving toward the audience at a measured pace. As it drew closer, the music increased in volume. A hush fell over the crowd.

It was Alan's painting, depicting Sylvester as Christ on the cross.

The beam of light, focusing tightly on Sylvester's figure, made it look as if it were floating in space. He was handcuffed to the cross at the ankles and at one wrist. With the other hand he held a movie camera to his eye, his body leaning forward sharply to face the viewers with a wide, mocking grin. The perspective of the figure was so well drafted that he appeared to be swinging lifelike out of the canvas. In every respect the painting was a superb piece of realist art, combining the techniques of the classical and romantic traditions with a content of contemporary satire.

As the music rose to a stirring climax, the audience began to applaud and cheer. The house lights came up, revealing the painting sitting on a movable easel. Everyone crowded forward to look at it more closely.

Alan was brought out and introduced to another round of applause. Photographers snapped pictures of him and Sylvester standing in front of the enormous canvas. When Jordan and Grace made their way through the crowd to his side, Alan saw to it that more pictures were taken of him and Jordan. A writer for *Art News* took quick notes for an interview; people shook his hand and asked questions about his training and background.

Meanwhile the loft was cleared and buffet tables were set up, trays of food were put out and a bar was opened. A rock group began to play and a party ensued, with the remaining guests and actors loudly arguing the merits of the presentation.

Through the crowd surging around him Alan caught a glimpse of Olivia and David standing at the back of the loft. For a moment he hoped that by some miracle Dorian might be with them. By the time he shoved through the crowd to get to them, he saw that they were alone.

"Alan, my dear—" Olivia cried, hugging him.

David exclaimed, "Your painting is sensational! It's the only thing of any merit in the whole ridiculous, incredible show."

"Incredible is the precise word to describe it," Olivia said primly. "But I agree with David—your painting is quite extraordinary."

She looked around the crowded room. "Isn't your father here? I was hoping to see him again."

"He couldn't make it; he's selling our house in Bay Shore and moving to Connecticut to live with my aunt. But I'm so glad the two of you are here," Alan said. "Can you stay for the party?"

"I'd rather not," Olivia said, shaking her head. "I've had quite enough for one evening. But do call me—we have many things to discuss. I want to hear about everything that's been happening to you."

After she left David said, "I can stay for a while; it's been too long since we've seen each other. You look wonderful—I like the long hair . . ."

"There hasn't been time to cut it, or do anything except work. I should have called you—"

"I understand. Can we find someplace to talk for a while?"

"I doubt it—but stay as long as you can; we may go back to my place later."

A dazzling light show set the party off like fireworks. David followed Alan through a cluster of people who were dancing, noting that some of the couples were men. He was surprised that Alan seemed oblivious to the number of gays in the crowd, but he quickly realized that no one else was paying much attention to the camping and shrill laughter. A few of the actors were still in costume, and he tried to keep his eyes from straying to young boys wearing skimpy togas and the heavily built men in black leather.

While they were making their way to the front of the room, Alan was stopped several times to be congratulated by people whom David recognized as acquaintances of Olivia's. They nodded to him, but Alan was the focus of their attention. David felt pangs of envy, an old stirring of jealousy at Alan's talent and accomplishments. Yet this feeling was mixed with a desire to be closer to him, a need to be more involved in Alan's life, as if in that way he too could find recognition. His wealth and position suddenly had little meaning for him.

They finally reached Layla, and Alan introduced him. "So you're Olivia's nephew," she said somewhat curtly. "Alan's told me about you and your sister—"

"All good things, I hope," David replied cordially.

Alan had his arm around her, and she offered him a drink from her glass. David guessed that they were lovers.

Charlene, the girl who had been in the opening scene, pushed forward to meet him. She stared at David with eyes that looked as if a torch had been ignited behind the lids.

"You wanna dance?" she asked, moving closer to him.

Seeing Alan and Layla watching him, he answered, "I'd like to very much." The lie almost choked him, but he led her onto the dance floor with all the charm he could muster.

Out of the corner of his eye he watched Alan dancing with

Layla, wincing inwardly when they stopped to embrace. He glanced at his watch and saw that it was growing late; Jennings was waiting for him—he should leave.

Charlene rubbed up against him. "You're really gorgeous," she said in a breathy whisper. "You straight? Don't be offended—it's just that most of the guys I go for are gay . . ."

David felt a momentary panic. The girl's crudeness repelled him, and for an instant, he wanted to say, "That's right, you empty-headed, illiterate little bitch! I'd rather have any one of those numbers in black leather!" But instead, he said, "I think you're terrific." He smiled, enjoying the ambiguity of his reply. For the next hour, he slipped into the cover performance he had used with girls in college. Charlene bought it, too stoned to detect the fraud.

As the evening wore on David danced with Layla and some of the other girls, and many times with Charlene. He got a little drunk, and at one point found himself necking with her in a darkened corner behind some of the flats. When the festivities began to wind down and guests were leaving, Alan, still high from his success and a little stoned, insisted that they join him and Layla at his studio to continue the celebration.

The four of them staggered out of the loft and into a cab, crowding against each other in the back seat. Charlene crawled into David's lap and began kissing him, moving his hands to her breasts. David closed his eyes, letting her tongue slide into his mouth. But it was the awareness of Alan's body pressed tightly against him that excited him. He began to feel as though he'd lost all control over his responses; what Charlene was doing aroused and repulsed him, but with Alan so close, he didn't want it to stop. He saw that Alan and Layla were making love, and wondered if it would continue when they got to the studio; for the first time he might have a chance to see what he had only fantasized. The thought was at once exciting and terrifying, and the terror aroused him even further.

At the studio they lit some candles and Layla rolled a few joints. The four of them sat on the bed next to each other; conversation was desultory, the room grew warm. Alan lay back against the pillows, bringing Layla with him. They began to make love.

David watched them like a witness to a crime, with a mixture of fascination, morbidity and excitement. He thought of Alan and Dorian's trysts in the boat house during the summer, remembered the exhilarating fear and fierce jealousy he had felt. Now he had the sensation of being in an erotic dream. Clothes began to disappear, until they were all naked. Candlelight filled the room with flickering shadows, and flesh took on a warm amber sheen. He studied the changes of expression on Alan's face, the movements of his body, the startling, beautiful contrast of his pale skin against Layla's dark coloring. Gazing at them he felt an eerie euphoria, and suddenly identified with Alan completely, as if he, David, had ceased to exist and were merely Alan's shadow, like one of the dark figures wavering over the walls.

David felt Charlene go down on him just as Alan began fucking Layla. He got to his knees to better watch him, and now they were side by side. Tentatively, he placed his hand on Alan's back to steady himself. Alan turned at his touch and gave him a sweetly drugged smile. In a surge of recklessness, David slipped his arm around Alan's waist, gripping him tightly.

Alan threw his head back and laughed. His teeth were bared and gleaming in the candlelight, and his face glowed with a thin film of sweat. "I'm gonna come," he moaned.

David closed his eyes, feeling Charlene's mouth on him like wet fire and Alan's body shaking against his. He struggled to hold him closer, trying to complete the union of his shadowy self and Alan's flesh. Then, driven by an irresistible compulsion that obliterated all sense of reason, he grabbed Alan's head and kissed him deeply as they both climaxed.

The moment transcended its own physicality; it was a consummation of all of David's emotions and desires, an explosive end to his self-denial. For those few brief seconds, he was absolutely free.

Then, like a drunk who is suddenly made aware of his condition, David dimly realized that Alan was fighting to get free of his grasp. For a moment he fought to keep him in his arms, then abruptly let him go. Shock swept through him like an icy chill, leaving him paralyzed. Charlene backed away from him, and Layla stared. Blindly he searched for his clothes, struggled to get into them, afraid to look at Alan, to see what was on his face.

David rushed out of the studio and plunged down the stairs. On the darkened street he felt waves of nausea rise in his throat and began to choke and cough. He darted into an alley and fell to his knees, vomiting against a stack of garbage. Shuddering and gasping for breath, he rose weakly to his feet, wiped his mouth with a handkerchief, then threw it away. He leaned against the brick wall, and pressed his face to the rough surface. His throat was raw, his mouth tasted foul. Straightening up, he ran his fingers through his hair, brushed at his clothes and stepped back out into the street, walking slowly, mechanically. He saw a phone booth on the corner and went to it, searching in his pockets for change. Once inside, he closed the door, dialed a number and waited, covering his eyes from the harsh overhead light. The phone rang several times before it was answered.

"Hello? Who is it?" Jennings's voice was thick with sleep.

For a few seconds, David couldn't answer. Then, tears flooding his eyes, he said hoarsely, "Jennings—it's me, David . . . David . . . I need you—"

༜

London: May

The small crowd assembled around Speaker's Corner in Hyde Park laughed at the elderly man shaking his fist at a young bicyclist with whom he'd been arguing.

"If it wasn't for the bloody capitalist-imperialists conspiring with the fascists," he yelled, "there wouldn't be any wars, mark my words! We Trotskyists believe that the communist revolution will never succeed until the reactionary elements of the Soviet government have—"

"Oh, come off it!" the young man said, laughing. "I've been hearing that Marxist rubbish from me dad since I was a kid."

There was a sprinkling of applause in the crowd, and the old man stepped down indignantly, the furrows and wrinkles in his face showing deep in the bright midday sun.

Dorian focused her camera and snapped the shutter repeatedly, capturing the old man's bent walk and dejected air. She turned back to the crowd, seeking more subjects in the viewfinder.

Vivian waited impatiently for her to finish. "I don't understand—are these pictures for some assignment you've been given?" she asked.

"No—these are just for me, just practice. I'm trying out a new lens . . ." Dorian watched three old women in frayed sweaters chattering animatedly to each other, then snapped the shutter.

"I thought we were going to have lunch," Vivian complained.

"We will, eventually. The weather is so perfect today, I didn't want to pass it up."

Dorian crouched to take a few shots of a little girl playing nearby. Her miniskirt rode up her thighs, and a young boy made a cooing sound as he passed by.

"Dorian, must you wear those clothes?" Vivian said under her breath. "The skirt is so short it's indecent!"

Dorian chuckled. "In my business, I can't go around looking like a throwback to the fifties . . ."

"Your business?" Vivian inquired sarcastically.

Dorian straightened up and replied cheerfully, "Yes, my business. I've had three assignments in the last couple of months."

"I'd hardly call three assignments a business. A hobby, perhaps, and one I think we've indulged you in long enough."

"You haven't indulged me in anything since I was eight!"

"I won't argue with you in public," Vivian said primly, taking Dorian's arm and leading her away from the crowd.

"Why argue with me at all?"

"Your father and I are simply concerned about the way you've been living. The gossip columns have been filled with stories about you and that Frenchman!"

"If it hadn't been for Claude, I wouldn't be doing anything!" Dorian declared hotly. "He got me the opportunity to take stills on the film he was doing publicity for—and everyone loved the pictures I took; he even used them in his campaign!"

"That's hardly a reason to live with him!"

"How I live and work is really none of your business!"

215

"Your father is threatening to cut you off—"

"Is that why you called me? That's why you're here? To tell me that? You know I came into my trust from Grandfather when I turned twenty-one, so stop threatening me! I can live quite comfortably on what I have and earn the rest!"

"Can't you see that you're being used by the people who employ you? That they're only interested in you because of who you are?"

"That's not true! My pictures are good!" She whirled on her mother furiously. "You're just jealous because I'm living my own life—something you've never had a chance to do! You were jealous of me when I wanted to go to New York to live with Alan. Well, you made a mess of that for me, you and father and Uncle Jonathan, but you can't touch me now—I won't let you!"

"Dorian, you're still a child! You don't realize what you're doing!" Vivian cried helplessly. "Everyone we know is talking about you—it's embarrassing, and your father is furious!"

"I'm not going to change for him, not like David has."

"At least David is trying—"

"He's miserable, and you know it!"

"Yes, I know it, I know it!" Vivian cried in a burst of frustration. "But what can I do? It's always been this way, and it gets worse all the time! What do you think it's been like for me, all these years? Your father never admits to being wrong about anything, I'm expected to keep the peace in the family—and for what? None of you have shown me any consideration or respect, ever!"

"I'm sorry," Dorian said stiffly.

"No you're not," Vivian said in a defeated tone.

The two women walked in silence toward Vivian's car. "Let's skip lunch," she said. "I'm not very hungry."

Dorian nodded, subdued. When her mother was seated behind the wheel she stood by the door and said, "If it helps any, you can tell father that Claude and I broke up a few weeks ago. I'm moving into my own place in a couple of days . . ."

Vivian regarded her daughter sadly. "I'm sorry, dear. I wish there were more I could do for you, but even if there were, I know you wouldn't let me . . ." She started the car, then added, "Take care of yourself."

Dorian walked slowly back through the park. A last connection between herself and Vivian had been severed, and for the first time in her life she felt that she was on her own. The realization was sobering; it was what she had desired for years, fought to attain, and now it was here. But there was no elation, no feeling of triumph; there was instead a sense that something crucial had occurred, a change she had brought about that she was not quite prepared to deal with.

❦

"David, speak up, there's static on the line—" Dorian said.
"Can you hear me now?"
"Yes, why haven't you called before? It's been months!"
"Blame dear Daddy—he's been a terror since he and mother came home . . . what's happening to you that I haven't already read about in the columns?"
"Not much—a couple of my assignments fell through, so I've been coasting, just enjoying my freedom . . ."
"So I've read. Be careful, or Daddy will drag you home and chain you up in the cellar!"
Dorian laughed. "It's all just gossip. What about you? Still hiding in the closet?"
"Knock it off! As a matter of fact, I have been seeing someone."
"Oh, David, really? Who is he? Tell me about him!"
"Not on the phone—I'll write you later."
Dorian paused, then asked, "Have you seen Alan? I read about a painting he did for some art event a few months ago."
"Yes, I was there."
"Did he ask for me?"
"—Yes . . . Dorian, when are you coming home? I miss you—"
"I miss you, too—Christ, there's nobody here I can talk to. But I can't come home, not yet. I've got to do something first, back up all that screaming I did for independence with some accomplishment. If I don't, Mom and Dad will find a thousand ways of saying 'I told you so' without ever using the words, and I couldn't stand that."

"Are you really having a thing with that Welsh actor, Derek Kingston? Or is that just more gossip?"

"I've been seeing him, but it doesn't mean anything. Oh shit, David, I've been seeing a lot of people who don't mean anything . . ."

"Dorian, I'm being buzzed—I've got to run. Call me next week?"

"David, don't go! I want to—"

The line went dead. She put the phone down and sat back, staring at it. Silence hung over the room like a shroud. She lit a cigarette and got up, walking around distractedly. At her desk she stopped and fingered through some messages: an invitation to a dinner party, a request to endorse a new perfume, another to be the hostess at the opening of a new boutique, a scrawled note asking her to accompany some people she hardly knew on a Mediterranean cruise. A few magazines lay opened to pictures taken of her at theater openings, in a night club, at a ballet gala. Under each was the caption, "Miss Dorian St. Clair, daughter of the hotel magnate, Alexander St. Clair . . ."

Angrily she swept the magazines and messages to the floor. The phone rang, and her face brightened. She eagerly reached to answer it. "David, I hoped you'd call back . . . oh, yes—hello Derek—"

৩

The cab drew up to the small private club just off Grosvenor Square and edged to the curb.

"Derek, do we have to do this?" Dorian asked. "I'm really tired. Why don't you just drop me off at my place and then come back here alone?"

"But my darling girl, I don't want to be alone," Derek Kingston said sulkily. "I've just given the worst performance of my life in the most ill-conceived, misbegotten play ever presented on an English stage. I shall probably receive notices that will send me howling into the streets, and I *need* the tender comfort of your presence."

"Don't you ever answer a question simply, without making it sound like a second act curtain?"

"That's the trouble with you Americans—you're all used to speaking in shorthand." He grabbed her arm and pulled her from the cab. "Come along like a good girl. We'll have a few drinks, listen to that noise they call music, and then go back to my place and fuck. See, I can speak very simply."

Over the din of a rock quintet Derek ordered drinks, then looked around, waving at people he knew. The dance floor was a solid jam of bodies, and just off the dining area, in a large room for gambling, a crowd was gathered around the tables playing blackjack, roulette, chemin de fer and poker.

Dorian lit a cigarette, trying to ignore the noise and confusion exploding around them. She shouldn't have come with him, she thought; he could be so difficult when he got drunk. They had received enough publicity in the gossip columns as it was: the young American heiress and the famous Welsh star of stage and films, and never mind that he had a wife and three children living just outside London. Christ, what the hell was she doing?

Derek was on his fourth whiskey when she decided to leave. "You stay and have a swell time," she said, getting up from the table. "I've had enough of this—I'll take a cab home."

He reached out and clamped a large hand on her wrist. "Sit down, you provincial little nit!" His voice was threatening. "Everyone is staring!"

"So what? Most of them have seen you drunk before, and they'll probably see you drunk again. Now let go of me, I want to get out of here!"

She tried to twist out of his grasp and he tightened his fingers, bruising her wrist. Dorian let out a cry and a few people looked over at them.

"Don't you dare make a scene in here," Derek hissed.

"If you don't let me go, I'll turn this place into a shambles!"

A waiter hurried over and tried to help her. "Perhaps you should let the lady go, Mr. Kingston," he said anxiously. "You're disturbing the other guests in the club."

"Disturbing the other guests?" He stared at the man blankly. Then he gave him a wide smile that was full of charm. "My dear fellow, why don't you piss off!"

Dorian yanked her hand out of his and reached for her purse. He snatched it up and held it away from her.

"Derek, for Christ's sake, you're acting like a child!" Dorian made a lunge for the purse and stumbled into a couple trying to get to their table. Furious, she tried once more to retrieve her purse, then, giving up, slapped him hard across the face.

"You bitch!" he roared, staggering to his feet and swinging at her wildly.

Tears blurred her vision as she tried to elude him. His fingers caught the top of her dress and ripped it open across her breasts. A woman yelled and several men rose from their tables to stop him. As Dorian fell back against a chair, someone seized Derek from behind, turned him around and punched him in the face. He went crashing into another table and an outcry went up. Dorian scrambled for her purse and fled, sobbing.

On the street, she tried to pull herself together, clutching at her dress and wiping tears from her eyes. A man came hurrying out of the club after her.

"Are you all right?" he asked. "Did he hurt you?"

"Only my dress and my pride." She walked to the curb, searching the street for a cab.

"Won't you let me take you home?" the man asked, following her.

"Thank you, I can manage—"

"Please, I can't go back into the club—I just knocked Kingston out. And I don't want to leave you here alone . . ."

Dorian looked up at him. He was a tall man, with thick silver gray hair, distinguished features, and a wide, pleasant smile.

"You knocked him out?" She returned his smile. "Thank you."

"Do let me take you home, Miss St. Clair, otherwise my good deed will remain incomplete." He took her arm gently and began leading her to his car.

Dorian asked, "Have we met before?"

"Yes, a few months ago, on Jack Clayton's set of *Our Mother's House*. You were with a young man, Claude Girard, who was doing the publicity . . ." He opened the door of a black Mercedes, helped her in, then got in on the other side.

"I'm sorry, I don't remember," Dorian said as they sped away from the club.

"We just said hello. I saw your pictures, though. They were wonderful, particularly the shots of the children, Pamela Franklin and Mark Lester. And the studies of Jack working with Dirk Bogarde were excellent."

"You really liked them?"

"Very much. You seem surprised, or is that just modesty? I also saw the pictures you did of your family's hotel in that architectural design magazine. You're very talented, but I prefer the work you did on the film. Are you doing any more assignments on films?"

"No one has asked me," Dorian replied with a rueful smile. "When Claude and I broke up, he said some rather nasty things about me to other producers . . ."

"That's a shame. Spurned lovers can turn ugly—"

"I seem to have a knack for attracting them," she said almost to herself.

He glanced over at her. She was staring out the window with a distant, thoughtful expression, one hand holding the torn dress together, the other lying limp in her lap. He thought she looked like a rumpled child who had just come in from playtime.

She turned and saw him staring at her. "I must look a mess."

"Not at all. You're very beautiful. I'm surprised that no one ever suggested you work in front of a camera instead of behind one."

She laughed. "Now you sound like a few producers I've met. Are you in the business?"

"As a matter of fact, I am—but I'm a director." He named some of the films he had done, and she looked at him with more interest.

"I've seen a few of them—I especially liked *The Rogue.*"

"Yes, that was one of my favorites. Are we almost there? I read that you'd taken a house near Regent's Park . . ."

"Yes, just down the street and turn left. You seem to have been keeping track of me . . ."

He smiled. "I do, don't I—I hope you don't mind. Ah, here we are, safe, if not quite sound."

He stopped the car and faced her. "Are you feeling better now?"

"Much. Thank you, you've been very kind."

"May I call you tomorrow? Perhaps we could have lunch?"

"Yes, I'd like that—but I'll take you to lunch."

He laughed and helped her from the car. They walked up to her front door, and Dorian said, "I can manage from here. Thank you again, Mr.—I don't even know your name!"

"It's Graham Bentley—and not Mr., just Graham."

"Good night, Graham. Call me tomorrow—"

She fitted her key into the lock, opened the door and closed it softly behind her. Graham stood for a few moments, looking after her, then returned to his car. Driving away, he whispered to himself, "Yes, I will call you tomorrow—and the day after that . . ."

16

New York: July

ALAN HELPED LAYLA from the cab in front of Jordan's building. In the elevator she said, "Tonight should be interesting—Grace told me that they've invited the big name troops, including your patroness, Olivia St. Clair."

"Why do I hear a menacing note in your voice everytime you mention her name? What the hell do you have against Olivia anyway?"

"I'll tell you about it sometime," she replied as the elevator came to a stop and the doors slid open.

A maid was waiting to take their coats. Sounds of music and conversation could be heard from the drawing room. Alan and Layla walked down the hall and stood in the doorway, surveying the gathering. He recognized some of the people he had met at the happening: artists and gallery owners, musicians and writers. Van Cliburn was sitting at the Steinway playing Gershwin preludes and chatting with Grace; Jordan was with John and Dora Koch and Moses Soyer. White-jacketed servants offered drinks, and visible through a wide archway was the dining room, where a sumptuous buffet was colorfully arranged amid gleaming silver and fine china.

"Every time I come to one of these evenings, I feel like I've stepped into another world," Alan said.

Layla chuckled. "Positively opulent, isn't it? The man entertains like a prince. He and Grace have created and maintain what must be one of the most elegant salons in New York. And tonight it's all pure Establishment, a gathering of the conservative elite, with the exception of yours truly."

"Layla, please," Alan warned. "No arguments for the avant-garde, no sniping at tradition—not tonight, okay?"

"Stop worrying—I love Jordan and Grace. Besides, you know I have a sense of decorum."

"No, I didn't know that," Alan said with feigned surprise.

She pinched his behind unexpectedly, propelling him into the room. He recovered himself swiftly and saw Olivia coming to greet him.

"Alan, I was so pleased when Jordan said you'd be here tonight. There are some people who are very anxious to meet you—" She paused as Layla came up beside them.

"Hello, Olivia," she said. "I'm sorry I missed talking with you at Sylvester's show. It's been a long time . . ."

Olivia seemed flustered for a few seconds, then answered politely, "Yes, it has. How are you, Layla? I heard that you were traveling in Europe."

"Yes, I was. But it's good to be home, back with my friends."

An awkward silence ensued. Alan sensed a strong current of animosity between them, and shifted uncomfortably.

"You look wonderful, as always," Olivia said, her eyes sweeping over the vividly patterned, almost transparent material that was wound sari-style around Layla's figure. "Your gown is lovely. Paris?"

"No, just something mother whipped up for me the other day."

"Ah, yes, your mother—she was always so clever with the needle."

Alan felt as if they were speaking in code; messages were being transmitted between them that he couldn't understand.

Olivia took Alan's arm and said, "There are some friends of mine here that I'd like you to meet." She glanced at Layla. "May I steal him from you for a moment . . . ?"

"He's all yours," she said graciously. "But only for a moment."

Olivia led Alan across the room. "Have you known her long?" she asked.

"Just for a few months." He hesitated to say more, then finished haltingly, "She's a wonderful model—"

"Yes, I know."

There was a bitter edge to her voice. Alan was more confused than ever; whatever had happened between the two women wasn't pleasant. He'd have to get the story from Layla.

Olivia took him to two men who were standing by the fireplace, and introduced him. "Alan, I want you to meet Robert Benson and Sidney Rabin. Gentlemen, this is Alan Conway."

Alan recognized them as the owners of a small, prestigious gallery on Madison Avenue. Benson was short and youthful-looking, with bright pink cheeks and thin, curly blond hair, a quick smile and darting gray eyes. Sidney Rabin was older, with receding dark hair and a calm, thoughtful expression on his face.

"We were at the show, and saw your painting of Peake," Benson said. "It was a revelation, after all that Hellzapoppin' chaos Sylvester is so famous for. Quite remarkable, really . . ."

"Jordan tells us you're one of the most talented artists to come into his studio in a long time," Rabin added.

"Believe me, he's exaggerating," Alan said.

"Perhaps," Rabin said agreeably. "But I've never known Olivia to exaggerate. Her instinct for spotting young talent is infallible. You have a great champion in her. In fact, we've already seen another example of your work—so you see, this meeting is not as casual as it may appear."

"I don't understand."

"After they saw your painting at the show, Robert and Sidney had dinner with me a few days later, and they saw the portrait of Dorian and David," Olivia explained.

"Which was precisely why we were invited to dinner," Rabin said.

"Sidney, you make me sound quite devious," she laughed.

"You are, my dear, but more graciously and intelligently than most people, for which Robert and I have always been grateful. We understand and appreciate your enthusiasm where new talent is concerned."

Benson said to Alan, "Jordan told us that there are several of your canvases here, in his studio. May we see them later?"

"Yes, of course," Alan replied, beginning to understand what was going on.

When the two men had moved off, Alan said to Olivia, "I appreciate what you're doing, but do you think I'm ready for a show . . . ?" He felt a little uneasy about her tactics.

"Andrew Wyeth had his first show at the Macbeth Gallery when he was twenty. You're as good a draftsman, and in my opinion a much better painter," she responded briskly. Then, seeing his look of concern, she added, "They will make the final decision—I'm just helping to speed things up a bit."

"You're a hell of a manager, At this rate, whatever career I have I'll owe to you."

"Not at all," she protested, but looking pleased. "The ultimate measure of your success is in your own ability." She examined him critically. "You look wonderful—more handsome than ever. I see you've let your hair grow longer. I like it, but not too much more; I don't care for this new look in artists—all shaggy and ragged. A sense of style is still very important, despite the changing fashion trends."

"Yes, I guess so—" Alan murmured. He had a sudden image of himself as a schoolboy being lectured to by a teacher.

"And you're thinner," Olivia went on. "But that's all right—I've always thought artists should look a bit haunted; it adds a certain romantic quality. There's something complacent-looking about a fat artist."

"I heard that!" a rotund man said, coming up to them and smiling jovially at Olivia.

"I was talking about artists, Oscar, not critics," Olivia said, embracing him. "Alan, this is Oscar Laurence, whom I'm sure needs no further introduction."

Alan shook hands with him. "I've read your reviews and articles, Mr. Laurence, and your latest book—"

"Ah, yes: *Today's Art, A Madness In Our Midst.*" He recited the title with obvious relish. "It's quite true, you know," he went on, as if sharing a confidence. "There is no art today. Wire constructions! Things made of plastic, rubber and bits of wood! Paintings that are cartoons or the dribblings of childish minds! The entrepreneurs are passing off garbage at extraordinary prices to people with no taste or education, but simply a mad desire to be *au courant!* I promise you, in twenty years or less most of today's so-called art will be found packed away in cellars and attics, and be thought of as an embarrassment by their owners."

"But not this young artist's work," Olivia said, interrupting his breathless discourse. "Alan did the painting of Sylvester Peake at his Easter Happening a few weeks ago—"

"Ah yes!" the critic exclaimed. "I was there. A ridiculous exhibition of bad taste, except for your work. It's a beautifully crafted piece for one so young. I know that I stand like a battered fortress against the rising tide of New York critics who favor the new expression, but I believe there is still hope for the survival of the great traditions in art, traditions for which you obviously have a reverence, young man."

Layla left a group she was chatting with and joined them. Oscar greeted her zestfully, exclaiming, "The most beauteous model in New York! It's good to have you back!"

"And it's comforting to find you as dense as ever, dear Oscar," she replied cheerfully. "You're still clinging to the romantic bullshit of the Ashcan school era. What a darling anachronism you are."

Alan shot her an angry look, but the critic took her ribbing goodnaturedly. It was Olivia who seemed offended.

"Oscar has great taste, a quality sadly lacking in today's world!" she snapped.

Layla answered her calmly. "Taste is wonderful in the drawing room, but I don't think it has much to do with producing art, only its selection by collectors."

Alan broke in quickly. "That isn't to say there isn't room for those artists who defy the current trends and create their own unique place in art. Certainly Jordan is the best example of that, along with Koch and the Soyer brothers . . ."

"And yourself," Olivia added, darting a furious glance at Layla. "I think Alan's work will eventually exemplify the best of traditional painting and stand head and shoulders above the so-called innovative, self-indulgent *crap* we are being offered today!"

"Alan has a long way to go," Layla declared, her voice rising a little. "He may change, broaden his outlook. Unless, of course, he becomes a success at what he's doing. Money often makes the difference between vision and complacency."

Olivia's shoulders stiffened and her dark eyes flashed angrily. Before she could respond, Jordan, who had joined the group while Layla was speaking, said quietly, "You've always had such positive views, Layla. But in a way, I must agree with you. While I enjoy my success and acceptance, I don't feel that what I'm doing is really important—that is, I don't make vital statements or break new ground. Nor, may I add, do I want to; it's not in my nature as an artist. Sometimes, however, I must admit to feeling a little archaic, and wonder if I haven't traded all this"—he looked around the room—"for something with more meaning."

Olivia and Oscar began to protest, but he cut them off. "No, don't disagree with me. Olivia, you and I have chosen to create our lives in the most civilized fashion possible, no matter how the world is changing around us. And we're both happy with our choice. It's just that every once in a while I question it, whereas you have far more confidence in the rightness of how you live."

Alan listened to Jordan, surprised by what he was saying; it was the first time he had heard the artist express any doubts about himself and his work. Just then Grace announced that the buffet was being served. Oscar seized Olivia's arm and hurried her off to the dining room.

Alan turned to Layla, but she and Jordan had abruptly slipped away and were walking out of the room. He was about to follow them when Grace intercepted him to chat for a moment. By the time he broke away from her they had disappeared.

A few minutes later, Robert Benson and Sidney Rabin, accompanied by Olivia, came up to him.

"Robert and I have to leave soon," Rabin said. "Could we see your paintings before we go?"

"And may I come along?" Olivia asked. "I promise to be quiet and not play 'agent.' "

Rabin took her arm and Alan led them to the studio. He turned on the lights, drew up some chairs for them and got out his canvases. Once the paintings were set up he stepped aside and stood quietly with his arms folded, trying not to appear nervous.

Benson and Rabin moved slowly from one painting to another, pausing to examine them up close, then stepping back for a more critical view. Alan watched their faces anxiously, thinking about what Layla had said earlier and the private conflicts they had had about his work. From the beginning she had urged him to experiment more, not to be confined by what she called his "narrow, academic vision." But Alan had stubbornly held to his own beliefs, refusing to be swayed by her arguments. Yet what Jordan had said a few minutes earlier began to nag at him, make him feel uncertain about what he was doing.

His thoughts were jarred when Rabin turned to him and said, "These are very good, Alan. How many canvases can you have ready by late summer—say August?"

For a moment, Alan stared at him, incredulous. All doubts and fears faded with the look of approval he saw in the eyes of the two gallery owners.

He took a deep breath and answered confidently, "Enough for a one-man show."

Olivia smiled with satisfaction as the three men shook hands.

On the way home in a cab, Alan told Layla about getting the show. She received the news with subdued enthusiasm and grew quiet, almost sullen. By the time they reached his studio he was beginning to feel angry.

"You don't seem very happy about my getting a one-man show," he said.

"It's what you want—I'm happy for you," she replied, then added sarcastically, "And you didn't get the show—Olivia got it for you."

"She didn't paint the pictures!"

"But she has the connections! Do you think they'd have paid as much attention to you if it hadn't been for her?"

"You're damned right I do! And what the hell do you have against her anyway? You were rude and bitchy to her all evening."

"She makes it easy! And I don't like seeing her do the same thing to you that she did to her husband."

"What do you know about her husband?"

For a few minutes, Layla was silent. She slumped into a chair and rummaged in her purse for a joint. Lighting it, she put her head back, drew deeply, then released the smoke with a deep sigh.

"He walked out on her because of the way she controlled his life and directed his work. Because she made him a success on her terms."

Alan sat down on the bed, staring at her with surprise. "How do you know that?"

"Scott and I were lovers."

"Did she know that?"

"Yes."

"Why didn't you tell me this before?"

"I didn't expect her to try the same thing with you—and I didn't know that you'd let her!" She looked at him accusingly.

"What did she do to Scott?"

"Everything. Arranged his shows, influenced the critics, dragged him to parties to meet wealthy collectors."

Layla stood up and began to pace the room. "She told him how to dress, to talk, and many times what to paint. He was a sweet, sensitive man, much too weak to defy her, and afraid of *not* being successful."

"Okay—so he was a weak man who let her run his life. What the hell does that have to do with me?"

She whirled about, facing him angrily. "He was kind and gentle. She broke him down with her money and ideas of prestige, made everything so easy for him he didn't have to struggle—just slide into success!"

"You really cared for him, didn't you?"

"Yes, more than she ever did. When the poor son of a bitch left her, she didn't even keep his name!"

"Maybe she did that because sweet, sensitive Scott was fucking you and she knew it!" Alan's voice rose harshly. "And maybe she knew he needed her to hold him up!"

"That's not true—"

"How would you know? I think you and Olivia have a lot in common—you both want things done your way! And now you have me to fight over. Well, screw that shit! I'm not Scott—I'm not gutless, just ambitious. I'll take every bit of help I can get, from Olivia, Jordan, Benson and Rabin, even from you. I can be helped, but not pushed!"

Layla was shocked into silence by his outburst. Alan reached out, took the joint from her fingers and took a hit. Then he gave it back to her and held out his arms.

"Now that we understand each other, let's go to bed and celebrate my ill-gotten gains."

She came toward him slowly. "You've got some mouth on you, *boychik*," she whispered. "I never heard you talk like that before."

He took her in his arms. "With you around, who gets a chance to talk?"

She stood quietly, her body still tense. Alan sensed that some irrevocable change had taken place between them, a small fissure in the bond of their relationship that he knew would grow and widen as time went on.

"You're going to go through with it, aren't you, despite what I've told you?" Layla asked.

"Of course I am. I have to go my own way."

She pulled away and looked at him with a mocking smile. "You mean the St. Clair way, don't you?"

"That's what I like about you—you never give up," he laughed, slipping his hands inside her dress.

"But it's true," she said, letting him undress her. "Look at the way your life has changed since you met them: your love affair with Dorian, what happened to your mother, the way Olivia has taken over your career—"

"Careful," Alan warned.

"Okay—the way she's *furthered* your career! And what about David? The poor bastard is buried in the closet and in love with you at the same time. If you ever see Dorian again, you'll have his feelings to contend with . . ."

"Thank you for enumerating all my involvements. Now can we go to bed? I get very horny when I see you naked."

"But Alan, you know what I'm saying is true—"

He cut her off with a kiss, picked her up and carried her to the bed.

Hours later he lay awake in the dark beside her sleeping figure, thinking about what she had said. He was reluctant to admit that it was true, yet he knew that his life had become enmeshed in tangled strands that bound him to the St. Clairs. The incident with David was still vivid in his mind; at least now he understood the enigma of their friendship. But what could he do about it? He had wanted to call David, but had been afraid of embarrassing him further, and was uncertain of what to say. He supposed that Dorian knew about her brother; that would explain their mysterious, exclusive relationship, the private world they shared. Falling in love with her had made him a part of that world, and now he wasn't sure if he were unable or unwilling to extricate himself from it.

Alan fell into a troubled sleep, thinking of himself and Dorian and David as three points in an ever-changing triangle, knowing that however they might be separated in the future, they would always form a single shape.

17

New York: October 1967

"COULD YOU LOOK slightly to the left—yes, that's it . . ."

Alan worked rapidly, sketching an indication of Mrs. Whitemore's eyes. He forced himself to concentrate. There were so many distractions in the room: the garish decor, bad art on the walls, an obsequious secretary who interrupted every five minutes, but mostly the subject, Mrs. Abner Whitemore. Overdressed in a pink ball gown she had chosen to wear for the portrait, and bedecked with a glittering array of diamonds, she sat fidgeting in her chair.

"Try to keep still, Dorothy," Olivia chided her from a corner of the room.

"I simply didn't expect to be kept prisoner in this chair all afternoon," Mrs. Whitemore petulantly replied.

Olivia poured herself another cup of tea and sat back, looking amused. "A little patience, and you'll be greatly rewarded. A few years from now, you can tell all your friends that you were one of the first to commission Alan Conway for a portrait."

"Oh, I do believe you, Olivia. It's just that I had to cancel so many appointments—"

"Could you put your arm back where it was?" Alan asked, straining to be polite.

"I wasn't aware that I had moved!"

He set his teeth and worked in silence. The tug of war between them had been going on for a week. He had finally called on Olivia for help. Now he wished he hadn't. She was doing her best, but the resulting tension was becoming unbearable. He had used photographs to block in the canvas, and now needed only a few sittings to complete the painting. But Mrs. Whitemore seemed determined to make it into a never-ending project.

233

He looked up from the easel to see that she had moved again. For a few minutes he tried to fix the woman's face in his mind so that he could work from the mental image, but all he saw were the flaws: her double chin, watery blue eyes, puffy cheeks and thinning hair tinted a champagne color. The painting would emerge a caricature if he continued with that image, he thought despairingly.

Just then, the secretary, a dour little woman with a subservient expression, appeared at the door.

"Mr. Whitemore is on the phone from Philadelphia," she announced in a high, tremulous voice.

"I must take that call!" Mrs. Whitemore exclaimed, bolting from the chair. Alan watched her race from the room, thinking that she looked like a diamond-studded freighter under full steam.

"Don't be cross with her," Olivia said, coming over to him. "Dorothy is a graceless, silly woman, but she'll talk you up to everyone she knows, and it could lead to more commissions."

"I never thought it would be this trying," Alan said wearily.

Olivia looked at the painting. "You astonish me," she said with a smile. "Despite all your trials with her, the painting is beautiful. You've even managed to give her a dignity she has *never* possessed!"

"I think I'd rather paint her as the old cow she really is."

Olivia frowned at the remark, but remained silent.

Bustling back into the room, Mrs. Whitemore spoke quickly about having to leave immediately to join her husband.

"But I'll be free next Tuesday for another sitting," she concluded breathlessly.

Later, in the café of the Metropolitan Museum of Art, Alan and Olivia sat at a table near the edge of the large pool, where life-sized sculptures of figures riding dolphins seemed to glide across the surface of the water. It was the work of the Swedish artist Carl Milles, and was called "The Fountain of Muses." Thinking of this, Alan wondered if his muse had taken the month off.

Olivia watched him thoughtfully as she sipped her coffee. "Sidney called me this morning," she said. "He was very excited—they just sold the last canvas from the show. It was altogether a great success . . ."

"That's wonderful," Alan sighed.

"You don't seem very pleased."

"I am, really. Right now I'm just tired."

"It's difficult, isn't it, to discover that being a portrait artist isn't as romantic as you believed it would be?"

"I suppose so—and I guess at heart I am a romantic." He laughed cheerlessly. "I had visions of myself as another Rubens, doing sittings in graceful surroundings with worldly, elegant people . . ."

"Oh, my dear, aristocracy is much the same from century to century. Only their settings change. I'm sure that Rubens, Whistler, Van Dyck and Sargent's subjects gave them as much trouble as Dorothy Whitemore is giving you."

Alan lit a cigarette and nodded. "I guess you're right. I still have a lot to learn, even though I seem to be losing my romantic illusions on a daily basis."

"Well, I think you've been very patient with Dorothy, and I have a reward for that patience."

Alan began to protest. "Olivia, please, you've done so much for me already! The one-man show, this commission—"

"Alan, do shut up," she laughed. "The reward is not from me, but by way of me."

"I don't understand."

"I received a call from Dorian last night," she began tentatively. "She's coming back to New York sometime next week, and asked me to tell you."

Alan went a little pale. "She's coming home?"

"Yes. She told me that you hadn't kept in touch—but she said she wanted to see you—that is, if you wanted to see her . . ."

"When will she be here?"

"She hadn't made her flight arrangements when I spoke to her. She's calling me the day she leaves." Olivia regarded him closely, "I know how you feel—at least, I think I know. But it's been over a year, and I thought—well, I thought you might be pleased."

Alan stubbed out his cigarette with trembling fingers. "I don't know how I feel. She's probably changed a great deal—"

"But so have you, don't you think?"

"Yes, I guess so . . ."

"When she calls, shall I tell her you want to see her?"

❦

Alan finished the portrait of Dorothy Whitemore, then secluded himself in his studio to wait for Dorian's call. He tried to work on a few unfinished canvases to make the time pass quickly, but none of them were going well; they lay on the floor around him, like fragments of thoughts, incomplete, lifeless. His attention wandered at every sound in the hallway or on the stairs; he stood by the windows searching the streets, or stared at the phone, as if willing it to ring.

The air in the studio was bad; cigarette smoke hung like a cloud, diffusing the light, turning it a hazy, toxic blue color. Alan squinted bloodshot eyes at the painting on his easel. He raised his brush, touched it to the canvas and stopped; the stroke was weak, indecisive. He dropped the brush to the floor and cursed. Catching sight of himself in the mirror, he grimaced; he was dirty and had a two-day growth of beard, his clothes were wrinkled and paint-stained. He couldn't remember when he had slept or eaten last. It didn't matter, he wasn't hungry. But exhaustion made him fall to the bed; he had to sleep, it was pointless to fight it any longer.

He awoke abruptly, his heart pounding from a nightmare; he had seen Marie, her swollen face white and bloodless in a glare of light. He sat up, his face wet with tears, and staggered into the bathroom, where he stripped off his clothes and ran a hot shower. He thought of calling Layla, but decided against it; their relationship had deteriorated in the last few months. With the success of his one-man show, and the commissions that were coming in, she was more argumentative than ever about his driving ambition. They were still friends, if only casual lovers, spending one or two nights a week together.

Revived by the shower, he wrapped a towel around his waist and began to shave, replaying in his mind the scene he'd been going over and over during the last week: seeing Dorian again. How would he act, what would he say to her? Recriminations sprang to his lips, but the thought of seeing her again silenced them. He'd be casual, off-hand—perhaps a little indifferent?

A few minutes later, while splashing water on his face and reaching for a towel, he heard a light knock at the door.

"It's open," he called out. "That you, Layla?" He walked out of the bathroom, drying his face. "I was thinking about calling you—soon as I'm dressed, let's get some food. I haven't eaten in days . . ."

"Take the towel away from your face, dummy, it's not Layla, whoever she is . . ."

The familiar voice went through him like the sharp thrust of a knife.

"That is Alan Conway behind the towel, isn't it?" the voice asked uncertainly. "Or do I have the wrong artist's studio?"

Alan dropped the towel to the floor. "No, this is the right studio," he whispered, barely able to speak. "Welcome home."

And then Dorian was in his arms.

ॐ

"Have I changed?" Her voice was a whisper in the darkness.

"No—yes, you're more beautiful. Have I changed?"

"Yes. You're more beautiful, too." She ran her fingers through his hair, filling her hands with it, like a just-discovered treasure. "And you're becoming successful, just as I knew you would . . ."

"Do you approve?"

"I think so—yes, it's exciting. And I envy you . . ."

"Me—?"

"Of course—David and I both envy you—we have from the first."

"Why?"

"Because you have talent and ambition, and because you're doing something with it. I read the reviews of your show and Olivia wrote me how it had sold out . . ."

"But you and David have everything! You have the world!"

She laughed and held him close, kissing him fiercely.

She came out of the bathroom wearing his flannel robe.

"Very chic," he commented, sitting up in bed.

"I feel like I'm camping out—is that fresh coffee I smell?"

"On the stove. Shall I make breakfast?"

"Absolutely! One of your gourmet omelettes!"

He held out his arms. "Give us a kiss first."

She went to him and let him open the robe to explore her body with his hands and lips.

"If you keep that up, we'll never get to breakfast," she murmured.

He pulled her down beside him. "Yes, we will—eventually."

They explored the city like children roaming through an enchanted kingdom. Alan took a drawing pad with him and did quick sketches in Little Italy and Chinatown, drawings of bearded merchants displaying their goods on Orchard Street, and of the chess players in Washington Square. They had lunch at the Russian Tea Room, ice cream at Rumpelmayer's, and strolled in Central Park with clasped hands.

Alan took her to see his favorite works of art, paintings and sketches that all reminded him of her: a languorous nude by Modigliani at the Museum of Modern art, Degas pastels of young dancers at the Metropolitan, and at the Frick, the cool beauty of the Ingres portrait of the Comtesse D'Haussonville. They wandered into the court and sat under the barrel-vaulted skylight, surrounded by flowering shrubs, coupled marble columns and stone colonnades. Alan watched pale blue shadows softly tint her slender throat. He put his lips to the shadows and whispered, "I love you more than I thought possible."

On the Staten Island ferry they stood at the rail with their arms around each other. Overhead, white clouds were sharply etched against the blue sky, and behind them the towers of Manhattan rose like a fortress of sharp angles and harsh stripes of light.

Dorian glanced up at Alan. He was staring out over the water, his strong profile in striking relief against the sky. A red scarf she had bought him was wound around his neck, and his dark hair tumbled over his head, curling up where it touched the red cloth. His eyes caught the sparkle of light from the water, and his cheeks and lips were moist from spray. She put her head on his shoulder, trying not to think about the future, but wanting only to isolate these moments, capture them forever in an unbroken sequence, like a perfectly matched strand of pearls.

In his studio, they sat across from each other in the dusty twilight. Alan told her about his work with Jordan and meeting Layla. Dorian listened quietly, making no comment. When he was finished she recounted her lonely months in Paris, going to London with Claude, and her efforts to become a photojournalist.

"But now we're together," he told her. "You can do more work here—the city is rich and vital, and you can capture it."

"Not the way you can," she countered. "Mine is a small talent, and I know it."

"That's silly! You haven't had time to develop it. But now you can—I'll find a larger place, we can fix up a dark room for you, live and work together just as we planned. I'm making more money now. Benson and Rabin are taking everything I give them, and Olivia has two more commissions lined up for me . . ."

"Alan, wait, you're going too fast—"

"Too fast? But what's to stand in our way? Dorian, it's what we both talked about, it's what we wanted."

"It's what you wanted," she said. "But I can't do it, now . . ."

"You can't? Are you still afraid of your parents?"

She laughed mirthlessly. "No, that's all over. There's nothing they can do to me anymore."

"Then what is it?" he demanded.

A flush of anger spread over her face. "Alan, don't do this to me! You're backing me into a corner! I'm not as positive as you are; I need time to think. You've always known exactly what you wanted to do, and then you did it. I *never* knew what I was doing; I just let things happen to me . . ."

"Like you let me happen to you?"

"Yes—but you were different! I wasn't prepared for that—I didn't realize . . ."

Her voice trailed off and she grew silent. Alan was suddenly aware of a change in her he had not noticed before, a kind of weary sadness that lay behind her dark eyes, and a hint of pain that blunted her reckless vitality. He reached out and took her in his arms.

The twilight turned to evening, and darkening shadows closed in around them. Alan's thoughts grew fearful; she was here and in his arms, but he was aware of the impenetrable barrier between them that he didn't understand, and couldn't surmount.

"I wanted us to have lunch with David," Dorian said the next morning. "But he refused. I know what happened between you—and I hoped you could make it up."

"There's nothing to make up. I'm not angry at David. If anything, I feel terrible about not having the courage to call him. He must be very upset . . ."

"It's hard to tell—you know David, he covers his feelings, he always has; Father taught him how to do that." She sighed and looked despondent. "We used to be so close, confiding in each other, sharing everything we thought and felt. But that's all changed. Everything began to change during the summer on the Island . . ."

"For all of us," Alan added.

She looked at him vaguely, as if from the perspective of a great distance. "Yes," she agreed. "For all of us."

She left him to return to the hotel.

"I have girl things to do," she told him when he protested. "Shopping, a visit to a beauty salon . . ."

"You don't need a beauty salon."

"You're an animal; you just want me to stay in your bed until I become a hag." She kissed him lightly. "I'll call you tonight."

By evening he hadn't heard from her. When he called the hotel he was told that she had gone out and they didn't know when she would return.

Two more days went by with no word from her. Alan was frantic. He called Olivia, and found that Dorian was there.

"I was going to call you," she said. Her voice sounded tense. "Please, don't be angry—something unexpected came up—"

240

"I'll come and get you."

"No, don't," she said hastily. "Come tomorrow, around one."

"Dorian, what's wrong? What's happened?"

"Tomorrow. I'll explain tomorrow."

He thought he heard her begin to cry before she hung up.

Olivia opened the door for him. She appeared tense. "Dorian's in the library, waiting for you," she said.

"What's wrong? Is it her parents? Have they returned?"

"No—no, it's not that—" She hesitated, then sighed deeply. "Dorian will have to tell you herself."

In the library, he saw Dorian standing by the windows. She looked up nervously when he entered the room.

Alan went to her and took her in his arms. She pulled away from him. "Darling, what's wrong?" he asked.

Tears filled her eyes and she wiped at them with an angry gesture. "Shit! I don't know how to do this!" she cried.

"Do what?" He took her arm and started to pull her toward the door. "Let's get out of here—we can talk at my place—"

"No, I can't leave! My husband will be here in a few minutes!"

He stared at her, disbelieving.

"I was married in London, a few months ago. Nobody knew, not Olivia or David, not even my parents." Her voice began to crack and tears ran down her cheeks. "I was going to go back in a week, but he got a call from Hollywood— he's a director—and they offered him a film. Now he's here, that's why I haven't called you." She was crying openly. "I meant to tell you. I wanted to tell you—his name is Graham Bentley, and he's been very good to me, very kind—"

"I don't want to hear about him!" Alan cried. "Just tell me why you did it! Or did you just let it happen—the way you let everything happen to you?

"Alan, please, try to understand . . ."

"Understand what? That you're still the same selfish, spoiled little bitch you were when I met you?"

He turned to leave but Dorian caught his arm. "Alan, don't go—not like this, please . . ."

In one violent move he wrenched his arm away and

slapped her hard across the face. "Don't you ever think of anyone but yourself? I feel sorry for the poor bastard who married you!"

He slammed out of the house and ran down the street, running until his chest ached, pushing his legs painfully before him, not wanting to stop moving. His breath came in heaving gasps, and the streets were a blur in his tearing eyes. Finally he was in the Village, and made his way to his studio. Inside, he leaned weakly against the door, struggling to catch his breath. Then he threw himself across the bed. There was a lingering scent of Dorian's perfume in the sheets and on the pillows. In a last burst of fury, he ripped them from the mattress and threw them on the floor.

November brought ugly gray days. Cold winds swept in off the sea, and the city became desolate, as if overnight a blight had descended, laying waste to the autumn color. There was a biting chill in the air, and people grew irritable, fighting the traffic and the cold with angry impatience.

Alan returned to work in Jordan's studio, venting his frustration and rage in a furious outburst of painting. Yet oddly enough his canvases expressed none of his anger, but were more lyrical and tender than ever before. It was as if he sought to create a world removed from his pain, a romantic observation of figures and objects that seemed to give him solace from his personal torment.

Layla once more became a constant companion. But she was quiet now, undemanding and sympathetic. Late at night, when he cried out in his sleep, she held him in her arms, rocking and soothing him until he became calm. All the drawings of Dorian were removed from the walls of his studio and packed away in a portfolio, to lie in the closet like imprisoned spirits.

Alan spent more time with the Shaws; he would stay for dinner after working all day in the studio with Jordan, or join them on tours of new exhibits at the museums and galleries. Layla often accompanied them. She and Alan had come to an understanding in their relationship; there was little discussion about the nature of his work, and no mention of the St. Clairs whatsoever.

One night in his studio Alan was working on a painting of

her. Layla was posed sitting nude on a chair to catch the overhead light on her face, while the rest of her body receded into deep shadows. After an hour or so Alan put his brushes down and rubbed his eyes. "That's it, I can't see a damned thing anymore," he said wearily.

Layla sat up and massaged the back of her neck. "Don't you think you're overdoing it? You've been working on that portrait of Sylvia Singer all day."

"Doing this is a relief from working with the Broadway legend and now aging sexpot," he replied.

"She giving you trouble?"

"Today she decided that she didn't like the gown she'd chosen for the portrait. I explained that the painting was almost finished, but she wanted to change it. So tomorrow I paint in a new gown."

"You agreed to that?"

"Why not? She's paying me to make the change. Besides, the more proficient I get with difficult patrons, the easier it will be for me later."

"Well, that's perfectly logical, if somewhat cold-blooded thinking."

"Don't get cute with me tonight—I'm too tired for your clever barbs."

"Sorry—I still have trouble adjusting to your way of mixing art and business."

Layla slipped into bed and Alan took off his clothes. He climbed in beside her and lay with his hands behind his head, staring into space. Layla took one of his arms and put it around her.

"So she's an aging sexpot, huh? What will you do if she comes after you?"

"Fuck her brains out and tell her to tell all her friends—the commissions will come pouring in."

She pinched his nipple, making him yelp. "You probably would, too, you bastard," she laughed.

They were quiet for a while, then he asked, "How's Jordan? I haven't seen him since Sylvia came into my life."

"He's okay," she answered vaguely.

"He looked worn out the last time I saw him."

"You know Jordan—he's like you, works around the clock."

She reached under the blanket and touched his cock, felt it lengthen in her fingers. "Obviously all of you isn't tired," she said dryly.

"Obviously," he agreed, pulling her closer.

It was after two o'clock in the morning when the phone rang.

"Goddammit," Alan grumbled sleepily, turning on the light. He picked up the receiver and said hoarsely, "Yes, who is it?"

Layla stirred beside him and sat up. "Who's calling at this hour?"

"It's Grace . . ." He looked puzzled and listened for a moment. "She says she wants you, that she's been calling all over town looking for you—"

She tore the phone from his hands. "Grace, what's the matter? Oh God! . . . No, don't do that! Try to talk to him—tell him I'm coming right over . . . Grace, please, try to stay calm—what? Yes, I'll be right there—yes, I'll bring Alan with me."

She hung up and looked at Alan with frightened eyes. "Jordan's freaking out—we've got to get over there right away."

"Freaking out?" he repeated blankly.

Layla flung on her clothes with trembling hands. "He's an addict—he's been a junkie for years!"

"I can't believe it! Why didn't you tell me?"

"He didn't want anybody to know, especially you. No one knew, except Grace—and me. I scored for him."

"For Christ's sake! Why did you do it?"

"Stop yelling at me and get dressed! I did it because he was afraid to, by himself. I thought I could help—maybe ease him off the stuff!"

Alan rushed into his clothes. "How bad a trip is he on?"

"I don't know—Grace said he locked himself in the studio—"

They ran through the deserted streets for blocks before finding a cab. As it sped across town, Alan asked, "What are you going to do?"

"I've got some heroin with me; I can help him if he'll let me, if he isn't too far gone—"

244

"I just can't believe Jordan would do this."

"I've been after him to quit since I came back from Europe. Before I went away, he said he wanted to experiment a little—just to know what it was all about . . ."

The cab pulled up to the front door of the Shaw's apartment building and Layla ran up the steps while Alan paid the fare. At Jordan's apartment, they banged on the door. It opened quickly, as if Grace had been waiting behind it for them to arrive. Her face was a mass of bruises, one of her eyes was blackened and there were welts and cuts on her neck and arms.

She fell into Layla's arms, sobbing. "I tried to help him, and he hit me! Now he's locked himself in the studio!"

"Stay here, we'll talk to him," Alan said.

"No, I'm coming with you," she cried. "He needs me!"

They ran down the hallway to the studio, and Layla signaled them to be quiet. She put her face close to the door and said in a low voice, "Jordan? It's me, Layla. Open the door—I can help you."

There was a sound of something crashing to the floor.

"Jordan?" Layla said more urgently. "Open the door! Please, I've got some good stuff with me—"

An anguished cry came from inside the room.

"Oh God, I think he's collapsed!"

"Let me try to break the door down!"

Alan stepped back, then threw his weight against the door. It gave a little but remained closed. He tried again, and the lock broke. The door flew open and they rushed into the room. Grace screamed.

The studio was a shambles: work tables overturned, paints, brushes, pastels, canvases and drawings scattered across the floor. Paintings that Jordan had been working on were ripped and slashed, priceless objects that he had been using as props were broken or smashed . . .

Jordan lay amid the wreckage, half buried under a stack of mutilated paintings. His arms were outflung and a needle still dangled from where he had jabbed it into a vein. A moan escaped his lips and his body quivered uncontrollably.

Layla cried. "He's OD'd! We've got to get him to a hospital!"

"No!" Grace shouted. "The police would be involved—if

the news got out, he could never stand the humiliation! Isn't there something you can do?"

Layla crouched over him and pulled the needle out. Jordan's eyes blinked open and stared at her glassily. "Okay, baby," she said to him, "It's okay—we're going to help you. Alan, let's get him on his feet. Grace, make a large pot of coffee and prepare some cold compresses—I think we can bring him out of it."

Alan and Layla struggled awkwardly with Jordan, pulling at his dead weight and finally getting him between them. Slowly they moved out of the studio, a step at a time, straining to keep him upright.

For the next three hours they walked him back and forth the length of the apartment. Grace followed them silently, carrying the coffee and cloths. They made an eerie group, supporting Jordan's figure past the paintings and sculptures, the antique furniture, the accumulated wealth of the Shaws' possessions. The only sounds were Jordan's cries and incoherent mutterings.

As the first light of dawn filtered through the windows, he seemed to rouse; they took him into the bedroom, stripped off his clothes and wrapped him in blankets. He looked small and childish in the large bed, his face sunken, eyes filled with pain and confusion. He began to speak fitfully:

"I'm so sorry—so sorry—"

"Don't talk," Alan said. "Save your strength—"

"No, you must understand, Alan—it's important . . ." He took several deep breaths and went on: "An artist has to grow, and I didn't grow—"

"You're a great artist," Layla said gently.

"I never grew or changed in my work—that's why I did this—" He gave them a pathetic smile. "Even old Rembrandt changed, did his best work in his old age, but not me—I tried to break out of myself, but it didn't help. I could almost touch a new vision, then it would disappear—and I couldn't see anything, nothing but this goddamned apartment!"

Tears began to flow down his cheeks and he clenched his fists, beating them soundlessly against the blankets. The light in the room grew stronger and Grace went to close the drapes.

"He'll be all right now," Layla said wearily. "All he needs is rest."

Jordon lay back against the pillows and closed his eyes. "Alan?" he whispered.

Alan took his hand and held it tightly. "Yes, Jordan?"

"You were my best student, the only one besides Grace who didn't judge me. You have great talent, you know? You even began to get some of my commissions . . ."

"What?"

But Jordan had fallen into a deep sleep. Alan looked up at Grace. "What did he mean? What commissions?"

"His agent was trying to get the Whitemore portraits for him, but Olivia spoke to Mrs. Whitemore first—oh, she didn't know that Jordan wanted the commissions—she wasn't being underhanded to help you. It just worked out that way."

Alan's shoulders sagged. "Oh Christ," he muttered, "I didn't know."

"His work simply isn't as popular as it used to be, and the critics never had a kind word to say about him, only those men who were our personal friends . . ." Grace added, bitterly.

They left the bedroom and went out into the foyer. "I can never thank you enough for what you've done," Grace said. "In a few days, I'll take him up to our place in Maine—there's a small hospital there, run by a friend of ours."

"We'll come to visit you," Alan said.

"No, don't do that. I don't want you to see him, either of you."

"Grace, what happened wasn't my fault!" Layla protested.

"I know that. Please, try to understand me. I love you both, but I love him more. He's been badly hurt, and I'm the only one who can help him now. We've both had enough of New York—and I think it will be a long time before we come back . . . Please go now. There's nothing else you can do here."

Alan and Layla stepped outside, shivering in the early morning chill. They walked silently down the street. Alan's face was white and pinched with fatigue. Layla took his arm and said, "Grace was upset. In a couple of weeks we'll call her. I'm sure she'll let us come to visit Jordan."

"I don't think so," Alan said harshly. "Don't you understand? Jordan saw himself in me; that's why she doesn't want him to see me. And that's what he was trying to tell me when he said that he hadn't grown, that his work didn't change as he became more successful; he saw me going the same way. Christ, I even began to get his commissions!"

"But that happens," Layla protested. "There will always be new artists who are taken up by the public and become fashionable. Jordan knew that long before he met you. And he knew how limited his talents were; that's why he took drugs—hoping to find something that just didn't exist within him. It was foolish, stupid! I told him that, so did Grace—"

"He was frightened and desperate! It's not enough to find a successful formula and stay with it, not if you want to do something that has meaning. That's what he's afraid will happen to me!"

"But you're not afraid of that, are you?"

The question brought Alan up short. He suddenly thought of something he had said to Olivia the first time they had met in the library of the St. Clair estate: "I don't intend to compromise myself."

But he had done exactly that from the moment he had fallen in love with Dorian. All of his efforts had been to achieve importance in her eyes, and the eyes of her family. Now he felt a sense of waste, the futility of that ambition.

"Alan, what are you afraid of?" Layla asked.

He shook his head wearily. "I thought I knew exactly what I wanted and how I was going to get it. Now I'm not sure. That's what I'm afraid of."

❦

Alan flipped his cigarette into the swollen, icy waters of the Connecticut River and hunched his shoulders against the cold. A silvery mist floated through the fading twilight, and he wondered idly what colors he would mix to achieve the ghostly appearance of the trees and shrubs crouched along the shoreline. More snow had fallen the night before, and lay over the stark limbs and branches like a sprinkling of fine powder.

It was late December; he had been here with his father and Aunt Margaret for almost a month.

After Marie's death, George had decided to remain in Connecticut with his widowed sister. He had sold the house in Bay Shore, and moved into her large, ramshackle white frame house. In time he had gone back to work, restoring homes in the area.

Shaken by Jordan's suicide attempt, Alan had called George, who insisted he come at once.

He had stayed on for Christmas, an old-fashioned affair with neighbors dropping in, gifts exchanged, large meals and hot toddies by a roaring fire. Gradually Alan had come out of his depression, and logic began to replace emotion, giving him a perspective on the events of the last year.

Alan watched evening descend over the swiftly moving waters of the river and thought about his plans for the future. He heard his father call out to him from the top of the hill, and started trudging up the road, his boots crunching into the hard white pack beneath his feet.

That evening, after dinner, he discussed his plans with George.

"I've decided to go away for a while," he began tentatively. "I don't want to go on living and working in New York."

George nodded his head and smiled. "I expected as much, and I don't blame you. When will you leave for Paris?"

Alan looked up at him, surprised. "How did you know I wanted to go to Paris?"

"I've known ever since you were fifteen and won the first prize in the high school art show. That's what Marie said you would do."

Alan laughed, remembering the event. "Yes, she did say that one day I would go to Paris and paint, didn't she."

George's sister came in from the kitchen carrying a tray of coffee and cake. "It's devil's food," she told Alan, cutting him a large slice.

"God, by the time I leave here, I'll be fat!"

"Well, you'll certainly look better than when you arrived," she said, sitting down at the table with them. "So, when are you leaving for Paris?"

Alan and George began to laugh and her round, pleasant face turned red with embarrassment. "The door was open, and I couldn't help overhearing . . ." she protested.

Alan leaned over and kissed her cheek. "Don't apologize. It's obviously no surprise to either of you."

"How will you manage?" George asked.

"I've saved a good deal of money, and the gallery owes me a sizable check from the last few canvases they sold."

"Will you be studying with a teacher?" Margaret asked.

"No—Cézanne once said that the Louvre was his teacher, and that will do for me. Benson and Rabin have an affiliation with a gallery there, and I'm shipping some new canvases to them. Olivia St. Clair said she'd give me some letters of introduction. So I won't be altogether alone. My French is still pretty good; I won't have any problems with the language."

George's eyes grew misty. "Marie would have been so happy to know that you are seeing her homeland."

"Yes, she spoke of Paris so often . . ."

George sighed deeply. Then he asked his son: "Do you ever hear from the St. Clair girl—?"

Alan's face darkened slightly. "No—she's in Hollywood with her husband."

"And her brother? You were friends with him."

"We don't keep in touch," Alan replied stiffly.

"It's sad, how things change. You were all so close that summer."

"It's not sad," Alan said curtly. "It's just the way things turn out."

On January 10, 1968, Alan stood with his father on the dock of Pier 5 in New York. Alan had booked passage on an Italian freighter bound for Marseilles.

"I still don't understand why you didn't want to fly," George said.

Alan smiled. "What could be more romantic for an artist than to sail to Europe on a freighter? Besides, I need the time to think about what I'm going to do."

George looked around. "Aren't any of your friends coming to see you off?"

"No—we said our goodbyes earlier this week. I just wanted you here with me." He glanced at his watch. "It's time, Dad."

"Yes, yes . . ." George's eyes filled with tears. He embraced his son and held him tightly.

"Take care of yourself, and write to me," Alan said. "Do you have the address of the gallery?"

George nodded. "Be safe," he whispered.

Alan picked up his bags and walked up the gangplank. A few minutes later he stood at the rail. It was early evening and the lights of the city glowed eerily in the overcast dusk. He watched the skyline of New York recede into the distance until there was nothing left but the dark sky and the water rolling against the prow of the boat like waves of black ink.

Fourteen days later Alan disembarked in Marseilles. After a few days of visiting the colorful port, he boarded the night express for Paris. Early the next morning he stepped off the train in the Gare de Lyon, and walked out into the brilliant sunshine of the morning.

Part Three

18

Paris: March 1968

THE CROWDS AT the outdoor cafés along the Boulevard Saint
Germain were beginning to thin out. Students left for classes
at the Sorbonne, businessmen sipped the last of their coffee,
and a sprinkling of tourists prepared for a day of sightseeing.
Waiters scurried to clean the tables, muttering under their
breath about the vulgarity of Americans, and slyly pocketing
oversized tips. A cool April breeze rustled through the clear
morning, and there was a din of traffic along the wide street.
The city was beginning to blossom with fresh vitality after
the long winter months.

Alan remained at his table and had another coffee and
croissant. Dressed in a black turtleneck sweater and gray cor-
duroy trousers, he had the appearance of a French student,
and was often mistaken for one by tourists who stopped him
for directions. He was amused at being thought of as a native, and proud of how quickly he had assimiliated; he spoke
more French than English, which impressed his concierge and
the shopkeepers in the neighborhood. He dined simply in local bistros, and spent weeks exploring the city. Recalling
Marie's reminiscences of her childhood, he often experienced
moments of déjà vu when he came upon a street or building
that she had mentioned.

The only place he gave a wide berth was the St. Clair Hotel. But that didn't help to disconnect him from the family;
Dorian was still in his thoughts, and Olivia's influence had
been responsible for establishing him with a well-known gallery.

Upon his arrival, he had contacted Louis Foucault, the
owner and director of the Galerie Foucault. A friend of Olivia's and an affiliate of the Benson-Rabin Gallery, Foucault
was expecting him. With his help Alan had found a studio

apartment on the Quai Voltaire that overlooked the Seine, and was within walking distance of Notre Dame, the Luxembourg Gardens and Montparnasse.

A few weeks later the canvases he had shipped from New York arrived at Foucault's gallery on the Rue de Seine. Within a month, three of them had been sold. Foucault took Alan to meet a well-known banker named Delane, who commissioned Alan to do a portrait of his wife. Madame Delane, a woman with demanding tastes, was delighted with the painting. The enterprising Foucault asked Alan for a one-man show, to be presented later that year.

All of this Alan dutifully reported in a letter to Olivia, who wrote back that she would try to be in Paris for the show. That he was still doing what Layla had accused him of—allowing Olivia to further his career—irritated Alan only a little; he was determined to use Olivia's contacts to his own advantage until the time came when he was no longer so inextricably linked to her.

Leaving his table at the café, Alan sauntered along the boulevard toward the Rue de Seine and the gallery; he had an appointment with Foucault to discuss the number of works for the show. On the narrow street he paused to glance in the windows of antique stores, into other galleries, and at the displays of meat and fowl in the windows and doorways of the butcher shops that were jammed between their more artistic neighbors.

At the gallery Alan opened a wrought-iron grillwork door and stepped into a centuries-old courtyard fronting the entrance. Foucault came out, greeted Alan warmly and took him to his office at the back of the gallery, where he offered him a glass of wine.

"Another painting was sold yesterday," the dapper Frenchman announced grandly, flourishing his cigar. "You are beginning to rival David Hockney in England, and your own Andrew Wyeth, with your youthful success."

Alan smiled politely. "Young artists are in vogue."

"So it would appear. For both our sakes, let us hope it continues."

They began to discuss the forthcoming show and Alan listened to Foucault attentively; the man had navigated the perilous transitions in art movements for over thirty years, and was regarded by his peers as an astute judge of talent and a shrewd businessman. He had gained a position of social prominence that insured, for the artists he represented, a high degree of access to wealthy Parisian society.

As they concluded their talk, Foucault's assistant came into the office. A tall, quiet young man, looking dangerously thin in a black suit, he waited silently until the director glanced up at him.

"Yes, what is it?"

"Mademoiselle Gautier to see you, Monsieur."

"Madeline Gautier? She hasn't been in for ages! Tell her I'll be with her as soon as I've finished with Mr. Conway."

"But she wishes also to meet Monsieur Conway . . ."

"Ah?" Foucault seemed surprised. He turned to Alan. "That is very intriguing, yes? So few people in Paris know you."

"Mademoiselle Gautier and I have a friend in common," Alan said stiffly; Dorian had mentioned her, and had told him that she was Jonathan's mistress.

Foucault smiled, sensing a morsel of gossip. A wily expression came into his eyes. "You are full of surprises, Mr. Conway."

They left the office and walked to the main gallery. "You know that Mademoiselle Gautier is an actress in films . . . ?"

"Yes—I've seen a few of them. She's very beautiful."

"Ah yes, but the beauty is quite fragile." Foucault sighed wistfully. "Soon it will fade."

Madeline was standing in front of Alan's paintings and drawings. Foucault greeted her gaily and introduced them. She seemed, to Alan, smaller, more petite than she appeared on the screen. Her lustrous blond hair was full and soft around her face, but he saw more irregularities than he had expected: the nose was short, her eyes widely spaced, and there was a hint of disdain in her delicately shaped mouth. But even so, she was fascinating, beautiful in the way of women who have heightened their best features into a captivating image.

Madeline said, "It's a great pleasure to meet you, Mr. Conway."

Her English was heavily accented, and to put her at ease,

Alan answered in French, *"Enchanté de vous rencontre, Mademoiselle."*

"Oh, please, do speak English with me—I hope to make a film in Hollywood some day, and need the practice."

"As you wish," Alan replied. The fact that she knew Dorian, and his knowledge of her relationship with Jonathan, made him more uncomfortable than he had anticipated; he fumbled nervously for a cigarette.

Madeline went on, "Last week I had the pleasure of seeing your portrait of Madame Delane, and knew that I must come to see your other works. What a fortunate coincidence that you are here today."

Alan saw a veiled glance pass between her and Foucault, and wondered if her visit to the gallery *were* a coincidence. He knew that Dorian had confided to her about him—perhaps she was just curious to meet him.

They talked for a few minutes about his paintings, then abruptly she asked Foucault, "May I speak with you privately, Louis?"

"Why, yes, of course." He called to his assistant who was hovering nearby. "Show Mademoiselle Gautier into my office," he told him. Then he said to Madeline, "I will be with you momentarily."

Before leaving the gallery she turned to Alan. "Will you wait for me? I would like to speak with you further."

It was more a command than a request, and Alan felt a twinge of annoyance, but he nodded agreeably. When she was out of sight, Foucault said, "Do not be offended—she is used to being indulged."

"So I understand."

Foucault gave a helpless shrug. "Who knows, she may want to purchase one of your paintings."

"Does she actually buy her own paintings?" Alan asked sarcastically.

"On occasion," Foucault chuckled.

A half-hour passed and Alan grew impatient. When he heard them in the hallway he stubbed out his cigarette and assumed a pose of nonchalance. As soon as they entered the gallery he noticed that Madeline seemed very pleased with herself. Foucault, too, appeared to be in good humor.

"Thank you for waiting," Madeline said. "May I make up

for the inconvenience by taking you to lunch?" She gave him a dazzling smile.

He returned the smile, his irritation weakening before her persuasive charm. "That's very kind—thank you."

She took his arm and said to Foucault. "I shall be in touch with you soon."

"I'm sure you will." he responded warmly.

Madeline took Alan to a resturant called L'Auberge Basque on the Rue de Verneuil, a narrow street between Saint Germain and the Gare d'Orsay. It was a small place decorated with Basque heraldry and filled with pungent odors of patés, cheeses and fresh coffee. They found a table near a window and ordered wine.

On the way they had exchanged ordinary pleasantries, but once they were seated Madeline came directly to the point.

"Mr. Conway, I could see that you knew who I was when we were introduced."

"Yes, Dorian mentioned you—and please, call me Alan."

"Thank you, and you must call me Madeline—" She stared at him for a few seconds, a faint smile playing at the corners of her lips.

In the soft light of the room, he found himself more impressed with her beauty; the flawless complexion was luminous and her blue eyes took on a darker, sensual quality.

"Dorian spoke of you many times," she went on. "When I heard that she had married the English director, I was very sad—I knew how much she cared for you."

"Please, I'd rather not discuss her."

"I'm sorry, I didn't mean to intrude into personal—"

"I'd prefer to talk about why we're here," Alan interrupted. "What is it you wish to discuss with me?"

Madeline's eyes flashed a look of anger. "You Americans are so direct! You have a way of turning polite conversation into a struggle of wills!"

"I'm sorry, I didn't mean to sound so rude. It's just that the subject of Dorian, or any of the St. Clairs, is a very sensitive one for me."

"I understand," Madeline replied, her voice softening. "I, too, have suffered at their hands; that is why I wanted to speak with you."

"I'm not sure I understand . . ."

"I will try to explain," she began. "It was no coincidence that I came to the gallery this morning. After seeing your portrait of Madame Delane, I called Foucault and told him to let me know when you would be there."

"Why all the intrigue?"

"There were certain things I had to discuss with him before I felt free to ask you about doing a portrait of me."

"But if it is simply a matter of a commission—"

"Ah, but it is not that simple. I don't want a portrait just to please my ego—it must accomplish more than that. To be quite frank, my relationship with Jonathan St. Clair has interfered with my career; I haven't made a film in over two years. But in the last few months that relationship has changed. Now I need something that will recapture the interest of the public and bring me some attention."

Alan was puzzled. "I'm flattered that you think a portrait of mine would do that, but I don't see how it can."

"That depends on the nature of the painting—its content, I mean, and how it is promoted. That is where Foucault comes in; he has agreed to my plan, and has many contacts among journalists and newspaper people." She leaned forward and lowered her voice. "And he is an inveterate gossip."

"This is beginning to sound more like a plot than a portrait commission."

Madeline sat back and nodded, her eyes bright and mischievous. "That is exactly what I have in mind. And part of that plot is that you will paint me nude."

Madeline's apartment was in an old, stately building on the Avenue Foch. She requested that the painting be done in the drawing room and Alan agreed; it was spacious, and filled with sunlight.

He set his easel up before a bank of windows that overlooked a beautiful formal garden. He had chosen a large canvas that would allow him to paint her almost life-sized, and set to work blocking in the composition in charcoal. But he hadn't reckoned with the complexity of Madeline's plan.

She had created a setting for the portrait; she wanted to be painted lying on an Empire chaise lounge that was partly covered by a full-length sable coat. Behind the chaise she had set a long chest cluttered with a display of objects including a pair of porcelain vases of the K'ang Hsi period, a Georgian silver coffee service, a pair of ormolu and bronze candellabra, a Louis XV mantle clock, and a collection of nineteenth-century mosaic plaques. On a low table in front of the chaise were more personal items: a jewel-studded Spanish comb, an inlaid-wood music box, and a hand-painted gilt jewel box spilling over with gems.

Alan suggested that some of the pieces be removed to make the painting appear less crowded, but Madeline insisted that they remain, offering only to let him rearrange them. In an effort to please her he spent a few days doing sketches, trying to work out a balance that would encompass all of the rare pieces, but found it impossible.

Madeline steadfastly refused to remove anything, until finally he exploded.

"This is ridiculous! I've spent days trying to get a decent composition out of this incredible pile of shit you've put together! We have to get rid of some of these things and make it all more simple!"

"Shit? You call these museum pieces shit?" she cried, outraged.

"I didn't mean it that way—"

"Everything must be in the painting!"

"This is supposed to be a portrait of you, not an antique store! Either you allow me some freedom of design or we forget the whole thing!"

There was a moment of strained silence; then she began to laugh. "An antique store! Does it look like that?"

"Well, yes—in a way—" Alan's anger melted and he stood there feeling foolish.

Madeline fell into a chair and stared at her setting, still laughing. "You're right," she said finally. "I'm getting carried away with my scheme."

"Just exactly what is your scheme?" Alan asked. "Obviously being painted nude isn't all of it."

She sat up and clasped her hands on her knees. "I can see that I must take you into my confidence; otherwise it will affect the painting. Come, sit down, and I'll try to explain it to you."

He took a chair opposite her and listened.

"I've been Jonathan St. Clair's mistress for the last three

years," she began softly. "I took less interest in my career because of him, and I must admit, I enjoyed not working. Then, a year ago, a young producer came to me with a marvelous script that was too good to turn down. But he needed money to finance the film. I went to Jonathan and he agreed to put up the principal cash, and approach his friends for the rest. I was ecstatic."

She stood up and walked to the windows. The warm afternoon light silhouetted her slim figure so that she appeared shadowy and mysterious. Alan sat quietly, enjoying her flair for dramatizing the moment.

"Then he met a young model," she continued, her voice taking on a bitter edge, "the current rage of the fashion designers. At first I thought she was just another of his escapades—he'd had many while we were together . . ."

And my mother was one of them, Alan thought, but she probably doesn't know anything about that.

"But it was more serious than I realized . . ." Madeline was saying. "He began to see more of her and less of me. Then he withdrew his offer of money for the film, and his friends followed suit. I was devastated! I took the script to people in the industry with whom I had worked, but they were afraid to take a chance on me—I had been out of pictures so long. The project fell through. Now I am alone. I've saved some money, but it won't last long. I've sold a few things, and I can sell more—but then what?"

Alan nodded sympathetically, then gestured to the assemblage on the chest and asked, "What does all this have to do with your story?"

"They are gifts from Jonathan, things he gave me during the years we spent together. I want them in the painting so that everyone can see them. Foucault has agreed to spread the word to gossip columnists about it—he's referring to it as a visual history of my affair with Jonathan."

"That's very clever of him," Alan commented dryly.

"You see," she went on, "even though we were seen in public together countless times, Jonathan always made a great pretense of merely being my 'escort,' and denied all rumors to the contrary."

"Why? Surely having a woman as glamorous as yourself would be something for him to be proud of."

Madeline smiled at the compliment. "But the man is a fool," she explained. "He considers himself a playboy, a gift to *many* women. An affair, yes—a mistress, no. He is always worried that his image will be compromised, and worse, he's terrified of his brother and what he will say. But there is a group of influential people who were our friends, who knew about us and these gifts. I shall make sure that every one of them is invited to attend the opening of your exhibit. They will understand what I have done, and it will infuriate Jonathan to see it all made so public."

"Aren't you afraid that your plan will backfire and harm your reputation?"

"That is a risk I'm willing to take. Most of those people have little respect for him anyway, and as for myself—a little scandal can be quite profitable to an actress. So you can see, with your painting, I can—how do you say it?—kill two birds with one stone? I shall embarrass him and draw a great deal of attention to myself."

"And you're not concerned about being painted nude?"

"That has nothing to do with exhibitionism, only with business. If the painting is a good one, it will rise above criticism. As a matter of fact, if all goes well you, too, will receive much notoriety that can only help further your career."

It would do more than that, Alan thought; it would be an opportunity to publicly humiliate St. Clair—a small revenge for what he had done to his mother, but revenge nevertheless.

He said to Madeline, "You offer quite a challenge."

She walked over to him and held out her hand. "Do we have an agreement?" she asked.

Alan stood up and took her hand. "We have an agreement."

The following afternoon Alan returned to Madeline's apartment to work on the painting. She was out shopping and he spent a few hours alone, doing quick watercolor studies of the composition. When she returned, she joined him in the drawing room and studied what he had done.

"You have created a really splendid design," she said.

"I want to take that out," he said, pointing to an Italian marble bust of a young girl he had loosely sketched in. "And this—" He rubbed out an indication of a small Renoir in the background. "They crowd the canvas."

"I agree," she answered. "But there is one thing I want you to consider adding—"

Before he could protest, she went to her desk, opened the top drawer, and took out a silver-framed photograph of Jonathan.

"Just to make sure that no one misses the point," she said, handing it to him with a wicked smile.

"I can see you have no wish to be subtle."

"Subtlety plays well on the screen, but not always in real life."

"I do very good portraits," he warned her. "Everyone will recognize him."

"Oh, I hope so!"

They both began to laugh, and then Alan asked, "Could you pose for a little while today? I'd like to begin blocking in your figure."

"Of course. Give me a few minutes to get out of these clothes and bathe . . ."

"Good. Now we can get to the most important *objet d'art* in the painting."

Madeline regarded him with a playful smile. "You grow more gallant every day—more French than American."

Alan took her hand and kissed it, making a little bow. She withdrew her hand slowly and gazed at him intensely. A provocative silence hung in the air between them; then she turned and left the room, glancing over her shoulder at him once before closing the door.

Alan felt a tremor of excitement pass through him. He realized that he was still holding Jonathan's photograph in his hand, and grimaced. He took it to the chest and set it into the arrangement of the other pieces so that it was featured. Stepping back, he looked at it and grinned. "I'm gonna get you by the balls, you son of a bitch!"

A few minutes later Madeline reappeared wearing a loose flowing robe. Alan was working at the easel, absorbed in the drawing. She slipped off the robe and asked quietly, "What do you want me to do?"

He looked up and caught his breath. The smooth, firm lines of her figure flowed continuously in delicate curves, at once sensual and chaste. She stood before him as serene and confident as if she had just made an entrance in a play.

"What do you want me to do?" she repeated softly.

Alan pulled himself together and approached her. He took her hand and led her to the chaise. "Sit down, with your legs extended . . ." She settled back against the sable coat. "Yes—and cross your ankles, so—your arm here, this one behind you . . . good."

He continued to fix the pose, aware that she was watching him closely, and resisted the temptation to let his fingers linger on her.

Finally, he stepped away. "Yes, that's perfect. Are you comfortable?"

She nodded, and he returned to the easel. For the next hour he worked quickly, sketching in her figure and indicating a likeness. She was looking at him directly, as he had instructed; in the finished painting she would appear to be gazing at the viewer.

Alan found his concentration beginning to break down. Once he looked up and caught her eyes moving over him with an expression of undisguised interest. He flushed, and said sharply, "Please keep your eyes still and stare directly at me."

"I am staring directly at you," she answered lazily. "And I'm also getting a little tired."

"Oh, I'm sorry. Take a break and rest for a few minutes."

She stood up and stretched, arching her body in a delicately feline series of movements. Alan carefully avoided looking at her and continued to work. She walked over to him and stood at his side. "That's lovely," she murmured, touching his arm.

He turned and said, "I have a beautiful subject . . ."

"You must be tired too. Can I get you some wine? Is there anything you want?"

His eyes swept over the perfection of her body, and he felt his heart race a little. "Under the circumstances, that's a foolish question—"

She touched his cheek with her hand. "You think I am teasing you? Well, I'm not—you're a very attractive boy . . ."

His hands went to her waist, and he drew her closer. "I'm

265

not a boy, and if I told you what I wanted, we wouldn't get any more work done for the rest of the day."

Madeline's eyes widened slightly. "The whole day?"

He bent his head so that their lips were almost touching. "The whole day and probably a good part of the evening."

"You're boasting."

"Am I? We'll see . . ."

19

Hollywood: April 1968

DORIAN FOLLOWED GRAHAM into the small screening room. While he talked with the producer of the film she sat down and rummaged in her purse for a cigarette. Someone beside her held a lighter; she leaned forward, lit the cigarette, and slouched back into her seat. A voice called out, "Let's see it!" and the room dimmed. She closed her eyes.

When she opened them, her face was on the screen in a tight close-up. She stared at it coldly, as if watching someone else. The mouth moved, pouted, and smiled, the dark eyes narrowed or widened mechanically, the voice sounded curiously unfamiliar and wooden. The camera pulled away and she saw herself walk across a spacious, tastefully decorated room, then stop to deliver a line of dialogue, and leave.

Dorian winced, seeing herself as a puppet whose strings were gently pulled to guide her from scene to scene.

The man pulling the strings was Graham. He had suggested her for the part, that of a young girl who comes between a man and his wife. It was a small but choice role, and he had convinced her and the producer that she could do it.

In the beginning Dorian had scoffed at the idea; she'd had no training, and found the whole thing faintly ridiculous. But Graham had insisted, saying that she had a natural, unaffected quality that was perfect for the part. He patiently coached her through the script, tolerant of her mistakes and kind about her inexperience. Under his tutelage she began to take more interest in what she was doing, growing enthusiastic about the possibilities of working with him.

But the first time she saw the dailies she was embarrassed and humiliated, and fled the screening room in tears. Graham consoled her and continued to be encouraging, and so she went on working, despite the tension on the set over her ineptitude. More than anything, she was determined to justify his faith in her.

Now, after weeks of getting up before dawn and working into the night, she was tired beyond caring about the lifelessness of her performance. She knew that they had both made a mistake, even if Graham wouldn't admit to it.

When the screening was over, the lights came on. Dorian listened disinterestedly to the comments of the producer, the assistant director, and the others in the room.

"You were marvelous, darling . . ."

". . . can't take my eyes off her when she's on the screen . . ."

". . . her face has a love affair with the camera."

Dorian smiled politely, hating the sound of the clichés and the way they all curried favor because she was the director's wife. Under her breath, she said to Graham, "Please, let's go. I can't take much more of this."

They left the studio and drove through the stifling night air to the Normandy-style house in Benedict Canyon that they had leased. It had been occupied, in turn, by a famous forties actress, a German director, a well-known athlete, and the producer of a now defunct rock group. Dorian disliked the place intensely; they had taken it furnished, and kept finding small mementos of each of the former tenants.

"It's like waking up after a party and discovering that most of your guests have left something behind," she told Graham. "It makes me uneasy; I keep thinking that they'll all converge on us one night to collect their belongings."

While Graham parked the car in the garage, Dorian went into the house and headed for the bar in the living room. The maid, a thin Mexican woman who spoke garbled English, came in, gave her a few indecipherably scrawled messages and left. Dorian tossed them on the bar and mixed some drinks, reflecting sourly that the woman had about as much ability to be a maid as she had to be an actress. Yet it seemed right, somehow, that the two of them were so misplaced; everyone she'd met in Hollywood seemed to have an air of confusion about who they were and what they were doing here.

She took the drinks out onto the deck that overlooked the city. A gray pall of smog had blanketed the air all day, and now the stars emerging in the dark sky glowed more faintly than the furthest lights of their neighbors' swimming pools.

Graham joined her on the deck. His tall, slim figure was immaculate in tailored sports clothes, and his thick gray hair was perfectly combed. She wondered how he managed to appear so impeccable even after working all day. At first she had admired that about him; now, for some inexplicable reason, it irritated her.

"Are we finished?" she asked. "Is there anything that has to be reshot?"

"No, it's all over, at least for you. Oh, some dubbing, perhaps, but that's all. Then, a few months of postproduction, and we can leave."

He put his arm around her shoulders and she leaned against his chest. "Good," she sighed. "This is a terrible place, Graham." Her voice sounded small and tired.

"Yes it is, isn't it," he chuckled. "But we've done good work, and I'm very pleased with you."

"All things considered," she added sarcastically.

"Darling, don't finish my sentences for me," he chided her. "You were very good. You underestimate the effect you have on the screen; you're a very beautiful girl."

"That's what everybody says. In fact, that's all they talk about, the only thing they can genuinely compliment me on. Christ! If I simply stood still for two hours, without opening my mouth, the picture would be a smash!"

"Now you do sound like an actress—insecure, afraid, never pleased with what she's done—"

"Graham, I know what good acting is—" She moved out of his arms and faced him angrily. "I'm not an actress, and you know that. This whole thing was just silly!"

He smiled confidently. "You'll be amazed when the picture is put together just how good you really are. You're tired, now; you've been working very hard. For the next few months you can take it easy, relax and have some fun . . ."

"Fun? Here? Graham, living in Hollywood is not my idea of fun! I hate these people, with their sunburned bodies and bleached brains! They only pay attention to me for three reasons—because I'm your wife, the daughter of Alexander St. Clair, and you know the third—every man I've met thinks I'm ready to jump into his bed because of the difference in our ages."

"I must admit, they do want to take advantage of that particular situation, don't they?" he said lightly. But there was a pained look in his eyes.

Dorian went into his arms and held him tightly. "Darling, let's get the hell out of here as quickly as we can . . ."

"We will, I promise. I'll try not to leave you alone too much; we can keep to ourselves, avoid the whole bunch of them."

Dorian was momentarily reassured. She reached up and kissed him. Graham's arms tightened around her and the kiss grew more passionate.

"I love you very much, my dear," he murmured. "I want nothing more than to be with you and take care of you."

Dorian smiled. "You're the only man I've ever met that I didn't have to do battle with."

He picked her up and carried her toward the bedroom. "Can we postpone dinner for a little while?" he asked softly.

"Yes, for as long as you like." She put her head against his shoulder and lay in his arms like a child being soothed.

❦

New York

Jennings stopped to talk with one of the ushers in the theater, then hurried on to join David. As they walked out into the street, David asked, "Who was that? Someone new in your life?"

"No, just a kid I met last year. You're the new man in my life, didn't you know?" He took David's hand and squeezed it.

David pulled away roughly. "Don't do that in public . . ."

"Sorry." They walked for a few minutes in silence, then Jennings asked, "How did you like the play?"

They had just seen *Boys in the Band,* which had opened a few days before. David hadn't wanted to go, but Jennings insisted.

"Well, it certainly wasn't Noel Coward's *Design For Living.*"

"I don't understand—what do you mean?"

"I happen to enjoy comedies where elegant people in ele-

270

gant clothes move around elegant sets and make elegant witti-
cisims."

"How terrifically elegant for you! I take it you didn't like
Boys in the Band because it wasn't elegant?"

"It was shit! Self-indulgent, hysterical, not particularly
funny—and it didn't have a second act!"

"Are you sure you didn't like it?" Jennings asked innocently, making David laugh. "Seriously," he went on, "I
thought it was a very brave and honest play. Look how the
audience responded."

"That group of giggling faggots was no audience," David
said loftily. "They're masochists who enjoy being whipped
with a public display of their own perversions."

"Christ! Thank God you're not a critic. Okay, sweetie,
bury your head in the sand and your ass in the closet, if that
makes you happy. Where would you like to go now? Home
to be perverted with me, or to the baths, where you can
spread it around in greater numbers?"

"Fuck off, you fairy dancer! And don't call me sweetie!"

Jennings danced ahead of him, bowing low as he skipped
backwards. "Yes, master, whatever master wishes . . ."

"You asshole, behave yourself!"

Later, sitting in a restaurant in the village, David talked
about Dorian. "She's just finished making a film in Hollywood with her husband. They'll be going back to England in
a few weeks. I talked to her last night. According to her,
we should go out there for a vacation—the blond, blue-
eyed beach boys are as ripe as the oranges. She asked for
you . . ."

"I really enjoyed meeting her when she was here. What
else did she say—about me, I mean."

David smiled. "Only that she thought you were good for
me, that I needed someone like you to keep me from going
bonkers."

"Do I?"

"Do you what?" David teased. "Yes, you help, but don't
push your luck."

"Massa goin' to beat me?" Jennings laughed. He saw a
dark look cross David's face, and said quickly, "Sorry, that
was an inappropriate thing to say."

271

David leaned forward and whispered angrily, "I didn't hurt that kid at the baths—I was just drunk!"

"I know—but you might have, and just because he resembled Alan."

"You really are a prick!"

"You're right! I also happen to care a great deal about you."

David remained silent and Jennings went on quietly, "You've been flagellating yourself about that incident with Alan ever since it happened a year ago! I understand why you turned on that kid at the baths, but you weren't drunk, just angry—and not at Alan, but yourself . . ."

"Don't play living room psychiatrist with me!"

"If I don't, who will? Your father?"

Suddenly David began to laugh. "I know you're trying to help, but please, don't bring my father into this—I may lose my dinner!"

"Christ, you're impossible! That's probably why I love you."

A woman sitting nearby looked up at them sharply, and David blushed furiously. But Jennings saved the moment by proclaiming, "You're the best brother a man ever had!"

On the street a few minutes later, David asked, "Do you want to stop in at Julius's for a drink?"

"No—it's late, and I have a rehearsal in the morning. Besides, I've heard that the cops have been harassing all the bars in the area . . ."

"Okay, then we'll catch a cab at the next corner and I'll drop you off."

"Why don't you stay over? I'm not that tired."

"I've got a staff meeting in the morning. Dear old Dad is demanding a weekly account of all my doings."

They walked along the deserted streets, hearing the sound of their footfalls echo lightly in the stillness. Jennings looked over at David and smiled. "We've known each other a year," he said softly.

David nodded. "I know—want me to get you an anniversary present?"

Jennings moved closer and put his arm around David's waist. "You're all the present I want."

Just then, out of the dense shadows of a narrow alley that lay between two buildings, they heard someone whisper, "Hey faggots, wanna suck some stiff dick?"

David froze in place. Jennings took his arm and urged him on. A young Puerto Rican boy stepped out of the shadows and called, "Hey, look what I got for you."

David turned around. The boy was rubbing his crotch and smiling. In the pale street light his face was sallow and corrupt; a ragged moustache drooped incongruously over childish lips, and his eyes were darkly taunting.

David took a step forward and said, "Fuck off, spic!"

"Oh, a tough guy!" The boy made sucking noises with his mouth.

David began to go for him when a knife blade suddenly gleamed in the boy's hand and two other boys stepped out of the darkness behind him.

"You gonna take us all, cocksucker?" the youth jeered.

For a tense moment, no one moved. Then David yelled, "Yes, you little bastards—all of you!"

He lunged forward, taking the boy by surprise, and grabbed at the hand holding the knife. It swept over his arm, cutting through his coat. He lashed out, his fist connecting with the boy's throat. Behind him, he heard Jennings groan from a blow; the other two boys had him pinned against the wall and were hammering at him with their fists. David threw himself against them, catching one in the groin with his foot, and smashing the other in the head.

"David, look out!" Jennings cried.

The boy with the knife had recovered and was coming at him, the blade upraised. David ducked as the knife flashed down and landed a solid punch in the boy's stomach; the boy doubled over with a gasp and dropped the knife. David grabbed him by throat and began choking him. Then, holding him down, he punched him again and again.

Jennings tore at his arms, yelling, "Stop it, you're killing him!"

David let the boy go and looked up, his eyes blinking wildly. "What—?"

Jennings pulled him to his feet. "The other kids have run off—let's get the hell out of here!"

David's face was white, his mouth slack. "Did I kill him?"

"I don't think so—he's moving. C'mon, the cops may be along any minute!"

They staggered up the street in a half run, until they neared a well-lit intersection. Jennings hailed a cab and they fell into the back seat.

David's sleeve was ragged from where it had been cut, and there were bruises on his face.

Jennings said, "You'd better come to my place and clean up."

"If you hadn't stopped me I would have killed that kid." David looked at Jennings's face and cursed. "Christ! They hurt you!"

"I'll live—I've had worse. But you were great, a real tiger!"

"You've had that happen to you before?"

"Many times," Jennings sighed. "It goes with the territory."

"Shit!"

At Jennings's apartment they cleaned each other's bruises tenderly.

"We look like a couple of pugs who just came out of a boxing match," Jennings said.

David grimaced and picked up his drink. He sat down on the bed and stared ahead, a haunted, fearful expression on his face.

"Hey, snap out of it," Jennings said cheerfully. "We've just had a good old-fashioned New York mugging, that's all."

David stared up at him thoughtfully. "I liked it," he said, his voice expressionless.

"What?"

"I liked beating up that kid. I enjoyed it . . ."

"What do you mean, you enjoyed it?"

David smiled crookedly, but tears glistened in his eyes. "I got a kick out of it . . . it excited me, here." He gripped his crotch.

Jennings sat down beside him. "That doesn't mean anything," he said quietly. "I've heard that men in battle experience the same thing—"

"I was excited. I still am . . ." He looked at Jennings steadily.

The dancer smiled and drew him into his arms. "That's what I'm here for," he said softly. "Just remember, you don't have to hit me."

20

Paris

ALAN LEARNED THAT Madeline's scheme included more than
just humiliating Jonathan; she was out to promote herself,
Alan, and her portrait.

With the singlemindedness of an ambitious publicist, she
saw to it that she and Alan were seen in public as often as
possible. They spent many evenings dining at exclusive
restaurants, going to the theater, making the rounds of night-
clubs and cafés. Madeline was recognized everywhere they
went, and gossip columnists began to comment on their ap-
parances together. Alan's fall exhibit was mentioned frequently, and Madeline made sure that everyone knew it
would include a portrait of her that would cause a sensation.
Journalists made repeated references to her former affair with
Jonathan, which delighted her; she knew how uncomfortable
that would make him. Alan, thoroughly enjoying the attention they received, also took pleasure in the thought of Jonathan's discomfort; not only was he working on a painting that
might ruin St. Clair socially, but he had become the lover of
the man's one-time mistress. But that wasn't enough to make
up for Jonathan's betrayal of his mother; the bitter, painful
words Marie had written in her journal still haunted him.

Late one night, as they lay in bed, Madeline chuckled
while reading the latest accounts of their activities in *Paris
Match*.

"It's going well, this little plan of mine," she said with satisfaction. "I've made the columns more in the last few weeks
than I have all year. Everyone is intrigued by the brilliant
American artist I am being seen with, and they are all curious about the painting. I have even received calls from pro-

ducers who thought I had died or gone to Hollywood! Ah, here's another mention of Jonathan—he must be furious!"

"He doesn't like publicity, does he?"

"No, he loathes it. He's so afraid his brother will find out what kind of a life he really leads. That does not stop him, of course, from behaving like an idiot, with his women and gambling. If his family only knew what he was involved in . . ."

"Oh? Something illegal?" Alan asked casually, to hide his interest.

But Madeline had found another story about them in the magazine and started reading it aloud. When she was finished, she tossed the magazine to the floor impatiently. "Journalists! They are just so many parasites. It's ridiculous to have to sell one's self this way instead of being able to depend on the quality of one's talents."

"I thought you were enjoying all of it."

"I've been doing this for years. The enjoyment is only in seeing them dance as I snap my fingers. For the rest, it is very demeaning—"

"And tiring," Alan agreed, yawning.

"Ah well, sometimes even great talent must be heralded by bullshit!"

Alan laughed and kissed her lightly. "Very neatly put. But it's beginning to wear me out. I can't party all night and work all day; I need some rest in order to be brilliant, or else my paintings will begin to look like the work of a deranged abstract expressionist."

"It is not parties that keep you up all night," she whispered, running her fingertips over his thighs.

Alan pulled her close and slipped his legs between hers, moved his hands down her back to her hips.

"You see," Madeline sighed. "You have absolutely no self-control."

"You're right, but it's more fun staying up for this."

℘
.

Jonathan was in his office at the hotel, taking a call on his private line. His face was taut as he listened to voice on the

276

other end say, "We're very concerned—you've been mentioned so frequently in the papers these last few weeks."

"It's nothing to worry about, Ellis," Jonathan replied. "You know how columnists exaggerate."

"I suggest you try to be more careful—we have too much at stake to take any risks. Does she knew anything about our operations?"

"Madeline? Of course not! I've never confided in her—or anyone. Now tell me what you want, or did you call merely to criticize my social life?"

"A man named Emile Bernard is coming in from Marseilles. He will be checking into the hotel tomorrow night. On Thursday he will leave for London, then he will go to Amsterdam on Friday. See to it that all the necessary arrangements are made."

"Will he be using the name Bernard at each hotel?"

"Yes. He's also requested some entertainment; he prefers not to go out, so you will arrange something? He has somewhat peculiar tastes—be careful who you send to him."

An expression of disgust crossed Jonathan's face. "How many girls? Or is it boys?" he asked impatiently.

Ellis Morel laughed. "Girls—and two should be sufficient."

"Is there anything else?"

"No, that's all for the moment." Morel's voice abruptly became warm and friendly. "Will I see you later at the club?"

"Yes, I'll drop by later this evening . . ."

"Good, we can have a drink together."

The line went dead and Jonathan hung up the receiver; beads of perspiration dotted his forehead. He took a handkerchief from his pocket, patted his face, then looked down at the newspaper on his desk. A photograph of Madeline clinging to Alan's arm stared back at him.

※

It was the early part of May; Alan had been in Paris a little over four months. Despite his affair with Madeline, thoughts of Dorian and the summer they had spent together emerged at odd times of the day or night to fill him with anger and despair. He turned to his work for solace, and to Madeline for escape from the persistent memories.

He felt obligated to keep in touch with Olivia, reporting only the progress he was making in preparing his show, but not mentioning the portrait of Madeline. She wrote back that she hoped to be in Paris for the opening, that Benson and Rabin were pleased by his success with Louis Foucault, and that his attempts at discretion were wasted; even in New York they read *Paris Match*.

Alan continued to work, not only on Madeline's portrait but on other canvases and sketches of people he saw in the parks and on the streets: workmen carrying their loaves of bread under each arm early in the morning, couples strolling through the Luxembourg Gardens, children playing at the pond in the Tuileries. Foucault expressed great enthusiasm, adding that all the publicity he was receiving with Madeline would guarantee many sales.

Totally absorbed in his own pursuits, Alan was only marginally aware of events taking place across the world: the escalation of the war in Viet Nam, the assassination of Martin Luther King, the Soviet intervention in Czechoslovakia. In the neighboring countries of Spain, West Germany, Italy and Poland, there were student uprisings protesting government policies.

But all of this meant little to Alan; he felt as removed from the increasing turmoil as if he were living in another time. Even when Madeline brought these events to his attention, he remained uninterested.

But on May 3, an incident took place that began to erode the shell of his indifference.

Daniel Cohn-Bendit, a student leader from the suburban Nantorre University campus who had already led a small and little-publicized protest there, inspired hundreds of Sorbonne students to demonstrate against repressive government control of the university system. When the police were called, a riot ensued. There were fights, injuries and arrests. And that was just the beginning.

The following morning Alan was at Madeline's, working on the painting while she read the somewhat sketchy accounts of the Sorbonne demonstration. When she had finished, she exclaimed, "Bastards! They think they can preserve the government's credibility by distorting the facts. They are making a big mistake, but the fools won't realize it until the situation is out of control!"

Alan held a mall stick against the edge of the canvas to steady his hand and carefully brushed in the design of a porcelain vase. "I'm surprised to find you political," he murmured. "It's so far removed from the kind of life you lead."

She turned on him with uncharacteristic vehemence. "I am not 'political,' I am human! What happens anywhere affects all of us, eventually. You've been fortunate; you escaped the sufferings of war and deprivation. It is different for Europeans, but you are too young to understand that. All you are concerned with is your work!"

Alan stopped painting and looked at her calmly. "It has more importance in my life than anything else."

Later, when he was alone, he began to think seriously about what she had said. He had always been apolitical, and now realized it was because of his mother. Despite the horrors of her war-time experiences, or because of them, Marie had refused to take any interest in contemporary political events. In the process she had removed herself, and Alan too, from all concerns outside the security of their provincial existence in Bay Shore, and his artistic talent.

But now he was living only a few blocks away from the beginnings of a political hurricane—the Sorbonne.

Between May 6 and May 11, increasing numbers of students had daily confrontations with the police and the Compagnies Républicaines de Sécurité, commonly called the CRS, a government security force that was notorious for its brutalities.

In streets around the university students erected barricades constructed of overturned cars, tree grilles, pieces of timber and the cobblestones beneath their feet, the same stones that had armed the peasants in the Revolution of 1798. Police wearing gas masks and helmets and wielding long hardwood clubs advanced, and were met by a barrage of rocks, bottles and chunks of wood. They fired back tear gas grenades until the air in the Latin Quarter was unbreathable. Throughout the nights more barricades were erected, and the battles raged, involving even innocent bystanders on the streets.

The ranks of demonstrators swelled as previously apathetic

students and young unemployed workers grouped together, finding a common voice to express their anger and frustration at the monolithic workings of an archaic government.

Alan thought of the demonstrations as similar to the sit-ins taking place in American universities and the civil rights marches he remembered from the early sixties. His initial shock at seeing the violence in the streets had quickly given way to a desire to capture what was happening. Skirting the periphery of the demonstrations, from the vantage point of shadowed doorways, he sketched with the cool detachment of an observer. Although his sympathies were with the students, he enjoyed the distance he kept from their struggle, seeing himself not only as an outsider, but as someone who could seize the moment to depict it in art. He believed that these protests, like their American counterparts, would be over in a few days and everything would return to normal. But he was mistaken.

The unions, sensing that the time was right to press their own long-neglected demands, decided to stage a nationwide general strike. By May 13, one could not get a taxi on the streets of Paris, and only a few of the Metro trains were running. On that day hundreds of thousands of workers, students, and other citizens marched through the Left Bank in protest against the government.

Strike actions began to take place all over the city: the national television and radio network struck for greater freedom of production, and even the Folies Bergére closed, the chorus girls trading their costumes for picket signs.

City services passed into memory. Gas and electricity were intermittently provided. Garbage removal had ceased, and soon there were ten-foot-high mounds of refuse along the famous avenues and boulevards, causing a threat of rats.

With the refineries on strike gasoline supplies dwindled, and cars were abandoned or left at home. The usually congested thoroughfares were virtually empty of traffic.

Food supplies were scarce, and snatched up the day they arrived on the shelves.

On the night of May 24, when President de Gaulle was scheduled to respond to the strikers' challenges, the entire city was at a standstill.

That evening Alan was in his studio, working on some watercolors of what he had seen in the streets: students taunting the police from the tops of barricades, blackened autos piled up like charred corpses, people crouched against walls covered with political posters, their faces reflecting grim determination and undaunted anger.

When he finished, he glanced at his watch; de Gaulle's speech had already started. He turned on the radio and stretched out on the bed to listen to it.

The president's message was long, rambling and conversational. Its conclusion was an offer to the French people: a referendum would be held, and citizens would have to vote on his proposed reforms for a new society. Then he added a threat: if they voted against him, he would step down from office.

Alan thought de Gaulle was trying to convince the people that the alternative to his rule would be total chaos. He wondered how they would react. As the strains of the *Marseillaise* concluded the program, he fell asleep.

He awoke to a darkened room and the sound of buzzing static from the radio. He switched it off and turned on a light. It was nine-thirty. Madeline was supposed to have picked him up for dinner around eight. He grew concerned; she had told him that there would be several demonstrations tonight in different parts of the city.

Still drowsy, he opened a window and leaned out for a breath of air. The stench of garbage assailed his nostrils; a mound of refuse outside his building had risen to almost six feet.

"I might as well have stayed in New York," he grumbled. "At least there the garbage complements the neighborhoods."

He looked to see if anything was happening, but the streets were ominously quiet. There was only the sound of a single siren in the distance.

Suddenly the phone rang, and he hurried to answer it.

"Alan, it's Madeline." Her voice sounded anxious.

"Where are you?"

"I ran into traffic barricades at the Place de la Concorde, and when I tried to go another way, I ran out of gas. I'm stranded, and a large group is starting to converge nearby.

I'm afraid of trying to get to your place alone. Can you come for me?"

"Where are you?"

"About a block from the Bourse, at the corner of Rue de Richelieu and Rue du 4 Septembre. Do you know where that is?"

"Yes. I'll leave at once."

"Please be careful. People on the streets are very angry about de Gaulle's speech . . ."

Alan made his way across the Pont Royal to the Right Bank, and through the avenue that divided the Tuileries from the Louvre. Despite the increasing number of people gathering, there were no police or CRS in sight. He heard someone say that they were dispersing crowds at the Gare de Lyon, and felt relieved; perhaps he and Madeline could get back without being caught in a confrontation on this side. Once they were over the Pont Royal, it was only a few steps to his apartment, where they would be safe.

As he approached the Place de la Bourse, his confidence was shaken by the sight of thousands of demonstrators filling the streets. He tried to see the corner where Madeline was waiting, but the dense mass swirling around him made it impossible. He pushed and shoved to keep from being driven backwards. Then there was a sudden change in the direction of movement; the crowd shifted toward the Bourse. Alan slipped out of the mob to get a clearer view of the streets ahead of him. He saw Madeline standing under a shattered streetlight, trying to avoid being pulled into the crowd surging past her. He fought his way to where she stood and swept her into his arms as the tide of demonstrators carried them into the center of the throng surrounding the Bourse.

The air was filled with cries of "Burn the Bourse!" The building was the stock exchange, a monument to the elite who dominated the government. Now it was under attack by the workers whose labors were its foundation. Alan and Madeline watched helplessly as two or three hundred people rushed up the steps, crashed through the wrought-iron fence that encircled the entrance and smashed the plate-glass windows in the front doors. They swept inside like a rushing flood and a triumphant cheer went up through the crowd. Inside the lobby, the frenzied mob went on a rampage of destruction, hurling rocks at two iron and glass chandeliers swinging from long suspension cables, and tearing apart wooden telephone booths used by brokers. Outside the building others collected packing crates and piles of rubbish, and carried them into the lobby. There was a sound of exploding Molotov cocktails, followed by the shrieks of people trying to escape the hail of broken glass and leaping flames. The Bourse was engulfed by fire.

The crowd gave vent to wild cheers as the blaze crackled and soared against the black night. Over the din came the sound of sirens; firefighters were on the way. While a few people stayed to erect barricades in front of the burning building to keep it from being saved, the main body of the mob turned to leave, sweeping Alan and Madeline along. The crowd poured into the Rue de Rivoli, smashing windows indiscriminately. Alan held Madeline tightly to keep from being separated. Shards of glass sprayed over them; several pieces struck her and drew blood.

They crossed the Pont Neuf. Below them the waters of the Seine coursed darkly, and a chill breeze blew against their faces like a whispered warning. On the other side of the bridge the crowd merged into the streets of the Latin Quarter, where thousands of people were collected. Over the noise and confusion came the cry, "The CRS!"

The black-helmeted troops in their gray vans began to launch tear gas grenades, sending clouds billowing out through the streets. The crowd responded by throwing cobblestones, and troops charged into the heavily gassed areas to beat the choking, blinded demonstrators.

Alan and Madeline began to run, their eyes stinging from the gas. They had been driven past Alan's neighborhood by the crowds, and now their only thought was to find a place to hide. The CRS was making hundreds of arrests and beating people indiscriminately with their truncheons.

On the Boulevard Saint Germain, Alan pulled Madeline into a narrow alley. They crouched in the shadows, gasping for breath, as the search-lights mounted on the top of CRS vans swept over the street, looking for anyone seeking shelter in doorways or behind cars. Fearful of being discovered, they moved further out of sight into a nearby heap of rotting garbage. As one of the vans passed them, its light illuminated the

283

refuse for a moment and Alan caught a glimpse of more than a dozen startled rats.

Madeline muffled the screams with her hands, and as soon as the van was gone they raced from the site. Sirens shrieked all around them and the air was thick with cries of pain and the crackling of fires.

"I can't run any more," Madeline gasped, leaning against a wall.

"We can't stop now—" He saw a figure beckoning to them from a doorway across the street, and said, "There's someone who can help us!"

Madeline trembled; she was on the verge of collapse. Alan picked her up and dashed across the street as more CRS vans turned the corner and headed toward them. A young boy thrust open the door and gestured to the stairs leading to the second floor. As soon as they were inside he closed and bolted the door and followed Alan, directing him to a room overlooking the street.

Alan put Madeline down on a cot near the windows and anxiously rubbed her hands. She looked up at him weakly. "I'm all right," she whispered. "Are we safe?"

"Yes, I think so. Don't try to get up—just rest."

The boy was standing by the windows, staring out into the street. "They've passed," he said softly. He came over to them and looked down at Madeline. "Is she all right?"

"Yes—just exhausted. We got caught at the Bourse when they set it on fire." Alan looked around the darkened room. "Could we turn on a light?"

"No, it's better this way; the building looks deserted." His thin face was pale in the light coming from the street, and Alan saw that they were about the same age. The boy's clothes were torn and dirty, and a pants leg was ripped, revealing a crust of dried blood on his leg.

"I can't stay," he told Alan. "I have to get back to the Sorbonne and help."

"But you'll be caught if you go out; they're beating and arresting everyone on the streets."

"I shall have to take my chances—my friends are waiting for me. I came back here for some food and cigarettes." He pointed to a cardboard carton on the floor.

"Is there anything I can do?" Alan asked.

The boy stared at him for a few seconds. "You are an American, yes?"

Alan nodded.

"You speak French very well." He went back to the windows. "I think I can make it now, the street is quiet. Will you watch from the window for me? I shall wait at the bottom of the stairs. If no one appears, call my name and I will run." He took Alan's hand and shook it. "I am Alain Cicoli," he said.

Alan smiled, pressing his hand warmly. "I'm Alan Conway."

"Ah," the boy grinned, "we are namesakes."

He picked up the carton and went to the door, then stopped to look back at Madeline. "She is Madeline Gautier, the actress, isn't she?"

"Yes—"

"I am a great fan of hers. Take care of her, and when this is all over, tell her I want an autographed picture."

"Yes, I will . . ."

The boy nodded and left the room. Alan went to the windows and looked up and down the street. There was no one there. He called Alain's name softly, and a moment later saw him running across the street and down the block. Suddenly three riot officers appeared out of an alleyway and took off after him. The first one caught up with him and dealt a swift blow to the boy's head with his truncheon. The boy fell, spilling his carton and trying to cover his face as the other officers circled him, swinging their clubs.

Alan turned away from the sight, choked by nausea, his eyes blurred with tears. A terrible sense of weakness shot through him, as if the ground had given way under his feet.

He awoke to the sound of Madeline moaning in pain. In the cold dawn light her white skin showed bruises and dried blood where her arms and legs had been scratched and cut. Alan lifted her from the cot and they staggered down the stairs to the street.

They walked cautiously through the early morning. There were signs of devastation everywhere; automobiles overturned and gutted, trees lying uprooted as if torn by a hurricane, garbage scattered haphazardly, debris, political posters and pamphlets covering the streets. A few dazed shopkeepers stood bewildered in front of their stores, surveying the damage.

At Alan's apartment, Madeline withdrew to the bathroom to bathe while Alan made a pot of coffee. He caught a glimpse of himself in the mirror; his face was hollow-eyed and drawn, etched with grim lines. There were streaks of dirt and ash in his hair, and his clothes were torn.

Madeline came out of the bathroom wearing his robe and a towel around her head. She sank into a chair and picked up her torn dress. "I'll need some pins to keep this together until I get home," she said dully.

Alan put a cup of coffee on the table beside her. She looked up at him and asked, "What happened to the boy who helped us?"

"The police got him."

"Oh God," she sighed.

Alan knelt beside her and put his arms around her. "Do you want to sleep for a while? I'll go out and try to find some food for breakfast."

"No, I'll be all right—the coffee is enough." She stood up and went to the mirror, dried her hair and began to brush it out. "You look worse than I do," she said to him. "Go take a shower—I think there's still some hot water left."

Alan went into the bathroom. A few minutes later he emerged, clean and in fresh clothes.

Madeline was standing by his worktable looking at the sketches he had finished the night before. "When did you do these?" she asked.

"During the last week—do you like them?"

"They are wonderful, so different from your other work . . ." She spread the drawings out on the table. "They are powerful, frightening . . ."

"I'm taking them to Foucault. I want them in the show."

"He won't accept them. He is unsympathetic to the student cause, and won't risk offending his clientele with radical art."

"But I'm not a radical! These sketches are good, they're the first work I've done that contain some truth, that aren't just pretty pictures!"

He stopped, suddenly realizing what he was saying, then laughed.

"Christ, it's really ironic. I've finally learned something important about myself and my art, and I can't do anything with it. I've trapped myself into a successful image, and now I have to go on cultivating that image in order to continue being successful."

"But you are young," Madeline said. "You will find that success can make you free to go on doing important work. Isn't that what you wanted? I assumed that's why you worked so hard—to earn enough to be free to live and paint as you like."

That should have been the reason, he thought, but it wasn't; his ambition for success had been fired by the sight of a great estate on Long Island, and falling in love with the girl who lived there.

"You are smiling," Madeline said. "Is it because you agree with what I've said?"

"No—it's because I've just realized how foolish I've been."

"Then you have learned something very valuable." She kissed him softly. "Now give me another cup of coffee, then I must leave."

Alan turned on the radio and they listened to a description of the casualties of the evening before: one thousand demonstrators had been injured, two hundred hospitalized; two men had died.

And in that carnage, something else had died, Alan thought: the naiveté of an artist whose values had been distorted by absurd, romantic dreams.

21

London: September

GRAHAM TAPPED LIGHTLY at the door to Dorian's bedroom. When there was no answer, he opened it and walked in. She was lying in bed, arms tucked under the pillows, her dark hair trailing across her shoulders. He tiptoed closer and watched her for a few minutes, taking secret pleasure in seeing her asleep. He missed waking up beside her, missed the warmth and scent of her body; it had been weeks since they'd been together. He felt a sharp ache of desire, and turned away, only to catch a glimpse of himself in the mirror over her vanity.

He approached it warily, as he would an enemy. The pouches under his eyes had grown thicker, the lines across his brow and around his mouth deeper. Small folds of flesh were apparent below his chin, and when he moved his head, his neck wrinkled into a fine web. He glanced at Dorian's reflection, then back at himself. I'm fifty-four, he thought bitterly, and I still want her like a boy of twenty.

Dorian turned over and flung an arm across the covers. Graham walked up to the bed and sat down beside her. "Are you awake?" he asked softly.

She gave a muffled reply and opened her eyes to narrow slits. "What time is it?" she asked raggedly.

"Almost nine. I have to leave for a meeting. Are you awake enough to hear me?"

She sat up, rubbed her eyes and nodded. "I can hear you."

Lowering his eyes to avoid seeing the movement of her breasts under the thin silk nightgown, he noticed his hands. They looked veined and crabbed against the white sheets; he shifted them to his lap, covering one with the other.

"I'm giving a dinner tonight at Claridge's for some men

who are interested in investing in the new film," he told her. "Can you be there?"

"Why?" she asked sullenly. "You know that sort of thing bores me."

"I know how deadly they can be, darling, but I would appreciate it."

"And I would loathe it," she replied, stifling a yawn.

He smiled to cover his disappointment and leaned over to kiss her, hoping to tease her into a better humor. But she drew back so that his lips only grazed her hair.

"Come on, sweetheart," he cajoled. "Help the old boy scrounge some money from the stiffnecks with your girlish charm." He grinned rakishly, feeling like a fool.

Dorian slid back against the pillows and sighed, "All right, all right—for God's sake don't beg! I'll be there, with my 'girlish charm' going full tilt."

Graham flushed with anger and resentment. He stood up and said stiffly, "Thank you, my dear. I'll see you tonight." He left the room, restraining himself from slamming the door.

Dorian looked after him, feeling ashamed. A desperate sadness came over her; why had she deliberately hurt him like that? He didn't deserve what she was doing to him—it wasn't his fault that their marriage had degenerated into a series of small, tense struggles. She tried to remember what had attracted her to Graham, what she had found in him that was amusing or romantic. But all she could think of was her own unhappiness, her feeling of being trapped.

I'll make it up to him tonight, she decided wearily. I'll wear something exciting, arrive early to greet his guests, be the charming hostess. Suddenly she thought of her mother. She could hear Vivian's voice with a frightening clarity: "Leave the arrangements to me, Alex. I'll take care of everything—the menu, the flowers, the wine—yes, dear, I'll seat them according to your plan . . . yes, dear . . . yes, dear—"

Tears began to flow, tears of anger, self-pity and fear. She turned her face into the pillows with a muffled sob.

❧
Paris: October

Alan was nervous; tonight was his opening at the Galerie Foucault. He checked his appearance again in the mirror. The suit looked good; expensive, fashionable, beautifully tailored. His thick, dark hair had been cut so that it fell a little below his collar, and he had shaved so close that his skin gleamed. He appeared the picture of youthful success—exactly the right image for tonight. He gave himself a cynical smile, turned out the lights and left the apartment.

It was a balmy autumn evening, and he decided to walk the short distance to the gallery. Seeing the streets so calm and undisturbed gave him a curious sense of unreality; it was as if the May riots had never occurred. Only shredded remnants of political posters still clinging to brick walls and unrepaired breaks in the pavements were left as reminders of the fragility of social order. Those savage nights had left him with a better understanding of the city; its beautiful façade thinly disguised dark and turbulent depths, and mirrored his own understanding of himself. Tonight he was like the city—underneath his carefully groomed appearance lay a turmoil of conflicting ideas, fears and desires. The thought sobered him as he hurried toward the gallery.

Turning the corner of the Rue de Seine, he saw cars crowded along the narrow street and cabs depositing guests. Newsmen and photographers were busy taking pictures of the arrivals and making notes on the distinguished names in attendance. Madeline had invited many friends in the film industry, and Foucault had carefully selected a list of his most esteemed clients: lawyers, industrialists, bankers, and diplomats.

Madeline and Foucault had done their work well; everyone in their circles knew about the painting of the actress, and tonight they undoubtedly anticipated a scene. Well, Alan decided, if success means riding in on the coattails of a scandal, let's do it.

Shouldering his way through the press at the front door, he searched the gallery for Madeline. She was standing by the bar with friends, and, catching sight of Alan, waved him over.

"It's going beautifully," she whispered.

"Has Jonathan arrived yet?"

"No. Olivia called Foucault earlier this afternoon and said they would be late. Did she call you?"

"Yes, but only to say that she'd see me here." He stepped back and looked at her. "You're a vision tonight."

Madeline laughed and turned gracefully, making the skirt of her Schiaparelli gown unfold like a slow-moving cloud.

"This looks familiar," Alan said, touching the ruby, emerald and pearl choker fastened around her throat. It was a gift from Jonathan.

Her eyes gleamed maliciously. "In the painting it is all I am wearing. I thought the photographers might enjoy seeing it—"

"You'll be lucky if Jonathan doesn't rip it right off your neck!"

"I depend on you to protect my honor."

"I don't think either of us have any left."

Foucault came up to them, beaming. "It's a great success, my boy! We've sold half the paintings and there have been several inquiries about portrait commissions." He took Madeline's arm. "Come, they want to take pictures of both of you in front of the portrait."

They spent the next hour posing in the smaller gallery, where the painting of Madeline dominated the room. Waiters passed among the guests with trays of champagne, everyone offered Alan their congratulations, Madeline introduced him to a dizzying succession of well-known film personalities and Foucault made sure that he spoke with an art critic from *Réalités*."

Alan broke away and stepped out into the courtyard for a breath of air. He stood in the shadow of a chestnut tree, where he would be unnoticed. His head was swimming with excitement and champagne. The evening had been a great success so far, but he was more painfully aware than ever that it all hinged on his painting of Madeline. He had heard the whispered comments on the audacity of the portrait, seen the guests looking for Jonathan's arrival. Everyone was waiting for the evening's denouement.

Of course, he had been praised for his talent: his sense of color, draftsmanship, technique. And almost everybody had remarked on his youth. He had even overheard Foucault say that "early Conways" would grow more valuable as Alan matured in his abilities and became famous.

"Famous"; the word sounded foreign on his lips. For the first time he was aware of his effect on a large number of people. His underground success with the portrait of Sylvester Peake, the show in New York at Benson and Rabin's, had been only the first stirrings of what was happening here. Tonight had launched him into the world of success. The thought filled him with a sense of power and a feeling of uneasiness. Since the nights of the riots he had begun to think about his obligation as an artist—not to the people who were scurrying to buy his paintings tonight for their investment value or as a souvenir of a scandalous event, but to the drawings and watercolors he had done in the streets during the riots. In the last few months he had come to realize that if success were to have any real meaning for him, it would have to be in paintings that had more universality than those on display tonight.

He was about to leave his hiding place and return to the gallery when a car pulled up to the entrance. An attendant opened the back door and Jonathan stepped out. Alan drew deeper into the shadows, his heart pounding; this was the first time he had seen the man since the night on Long Island. For a moment he remembered being held in the grip of Alexander's hands while Jonathan beat him. As he started forward he saw Olivia emerge from the car, then he froze in disbelief. There was someone else with them—Dorian!

Standing on the sidewalk, she paused to search in her evening bag and drew out a cigarette. Simply gowned in black silk, with no jewelry and wearing her long dark hair combed back, she had the elegant, haunting beauty of a dancer poised at the edge of a stage. Jonathan held a lighter for her and the bright flame momentarily illuminated her face. In that instant, all of Alan's bitterness and resentment disappeared.

As they started toward the gallery, one of Foucault's assistants saw them and signaled to the others inside. They were stopped at the door by a crush of journalists and photographers. Dorian and Olivia fell back, but Jonathan, glaring furiously, strode through the crowd.

Alan took a deep breath and stepped out of the shadows.

Sensing someone near her, Dorian turned and saw him. Her eyes searched his face for a sign of welcome.

"I didn't expect you," he said in a husky whisper.

"It was Olivia's idea . . . I wasn't sure you'd want to see me."

Olivia approached them and Alan embraced her. "I'm glad you came," he said.

She stepped back and examined his face anxiously. "Are you sure you can handle seeing Jonathan again?"

Alan smiled. "Yes, I'm sure—" He gestured to the filled gallery. "This is all for me; he's on my turf tonight."

Olivia glanced through the door at the clamor of people around her brother. "There's obviously more than just an exhibit opening going on, with all these photographers and newspaper people. What's it all about? Jonathan's been foaming at the mouth all day, but he refused to tell me anything."

"Didn't Foucault tell you?"

"Tell me what?"

Alan groaned. "We'd better get inside; I'm sure the action has already started."

He steered the two women through the main gallery to the smaller room where they could hear Madeline's voice raised in anger.

"How dare you speak to me that way?"

Jonathan was standing in front of the painting, his face white with rage. He turned to leave and saw Alan in the doorway with Olivia and Dorian. Staring at Alan with an expression of contempt, he said loudly to the newsmen pressing around, "I do not consider this painting worthy of so much attention, gentlemen. It is the work of a publicity-hungry, opportunistic young man of meager talent."

A gasp went up in the room, and he turned to Madeline, saying in a voice filled with disdain, "This ugly little scene you have staged will do nothing to help your fading career. All that you have accomplished is to confirm what everyone had long suspected—that you are simply an aging courtesan!"

Madeline let out a cry and struck him across the face. Jonathan threw up his arm before she could slap him again, and gave her a glancing blow that made her stumble back against the wall. Alan broke through the crowd and grabbed Jonathan by the shoulder. Spinning him around, he punched him in the face, knocking him to the floor as flash bulbs went off like a burst of firecrackers.

Over the shouts of guests Foucault rushed to help Jonathan to his feet, and hurried him out of the room. Alan went to Madeline and asked, "Are you all right?"

She looked up at him with a smile of triumph. "Of course! He behaved true to form, with a little help from me!"

Olivia and Dorian came forward, Olivia said, "So much for being able to handle seeing him again, Alan! Now what the hell was that all about?"

Alan gestured to the painting. "I'm afraid this is what stirred up all the heavy emotion."

Dorian recognized the sable coat and all the other gifts that her uncle had given to Madeline. When she saw Alan's portrait of his photograph peering out from among the objects, she began to laugh. Turning to Madeline, she exclaimed, "Oh, what a priceless idea! It's wonderful!"

"Forgive me, *ma petite*," Madeline said, embracing her. "I did not expect to see you again under such bizarre circumstances."

"I wouldn't have missed it for the world!"

Olivia quickly grasped the intent of the painting and turned on Alan like a scolding mother. "Did you think that you needed to do something like this to create interest in your work? I have no great love for Jonathan, and I'm sure Mademoiselle Gautier has a legitimate reason for wanting to embarrass him. But was it necessary for you to be a part of it?"

Foucault had come back into the room while she was talking, and said, "My dear Olivia, we have sold almost every piece in the show, and there are a half-dozen requests on my desk for portrait commissions. I think that answers your question."

"I credited you with more taste than to allow an incident like this in your gallery, Louis!"

"Taste, dear lady, does not always pay the bills. The art market in Paris is no less precarious than in New York. One must do what one can. As for Alan, he is a genuine talent. In time, this little excitement will be forgotten—but not his work. And now, I suggest that you see to Monsieur St. Clair; he wishes to leave immediately."

Alan put his arm around Olivia's shoulders. "Don't be angry," he said. "I'll call you and we'll have lunch together."

She glanced at Dorian and he added, "I'll see that she gets home safely . . ."

Olivia shook her head with a smile of mock despair. "You've been surprising me since the first day I met you." She took Foucault's arm and left the room.

Madeline whispered something to Dorian, then said to Alan, "I have some friends waiting for me. We'll talk tomorrow. Call me, but not too early; I suspect this will be a very long evening."

When they were alone, Dorian laughed nervously and said, "It's suddenly very quiet in here."

"They all got what they came for."

"And you—?"

"More than I expected. What did Madeline say to you before she left?"

Dorian looked up into his face. Tears started in her eyes. "She told me not to worry—that you still belonged to me . . ."

Her voice broke, and Alan moved swiftly to take her in his arms. "She was right," he whispered.

A little while later they sat across from each other in a small neighborhood bistro. Alan was listening to Dorian, a cigarette burning low between his fingers.

". . . after we got back to London, Graham and I agreed that I wouldn't do any more films."

"Was it really that bad?"

"Worse. It died in the previews and they gave it a quick, multiple-theater release before selling it to television. The critics panned everything about it. Graham didn't mind as much as I did—he's had that happen before, but I hated it, and ended up blaming him for the whole fiasco."

She went on to tell him how Graham had started work on another film, and of her growing restlessness trying to fill the role of wife and hostess. "I didn't do that very well, either," she said ruefully. "I really wasn't cut out to be a twenty-one-year-old matron."

"Dorian, why did you marry him?"

She flushed, and looked away. "An impulse, I guess. I was

having a rough time. Mother and Father were on my back to go home with them, and Graham came along. He was kind and attentive—and I thought that with him I'd be free. I was wrong. Poor Graham. Having me for a wife did a lot for his ego, but not for long—"

"What happened?"

"I met other men—no one important to me, just other men. Graham was patient and tried to be understanding, but the rumors and gossip made it difficult, if not impossible. A few weeks ago we agreed on a divorce. I moved into the hotel in London, Olivia called to tell me she was coming to the opening of your show—and here I am."

Alan tried not to show the leap of excitement he felt at her news. "How do you feel about the divorce?" he asked cautiously.

"Well, it solves the latest of my idiotic mistakes, but that's about all," she replied matter-of-factly. "I never had a very good model for marriage, you know; a dictatorial, narrow-minded father and a mother trapped into playing her life like an outdated comedy of manners."

"But it doesn't have to be the same for you, does it?"

"I don't know what it's going to be for me, whatever 'it' is," she answered bitterly.

He found no encouragement in her reply to the questions he was aching to ask: Could she stay with him? Could they finally have the life they had planned during those summer nights on Long Island? He was once more aware of her fearful insecurity; in that way she had not changed at all.

Dorian went on more cheerfully, "I *have* done something that I'm proud of. While Graham was working, I went back to my photography and took pictures all over London. Not the tourist kind of thing, but of people and places you rarely see in travel books." She added, almost shyly, "I used Cartier-Bresson as my inspiration, just as you told me you were inspired by Van Dyck and Sargent . . ."

"That's wonderful. I always said you had the eye of an artist."

"I showed them to a publisher in London, and he said that they might do a book with them. Mick Tolo offered to write the captions—"

"Mick Tolo? The rock musician?"

She lowered her eyes. "Yes—he's a friend of mine . . ."

Alan remained silent. She looked up, waiting for him to speak.

Finally he said, "I like his songs."

She reached across the table and took his hand. "He doesn't mean anything special to me, Alan. He's just a friend, like Madeline is to you." There was a hint of sarcasm in her voice that did not escape him.

"We've had our separate lives, haven't we?" he said.

She nodded, and touched his cheek, her fingertips tracing the shape of his lips. He felt a familiar excitement stir within him, and asked, "I live close by—do you want to come home with me?"

She nodded again, almost imperceptibly.

In the darkened room, as they made love, memories were reawakened of the boat house and stolen moments on the beach. Dorian cried out and Alan strained to hold back, but was unable to resist the impulse to a quickened pace. She drew her breath in sharply, Alan covered her lips with his, and they were flung into a suspension of time where nothing existed but each other.

Later, Alan lay motionless, watching her. Moonlight cast a pale glow over her body; her hair was a dark, serpentine mass against the white pillows. She looked serene, the long lashes of her closed eyes making light feathery shadows on her cheeks.

Alan felt a sense of longing, as if their union had not yet been achieved. She seemed, even in sleep, more elusive, more illusory than ever. It's all so simple, he thought, we belong together. Yet he knew that there were forces at work in her that he could not reach, forces that would continue to take her out of his life until she could deal with them. In a way, he understood; Dorian was very like himself, striving for a goal as yet unobtainable. Only he had defined his goal long ago—and she had not.

He bent down and kissed her. She stirred, reached up and enfolded him in her arms, whispering his name as in a dream.

In the morning, when he awoke, she was gone.

22

PRESS COVERAGE OF Alan's exhibit was extensive, including many favorable reviews of his paintings. But more space was devoted to the fight between him and Jonathan. In one interview, Madeline was quoted as saying, "Monsieur St. Clair should be more careful whom he publicly insults. Neither his personal life nor his questionable business practices leave him above criticism."

It was the kind of innuendo that was safe to publish; there was nothing libelous in it. But the statement triggered an unexpected chain of events.

Sensing the hint of a bigger story, the newspapers sent out reporters to investigate Madeline's charge of "questionable business practices." Within a week, several articles appeared that speculated on Jonathan's acquaintance with prominent figures in an organized crime syndicate, men who had long been under police surveillance.

Jonathan cloistered himself in his office, refusing to give interviews or respond to the allegations. Alexander called from New York daily to berate him, insisting that he take action to quash the rumors that threatened to damage the family's prestige.

But Jonathan had more to fear than Alexander realized.

His involvement with the syndicate had begun two years earlier, when he had fallen deeply into debt at the private club where he gambled. The owners of the club made him an offer: they would cancel the debt in exchange for his help. They needed a place for illegal transactions, a location that would be above suspicion from the police. Jonathan was to arrange a suite of rooms at the hotel to be kept available at all times for their agents to use.

At first the request seemed easy enough to comply with.

The hotel staff was told that the suite was for Jonathan's friends and visiting guests. He never asked what transactions took place, and everything went smoothly. But within a few months he was pressured into making the same arrangements at the St. Clair hotels in other countries. His incessant gambling involved him more deeply, and he was called upon to provide other services: private cars and drivers, and prostitutes who had to be smuggled into the hotel without being seen by the other guests.

Jonathan foolishly thought of all this as an adventure, a game; in his inflated self-conception, he saw himself as an international figure dabbling in the dark area of the underworld. It also pleased him to think that he was doing something that would outrage Alexander.

But Madeline's vindictive statement to the press had changed everything. Now reporters were swarming over the hotel, searching out information and gossip.

And Jonathan had begun to receive threatening phone calls on his private line.

One morning about three weeks after the night of Alan's opening the scandal broke. A reporter had bribed a desk clerk for a look at the hotel register and recognized an alias used by one of the syndicate men. The police came to question Jonathan. He denied any knowledge of the man, claiming that he couldn't possibly know who all of the guests in the hotel were, or what they did in the privacy of their rooms. The police advised him not to leave the city until they had completed their investigation.

In a state of panic, Jonathan called Alexander, confessed everything and asked for his help. Then he assigned a hotel security guard to be at his side around the clock.

✿

Jonathan sat up abruptly, his eyes wide and staring in the darkness of his bedroom. What was that sound? He reached out and turned on the light. The room sprang to life, illuminated in every corner, but nothing was there.

Nerves, he thought, just nerves. He got out of bed, slipped on a robe and walked into the living room of the suite, turning on lamps as he went. He glanced at the clock on the mantel; it was a little after two in the morning. In a few hours Alexander would arrive. As much as he hated to admit it, he was relieved that his brother would be here to help him; Alex had many friends who were high officials in the government. Favors would be exchanged, money, if necessary, and the whole ugly business would be over. Their lawyers would see to it that he was granted immunity by the police for giving evidence against the syndicate, and then he would get out of Paris.

His stomach gave a lurch, and he realized he was hungry; he hadn't eaten since that morning. He went to the phone and called the kitchen, asked for some food to be sent up, then went to the front door of the suite and unlocked it.

Guillaume, the hotel security guard, was sitting in the hall by the door, his chair tipped back against the wall. Seeing Jonathan, he stood up quickly.

"Yes, Monsieur St. Clair—do you wish something?"

"No, I just wanted to tell you that the kitchen was sending up a tray for me."

"Oui, Monsieur."

Jonathan closed and locked the door, paced the floor for a few minutes, then wearily sank into a chair, thinking how it had always been like this—getting involved in something he couldn't handle, and having to call on Alexander for help. It had been the same since they were children; Alex always concerned about preserving appearances, and Jonathan the irresponsible baby brother, opposing him, becoming a playboy not only because he enjoyed it, but because it was the absolute antithesis of Alexander's somber, respectable life.

He couldn't erase his brother's scowling face from his mind. Suddenly he thought of the ugly scar on Alex's forehead, the scar that he had put there when they were young men.

It had been a terrible fight. They were arguing about a girl Jonathan had been seeing. Alex called her a whore, and threatened to tell their father if Jonathan didn't stop seeing her. Insults were exchanged, then Jonathan struck him. Alex fell, hitting his head hard against the brick edge of the fireplace mantel. Later, he passed the scar off as a memento of one of his hunting trips, but Jonathan never lost the sense of pleasure he had felt at bringing his brother down.

A knock at the door brought him to his feet. "Yes?" he called out.

Guillaume's voice replied, "Your tray is here from the kitchen, Monsieur."

Jonathan went to the door and opened it. A waiter was standing to one side of the trolley cart. As Jonathan opened the door wider the waiter's hand came up holding a gun with a silencer attached to the barrel. He fired point blank at Guillaume, then whirled on Jonathan as the security guard crashed into the trolley.

"Why?" Jonathan gasped.

The man's face was devoid of expression. "I only do what Monsieur Morel tells me," he said, and fired a second time.

It wasn't a clean shot; Jonathan had turned his head and the bullet shattered his jaw, scattering gold-crowned teeth and blood across the carpet.

The next shot was more accurate.

❦

Alan stood in front of the painting of Madeline. Foucault's assistant hovered close by, speaking in a hushed whisper. "It has become a major attraction in the gallery, ever since the death of Monsieur St. Clair . . ."

"Yes, I'm sure it has," Alan remarked dryly. "Will Louis be free soon?"

"In a few minutes—he's on a long-distance call. I've told him that you are waiting—"

The assistant slid out of sight and Alan continued to gaze at the portrait. He decided that technically it was a good piece of work; the brush strokes were sure and direct, the color was muted and well balanced. He had handled the clutter of *objets d'art* so that they were integrated into the overall design of the canvas, and not obtrusive. A good display of virtuosity, he concluded, with about as much meaning as the decoration on a lid of a candy box.

His eyes were drawn to the silver-framed picture of Jonathan in the painting. The handsome, arrogant face seemed to be peering at him directly, accusingly. Alan turned away; a small chill traveled through him. This was the first time he had looked at the portrait since Jonathan's murder, over a month ago.

Before leaving the room he glanced back at the painting, wondering what his mother would have thought of it. He couldn't help smiling at the irony of the situation: Jonathan had betrayed her trust and precipitated her suicide, and her son's painting had been an instrument of his death. The score was settled; whatever thoughts of revenge Alan had harbored these last two years no longer existed. But the realization left him with an inexplicable feeling of uneasiness and regret.

Foucault came into the gallery. "You're looking very thoughtful this morning, my friend," he greeted Alan. "What is troubling you?"

"Profits, Louis . . . profits," Alan responded quietly. "I've sold all the paintings, Madeline has been offered a large advance by a publisher for her memoirs, a film in Hollywood—and your gallery has practically become a landmark on the Left Bank. And all it took was a scandal and a murder . . ."

"But you cannot blame yourself for what happened," Foucault said, then added philosophically, "One casts a stone, and sometimes it makes wider ripples than one believed possible."

"I like that, Louis," Alan said with a cynical smile. "It takes the edge off the burden of guilt."

"You are only guilty of doing a good painting. Come back to the office—we have business to do."

Alan followed him to his office and sat down while Foucault took out his check book.

"I have money to give you," the gallery owner said. "That will cheer you up. And we must discuss the commissions you've been offered. There are six altogether."

"Good. That will keep me busy through the winter, and give me enough money to leave in the spring."

"Leave? Where are you going?"

"I'm not sure yet. I want to travel for a while, see the rest of Europe, and paint, of course."

"But you've made a great success here—you should stay, solidify your position . . ."

"No, Louis—I've learned a few things about my art and

myself, now I must learn more . . . but we can talk about that later."

"As you wish." Foucault made out a check and handed it to Alan. "Have you spoken with Madeline?" he asked.

"Yes, a few days ago. She's leaving for Spain tomorrow . . ."

"I know—this whole episode unnerved her terribly." Foucault sighed deeply, and added, "As it did us all—"

Alan remained silent. He pocketed the check thinking, You old fraud, you're no more unnerved than she is. For a moment he wondered if anyone had really grieved for Jonathan. He had seen photographs in the papers of Alexander and Vivian at the airport, taking the body back to New York for burial. Their faces were like masks, revealing nothing of what they thought or felt. Behind them, the figure of Dorian was no more than a blur, and the accompanying story said only that she was going home with them for the funeral. Alan had not heard from her since the night of his opening; he wondered if he would ever see her again.

He looked up and saw Foucault waiting to speak to him. "Let's talk business, Louis," he said briskly. "Tell me about the commissions."

23

New York: June 1969

DAVID GLANCED AT his watch. It was five o'clock; Jennings was expecting him for dinner at six. If he moved quickly, he could get away for the evening without seeing Alexander.

He started to leave when the phone rang. For a moment he was tempted not to answer; then he picked it up. It was his mother.

"David, your father wants to see you."

"Not now," he answered sharply. "I have an engagement in an hour . . ."

"David, please—it won't take very long, I'm sure." There was a desperate, ragged sound in her voice; she had spent the last month futilely attempting to keep her husband and son from each other's throats.

David relented. "All right, tell him I'll be there in a few minutes."

He hung up the phone and lit a cigarette. This couldn't go on much longer, he told himself.

It had started after Jonathan's funeral. Alex had returned to Paris to try to salvage the integrity of the hotel and the family name. He had stayed through the winter and returned to the estate on Long Island in the early spring. He had come home with a severe cold that lingered for weeks and finally turned into the flu. Refusing to go into the hospital, he had insisted on being moved into the family suite in the hotel, where a nurse was in attendance.

Dorian had been staying at the hotel since the funeral, to be with David. After Alexander returned, she went back to London. David couldn't blame her for leaving so abruptly; Alex had taken every opportunity to criticize the failure of her marriage.

Now his parents had been in the hotel for over a month,

making David's life miserable; Alex called down to the office on one pretext or another every hour, and demanded a full report of the day's events every evening. David finally had to resort to sneaking out in order to spend a few hours with Jennings.

Vivian was waiting for him when he got out of the elevator at the family penthouse. She was dressed in a deep blue chiffon gown and a pearl choker. Her blond hair was carefully done and sprayed, looking almost sculpted, and makeup lent her complexion the smooth finish of a porcelain doll. But nothing could disguise the tired, anxious expression in her eyes. She was holding a cocktail in one hand, and when David kissed her cheek he realized that she was a little drunk.

"Are you going out?"

"Yes, Olivia is taking me to see Lauren Bacall in *Applause*."

"It'll do you good to get out for a while."

"I'm not sure I should go—he's been so restless all day—"

"Go and enjoy yourself—you've put up with enough of his crap as it is."

She sipped her drink and stared at him moodily. "You're right—I have. Ever since Jonathan's death, he's been worse than ever . . ." She stopped, embarrassed by her confession, and went on quickly, "It's not that I don't sympathise—I do. He's been through a lot, but we all have! I just don't understand why everything has changed so. Nothing is the same."

An angry shout came from the bedroom. "David, is that you?"

"Yes," he called back. "I'll be there in a minute."

He put his arm around Vivian's shoulders. "Why don't you get out of here?" he whispered. "Go wait for Olivia in the lobby. I'll have breakfast with you in the morning and you can tell me all about Lauren Bacall."

"That's a wonderful idea." She gave him a conspiratorial smile, and picked up her purse and gloves from the hall table. She put her arms around him and held him close. "You're a darling," she whispered tremulously. "Sometimes I don't know what I'd do without you."

The emotion in her voice moved him. He could see how much she had changed: she was thinner, less able to conceal her tension, and she was drinking more, too.

The elevator arrived and she stepped in. "Try not to argue with him tonight, dear."

David smiled. "Why should tonight be different from any other night?"

The elevator doors closed on her anxious smile. David turned and walked briskly to his father's bedroom.

"What took you so long?" Alex asked.

"I was talking with Mother. What's up? You sound particularly disagreeable tonight," he answered breezily. "Shouldn't you be in bed?"

Alexander was sitting at his desk, wearing pajamas and a thin silk dressing gown. The long illness had taken its toll on his usually vigorous appearance: he was pale, and there were deep hollows under his eyes. The scar across his forehead seemed more prominent, like a dull red welt from the flick of a whip. He lit a cigar and David noticed that his hands were veined and wrinkled, covered with spots of age.

God, he's getting old, David realized. He's actually getting old! The thought cheered him.

"Pour me some brandy," Alex said gruffly. "And yourself one, too, if you wish."

David went to the bar glancing anxiously at his watch; it was getting late, and Jennings was waiting.

"What's the occasion?" he asked, bringing the brandy to his father. "Or are you just being pesky because the doctor told you to stay off cigars and spirits. Remember your blood pressure?"

St. Clair made a noise of disgust and lifted the glass, eyeing his son warily over the rim of the glass.

"What happened to Miss Prune Face, your nurse?" David asked.

"I dismissed her—I'm much better, now." He took a swallow of brandy and put the glass down. "I didn't ask you up here to discuss my health," he began. "I have something more important to tell you."

David sat up, alert. What was happening now? He had seen his father like this before: dramatic and crafty, springing a surprise like a trap.

"I've decided to send you to Paris, to take over the directorship of the European hotels," Alexander said.

David stared at him, stunned. He took a swallow of brandy and tried to remain calm. "Why?" he asked.

"Because I want you there," Alexander replied with deliberate exaggeration, separating each word as he would to a child.

"That's not much of a reason."

"It's enough reason for me."

"I'm not sure I want to go."

"What you want has nothing to do with it."

"It never does, to you!" David made an effort to control his rising anger. "I like working here, and living here. I'm comfortable with the routine and I do the job well—"

"It's a job anyone can handle," Alexander said curtly. "The situation in Europe is a bit shaky—I've sent Edmund Duclos, the manager of the Paris hotel, out to investigate the rest of the chain; I'm expecting a report from him any day now, and I doubt if it will be reassuring. Jonathan left quite a mess behind him." Alex finished his brandy, signaling that the discussion was at an end. "In the morning you can make your arrangements. I want you to leave within a week."

"I don't want to go," David said stubbornly.

"I don't give a damn what you want!" Alexander's tone was dismissive. "Now get out of here, I'm tired."

"You can't just uproot me whenever you feel like it! I've made a life for myself here, I have friends—"

"You'll make new ones!" St. Clair replied sharply. He stood up and came around the desk to face David. "I don't want to discuss it further. Just do as you're told."

David felt himself faltering. "I thought you said that you were going back to Paris in a few months," he said weakly. "You told me you were—" He heard the whining tone in his voice and paused, trying desperately to collect his thoughts.

"I have more important work to do here," Alexander said. "I've made several investments that I want to see through—a shopping complex in California, and some land developement in Arizona. So you see, you have to go."

"I don't have to do anything!" David cried. "You've shoved me around like a piece of furniture all my life, with no regard for my feelings—or Mother's, or Dorian's, for that matter! You've bullied and hounded all of us—!"

"How dare you!"

"Don't pull that shit with me!"

St. Clair lifted his arm and dealt a stinging blow to the side of David's face. Without hesitation, David lashed out with all his strength, striking his father so hard that the older man reeled back against the desk. Then David rushed from the room, ignoring the elevator and taking the fire stairs, running down flight after flight, his feet barely touching the steps.

꘎

"Yes, I hit him!" David told an astonished Jennings. "I hit the son of a bitch!"

Jennings began to applaud furiously, and David sat up from where he was lying on the bed and took bows.

"To the victor belongs the spoils!" Jennings sang out, throwing himself across the bed and into David's arms. "Take me and despoil me! You have fought the good fight and won your prize!"

David bent over him and leered, "Now, or after dinner?"

"Now, this instant. But be quick about it—I'm starved!"

"And you're crazy," David laughed, kissing him.

They grew quiet, content to be in each other's arm. Then Jennings asked, "What's going to happen? Will he leave you alone—let you stay here?"

David sat up and reached for a cigarette. "I don't know," he admitted slowly. "I guess I'll just have to keep saying no until he gets the message and drops the whole thing—"

"Do you really think that will happen? That he'll drop it? It doesn't sound like the raging megalomaniac we all know—"

"Hey," David complained, "not so many questions! I can only make one stand at a time. Look—" He held out his hands; they were trembling. "See? I'm still shaking."

Jennings took them and held them tightly. "I understand . . ." He hesitated, then said softly, "One more question— did you stand up to him because of me? So that you wouldn't have to leave me? I really have to know."

David took a deep breath before answering. "I thought of you, yes." He looked into Jennings's eyes and saw the larger, unasked question there. "I don't know if I love you, I don't even know what the hell love is, at least not the kind of love you've talked about. I do know that you've given me more concern and affection than anyone in my life, except for Dorian."

Jenning put his fingers to David's lips. "Don't say any more," he whispered. "That's good enough for me. Let's get out of here and celebrate your coming of age."

"Can we come back later and celebrate privately?"

"It's amazing how you read my mind."

They chose a quiet Italian restaurant in the Village, where they lingered over dinner, talking quietly, discussing plans to rent a house on Fire Island when David could get away for a week. Candlelight flickered over the room, and David grew relaxed, contemplative. He knew that Jennings loved him, and the knowledge gave him a feeling of security. Perhaps, someday, he would be able to assert himself with no fear, and live according to his own dictates, not those of his father. He was getting more used to gay society; was that because of Jennings? So little about him was stereotypical, which was important to David, despite Jennings's claims that it was pure snobbery on David's part to think that they were different from other, more overt gays.

"What about stopping off for a nightcap before we go home?" Jennings was saying.

"What? Oh, sure, if you want to. But not for too long, okay?" David grinned at him.

"Anxious to get home, huh?"

"Yeah, I want a long evening of celebrating."

They went to a bar a few blocks away, called the Stonewall Inn.

The atmosphere was warm, relaxed; men danced together to a rhythm-and-blues song, and a few, in elaborate drag, were performing as if they were on stage, acknowledging shouted encouragement with regal bows and graceful turns.

"I didn't think it would be this crowded," Jennings remarked, looking around.

"It's nice—I like it," David said. His words were a little slurred; he was on his third drink, and had taken a few hits of Saigon grass that someone from the next table had offered.

"I can't take you anywhere," Jennings said laughingly. "You're getting stoned to the tits. Once I get you home, you'll probably pass out."

David wagged a finger at him slyly. "Oh no I won't," he giggled. "I never pass out on attractive men."

A young dark-haired boy staggered up to David and threw his arms around his shoulders. "God, you're beautiful . . . ," he said drunkenly.

David disengaged the boy's arms. "That's true," he agreed solemnly. "But I belong to him—" He gestured to Jennings.

"Oh shit, that's the story of my life," the boy muttered, and wandered off.

Jennings said, "I think it's time to toddle off to bed . . ."

"Good idea! But first, we dance!"

"You're kidding! You've never danced with me in public before."

"Tonight's a night of firsts!" David exclaimed, getting up and holding out his arms. "Besides, you're not the only one who can dance, you know. Just stay on the ground, and no *entrechats*."

They began to move in time to the music, nudging aside one of the boys in drag. He turned and gave them a dreamy smile, revealing a light smudge of lipstick on his white teeth.

David returned the smile, and winked at him. "Cute," he said to Jennings. "I wonder what he looks like in pants."

The music rose in volume and people began clapping their hands. The dancing grew more boisterous, long hair and hips swinging freely, fingers snapping out the rhythm.

Suddenly the music was cut off.

Eight people were standing in the door: five men and two women in plainclothes, and one uniformed officer.

"Oh fuck, it's a bust!" a boy wearing beads and faded denims moaned.

David froze. He felt Jennings push him off the dance floor to lean against a wall. His heart was pounding violently and his breath came in uneven gasps.

"Take it easy," Jennings said.

The detective in charge brandished his badge at the bartender and began to recite, "You're under arrest for selling alcohol without a license. You have the right to remain silent—"

"We have no fucking rights!" a heavy-set man exclaimed, causing a ripple of nervous laughter through the crowd.

David broke out in a cold sweat and his face turned the

color of plaster. "Get me out of here," he whispered to Jennings. "I can't be arrested, I just can't!"

"They're only going to arrest the bartender and the owner—just relax, we'll be out of here in a few minutes."

An apprehensive silence fell over the bar as the police ordered everyone to leave, one at a time.

"Are they checking ID?" David asked in a choked voice.

Jennings gripped his arm. "There's over two hundred people here—they're not going to check ID."

In the line ahead of them, a couple of drag queens were taunting the officers, striking poses and swishing by them with limp wrists. Friends already outside cheered them on. Just then a paddy wagon arrived. The bartender and doorman and a few of the more blatant drags were shoved into it. Catcalls and boos went up from the crowd as the wagon drove off.

David lowered his eyes as he and Jennings approached the gauntlet of police. Once outside, they found themselves caught up in a swelling mob of protesting men. Before they could get through the crush, they were separated. A fresh cry of anger sounded over the struggle of a lesbian who had just come out of the bar; she was being forced into a waiting police car. Other gays had joined the crowd filling Sheridan Square, a tiny park directly opposite the Stonewall Inn. A Puerto Rican youth stood up on an overturned trash can and jeered, "When you faggots gonna stop taking this shit? Don't let the pigs fuck you over!"

The cry was picked up as the police car drove off. The temper of the crowd turned ugly. They began to throw a hail of coins, followed by bottles and bricks. The police, taken aback by the sudden eruption of anger, bolted into the empty bar and locked the door. The men in the street surged forward, throwing rocks and debris.

"Get the fascist cops!" someone screamed, and others joined in, "Get the pigs!" "Gay Power!"

The door of the bar crashed open under the pressure of the mob. Three of the officers rushed out to the sidewalk. One of them was hit in the face and began to bleed. Another lunged at a man standing nearby and started to beat him, pulling him down and dragging him into the bar by his hair. The door was slammed shut again, and the attack increased in fury. Rioters began to batter the door with an uprooted parking meter and hurled more bricks and bottles. The windows of the bar, boarded up on the inside with plywood, gave way with a crash of shattering glass and splintering wood.

David saw Jennings in the mob pressing against the door. He called out and Jennings waved his arms excitedly. They shoved through the crowd to get to each other.

"Do you believe what's happening?" Jennings cried.

"We've got to get out of here!" David said desperately. "More police will be along any second!"

"But we can't leave! They're fighting back! Don't you realize what that means? *We're* fighting back! We've got to stay!"

"I can't! I don't want any part of this!"

At that moment someone reached through the broken window of the bar, sprayed some fluid into the room, and followed it with a flaring match. There was a burst of flames, and a cheer of triumph went up.

David grabbed Jennings's arm and tried to pull him away. "Let's get the hell out of here!" he pleaded.

"No!" Jennings yanked free of him. "David, stay and make a stand. You made one earlier tonight, an important one. Make one now, for this; it's just as important, even more so. Don't run away and hide from it like you have all your life!"

David backed away from him angrily. "I can't do it!" he shouted over the din. The sound of approaching sirens filled the street. "Jennings, please, they're coming!"

"I'm not leaving! Go on, get out of here . . ."

Carloads of police turned into Christopher Street, red lights flashing and sirens screaming. People began to run, dispersing into alleys and side streets, but most of them remained and continued to harass the officers trapped inside the bar.

Jennings gave David one last pleading look, then turned away to join the crowds surging against the police.

David began to run in the opposite direction.

Back at the hotel, he hurried through the lobby toward the elevators, but the manager intercepted him. The man looked grave and anxious.

"Mr. St. Clair, we've been trying to reach you everywhere!"

"What is it, John—what's wrong?"

"Your father. He's had a stroke!"

"What?" David felt light-headed, almost faint. "Is he dead?"

"No—at least, I don't think so. He was alive when the ambulance took him to the hospital. We called Mrs. St. Clair at the theatre—she and your aunt are at New York Hospital now . . ."

David hurried down the corridors toward the intensive care unit. His heart was beating wildly, and the acrid smell of disinfectant made him slightly nauseated. He found Vivian and Olivia standing in the hallway with Dr. Steiner, the family physician. Vivian's face was pale and drawn. Tears had streaked her makeup, but her expression was hard and alert.

David reached to embrace her, asking, "How is he?"

She pulled back from him. "Where have you been? We've been waiting for you half the night!"

"I was out—with friends," David stammered.

"What happened after I left you with your father?"

Olivia took her arm. "That's not important now, dear . . ."

"Yes, it is!" Vivian said shrilly. "You had a fight, didn't you? And you struck him! There's a bruise on his face!"

"No—I didn't . . . that is—we argued . . ."

Vivian began to cry and Olivia led her to a chair.

Dr. Steiner said to David, "I'll give her something to quiet her nerves before you leave. She'll be all right as soon as she gets some rest."

"What about my father? What's his condition?"

"It's hard to say this early, but I think we can expect a partial recovery. His left side has been affected, and his speech—but his heart is strong and he's in good physical condition."

"Is there anything we can do?"

"No, but I think you will have to take over the business until he's better. Can you handle it? I'm sure that's the first thing he'll want to know when he's able to communicate with us."

David felt a small hysterical flutter rise in his throat and threaten to escape in burst of laughter. He drew himself up and answered firmly, "Tell him that I'll take care of everything."

He was awake most of the night, drinking and crying. After years of enduring humiliation at Alexander's hands, he was now in control. Yet the thought that he had almost killed his father filled him with guilt. He collapsed on the bed and closed his eyes, trying to blot out the nightmarish events of the evening. But even in sleep, his agony pursued him, he saw his father and Jennings, their faces merging one into the other, staring at him accusingly.

A few weeks later, Alexander was moved by private ambulance to the estate on Long Island to recuperate. There was a nurse in attendance, and a speech therapist and a physical therapist were installed in the guest house that George Conway had taken such pains to reconstruct.

David made arrangements with the family lawyers to take care of their holdings and follow through on the new investments. He spoke to the managers of the hotels across the country, informing them of what had happened, and referring them to the manager of the New York hotel or the lawyers if they had any problems. Then he made reservations for a flight to Paris.

Not once before he left did he speak with Jennings Talbot.

Part Four

24

London: 1972

GLENWAY HARCOURT WATCHED in dismay as the three large rooms of his gallery filled with people and equipment. Photographers were setting up lights, their assistants covered the floors with cords and cables, and a troupe of girls carrying makeup cases and clothes hurried from one room to the other, calling out questions that no one answered. A young woman rushed in, giving orders in a sharp voice, and two men wandered around, gesturing to the paintings on the walls and a group of sculptures arranged on pedestals.

Harcourt's thin, aristocratic face became creased with concern as one of the men lifted a marble bust. "Please don't move that!" he said, raising his voice.

"We'll put it back," came the reply.

"Is all this absolutely necessary?" he asked the other man.

"Oh yes, absolutely," was the cheerful answer.

A middle-aged woman wearing a tailored suit and a frightened expression came up to him. "Mr. Harcourt, I'm sorry to bother you—"

"Please, Miss Collins, I'm very busy," he snapped. "No—you can't take that painting off the wall!" he yelled to the young woman who was giving instructions to the others.

"Mr. Harcourt, please," Miss Collins persisted. "Mr. Conway has arrived. He's up at the front."

"Mr. Conway?" Harcourt's expression became desperate "Oh God, not now! He wasn't due in until later!"

"Well, he's here now, and he looks very angry."

"All right, all right—stay here and try to keep them from wrecking the place. I'll go talk to Mr. Conway."

"Yes, Mr. Harcourt," she answered. "Do be careful of the cables on the floor—"

Harcourt tripped and almost fell. "Damn!" he muttered, straightening up. "They'll kill us all!"

He hurried into the front room of the gallery and saw Alan standing by the reception desk with an angry scowl on his face.

"Mr. Conway," he said, smiling brightly, "we didn't expect you until later this—"

"What the hell is going on here?" Alan asked.

"Well, it's something that came up last week—I tried to reach you, but you were already in transit, and I wasn't sure where—"

"What is it all about?"

Harcourt replied, "It's a fashion layout using your show as a background, for a new magazine called *Styles*." Alan gave him a look of incredulity, and he hurried on "It's a very fine magazine, similar to your American Vogue, and I really thought it might be good publicity for the show—"

"And the gallery!" Alan finished.

Harcourt's smile was sheepish. "Well, yes, in a way—you'll be on exhibit for several months, and the magazine will be issued during that time . . ."

"Mr. Harcourt, I understand your motives and I appreciate the fact that the media has invaded all areas of culture, but I do not want my paintings used as a background for the latest fashion craze!"

Harcourt flinched before Alan's outburst, then both men turned in surprise at the sound of applause from a young woman standing nearby.

"Mr. Conway, you're absolutely right," she said. "But do try to understand how much this would mean to the magazine, too. We've just begun publication, and we're making every effort to achieve a presentation that has great prestige. We plan a section of full-color reproductions of your paintings, and a critical study of all your work. Won't you reconsider and allow us to go on? I'm the associate editor of the magazine, and I would personally be very grateful."

Alan's anger vanished. He said to Harcourt, "Give this young woman your full cooperation."

The gallery owner breathed a sigh of relief. "Thank you, Mr. Conway, that's very kind of you. Now, if you'll excuse me, I want to make sure that no one damages anything . . ."

He stopped, aghast at his slip of the tongue, then hurried to the back of the gallery.

The young woman laughed and said, "I thank you, too, Mr. Conway—and may I add that you look more handsome than ever?"

"And you more beautiful, Dorian . . ."

"If you don't kiss me very quickly, I may leap all over you."

Miss Collins appeared, her plain face blushing to a high pink as she watched them embrace.

"Excuse me, Miss St. Clair," she said. "I hate to bother you, but they want you in the back gallery . . ."

"Where are you staying?" Dorian asked Alan.

"I just got into town and thought I'd come here first. Can you suggest a good hotel?" he asked, smiling.

"Try the St. Clair—it's supposed to be marvelous," Dorian laughed.

"Are you living there?"

"No—I have my own place near Regent's Park. When I'm finished here, I'll call you."

"Can we have dinner?"

"I won't have time for dinner—there's some business I have to take care of at a club tonight—but you can come with me, if you like. Then we can go back to my place and catch up . . . God, Alan, it's been four years since I've seen you!"

One of the photographers called out from the back of the gallery, "Dorian, we're waiting . . ."

"I've got to run—they can't do a thing without me. I'll pick you up at the hotel around nine."

Alan stood to one side for a few minutes, and watched Dorian direct the models and photographers. She gave orders briskly, checked camera angles, corrected makeup, and set up the poses with authority and confidence. It seemed that time had brought about the changes she'd been seeking, but, he reflected sadly, it had also vitiated the bond between them; they had greeted each other as if they were no more than casual friends suddenly reacquainted by chance.

That evening she took him to a private discotheque that had a membership of rock stars, film producers, and other media celebrities. As they walked in Dorian nodded and waved to a few people, flashed her membership card at the hostess and said, "Take us to the MainMan table."

They were led through the club and seated at a table where a group of people were talking noisily over the blare of music coming from loudspeakers.

"Dorian!" a tall, bearded man said to her. "Where the hell were you Tuesday night? I waited nearly an hour, you bitch." His thick Cockney accent matched his aggressive manner. "Who's your friend?

"Alan Conway, this is Roland Stewart," Dorian introduced them. "Alan's an old friend from the States . . ."

"You in the business?" he questioned Alan.

"No, I'm a painter—"

Roland swung back to Dorian and said, "So—let's talk business, love—that's what we're here for."

"Where's David?" she asked.

"He called, said he and Marc will be along later. It doesn't matter, I can tell you whatever you want to know."

Alan listened to their conversation until his attention began to wander. Dorian was negotiating for a fashion layout with Roland's client, a David somebody—he'd picked up that much—but the rest of the talk—names he didn't recognize, references to parties and gossip—was meaningless to him. He watched the people on the dance floor; dressed in designer clothes, they moved listlessly, with expressions of ennui fixed on their faces, and gave the appearance of being animated mannequins.

"You know I don't work like that!" Dorian said loudly. The furious tone of her voice brought Alan's focus back to her and Roland.

He was saying with exasperation, "I don't want to do it during the day—it'll interfere with the recording sessions."

"And I can't be expected to provide a full staff of makeup people, photographers, lighting men and models in the middle of the night!" she retaliated. "It's out of the question!"

"Dorian, it can't always be done your way . . ."

She sat her eyes like steel pinpoints and said, "You asked me for this, Roland. You want the exposure for him, the publicity. It sells records."

320

"And you want him because he's a fashion trendsetter, and he'll sell that bloody rag of a magazine!"

Dorian sat back in her chair with a smile. "Agreed. Now let's see if we can arrive at an amicable compromise about when to do the layout."

"All right, all right, I'll discuss it with him!" Roland cried. "Maybe we can do it at seven or eight in the morning, before we go into the studio. Would that suit you?" His sarcasm was barely concealed.

Dorian laughed. "You're a darling—call me tomorrow and we'll set it up."

"Why don't I call you later," he said, leering. "We could set something up for tonight."

She reached out and stroked his beard. "Don't ever shave, or you'll lose what little charm you have."

A light rain had begun to fall as they drove back to Dorian's house. Turning a corner, she hit the brakes, making the rear wheels of the Aston-Martin screech on the wet streets.

"I see your driving habits haven't changed much," Alan chided her.

"Don't be silly—I'm a much better driver now."

"Who is the David you were so intent on getting for your photo layout?"

"David Bowie, of course."

"I've never heard of him."

She laughed. "That's so like you, Alan, not to stay in touch with what's happening."

"I've been accused of that before—a lingering fault."

"It's part of the pose, isn't it? The artist too involved in the depth of his vision to pay attention to trends?"

The remark was tinged with sarcasm and caught him by surprise; his answer was cautious. "It's not a pose . . ." He watched for a reaction, but her face reflected nothing.

"Anyway," he went on, "it's wonderful to see you so successful. I always knew you would be."

"It's not a bad job—I worked hard enough to get it. Besides, I'm better at organizing things and telling people what to do than being a photographer."

"But you still do some work of your own, don't you?"

"When the mood strikes me."

They lapsed into silence. Alan watched her out of the corner of his eye, thinking how she had changed; the line of her profile was as perfect as he remembered, but a thin, hard shell of makeup and the high-fashion gown she was wearing added a glossy veneer to her natural beauty. Sitting stiffly behind the wheel, she might have been posing for a photograph for her magazine.

Dorian's house on Ulster Terrace was decorated with expensive contemporary furnishings. Chrome and plexiglass was the dominant motif, and all the walls and woodwork had been painted a stark white. Alan found the effect sterile and chilling.

"It's not what you expected, is it?" Dorian asked a little defiantly. "Your father would be horrified at all the beautiful wood under the paint. How is he, by the way? Have you kept in touch with him?"

"He died last year of a heart attack," Alan replied quietly. "I was traveling, and didn't get the news until a month after the funeral."

"Alan, I'm so sorry." Dorian stood motionless, wanting to go to him, but feeling the barriers that time and distance had put between them. Finally, she asked with forced briskness, "What can I get you to drink?"

"Whatever you're having is fine."

While she mixed the drinks at an etched glass bar, he walked up quietly behind her and put his hands on her shoulders. She stiffened and let go of a glass she'd been holding; it fell to the floor and broke.

"Jesus! Don't do that!"

He backed away in surprise. "Dorian, I'm sorry—I didn't mean—"

"Forget it. I'm just a little on edge—Roland always does that to me . . ."

She bent down to pick up the pieces of broken glass, tossed them into a wastebasket and finished making the drinks in silence. Alan watched her cautiously. She handed him a glass and he lifted it in a toast: "To old friends?"

She nodded and downed the drink, then made another for herself. As she relaxed, she ran through her experiences of the last four years in a brisk, impersonal tone, as though she were reciting a resumé. Her professional life had been filled with setbacks and advances, people who had sabotaged her efforts, a few who had helped further her goals. Alan listened soberly, realizing that her fundamental complaint had not changed; she continued to be plagued by her name and status.

"I have no illusions about my position at *Styles*," she said with a trace of bitterness. "The owners are as mercenary a group as you'll find in publishing." She lighted a cigarette and added, "But whether they care or not, I know I'm doing good work, so I try to ignore the 'heiress' bullshit."

She stood up a little unsteadily and made herself another drink, offering one to Alan. He shook his head no, and she said, "You've certainly been making a name for yourself. I read about the portraits of Grace and the Prince, and the show in Berlin—'Conway Exhibit Sets Tone for Contemporary Realist Art!' You finally achieved what you wanted, didn't you?"

"Yes, that's true. But more, I've been using those commissions to subsidize the work that's important to me. I've been thinking about buying a place in Ireland, where I could settle in and devote some time to serious work; I'm getting a little tired of catering to the rich and famous."

Dorian laughed a little drunkenly. "We're never satisfied with what we get, are we? There's always something else, something more we want . . ." She staggered and Alan went to her, put his arm around her shoulders to steady her.

"Are you all right?" he asked.

"Yes, just a little tired and a little drunk." She sagged against him and put her head on his shoulder. "Sorry, I haven't made you feel very welcome, have I?"

"It's late," he said softly. "You need some rest. Why don't I call you tomorrow?"

She drew back and faced him. Her eyes were brimming with tears. "Alan, don't go. I want you to stay—please?" She pressed against him and kissed his lips. "I've been waiting for you," she confessed in a whisper. "When I heard that you were going to have a show at Harcourt's, I talked the magazine into letting me do the fashion layout and the article on your work—I planned the whole thing—please, stay?"

"Dorian, are you sure? I didn't think you wanted me to—"
She kissed him again, more urgently.

Alan came awake and realized that he was lying alone in
Dorian's bed. An old anxiety gripped him and he sat up in a
sudden, reflexive movement. "Dorian?" he called out.

"I'm in the kitchen making coffee," she called back. "I'll be
right up—"

He sank back against the pillows with a sigh of relief, and
looked around. Sunlight was pouring into the room through a
bay window, and he saw that it was furnished differently
from the downstairs; less contemporary and more comfortable, with deep easy chairs and fine wood tables. Then he noticed a painting hanging over the fireplace and sat up in
surprise; it was one of his that had been exhibited at
Foucault's gallery four years before. He had painted it in the
Luxembourg Gardens; in the foreground was the figure
of a young girl staring dreamily at the Medici Fountain.

"Did you think I'd run out on you again?" Dorian asked,
coming into the room carrying a tray of coffee and croissants.
Her long hair was tied back and her face was clean of all
makeup. She was wearing a soft rose-colored peignoir and
looked startlingly unchanged from their summer on Long Island.

"I didn't know you had bought that," Alan said, gesturing
to the painting as he sipped his coffee. "Foucault didn't tell
me."

"I asked him not to, I had the feeling you were thinking of
me when you painted it."

"You're right—I was."

Dorian sat down on the edge of the bed next to him. "I'm
sorry about last night. If I remember correctly, you very ro-
mantically carried me up the stairs and by the time we got to
bed, I had passed out—"

Alan smiled. "I'm not as fascinating as I used to be, and
you were very tired . . ."

"Don't be polite—I was very drunk."

"Are you feeling better now?" he asked, taking her hand.

"Yes—from the moment I woke up and saw you lying
there beside me."

He put his cup down and took her in his arms. "Oh God,

I've missed you—" he whispered, holding her close. He moved his hands inside her robe and found her naked flesh warm and silky to his touch. She trembled slightly and pressed against him, kissing his throat. "Ummm, you scratch," she murmured.

"Shall I get up and shave?"

"Don't you dare leave this bed."

"It's late," Alan said. "Shouldn't you be at the office?"

"I called in sick this morning—took the whole day off."

Alan laughed and settled her more comfortably in his arms. "Clever girl—but won't people talk? After all, we were seen leaving the club together last night."

"It won't be the first time."

"Have you become that infamous?"

"No, just talked-about. When David came to visit, we were seen everywhere together and the rumors went from snide to lurid—one very great lady of the English stage confided to me that she too had had a mad passion for her brother. David ended up spending the night with her son, and that shut her up."

"I read that he'd taken over the directorship of the chain after Jonathan's—death . . ."

Dorian saw that he was uncomfortable, and said, "You don't have to worry about talking about Jonathan; it wasn't your fault. Somebody would have killed him sooner or later—he was so careless with other people's lives. He left an ugly mess behind him, though; some of the hotels had to be sold, they'd been so badly mismanaged, they couldn't be saved . . ."

"What about David? Is he doing well? I haven't seen or talked with him since that night at my studio in New York . . . I still feel ashamed about that—not calling him or trying to see him."

"You really were innocent, weren't you? Didn't know for a minute how he felt, how much he loved and wanted you?"

"No, I really didn't. What's even stranger is that he was one of the few men I've ever made friends with—I mean the way we did that summer; I felt very close to him. He probably never wants to see me again."

"That's not true: we've talked about you a lot—you're the

only person he ever respected. I think he'd like to see you again very much."

"Perhaps we could fly over for a weekend, spend some time together like we used to—"

"We might," Dorian said hesitantly. "What are your plans? Are you going to stay in London for a while?"

"Yes—I took on a few more portrait commissions to help buy that place in Ireland I mentioned last night—" He paused, hoping for a response from her: they were circling each other cautiously, waiting for a sign to say what they felt.

"I suppose you'll be looking for a studio, then—" Dorian said.

"Yes, I can't work out of the hotel . . . can you recommend an agent to help me find a place?"

"Would you like to stay with me?" she asked in a small voice. "The top floor of the house is a loft. It wouldn't take much to convert it into a studio . . ."

Alan lay very still.

"It's quiet here," Dorian went on. "And I'm at work all day, so you could do the sittings without any distractions. Then, if you're free in a couple of months, we could go to Paris; I can take a week off in the late summer before all the fall fashion hysteria begins . . ."

Alan turned so that he was leaning over her. He pressed his fingertips to her lips and whispered, "The answer is yes, yes to everything . . ."

❦

During the following weeks, Alan settled into Dorian's house. The loft was converted into a spacious, comfortable studio, and he scheduled his sittings so that they could spend every free moment together. At first they shut out the world like young lovers, fiercely possessive of each other. She began to revive her interest in photography, and stole time from her work to photograph Alan painting. His first few commissions were of the wives of government officials, and Dorian saw to it that another article was published in the magazine, using his preliminary sketches, the finished portrait and her studies of the sittings. More commissions came his way from some of the leading names in theatre and films.

Suddenly they were in vogue: the bright new couple among the elite of society. Their efforts to remain private collapsed under a welter of invitations to attend the openings of new plays, the opera, for dinner parties and weekends at homes of celebrities. They were flattered and fawned over, as others had been before them, by a bored society searching for new vitality to sustain its flagging energies.

A London publisher asked them to do a book detailing Alan's work on a painting, accompanied by Dorian's photographs. Alan agreed, but somewhat reluctantly; he was growing weary of doing work he considered unimportant, and of a social life that had little interest for him. Dorian, however, appeared to thrive on the attention that was being paid to them.

She insisted they celebrate the signing of the contract for the book with a large party; they took over a private club for an evening. It turned into a crowded, noisy affair that went on until the early hours of the morning. Alan enjoyed it for a while, but grew uncomfortable as the evening wore on.

"Why so quiet?" Dorian asked as they drove home. "It was a wonderful evening!" She leaned over and kissed him. The kiss tasted of alcohol, and Alan drew back. "Oh Christ, you're turning moody on me," she sulked, drawing away. Then she said pensively, "Remember what you said to me on Long Island, when we were planning on going to New York together? How you would paint and I would take pictures of you and the famous people who sat for you? Don't you think it's incredible that it finally turned out that way?"

"Of course I do," he replied. "It's what I always wanted. But . . ."

"Oh shit, there's always a 'but'! What is it now?"

"Dorian, I don't want to argue—it's been a long evening and we're both tired—"

"—and I'm drunk, right? God, you can be a pain in the ass!"

Alan remained silent for the rest of the drive. In the course of the last few months, his apprehensions about Dorian had grown and crystallized into a persistent voice of discord. It spoke to him when she expressed frustration over her work, or when, after a day of maddening pressure at the magazine, she drank herself down from seething tension to a manageable stupor. He tried to understand, but his efforts to deny what he was witnessing, to overlay the situation with a patina of comforting lies, only increased his fears and convinced him of their veracity. Dorian was driving herself furiously toward an intangible goal that constantly eluded her. She would tell him that all she wanted was respect for her work, her talent; later she would say that she cared nothing for the opinions of her colleagues and social peers. In private, she despaired that her background was a trap from which she could never extricate herself, but in public she reveled in the attention paid to her. When Alan patiently tried to make her understand what was happening, she became argumentative and sullen.

They began to depend on sex as a means of evading this unresolved conflict; the euphoria of sensual pleasure disguised the pain of the wounds they were inflicting on one another.

One morning, while they were having breakfast, Alan opened a letter that had come in the mail. "This sounds wonderful," he exclaimed.

"Another request for a portrait?"

"No, it's from the real estate agent in Dublin. He's located a house in County Wicklow, in a place called the Vale of Clare. Another artist lived there and it has a large studio on the second floor, two bedrooms, a study, living room, two baths—"

"Sounds lovely," Dorian said quietly. "But a bit remote . . ."

"No, it's only twenty-five or thirty miles from Dublin, and we can get to London by plane in less than an hour."

She put down her coffee and looked at him questioningly. "You really want to do this, don't you? Move to Ireland?"

"Of course—I told you that months ago. Now I can afford it." He reached across the table and took her hands. "Dorian, we could make a home—"

"We have a home, here." Her voice was abruptly harsh. "We have this place, our work, our friends, all the things we do . . ."

"That's a schedule of activities, not a home! I want a wife, not a career woman, part-time society playgirl and mistress. And I want children!"

"Children!"

"Of course! Dorian, I want to marry you!"

"Stop it!" Dorian pulled her hand away and got up from the table. She turned her back on him, walked to the windows, and stared down at the small garden in back of the house.

"What is it? What are you afraid of?" he asked.

"I'm afraid of everything—all of it."

❦

In late August Dorian told Alan she was taking a week's vacation and wanted to go to Paris to see David. "He's reserved a suite for us in the hotel, and said he couldn't wait to see you."

"Sounds great—I could use a break. I have one more session with Mick and Bianca, and the painting will be finished."

"The timing's perfect! She told me she thinks you're a genius, and wants you to paint all their friends—"

"God help me!" Alan laughed. "Mick told me something more interesting the other day . . ."

"Oh? What?"

"They're thinking of getting married in September."

Dorian was silent, and Alan went on, "I told him we've been talking about that, too—"

"We haven't talked about it in months," she snapped.

"I know—but we'll have to soon; I've bought the house in Ireland."

"You know that as soon as we get back from Paris I have the fall issue to get out! I'll be working around the clock! I can't just take off!"

Alan said quietly, "Dorian, I've bought the house. I could go on ahead, get it set up and ready for us. We could be married here, after you've finished and the magazine has had enough time to get someone else. Try to understand—I don't want to go on doing one portrait after another. The money isn't that important to me, but my work is. I need the time to experiment, try out some new ideas. I'm getting too facile, stale, disinterested in my subjects . . ."

"I know, I know! You've been telling me that for months!"

329

"Then start listening to me! I need a change—and I think you do, too!"

She stared at him intently. "Would you go without me?"

"Yes, if I had to."

"You said that very quickly—didn't hesitate for a minute!"

"I've been thinking about it a long time." Alan waited, but she remained silent. "Am I asking you to give up that much?" he asked. "The book we did together was a success—didn't that prove anything to you? There's so much more we could do—"

"The book was tied to your work, to you!" she said angrily, beginning to cry. "They never asked me for a book of my own! If we get married, it will always be like that! First I had to fight being a St. Clair, now you want me to fight being a Conway!"

"Can't you see that it doesn't have to be that way?"

"No! You want a home and children, but I have a position here, one I fought like hell to get. People listen to me here!" She broke into deep sobs.

Alan took her in his arms. "I know how you feel. All I ask is that you think about it, really think about it." He sat down, let her curl up in his lap and rocked her gently. They sat quietly until she grew calm.

25

DAVID WAS WAITING for them at the airport. Alan saw him
first, and thought, How typical of David to appear so aloof
from the crowds swirling around him, as if he were part of
another setting altogether.

Dorian rushed up to him and hugged him ecstatically.
"God, how I've missed you! You look wonderful!"

"Liar! I look like shit!" He let Dorian go and extended his
hand to Alan with a trace of reserve. ". . . It's been a long
time."

Alan saw the apprehension in his eyes. He ignored the
awkward gesture and embraced him in a bear hug. "Too
long, David. It's good to see you again!"

They pulled apart, grinning foolishly at each other until
they heard the click of Dorian's camera.

"You both look like silly apes!" she exclaimed. Then she
linked her arms through theirs and began to run, pulling them
along until all three were racing through the airport.

At the hotel, David ushered them into their suite. There
were flowers everywhere and an ice bucket of champagne
and glasses had been set out.

"David, this is beautiful," Alan said. "Thank you."

"Nothing but the best for my nearest and dearest! Shall we
toast the occasion?"

"You two toast, I have to change and clean up, then we
can take off," Dorian said. She picked up her makeup case
and started for the bathroom. "You have twenty minutes to
catch up."

"Just twenty minutes?" David asked, laughing.

"It hasn't been all that interesting, at least not for you!"
she shot back, closing the door against the obscene gesture he
made to her.

"Some things never change," Alan chuckled.

"Don't you believe it—everything's changed." David opened the bottle of champagne and poured two glasses. He handed one to Alan and said, "To old times."

Alan echoed the sentiment and they drank. David studied Alan carefully.

"Do I pass inspection?"

'I remember you saying that the morning by the pool, when Dorian showed up *au naturel*," David said with a smile. "Yes, success looks good on you."

"You look pretty good yourself—the apple-cheeked boy has turned into a man of the world."

"I was never an apple-cheeked boy, and you know it!" He glanced at himself in a mirror and delicately touched his hair with his fingertip. "It's still not too bad, though, is it?"

The off-hand, effeminate gesture caught Alan by surprise; David had changed more than he realized. His face was thinner, and his lips had a pouty, sullen expression that reminded Alan of male models in fashion magazines. He was still extraordinarily handsome, but there was a hint of strain and restlessness in his amber-colored eyes, an uneasiness that had replaced the once calm self-assurance.

They were quiet for a few minutes then, both started to speak at once. Alan smiled and waved his hand, "You first—"

"I just wanted to get something out of the way up front, about the last time we saw each other . . ." David began.

"For Christ's sake, don't apologize," Alan broke in. "I behaved stupidly, not only then, but later; I should have called and apologized to you."

"Thank you," David murmured. "Now I don't have to do that old 'Christ-was-I-drunk' routine—"

"Not with me," Alan replied sincerely. "We were close friends once; let's be that way again."

Dorian came into the room dressed in a white blouse, dark brown culottes and boots, a wide-brimmed felt hat and a shoulder bag. "Okay," she announced, "I'm ready. How do I look?"

"Like you just bought that outfit off the rack in the UNICEF store," David muttered, then ducked as she threw an ashtray at him.

❦

Despite the August heat and the crowds of tourists, the three of them kept up an exhilarating pace of sight-seeing, shopping, dining and nightclubbing, breezing through the city as though they owned it. But with each passing day, it became increasingly difficult for David to be with Alan, who was even handsomer and more self-assured than when they had first met. David found himself confronting the same pain and terrors that had obsessed him years before. He saw Alan now as a man who lived as he pleased and did work that had meaning for him. By contrast, David viewed his own life as an empty ritual: during the day he worked at being gracious and charming to important guests, and, with the help of Edmund Duclos, the manager, kept track of operations at the other hotels on the Continent; in the evenings, when he wasn't involved in a business or social event, he haunted cafés and clubs, shabby rooming houses and dimly lit alleys. Experience had taught him to carry little money and false identification in case he was beaten and robbed by the tough young punks who provided the thrills and fear he now sought out. He was powerless to end his involvement in the dangerous exploits that had become so irresistible.

One morning, toward the end of the week of Alan and Dorian's visit, David stood in the bathroom shaving. When he was finished, he examined his reflection with the discernment of a jeweler inspecting a gem for flaws. His face was pale, and dark circles magnified his eyes. The strain of keeping up pretenses was evident in the fine lines of tension around his eyes and mouth. He was reminded of a line from Cocteau's *Orpheus*—something about how Death did not come at the end of one's life, you had only to look in a mirror to see him at work every day. The thought made him shudder.

He went into the bedroom and began to dress, recalling what had happened the night before. They had spent the evening making the rounds of clubs and discos, and had ended up in a gay bar that David rarely frequented; too many men that he knew in society had been seen there. But he felt safe with Dorian and Alan by his side. Many of the couples dancing together were men, and Alan appeared a little embarrassed. Dorian chided him for still being so naive, and David had daringly asked him if he wanted to try it. Goaded by Dorian, Alan agreed. Once he got over his awkwardness, he began to enjoy it; both he and David were good dancers. At one point he had laughed: "We're better than Kelly and Astaire!" Then Dorian cut in and the two of them finished out the dance while David watched from a table.

He could still remember the feel of Alan in his arms, the brief surge of joy he had felt at being with him like that. Now he was almost grateful that they would be leaving in a few days.

After dressing, he dialed their suite; they were supposed to have breakfast together. The phone rang several times before Alan answered it. His voice was low and sounded breathless:

"David? No—you didn't wake us . . ."

"Are we having breakfast downstairs, or shall I have something sent up?"

Alan hesitated before answering, "Uh—no, we're a little tired. These late nights have caught up with us . . . Why don't we meet you in the dining room in a couple of hours for lunch?"

David heard Dorian giggling in the background, then Alan whispering to her and laughing. His throat tightened and he said to Alan hurriedly, "Okay—I'll see you later—"

He hung up before Alan could reply, holding down the receiver as if to shut out the sound of their voices. His heart was pounding; they'd been making love when he called. He put the phone on the side table and fell back against the pillows, feeling tense and agitated.

❧

It was their last day in Paris. A soft rain had been falling all morning; the city had the silvery sheen of a steel engraving. Alan stood by the windows in their bedroom while Dorian dressed to go out to visit a few of the couturier houses and do some shopping.

"We've had such a great time, I really hate to leave," she said, slipping into a trench coat.

"Yes—it's been wonderful." He stared out at the slate gray day.

334

Dorian came up behind him and put her arms around his back. "Are you sorry to leave, too?"

"No. I have a lot to do when we get home . . ." He turned so that they faced each other. His eyes reflected the question they had ignored all week.

She pulled away from him. "You promised you wouldn't talk about Ireland until we got back to London."

"And I haven't. But tomorrow we'll be home . . ."

"Alan, please, let's not spoil the last day," she pleaded.

He sighed and kissed her. "Go shopping. Buy something outrageous and daring and we'll give the city one last shock before we leave."

She held him close and whispered, "I love you. You know that, don't you?"

"Yes, I know that. What time will you be back?"

"Before dinner. What are you going to do today?"

"I'm not sure—I may drop in at Foucault's . . ."

When she was gone, he remained at the windows, feeling restless and indecisive. There had been moments during the week when he had felt as if they were all performing for each other, being bright and witty in a brave attempt to re-capture the carefree days they had spent on Long Island. It had almost worked, like a drug that relieves a cold or a headache, but only for a few hours at a time.

The phone rang and he went to answer it. David's voice was cheery: "What's on the agenda for today?"

"Dorian's out shopping for the afternoon and I'm being artistically moody—can't decide if I want to go out and stare into the depths of the Seine or sit and watch the rain fall."

"I have a better idea—I'll have lunch sent up for both of us, then we can talk, drink, talk, drink some more . . ."

Alan laughed. "I like your plan better than mine."

"See you in a few minutes."

As soon as the waiter had wheeled out the table with the remains of their lunch, David went to the bar.

"Now we can get down to some serious drinking, a perfect antidote to a gray day in Paris."

He filled two glasses and brought them to where Alan was sprawled on the couch.

"Shall we make a toast?" Alan asked, taking his drink.

David sat down in a chair near him and replied," To hell with toasts—let's just drink!" He took a swallow and licked his lips. "Perfect—a rainy day, good liquor and an old friend. I'm glad we decided to do this, it's the first chance we've had to be alone."

"I really should do some sketches of you—you're so changed from when we first met. Are you happy being in Paris?"

"I like living here. Especially without dear old Dad crouched over me like a gargoyle. It's the first time I ever had a chance to be my own man, whatever that is."

"I must admit in all honesty that I was never fond of your father."

"Join the club." David took another sip of his drink. "He's pretty well recovered from his stroke, but the doctors won't let him travel, thank God. Oh, he still works from his office at home, of course; calls me every couple of days and bellows. But the sound is much weaker, almost mewling at times, I'm happy to say."

"Well, you've obviously been able to handle the business here—"

"What little there is left to handle. We've sold a good many of the hotels. Aside from the way Jonathan fucked up, the Japanese and the Arabs finally got to us with offers we couldn't refuse. There's still the chain in the States, of course, and the major ones here: London, Paris, Berlin and Rome— and I get letters every day with offers on those. Especially this one. But I've come to think of this place as home; I doubt if we'll ever sell it."

David leaned forward, cradling his glass between his hands. His face was getting flushed from drinking and his eyes were sparkling, mischievous. "Enough about the fortunes of the St. Clairs—what about you? What's next in your illustrious career?"

"I'll need another drink for that question," Alan said. David took his glass and went to the bar to refill it, pouring himself another one at the same time. He came over and sat down heavily next to Alan, handing him his drink.

"At this rate we'll be plastered by the time Dorian gets back," Alan muttered, taking a sip.

"Dorian can do her own drinking—and does," David said

woozily. "Tell me about your adventures. You've done a hell of a lot of work in the last four years; you've become rich and famous . . ."

"Not quite rich, and just a little famous," Alan said, smiling.

"Bullshit! I knew you were going to make it when you did our portrait . . . fucking talent is going to take you all the way!"

He stared at Alan morosely, then his face brightened. "Remember when we said we'd make you famous? That morning in the kitchen, after we skinny-dippped in the pool? And we did, didn't we?"

"Well, yes, I suppose so—"

"Suppose, hell! If it hadn't been for our portrait, and all the things Olivia did for you—even that show you had here, back in '68 . . . I saw that painting you did of Madeline. Christ, it was great. You really fucked Jonathan over! God, I wish I could have seen his face when he saw that painting! And you punched the bastard out, didn't you?" David laughed and threw his arm around Alan's shoulders, hugging him.

Alan began to laugh, recalling the incident. "The son of a bitch looked like he was going to have a heart attack!"

David tilted his head back and emptied his glass. Some whiskey dribbled over his chin and he wiped it away with the back of his hand. "The prick deserved to be killed," he said drunkenly. "After what he did to your mother, and the way he beat you that night at the house—I tried to help, Alan, you know that? I tried . . ."

"I know, I know," Alan nodded.

They were silent for a few minutes. Alan was aware of the rain pattering against the windows, and of David, sitting close to him. He leaned his head back against David's arm, still around his shoulders, feeling mellow and content. David was right—the St. Clairs had made him famous; they had been an integral part of his career and his life from the first day they had met. The thought wasn't galling any more; he was suffused with a warm flush of gratitude and impulsively took David's hand. "I have a lot to be grateful to you for—you, Dorian and Olivia," he said with boozy sincerity.

David gave him a timorous smile. His blond hair was

tousled across his forehead and tears glistened on his lashes. The muscles in his jaws worked painfully as he tried to speak. He pressed Alan's hand in his, then suddenly lifted it to his lips. "God, I love you, Alan, I always have . . ."

"I know, David—and I love you too," Alan said simply.

David shifted, trying to gather Alan into his arms. The move was awkward and unexpected; Alan found himself being tightly embraced. "Hey, wait—" he said, giggling a little. He struggled against him clumsily. "David, this is silly—"

"Alan, please, let me," David whispered. His voice sounded dry with fear and need. "Please—I've wanted you for so long . . ."

Alan felt David's warm breath on his neck, lips moving over his chin, seeking his mouth. "David, don't," he said weakly, pushing him away. "We're both drunk—"

Then David was kissing him, forcing his tongue into his mouth, one hand moving anxiously between Alan's thighs to his crotch. The kiss grew in intensity, and for a few seconds Alan accepted it, dazed by surprise and weakened by his intake of alcohol. Fingers were tearing at his belt, opening his fly and reaching inside his shorts. David's body was like steel, pressing him down into the couch. He felt a hand wrapped around his cock, pulling it free.

"I want to kiss it, suck it," David was moaning. "I want you to fuck me, fuck me like you did Dorian, all those times in the boat house, I used to watch you, wishing it was me . . . me!"

A terrible anger swept through Alan, rising into an uncontrollable rejection of what David was doing to him. He grabbed at his hair, pulled his head up sharply and smashed his hand across David's face.

David fell back, his mouth drawn into a grimace of anger and desperation. Suddenly he sprang at Alan and dragged him off the couch and onto the floor.

They grappled vainly, like children flailing senselessly at one another. Both of them were bleeding, but the injuries went unnoticed. They grew light-headed from the exertion and their strength was quickly exhausted. David fell across Alan's chest, breathing in hoarse gasps; trapped under his weight, Alan remained still, and tried to gather his energies.

"Don't you understand?" David cried brokenly. "All these years—what you've done to me?"

Alan heaved his body up, toppling David off him, and managed to get to his feet, but David lunged after him, catching him by the shoulders.

Enraged, Alan whirled around and struck him in the stomach. David doubled over and Alan lashed out again, punching him until he sank to the floor, unconscious.

At that moment, Dorian walked in.

Alan stood at the foot of David's bed while the hotel doctor finished examining him. Dorian sat beside her brother, clasping his hand.

"There's nothing broken," the doctor said, fixing a bandage over David's cheek and another near his left eye. "He's just badly bruised." He closed his medical bag and left the room, shutting the door discreetly behind him.

Alan started forward, but a glance from Dorian stopped him. Her face was streaked with dried tears, her dark eyes blazed with anger.

"Dorian, I told you, we were both drunk," Alan said. "David didn't know what he was doing, and I simply lost control of myself—"

"I don't want to discuss it," she said savagely. "Why don't you get the hell out of here?"

Alan drew back at the vehemence in her voice. "I'll wait for you in our room—we can talk then."

"Don't wait. I'm going to stay with David. I'll call the magazine and tell them I've been detained for a few days."

"Then I'll stay with you, of course," Alan protested.

"I don't want you here! Go back to London, tonight! As a matter of fact, you can pack up and clear out of my house and go to Ireland! That's what you really want to do, isn't it?"

"What the hell are you saying? We just had a fight, that's all! David, tell her what happened—we were just drunk!"

The two of them stared at him stonily, not speaking. Alan suddenly remembered them staring at him the same way in Kennedy Airport, the day he had come to pick them up. For a moment it was as if the years had dropped away, and he was once more the object of their disdain, excluded again from the private, secret world that only they inhabited. The fight with David had brought them full circle.

That evening, on the plane back to London, Alan reflected bitterly that Dorian had seized upon the incident as a means of escaping a final confrontation with him. In doing so, she had torn the last threads that had held them together. Whatever hope he'd had for a future with her was gone now. Yet he felt no sense of betrayal or outrage, as he had in the past. Instead, in a way that he could never have expected, she had given him something that he had not been able to attain by himself: his freedom.

26

Paris: September 1973

THE STRANGER WAS handsome in a way that few men are. In his mid-thirties, he had thick blue black hair that was slightly long and curled up where it touched the collar of his jacket. Equally thick eyebrows arched over large black eyes that gazed calmly from under a fringe of long, sooty lashes. His nose was short and straight, slightly thick across the bridge, his dark red lips full and boldly curved. He was tall, and when he moved the power of his body was markedly evident under impeccably tailored clothes. He carried himself with a nobility of bearing that suggested an aristocratic lineage.

David had noticed him when he got off the elevator. Now he watched as the man stopped near the entrance to the dining room and glanced around the lobby. He caught sight of David, and for a few seconds their eyes locked. The glimmer of a smile touched the corners of his mouth, then he turned away and began talking to the maître d'. David went over to the bell captain and asked, "Who is that man over there, talking with Gerard?"

"A new guest, sir. He checked in yesterday afternoon—I don't remember his name. Shall I ask the desk clerk?"

"No, don't bother. Thank you, Marcel . . ."

David watched until the man was led into the dining room and seated at a table, then he left the hotel to attend a dinner at the home of the banker Jean Delane.

Later that evening he returned to the hotel and stopped in at the small bar off the lobby for a drink. He was disturbed; on the wall in the library of the Delane house he had seen Alan's portrait of Madame Delane. A few brief words about Alan and his work had been exchanged, but out of respect for David nothing was said about the scandal involving

341

Jonathan, or Alan's part in it. David had left as soon as he could.

It was late now, and there were only a few people in the bar, listening to a woman sitting at the piano singing a song by Charles Aznavour. The plaintive melody only added to David's troubled feelings; seeing the portrait had reminded him of Alan, and of their irreconcilable separation.

He took a seat at the bar and ordered a drink, lighted a cigarette and stared into the smoked glass mirror behind the bar. His reflection was blurred, deeply shadowed in the dim lighting, giving the appearance of a ghost figure or an image seen in a dream: wavering and ethereal, lacking all substance. He smiled, thinking of himself as having more reality in the mirror than in life; during the last year he had succumbed to an existence that was as predictable and enervating as living out a prison sentence.

"May I join you?" a voice behind him asked.

In the mirror, David saw a figure standing behind him; it looked as if it had materialized out of the dark glass and was waiting for a word from him to assume life. He swung around and looked up into the face of the man he had seen earlier that evening.

"Yes, please . . ." He indicated the seat beside him.

The man sat down and ordered a drink from the bartender. He reached into his jacket and brought out a silver cigarette case. His hands were large and strong, and as he took out a cigarette and lighted it a diamond ring caught a flash of light.

"Have you had a pleasant evening?" he asked David.

"Not very. I attended a dinner with some business acquaintances. And you?"

"It was very quiet. After dinnner I wrote some letters and read for a while . . ."

His voice was soft and his accent hard to define; one of the Balkan countries, David thought. He felt a little nervous; they were sitting close together and he was aware of the man's body heat, the subtle scent of his cologne. "Are you staying in Paris long?" he asked.

"A week, possibly longer. It all depends on how my business goes."

"What kind of work do you do?"

"I represent a firm of importers. I used to live here, some years ago. I came here for dinner many times; the cuisine is superb."

"Where do you live now?"

The man smiled, revealing even white teeth. "I really don't know," he confessed, then laughed, "I've been traveling so much, I've come to think of Europe as my home. But I admit, I'm tired of moving about. And I miss Paris. It has changed so, since I was last here. I must take time to explore and rediscover it all over again . . ."

David sensed the hint of an invitation, but hesitated to speak; the man was a guest in the hotel, and from all appearances was straight. Yet there was something in the way he smiled, leaned close to him, that suggested the possibility of intimacy.

"And how long are *you* staying in Paris?" the man asked.

"I live here," David replied. "I'm David St. Clair; my father owns the hotel, and I'm the director of the chain—"

"Ah yes, the son and heir—I knew your uncle, slightly—we had a few drinks together—a charming man." His voice became sympathetic. "I was shocked to read of his—untimely death. Did they ever catch the man?"

"No, but the case is still open. I took over the operation after he died."

"But you are so young!" The man smiled warmly. "You must be very clever." He glanced at his watch and sighed, "It is late, and I have so much to do tomorrow. Perhaps you would join me for dinner tomorrow evening? There are few people I know in Paris, these days—I would be very grateful for your company."

The invitation was offered casually, yet David was aware of a subtle intensity in the man's voice.

"Yes, I'd enjoy that," David replied.

"Good!" The man rose and held out his hand. "Until tomorrow evening, then; shall we say about nine?"

David took his hand; it was warm and fastened on his with a quick powerful grip that shot through him like a small shock. "Yes, about nine," he stammered. "Thank you, Mr.—?"

"Oh, forgive me, I've not introduced myself. My name is Morel—Ellis Morel."

During the next few days they met several times for drinks or dinner. One morning Ellis called David and told him that he had the afternoon free, and asked if they could spend the time together walking in the city, then perhaps have dinner and see a show. David eagerly agreed; with each meeting he had become more intrigued by Morel, and not just because of his extraordinary handsomeness. He was intelligent, discerning, and solicitous of David, giving him his undivided attention when they were together, encouraging him to speak freely. However, he was careful to reveal little of himself; in the course of their meetings, Morel mentioned famous people he knew, countries he had lived in, schools he had attended, but maintained a vagueness about his personal life that added a darker color of mystery to his personality.

That afternoon, they wandered through the Tuileries, ending up at the Jeu de Paume, where they spent a few hours looking at the museum's collection of Impressionist paintings. Afterwards they strolled into the nearby terrace that overlooked the Place de la Concorde. The September day was overcast, the air warm and sultry. A slight breeze stirred through the trees, making the leaves tremble. David felt unsettled and a little apprehensive; Morel had been very quiet all afternoon.

Then he noticed two young men. One was seated on a bench a few hundred yards away, the other was leaning up against the trunk of a tree nearby. The boy who was seated suddenly stood up and stretched, showing off his athletic build in a white pullover and dark trousers. He glanced at the other boy, then made an elaborate show of walking by him casually, stopping to gaze at the view. In a few moments, the other boy approached, keeping a careful distance away, and also glanced at the view. David watched them intently, caught up in their charade.

"Charming, aren't they?" Morel asked, startling him out of his concentration. "In a moment or two, one will put a cigarette in his mouth, search his pockets for a match, then turn to the other with a helpless gesture and a smile—ah, there, you see—it's as I said. Now they will chat for a few minutes, and then—"

David remained silent, watching, until the two young men walked off together. With someone else, he might have made a joke, but in Morel's presence he was reluctant to comment.

Finally Ellis said, "I've not heard you mention any women in your life, aside from your sister, Dorian . . ."

The statement was uttered in a seemingly off-hand way, yet David knew what Morel was asking. He replied defensively, "And you—you've not mentioned a woman in your life." He searched Ellis's eyes for a response.

"I'm more comfortable in the company of men."

David was disarmed by the candor of his reply, and felt his pulse begin to quicken. Morel offered David his hand. "Come," he said. "I'm starved. Let's find a quiet café and have something to eat. Then we can discuss what we will do this evening—a play, perhaps, or a film? Or did you have other plans?"

As in a gesture of surrender, David gave him his hand. "No, I have no other plans. Whatever you want to do is fine with me."

Ellis smiled. "Then we are of one mind."

ℰ

In the evening they returned to the hotel and went directly to Morel's suite. Once inside, Ellis drew the blinds and turned on a small table lamp. He approached David and said, "You look very pale. Are you nervous?"

"Yes."

"There's no need to be."

"I know." David laughed self-consciously. "Usually I'm the one who is calm and the other person is nervous."

"Am I so different from the other men you've been with?"

"Yes."

"Good." Morel gave him a tender smile and drew him close. "I do not want to be thought of like the others. You, too, are like no one else I've ever been with."

They kissed, tentatively at first, then more deeply. A wave of excitement went through David and he moved against Morel aggressively, his hands urgently seeking to touch flesh.

Morel pulled away and said softly, "No, we shall do it as I say. Yes?"

It was not a request but a command, and David acquiesced. Morel began to undress him slowly. As each article of clothing was removed, David felt increasingly vulnerable. Morel's hands caressed his chest and stomach, traced down his hips and along the insides of his thighs until he was quivering; but Morel would not allow him to move, tacitly indicating with the pressure of his fingertips that he wanted him to remain still. When David was completely naked, Morel stood up and whispered, "Take off my clothes."

David obeyed with trembling hands. The sculpted figure was powerfully built, classically proportioned, and had the tense energy of an animal poised to spring at the slightest movement of its prey. David stood waiting breathlessly. Then, with a sudden, effortless grace, Morel picked him up, held him in arms as if he were a child, and walked into the bedroom.

ツ

The next morning, David was working in his office when his secretary admitted a delivery boy carrying a long florist's box. The boy handed it to him, saying, "I was told to deliver this directly to you, Monsieur."

When the boy and his secretary were gone, David opened the box. It contained a spray of rare orchids. There was a card, written in a fine script: "Like no one else I've ever been with."

He dialed Morel's room and waited impatiently as the phone rang. Morel answered and David said, "A man doesn't send flowers to another man . . ."

"But why not? Don't you like them?"

"Of course—they're beautiful. But what do I tell my secretary?"

"That they are from a dancer at the Folies Bergère whose life will never be the same now that she has met you."

David began to laugh, and said, "I just can't see you in tassels, net stockings and stiletto heels."

"I may surprise you one night," Morel responded. "Why

are you working on this beautiful morning? Can you take the day off? Or better still, the weekend?"

"Yes, I suppose I can. Why, what did you have in mind?"

"That is what you Americans call a loaded question. Stay where you are, but be prepared to leave at a moment's notice."

"Where are we going?"

"I shall surprise you."

An hour later David's secretary told him that a car was waiting for him in front of the hotel. David went outside and saw a black Mercedes limousine at the curb. A young man in a chauffeur's uniform stood by the back door, holding it open. Morel was inside, grinning at him.

"What is all this?" David asked, getting in beside him. "I have a car if you want to go somewhere."

"But not like this," Morel replied.

He pushed a button and opaque windows rolled up, closing them off from the stares of passersby. Another button controlled a window separating them from the chaufeur.

"Now we are alone," Morel said.

"But where are we going?"

"To Senlis. It's not far, only thirty miles or so, but I have always loved the city—it is out of another century. And you see"—he pointed to a wicker hamper on the floor—"I have brought a picnic lunch, and"—he released a catch and a small door opened revealing a bar—"chilled wine and glasses."

"You've thought of everything."

"Are you pleased?"

David leaned his head back against the plush seat and smiled delightedly. "What do you think?"

Morel's dark eyes gleamed in the pale light inside the car. He reached out and touched David's lips with his fingers. "I think you should take off your clothes . . ."

"Here? What about—?" He glanced toward the chaufeur.

"He can see nothing, and if he wishes to speak to me, there's a phone." Morel's voice sank to a whisper. "Take off your clothes, David."

In the late afternoon the car drew off the road and rolled to a stop near a tree.

"We need some nourishment," Morel said, kissing David lightly. "You bring the hamper and I shall bring the wine." He picked up the phone and gave a few quick instructions to the chauffeur, who got out and opened the door for them. A cloth was neatly folded over his arm. He preceded them to a grassy spot under the tree and spread the cloth, took the hamper from David's hands, and deftly set out a service of china and gleaming silver. He glanced up at David and smiled; in his haste to dress, David had left his shirt unbuttoned. Morel set down an ice bucket and glasses, dismissed the chauffeur with a wave of his hand and opened the bottle.

"I think he knows what's going on," David said worriedly, watching the young man return to the car.

"Ah, you Americans—so cautious and fearful, like children fumbling with each other in a locked bathroom. Of course he knows what's going on, but he's been well paid for his discretion." Morel glanced over at the young man, who was leaning up against the car. "If anything, he probably wishes we would ask him to join us—"

David's face reddened slightly and Morel laughed. He dropped down beside him and said, "Does the idea intrigue you? He's very young, only twenty, I believe—and rather attractive, don't you think?"

A wave of jealousy swept through David. "No, I don't," he said coldly.

Morel put his arm around David's shoulders. "You should not be upset. I was only thinking of you, what desires you might wish to gratify. For myself, I am content to remain only with you."

David relaxed into Morel's arm and said firmly, "Good, let's keep it that way—at least for the time being," he added slyly.

Early that evening they entered the city of Senlis, drove past the ruins of the Royal Palace and wound through ancient streets and down narrow alleys. In the fading twilight, the city appeared medieval, forbidding.

"Where are we staying?" David asked. "Or do you intend for us to spend the night in the car?"

"My God, no," Morel said, laughing. "There's only so much fucking that can be done on the back seat of a car,

348

even one as *formidable* as this! We are going to the home of a friend of mine, a business acquaintance who is, shall we say—sympathetic?"

David grew hesitant. "Is that wise? I mean, after all, we both have a position to maintain, and—"

"—we must fear for our reputations? Not here, David. You have nothing to worry about here—I have seen to that. You must trust me."

"I don't think I have any choice."

The car drew up to a crumbling wall covered with ivy, and turned into a courtyard that faced an old stone house. The dust of centuries seemed to have settled into the chipped, cracked Gothic arches, and field mice scurried through surrounding underbrush. Leaded glass windows glowed with a faint light from inside, casting pale rays on the cobblestones of the courtyard. The car stopped and the young chauffeur got out and opened the door for them.

"What the hell is this place?" David asked. "It has all the charm of the Bastille."

Morel smiled and took his arm, leading him up the steps to the thick wooden front doors. "It's a retreat for gentlemen—very out-of-the-way and very discreet. I'm sure you'll enjoy it."

He pulled the bell cord and a few seconds later the door swung open, revealing a flood of amber light. A young man in a close-fitting black shirt and trousers greeted them, then led the way down a wide hallway to a study, where an older man with thick white hair and a smooth, unlined face stood waiting.

"Ellis! It's good to see you again!" He and Morel embraced, then David was introduced: "This is Roger Severin, an old and close friend."

"Welcome, my boy," he said heartily, shaking David's hand. Severin was dressed in a long velvet lounging robe with a white scarf tucked around his neck. His small blue eyes were shadowed by bushy white eyebrows, and a neat vandyke beard disguised the soft line of his chin. After examining David carefully, he said to Morel, "Your room is ready; if you're hungry, simply ring the bell and a tray will be brought up by Jean—" He gestured to the young man in dark clothes standing silently by the door.

349

"Thank you, Roger," Morel said. "Perhaps we can have a drink later?"

"Of course, my friend. I shall be here all evening."

David and Morel followed the young man up a wide, curving staircase to the second floor, and down a gallery to the door of their room. In contrast to the dark, crumbling facade of the building, the interior was richly furnished and well lit. Teak paneling gleamed in the light of coach lamps, and thick rugs and tapestry wall hangings subdued the sound of their footsteps.

The young man opened the door of their room. Going in before them, he turned on lamps and opened the door to a bathroom, then left, murmuring, "If there's anything you need, Messieurs, just ring . . ."

David stood in the center of the room and looked around. "I would never have expected all this—"

A wide, canopied bed occupied one corner, and deep, comfortable easy chairs were grouped around a low table near an ornately carved stone fireplace with a high mantel. The walls were paneled in deep, burnished mahogany, except for one long area that was completely mirrored, making the large room seem twice as spacious.

"I thought you'd like it," Morel said, throwing himself across the bed. "I discovered it years ago, while I was living in Paris."

"Is it a private club?" David asked.

"In a manner of speaking," Morel replied, taking off his jacket and kicking off his shoes. He leaned back against a bank of pillows and smiled lazily. "Membership is very exclusive, and the place is only busy on the weekends; I was lucky Roger had a room left."

"But what do you do here? Besides the obvious," David grinned, sitting down next to him.

"You can do everything here," he replied, pulling David down beside him. "Anything you've dreamt, fantasies you've had since childhood, games you've always wanted to play . . ." He stroked David's crotch gently.

"I don't understand—and if you don't stop that, we may not leave the room this evening."

"I doubt if we shall leave it all weekend," Morel laughed.

He let go of David and stood up. "Come, I will show you what the entertainment is."

David followed him to the mirrored wall. "Turn off those lights," Morel said. David flicked off the lamps, plunging the room into darkness. "Now watch—" Morel told him. He reached out and touched a switch on the wall.

The mirrors suddenly lit up, becoming windows into several other, smaller rooms. In each were men, varying in age from eighteen to fifty, some clothed and some naked. All of them were engaged in sexual activity.

"Jesus Christ!" David whispered. "Can they see us?"

"Not at all, unless they want to. See—that room there is dark. And if you meet someone later in the evening whom you've seen, you say nothing, except perhaps to invite him to your room. Discretion is the rule of the club. What do you think?"

In one room a young boy was getting fucked by an older man, while another youth had the boy's head buried between his thighs. In the next room, a husky man in his forties lay on a narrow bed, while a masked man lashed his buttocks with a strap. In another room a delicately built young boy wearing a bizarre costume of veils weaved about in a sinuous dance before the glazed eyes of an elderly man reclining on several large pillows. In the last and largest room a group of ten or twelve men were in the midst of an orgy, their bodies arched, limbs entangled, moving slowly like some great, lethargic beast.

Morel had unzipped David's trousers and slipped his hand inside. "It's thrilling, isn't it—seeing all this?" he whispered.

"Yes." David's throat was dry, his heart pounding. He felt as if he had entered a secret world, where dreams and reality merged in a phantasmagoria of unleashed longings. He was dimly aware of Morel loosening his clothes and taking them off. The door of their room opened and two figures slipped in: Jean, the young porter who had assisted them, and the boy who was their chauffeur. Both were naked. In the yellow glow of light coming from the other rooms, David saw them glide across the floor like wraiths. A warm mouth fastened on his lips, a tongue fluttered across his chest, fingertips played over his buttocks. He reached out blindly with his hands, encountering smooth flesh and erect organs, felt Morel encircle him from behind with strong arms and press against him. Sensations burned through him like flames; he fell back in submission, was stroked and caressed, then lifted and carried to the bed. Other men joined them and David was possessed by a demonic fury, feverishly exploring the labyrinth of sexuality offered to him. He was master and slave by turn, experiencing the wonderment of pain given and received, achieving heights of ecstasy that made him cry out for surcease, then demand more. Through the long hours of the night, he enjoyed a power more liberating than any single moment he had known in his entire life.

❦

Late on Sunday night David and Morel returned to Paris. As they drove through brightly lit boulevards, passing crowded sidewalk cafés and throngs of people promenading, David felt as if he were emerging from a drug-induced state.

"Are you all right?" Morel asked with some concern. "You've been sleeping since we left Senlis."

"I shall probably sleep for a week," he replied, staring out the window with heavy-lidded eyes.

"My surprise weekend was too much for you?"

"Let's just say it was more than I expected."

"Are you angry with me for taking you there?"

"No, not at all—it was exciting, more thrilling than anything I've ever imagined. It's just that I—"

"It frightened you, perhaps?"

"Yes, a little—I'm glad I experienced it, and that you were there with me, but I'm not sure I want to do it again."

"Then we will not; it was merely an adventure I thought you might enjoy. After all, we have each other." Morel drew David into his arms. "That is enough for both of us, yes?"

David put his head against Morel's chest and closed his eyes, feeling content and cared for. "Yes," he answered, "more than enough."

A few days later David was in his office with Edmund Duclos, the manager of the hotel. Duclos was saying heatedly, "But we must inform your father of our predicament! The hotel has been losing money steadily over the past year despite all our efforts." He waved a letter he was hold-ing in his hand. "This offer cannot simply be ignored!"

"I don't want to argue the matter!" David declared. "We will not consider any offers to buy the hotel. I'm aware that we've had losses but in time the situation will improve—every hotel goes through a bad period . . ."

"This *bad period* started years ago, when your uncle was here!"

"I cannot trouble my father with this now—his health has been failing, and he depends on us to keep things going. We'll begin a new advertising campaign, reduce some of our room prices and try to make up our losses in volume."

"Monsieur, I beg you to reconsider. I do not wish to im-pugn your capabilities, but your father has conducted business longer than you, he understands the—"

"Duclos, the subject is closed! Contact the advertising agency we've been using and make an appointment with them to see me. We'll begin working on a new campaign at once."

Duclos drew himself up, made a stiff bow and left the of-fice. David let out a sigh of relief and sat back in his chair, feeling tired; he had spent the night with Morel, getting little sleep. He smiled, thinking about the hours they had spent making love, and the plans they were beginning to formulate. Morel had told him that the firm he worked for was thinking of establishing a home office in Paris, and making him the head of it. He had already contacted a real estate agent and was looking for a house he could buy, a place they could make their home. David had received the news with mixed feelings; people would talk, the news might reach his father.

"You are still the erring son, hiding from his father's wrath," Morel had laughed. "But I understand, and I have a solution. I shall lease a place large enough so that part of it can be converted into an apartment for you. Then I will merely be your landlord—exacting the rent in my own fash-ion," he added with a wicked smile.

They had gone on to talk of things they would do, vaca-tions they would take together, people they would allow into their lives, a plan of living together that filled David with happiness.

He went back to work, glancing at his watch; Ellis was

supposed to call and let him know where they were meeting for dinner. An hour passed and his secretary knocked and entered the office.

"A message for you, Monsieur St. Clair," she said, handing him an envelope.

"Thank you, Denise," He recognized Morel's handwriting on the envelope and waited until she was gone to open it. The note was brief:

Unexpected change of plans. Must leave immediately to confer with my superiors concerning opening of Paris office. I should be back within a few days, barring any unforeseen complications. I am enclosing Roger Severin's phone number if you get too lonely.

Yours, Ellis

David rushed to the front desk and asked the clerk, "Has Monsieur Morel left yet?"

"Yes, he checked out over an hour ago."

"Did he leave a forwarding address?"

"No, he did not, Monsieur St. Clair."

A week went by with no word from Morel. At first David was impatient, but as more time passed, he grew frantic; something had happened to him, an accident, or perhaps he was ill. By the end of the second week he was desperate. He tried to remember the name of the firm Morel worked for— had he ever told him? He couldn't remember, and began to call the importing companies in the city. None of them had ever heard of Ellis Morel. He called the house in Senlis and asked for Roger Severin, only to be told that Severin had left the country for an extended vacation. Yes, they knew Monsieur Morel, but had no idea of his whereabouts. But he had left word that Monsieur St. Clair was to be made welcome any time he visited the house.

Hearing the last relieved David somewhat; in a sense it was another message from Morel, letting him know that if he were delayed, David could enjoy the pleasures of the house with no feelings of guilt. He reasoned to himself that Morel had not called or written out of concern for David's fear of being discovered; letters or calls might arouse the suspicions

354

of his secretary or the desk clerk; even while Morel had stayed at the hotel, David had been careful that they not be seen together too often in the bar or dining room. But these excuses crumbled as more time passed. He began to think that Morel had found someone else, and tortured himself imagining the man in the arms of another. By the end of a month, he was convinced that Morel had left him.

An old and familiar despair became his companion once more. He was irritable at work, leaving more and more of it in Duclos's hands, drinking despondently in the evenings, and finally driving to the house in Senlis every few days to lose himself in furious sieges of sex. He called his sister several times, wanting to confide in her as he once had, but was met with a barrage of Dorian's own problems; she had lost her job at the magazine in a power play by the editors and publishers, and was currently in the throes of a divorce scandal in which she had been named correspondent.

He took to prowling the streets, engaging the services of young men, and even risked taking them back to the hotel with him. At times he grew violent, abasing them and himself. The hotel doctor was heavily bribed to become a confidant, dressing bruises and wounds, and even supplying David with drugs.

Late one morning David was lying in bed, his head buzzing from a hangover, his throat raw from smoking. A young boy was beside him, sound asleep, his naked body sprawled carelessly, like a doll that had been flung in the corner by a petulant child. The room was a shambles: chairs overturned, clothes strewn across the floor, the remains of a late-night supper piled onto a dining cart. David groaned and threw his arm across his eyes to shut out the morning light. The boy beside him stirred and turned over on his stomach, burying his face in the pillows. David glanced at him in disgust and started to rise when the phone rang. He ignored it and it rang again and again. Finally he picked it up, cleared his throat and answered. It was Vivian. She sounded frantic.

"David, can you hear me?" she asked over the static on the line.

"Yes, what is it?" he asked impatiently.

"Your father—he insists that you come home at once, by the first plane!"

"What? I can't do that—what the hell does he want? Is he ill?"

"I don't know—yes, I think so—the doctor is on his way. But he's demanding that you come home. David, please, he's been like a madman all morning . . ."

"Damnit, I can't just leave! What does he want?"

"I don't know—he won't tell me. Please, for your sake . . ." She began to cry.

"All right, all right, I'll get there as soon as I can. My secretary will call you and let you know what flight I'm coming in on. Have the car waiting for me."

He hung up and lay back with a deep sigh, muttering, "Just what I needed—a visit with the folks at home."

He looked over at the boy and shook his arm. "Get up, punk—I have to leave."

The boy rolled over and opened his eyes, then sat up. "What time is it?"

"Late. Get dressed and leave by the service entrance." David got out of bed and slipped on a robe. He watched the boy struggle to his feet and search the room for his clothes. "May I bathe?" he asked.

"No, there's no time," David replied.

The boy pulled on his shirt and looked around for his pants. His legs were long and smooth, and his buttocks firm, muscular. David slipped his hand under his robe and touched himself gently. The boy saw the gesture and smiled, arched his back slightly and came over to him. He opened David's robe and fondled him.

"Must I leave so soon?" His fingers were firm, insistent.

David reached out and roughly pulled the boy to him. "No, you can stay; this may be my last chance to do this for a while."

27

Shortly after three o'clock in the morning David's plane landed at Kennedy Airport. He had slept uneasily on the flight, beset by disturbing fragments of dreams. Awake, he had stared out at the black void of sky, wondering why he had been summoned home so frantically. Was the old man dying at last? He contemplated the idea with little emotion, feeling only a nagging dread at the idea of seeing him again.

Charles, the family chauffeur, was waiting for him, and they began the long drive home. David was exhausted and slept most of the way. He roused himself as the car turned into the driveway and pulled up before the front entrance. It was almost five o'clock now, and still dark. The air was cold and damp, and he could hear the surf rolling in against the beach. The house looked pale and indistinct in the darkness. A light suddenly went on in the foyer, and Mrs. Childress opened the door.

"Chilly, what are you doing up at this hour?" David asked, embracing her.

"I'm up at all hours now," she replied gruffly. "Come in, before you catch cold—the weather's been miserable."

David followed her into the house and looked around warily. Even in the semidarkness he could see that nothing had been changed, not a single piece moved or replaced. Familiar smells hovered in the air: the odor of flowers, the lemony spice of furniture polish, a stray scent of his father's cigars, and in the background, lending an unmistakable bite to the atmosphere, the sea.

The housekeeper took his coat and said, "There's a fire in the living room; go and get warm. I'll bring you some coffee." She padded off down the hall, leaving him alone.

David started across the foyer. He had the eerie sensation

of expecting to see himself as a child come through a doorway or walk down the stairs. For a moment he thought he heard the sound of Dorian's laughter from the gallery and looked up, searching for her in the gloomy light. Even the sound of his steps on the marble floor resonated with an almost tangible echo of the past.

Lamps had been turned on in the living room, and a fire was blazing in the fireplace. He stood in front of it for a few minutes, warming his hands, then went to the liquor cabinet to find something to drink.

"There's nothing there," Vivian said from the doorway. "We have to keep the alcohol away from your father."

She was dressed in a long robe, and her hair was pinned up loosely, looking slightly disarrayed. Her face was gaunt and worn, and when David took her in his arms, he felt how thin she had become. There was little strength in her embrace.

"Oh, darling, I'm so glad you're home," she whispered, clinging to him.

"Why aren't you in bed? You didn't have to get up for me."

"I didn't get up—I've been up, for hours." She let go of him and walked to the fireplace. "I lose track of time—" She sounded vague, distracted. He helped her into a chair and sat down on an ottoman beside her.

"What's wrong with Father? What did the doctor say?"

"He wouldn't see the doctor. Refused. We had a terrible scene. I don't know what's the matter with him; he just insisted that you come home, that he had to see you . . ."

Mrs. Childress came in carrying a tray of coffee and sandwiches. "Ah, there you are," she said to Vivian. "I thought you were going to try and get some sleep." Her voice was gently scolding.

"I did try, but it was impossible. Don't pick on me, Chilly," Vivian said sulkily.

"Maybe you can make her take better care of herself," Mrs. Childress said to David, putting down the tray. "If she keeps this up, she'll be worse off than your father."

When she was gone, David said, "I had no idea things were so difficult; you never mentioned any of this in your letters."

"It wouldn't have done any good. Oh, it wasn't so bad at first. He recovered from the stroke quickly, but it left him weak, and you know how he despises being incapacitated in any way. He pushed himself to get stronger, recovered the full use of his arms and speech. But his legs are almost useless, despite the therapy. He can manage on crutches, but is in a wheelchair most of the time."

"Christ, I can imagine what he's been like . . ."

"As always, demanding—only now more so. I manage to get away every so often for a weekend in the city with Olivia, but he resents me for that. He refuses to have guests here, and won't be seen in New York in a wheelchair. He's a very proud man, and his vanity has been shattered. Sometimes I'm sure that it's affected his mind."

She began to cry softly and David held her in his arms. "I should have come back sooner—I might have been able to help—"

"I don't think so, darling. I know how you feel about him, and I think I understand why he's always been so hard on you, so cruel." She wiped at her eyes with a handkerchief and sat back, sighing deeply. "He could never reconcile the fact that you weren't exactly like him. That's what he wanted, I think—a son who would have been his mirror image. And I was as much to blame—I never knew what to say or do to make him understand."

"You did the best you could," David said, comforting her. "Maybe if I stay for a while, I can help; Duclos can manage without me. I'll talk to Father about it after I've gotten some sleep."

"You have to see him now," Vivian said sadly. "He's waiting for you . . ."

"Now? You mean he's awake? In his condition?"

"We don't have any regular hours in this house any more. I think he's been awake since I called you. He's in the library; I'm sure he knows you're here."

Fatigue pulled at David's back and shoulders. He took a breath and stood up. "All right, I'll go see him. Try to get some rest; we'll talk later."

Vivian reached out and took his hands. Her fingers were cold and dry. "Don't say anything that will upset him, and don't mention the trouble Dorian is having with that divorce—I've managed to keep that from him."

David leaned down and kissed her cheek. "I'll be very careful, I promise. Now go to bed, or I'll set Chilly on you."

"In a few minutes. I just want to sit here for a while."

David started to leave the room. At the doorway, he turned and looked back at her. Vivian had curled up into the chair and was staring at the fire, her hands clasped tightly in her lap, a dreaming look in her eyes.

David opened the library doors and walked in. Alexander was seated at his desk at the far end of the room, near the French doors leading to the garden. David approached him slowly, feeling an apprehension conditioned by years of conflict. A small desk lamp was turned on, and a fire burned low in the fireplace, casting flickering shadows across the walls. Olivia's collection of paintings had been removed, and in their place were only a few pieces, making the room look empty, devoid of warmth. Over the fireplace mantel hung the Sargent portrait of Augustus St. Clair. The commanding figure seemed larger in the dim light, the stern eyes more intense.

David stood at the desk and looked down at his father, trying to mask his shock at Alexander's appearance. His cheeks were sunken and his eyes veiled, colorless. The once-strong jawline had succumbed to loose flaps of flesh disappearing into a thin, wrinkled neck, and his hair had turned an impure white. Only the scar across his brow had retained any color, a narrow red line slashing over the tautly stretched skin.

Alexander stared back at his son, and gestured to a chair. "Sit down, David." His words were a little slurred, but the tone of his voice was still crisp.

David pulled up a leather easy chair and sank into it. "How are you?" he asked.

"Just as I appear." Alexander gave him a faint, ironical smile.

"You look well—"

"Let's not lie to each other, not now. I think we're beyond those amenities." He stared into his son's handsome, eroded face. "You look tired—"

"I am. I've been up since yesterday morning. When Mother called, I took the first flight I could get on—" David ran a hand over his unshaven face, feeling self-conscious. "I didn't expect to see you until I'd gotten some sleep."

"What I have to say couldn't wait." He suddenly turned his eyes to the portrait of his father and was silent for a few moments. Then he said, "I've been thinking about him a great deal lately. He was a man of strange contrasts: he had a deep appreciation of beauty, but had no beauty in him. He was ruthless, and he terrified me. He provoked in me an anger that I never lost. He taught me many things, but the most profound lesson was fear—fear of being weak, and of weakness in others." Alexander paused, and suddenly smiled. "You will, I'm sure, agree that he taught me well."

David's initial response to his father's musings was one of confusion; he hadn't expected this quiet introspection. He knew Alexander well enough to be aware that there was something more behind what he was saying.

"Why are you telling me this?" David asked.

Alexander turned his eyes back to him and replied softly, "Because I'm dying."

David started to protest, but his father silenced him with a gesture. "No, don't say anything. I know I'm dying, and there's nothing either of us or any doctor can do about it. At this point the fact of my approaching death is unimportant. However, what is important to me is what I leave behind."

He paused and looked back at the painting of Augustus. His eyes grew wide, as if he were peering into the depths of his own past. When he continued, his voice was harsh. "He had a vision of graciousness and civility, a vision I was determined to continue in my own life and in the lives of my children. The world intruded with changes that I couldn't control, changes that were labeled 'progress.' What I tried to preserve became ridiculous, outdated. But I still hoped that some spark of that vision would be carried on by my children. I was wrong."

David watched him uneasily; despite his illness, Alexander was still using his old tactics: manipulation mingled with an underlying threat. But what threat? he wondered.

"Dorian, with her headstrong defiance, has made a shambles of her life," Alexander went on. "She has no strength of her own, only the strength of her name and fortune—"

"That's not true!" David broke in angrily. "You know nothing about her, as you know nothing about me! You never took the time to hear anything we said . . ."

Alexander cut him off. "I know about Dorian, and now I know everything about you!"

A rush of fear swept over David. "What do you mean?" he asked faintly.

Alexander opened the top drawer of his desk and took out a large manila folder. He handed it to David, his eyes fixed and stony. "Open it," he commanded.

David hesitated, sensing that his father was imposing some final act of terror on him. He opened the folder slowly and felt his entire being turn to ice. A group of photographs separated beneath his hands, photographs that had been taken at the house in Senlis, showing him in the basest of postures, the grotesque contortions of perverse acts. Yet the searing pain that burned through him was not due to this ugly revelation of his secret life, but the realization of his betrayal by Ellis Morel. Tears blinded his eyes as he stared at the pictures; Morel did not appear in any of them.

"There's a letter," he heard Alexander say, his voice sounding as if from a great distance. "There's a letter," Alexander repeated with deliberate emphasis. "I want you to read it— out loud."

David wiped his eyes with the back of his hand and searched through the photographs until he found the letter. It was neatly typed on a piece of familiar-looking gray stationery. He knew it was Morel's, even though there was no signature.

"Read it," Alexander said sternly.

David began, his voice faltering, "You are advised to begin negotiations for the sale of the St. Clair Hotel in Paris immediately. If you fail to do so, these photographs will be made public. When the sale is completed, you will receive the negatives. Please contact J. Belloc at the following address for further instructions."

When he was finished, David slowly looked up at his father. Alexander's face had turned the color of ruined marble; his fists were clenched and shaking. "Well? What do you have to say?" he demanded.

David felt dazed, light-headed. He watched his father's lips forming the question over and over, but all he could hear was the sound of his own heartbeat. The room seemed to grow larger, separating them, and he closed his eyes, engulfed in a sensation of falling through darkness. Alexander's question became a shout, and he opened his eyes. In that single instant, the entirety of his life focused with supernal clarity. The infinite complexities of his existence were reduced to a single realization: he had wasted his life in a futile struggle, not against his father, but against himself. All his anguish, all his deceptions became as insignificant as a speck of foam generated by a crashing wave. Fear had made him live for nothing, create nothing, be nothing. But now the fear was gone, and knowing that, he was finally free. And his first act of freedom was laughter, unashamed, uncontrollable laughter.

Then he saw the gun in Alexander's hand.

Laughter bubbled away to a ghastly silence as he became aware of the finality of his father's expression. He saw the uselessness of trying to stop him, and felt only a momentary regret at the waste they had made of their lives.

"What are you going to do, kill yourself?" he asked hoarsely. "Are you going to spare yourself from seeing your noble vision, and his"—he glanced at the portrait of Augustus—"come down around your head in ruin and scandal? Will that be your last act of terrorizing me?"

Alexander remained silent, lifted the gun slightly and gripped it with both hands.

"Or are you going to kill me?" David rose from the chair slowly and leaned over the desk, bringing himself inches from the barrel of the gun. "Is that what you're going to do? Kill me?" He gave his father a wide, beautiful smile. "Yes, kill me. It's your right, your privilege! You should be the one to destroy what you gave life to . . ." His voice grew stronger, his words mocking. "Oh yes, kill me! Kill your useless, degenerate, perverted son!"

Alexander seemed to be in a trance; his body was rigid, his face bloodless.

"Please, please," David begged, "be the man you always claimed you were. For God's sake, don't disappoint me—not now, not after all these years—"

The sound of the shot echoed in the large room. David felt a single moment of unbearable pain. His eyes widened, and in a radiant flash of light he saw himself and Dorian, fixed on the canvas of Alan's portrait, close together, their hands touching. He fell across the desk, his arms outstretched to his father. Alexander jerked back, gripped by a terrible seizure, then slumped forward and was unmoving, without life.

Epilogue

November 1973

AN INQUEST WAS held, and the official verdict was accidental death: David, in an attempt to prevent his ill and despondent father from committing suicide, had been shot to death, and Alexander had subsequently suffered a massive, fatal stroke.

In the living room of the St. Clair estate, Alan listened to Olivia finish telling him what really happened.

"So I burned the photographs and the letter before the police arrived, and at the inquest, Dr. Steiner testified that David had been shot while struggling with Alex for the gun. Even Vivian doesn't know the truth—she collapsed when she saw them from the doorway of the library. She never got close enough to the desk to see the pictures."

"What about Dorian?"

"She knew—she guessed what had happened even before I told her. We called our lawyers in Paris, and the hotel has been sold, the negatives destroyed. Thank God it's all over," she concluded, beginning to cry.

Alan held her, trying to offer some comfort. His own shock at the news had diminished during his flight from Dublin to New York; all he could think about was Dorian, and how she would be affected by what had happened. What could he say to her? They had not seen each other in over a year, and the memory of her bitterness toward him in Paris was still a painful one.

"Does Dorian know that I'm here?" he asked Olivia.

"I didn't tell her that I cabled you. I'm terribly worried about her, that's why I wanted you here—I can't do anything to help her."

"Can I see her now?"

"I think she's somewhere on the beach—I saw her go across the lawns in that direction just before you arrived."

"I'll go find her. You should get some rest . . ."

"Yes, I will. I'll have Chilly unpack your bags; you will stay with us, won't you?"

"Of course, for as long as you need me."

Alan left the house and started for the beach, turning his collar up against the cold November afternoon. At the sight of dark clouds massing low on the horizon he walked more swiftly, automatically turning toward the boat house. Beyond it, in the rock cove that had been David's hiding place, he saw Dorian. She was staring out at the white swirls of foam breaking over the shore, her body tensed against the wind sweeping in from the sea. At his approach, she looked up; her face was gaunt and white, drained of all color and expression.

"I thought you might be here," Alan called out softly.

She turned and began to walk away from him.

"Dorian, wait!"

She whirled, her eyes narrowed, fists clenched. "Olivia sent for you, didn't she! Why did you come? You didn't give a damn about David!"

"That's not true, and you know it. I couldn't return David's feelings, but that doesn't mean I didn't care for him!"

"Nobody cared about him but me! I was the only one who understood what he was going through!"

"But you couldn't help him. David was responsible for his own life. There was nothing you could do for him, nothing that would have made any difference."

"What the hell do you know about it?" she said viciously. "You never understood David—or me!"

His sympathy gave way to anger. "Maybe I didn't! But you can't justify the waste David made of his life, or the useless way you've spent your own!"

She struck him hard across the face. "Get the hell out of here!"

"You hypocrite! It isn't me you're angry at—it's yourself! It always has been. And you made me and everyone else around you suffer for it!"

"That's not true!"

"It is, and you know it! You wrecked your happiness with every selfish decision you made, every excuse you used for your own failures! I loved you and wanted us to share our lives, but you refused to understand that!" He turned his back on her and began to walk away.

Dorian's anger crumbled under the weight of his accusations. David's death had deprived her of the only real support she had ever known, and more, it magnified all of her own failings and weaknesses. She felt stripped of every illusion she had tried to maintain. What Alan had said was true, and hearing it had destroyed her last source of strength—her pride. Seeing him walk away from her, she was suddenly terrified. "Where are you going?" she cried out.

"Home, back to Ireland. I thought you might need me, but you don't—you don't need anybody!"

"Wait!" She ran after him.

"For what? More abuse? I'm sorry about David and your father, but nothing can be done for either of them now. As for you"—he touched his face—"you've made yourself perfectly clear."

After a silence, Dorian managed to say, "You're right about David—and you're right about me; I don't have the slightest idea of what I'm doing any more."

A light rain began to fall, washing down her cheeks like tears, but her eyes were dry and hollow. They started back toward the house, together.

He said, "Come back to Ireland with me, even for a few days. It's quiet there; you can rest, and we can talk. We can't do it here."

"All right, just for a few days," she whispered. "I've never been so tired in my life."

A week later Dorian and Alan returned to Ireland. They had reestablished a relationship, but it was tenuous; he was thoughtful and solicitous, she was wary of his attentions. When they arrived at his house she followed him through the cheerful rooms, quietly expressing her approval. Alan watched her cautiously, aware of the strain she was under.

"Would you like to see the studio?" he asked.

She nodded, and they went upstairs to the second floor. He led her into the spacious room, and she walked around slowly, examining the paintings and drawings hanging on the walls. "These are wonderful," she said. "More beautiful than anything I've seen you do." She sat down on the window seat and looked through the bank of windows at the valley stretching away to the mountains. "I can understand why you wanted to come here to live—it's beautiful, and peaceful."

She reached into her shoulder purse and pulled out a package wrapped in white tissue. "I have a gift for you, and this seems the perfect time to give it to you." She handed him the package. "I should have done this years ago, but somehow I couldn't . . ."

"I don't understand—what is it?" Alan unwrapped the tissue and stared at the book in his hands. It was Marie's journal.

Dorian said, "That night you came to the house and had the fight with Jonathan, I picked it up and kept it. I was going to give it to you when we were living in London, but I didn't—I don't know why. I've read it many times—I hope you don't mind."

Alan leaned forward and gently kissed her cheek. "I don't mind. Thank you for keeping it, and for giving it to me now."

Dorian moved a little away from him, and glanced nervously at the covered painting sitting on the easel. "What are you working on?"

"It's a gift for you."

"For me? Were you that sure I'd come back with you?"

He smiled and shook his head. "I didn't know when I'd be able to give it to you, but I painted it for you—for both of us, really."

He went to the easel and took off the cover. In a masterful composition that ranged across the large canvas, they were all there: Alexander, Vivian and Olivia, sitting together at a white garden table; Marie, standing alone in faint shadows cast by the cottage, and behind her George, half turned to his work; opposite them, Jonathan, his arms folded in a self-assured pose; and in the foreground, lounging beneath the wide-spread limbs of a tree, David and Dorian, and Alan close by, holding a sketchbook on his lap.

It was unlike any work he had ever done. It was not reportage, like the sketches of the Paris riots, but there was a quality of arrested motion in it that reflected what he had learned during those days of violence. It was not portraiture in the strict sense, although it had taken all his experience as a

370

draftsman to create the subtle nuances that brought the work to life. He had done more than refine his technique and synthesize his ideas; he had finally found the way to infuse himself completely into his work. In the process of doing so, he better understood the simple truth that art is the act of making order out of chaos; the figures in the painting were in harmony, as nothing in life can be. Sunlight seemed to come from within the canvas, flooding the entire painting with an atmosphere of serenity. In the lower left-hand corner, just above his signature, Alan had carefully lettered, "The St. Clair Summer."

"It took me a long time to finish it," he said, "but I knew I had to do it; it was my way of being able to look at the past and close the door on it, once and for all. I want you to have it, if you like it."

Dorian stared at the canvas, transfixed. In her face Alan read the familiar signs of conflicting emotions, the expression of envy and frustration tempered with resignation and love. He understood that her struggle for happiness and fulfillment was not over, and realized, with some regret, that she would never be as perfect as his paintings of her.

Dorian's eyes began to brim with tears. Alan took her in his arms and held her close, thinking that whatever they had lost through the years was impermanent, fated to be lost. Now there was a strand of hope—scarcely more than a thread, but still, it was there.